STORIES
FROM
THE QUARTO

STORIES

FROM

THE QUARTO

Edited by

LEONARD BROWN

CHARLES SCRIBNER'S SONS *New York*

PUBLISHER'S PREFACE

A *Quarto of Modern Literature* has endured for three decades as a superior anthology of 20th century writing. It is our belief that the continuing appeal of the Quarto is largely attributable to an outstanding section on the short story. We have been encouraged in this belief by many of the educators who have enjoyed teaching these stories as part of the larger collection and who have, from time to time, expressed an interest in a separate collection of the stories.

It is with pleasure that we offer *Stories from the Quarto* as a separate collection for the first time. The stories were selected to offer the most representative selections possible from the pens of outstanding 20th century writers, and to offer, as well, selections which reflect something of the thematic and stylistic scope of the 20th century short story.

TABLE OF CONTENTS

THE APPLE TREE

JOHN GALSWORTHY

JOHN GALSWORTHY (1867–1933) came of a Devonshire family, was educated at Harrow and for the law at Oxford, traveled widely, and at twenty-eight drifted into writing largely at the suggestion of the woman who later became his wife. After eleven years "without making a penny, or any name to speak of" he published *The Man of Property*, the first of the novels in *The Forsyte Saga*, his fictional study of British middle-class society; in the same year, 1906, *The Silver Box*, his first play, was produced. "A drama must be shaped," he tells us in *Some Platitudes Concerning Drama*, "so as to have a spire of meaning. Every grouping of life and character has its inherent moral; and the business of the dramatist is so to pose the group as to bring that moral poignantly to the light of day." He wished "to set before the public no cut-and-dried codes, but the phenomena of life and character, selected and combined, *but not distorted,* by the dramatist's outlook, set down without fear, favor, or prejudice, leaving the public to put down such poor moral as nature may afford. . . . A human being is the best plot there is," he continues, "he is organic. . . . The dramatist who hangs his characters to a plot, instead of hanging his plot to his characters, is guilty of cardinal sin. . . . Take care of character: action and dialogue will take care of themselves. . . ." His theories on the writing of fiction will be found in "A Novelist's Allegory" (*Inn of Tranquility*, 1912), and in *The Creation of Character in Literature*, 1931. Galsworthy was awarded the Order of Merit in 1929, the Nobel Prize in 1932.

"The Apple-tree, the singing, and the gold."
—MURRAY's *Hippolytus of Euripides.*

O N their silver-wedding day Ashurst and his wife were motoring along the outskirts of the moor, intending to crown the festival by stopping the night at Torquay, where they had first met. This was the idea of Stella Ashurst, whose character contained a streak of sentiment. If she had long lost the blue-eyed, flower-like charm, the cool slim purity of face and form, the apple-blossom coloring, which had so swiftly and so oddly affected Ashurst twenty-six years ago, she was still at forty-three a comely and faithful companion, whose cheeks were faintly mottled, and whose gray-blue eyes had acquired a certain fullness.

It was she who had stopped the car where the common rose steeply to the left, and a narrow strip of larch and beech, with here and there a pine, stretched out towards the valley between the road and the first long high hill of the full moor. She was looking for a place where they might lunch, for Ashurst never looked for anything; and this, between the golden furze and the feathery green larches smelling of lemons in the last sun of April—this, with a view into the deep valley and up to the long moor heights, seemed fitting to the decisive nature of one

who sketched in water-colors, and loved romantic spots. Grasping her paint box, she got out.

"Won't this do, Frank?"

Ashurst, rather like a bearded Schiller, gray in the wings, tall, long-legged, with large remote gray eyes which sometimes filled with meaning and became almost beautiful, with nose a little to one side, and bearded lips just open—Ashurst, forty-eight, and silent, grasped the luncheon basket, and got out too.

"Oh! Look, Frank! A grave!"

By the side of the road, where the track from the top of the common crossed it at right angles and ran through a gate past the narrow wood was a thin mound of turf, six feet by one, with a moorstone to the west, and on it some one had thrown a blackthorn spray and a handful of bluebells. Ashurst looked, and the poet in him moved. At cross-roads—a suicide's grave! Poor mortals with their superstition! Whoever lay there, though, had the best of it, no clammy sepulcher among other hideous graves carved with futilities—just a rough stone, the wide sky, and wayside blessings! And, without comment, for he had learned not to be a philosopher in the bosom of his family, he strode away up on to the common, dropped the luncheon basket under a wall, spread a rug for his wife to sit on—she would turn up from her sketching when she was hungry—and took from his pocket Murray's translation of the "Hippolytus." He had soon finished reading of "The

Cyprian" and her revenge, and looked at the sky instead. And watching the white clouds so bright
against the intense blue, Ashurst, on his silver-
wedding day, longed for—he knew not what. Maladjusted to life—man's organism! One's mode of life
might be high and scrupulous, but there was always
an undercurrent of greediness, a hankering, and
sense of waste. Did women have it too? Who could
tell? And yet, men who gave vent to their appetites
for novelty, their riotous longings for new adventures,
new risks, new pleasures, these suffered, no doubt,
from the reverse side of starvation, from surfeit. No
getting out of it—a maladjusted animal, civilized
man! There could be no garden of his choosing, of
"the Apple-tree, the singing, and the gold," in the
words of that lovely Greek chorus, no achievable
elysium in life, or lasting haven of happiness for any
man with a sense of beauty—nothing which could
compare with the captured loveliness in a work of
art, set down forever, so that to look on it or read
was always to have the same precious sense of exalta-
tion and restful inebriety. Life no doubt had moments with that quality of beauty, of unbidden flying
rapture, but the trouble was, they lasted no longer
than the span of a cloud's flight over the sun; impossible to keep them with you, as Art caught beauty
and held it fast. They were fleeting as one of the
glimmering or golden visions one had of the soul in
nature, glimpses of its remote and brooding spirit.
Here, with the sun hot on his face, a cuckoo calling
from a thorn tree, and in the air the honey savor of
gorse—here among the little fronds of the young fern,
the starry blackthorn, while the bright clouds drifted
by high above the hills and dreamy valleys—here and
now was such a glimpse. But in a moment it would
pass—as the face of Pan, which looks round the
corner of a rock, vanishes at your stare. And suddenly
he sat up. Surely there was something familiar about
this view, this bit of common, that ribbon of road,
the old wall behind him. While they were driving he
had not been taking notice—never did; thinking of far
things or of nothing—but now he saw! Twenty-six
years ago, just at this time of year, from the farm-
house within half a mile of this very spot he had
started for that day in Torquay whence it might be
said he had never returned. And a sudden ache beset
his heart; he had stumbled on just one of those past
moments in his life, whose beauty and rapture he had
failed to arrest, whose wings had fluttered away into
the unknown; he had stumbled on a buried memory,
a wild sweet time, swiftly choked and ended. And,
turning on his face, he rested his chin on his hands,
and stared at the short grass where the little blue
milk-wort was growing. . . .

And this is what he remembered.

I

On the first of May, after their last year together at
college, Frank Ashurst and his friend Robert Garton
were on a tramp. They had walked that day from
Brent, intending to make Chagford, but Ashurst's
football knee had given out, and according to their
map they had still some seven miles to go. They were
sitting on a bank beside the road, where a track
crossed alongside a wood, resting the knee and talking of the universe, as young men will. Both were
over six feet, and thin as rails; Ashurst pale, idealistic,
full of absence; Garton queer, round-the-corner,
knotted, curly, like some primeval beast. Both had a
literary bent; neither wore a hat. Ashurst's hair was
smooth, pale, wavy, and had a way of rising on
either side of his brow, as if always being flung
back; Garton's was a kind of dark unfathomed mop.
They had not met a soul for miles.

"My dear fellow," Garton was saying, "pity's only
an effect of self-consciousness; it's a disease of the
last five thousand years. The world was happier without."

Ashurst, following the clouds with his eyes, answered:

"It's the pearl in the oyster, anyway."

"My dear chap, all our modern unhappiness comes
from pity. Look at animals, and Red Indians, limited
to feeling their own occasional misfortunes; then look
at ourselves—never free from feeling the toothaches
of others. Let's get back to feeling for nobody, and
have a better time."

"You'll never practice that."

Garton pensively stirred the hotch-potch of his
hair.

"To attain full growth, one mustn't be squeamish.
To starve oneself emotionally's a mistake. All emotion
is to the good—enriches life."

"Yes, and when it runs up against chivalry?"

"Ah! That's so English! If you speak of emotion
the English always think you want something physical, and are shocked. They're afraid of passion, but
not of lust—oh, no!—so long as they can keep it
secret."

Ashurst did not answer; he had plucked a blue
floweret, and was twiddling it against the sky. A
cuckoo began calling from a thorn tree. The sky, the
flowers, the songs of birds! Robert was talking
through his hat! And he said:

"Well, let's go on, and find some farm where we
can put up." In uttering those words, he was conscious of a girl coming down from the common just
above them. She was outlined against the sky, carry-

ing a basket, and you could see that sky through the crook of her arm. And Ashurst, who saw beauty without wondering how it could advantage him, thought: 'How pretty!' The wind, blowing her dark frieze skirt against her legs, lifted her battered peacock tam-o'-shanter; her grayish blouse was worn and old, her shoes were split, her little hands rough and red, her neck browned. Her dark hair waved untidy across her broad forehead, her face was short, her upper lip short, showing a glint of teeth, her brows were straight and dark, her lashes long and dark, her nose straight; but her gray eyes were the wonder—dewy as if opened for the first time that day. She looked at Ashurst—perhaps he struck her as strange, limping along without a hat, with his large eyes on her, and his hair flung back. He could not take off what was not on his head, but put up his hand in a salute, and said:

"Can you tell us if there's a farm near here where we could stay the night? I've gone lame."

"There's only our farm near, sir." She spoke without shyness, in a pretty, soft, crisp voice.

"And where is that?"

"Down here, sir."

"Would you put us up?"

"Oh! I think we would."

"Will you show us the way?"

"Yes, sir."

He limped on, silent, and Garton took up the catechism.

"Are you a Devonshire girl?"

"No, sir."

"What then?"

"From Wales."

"Ah! I *thought* you were a Celt; so it's not your farm?"

"My aunt's, sir."

"And your uncle's?"

"He is dead."

"Who farms it, then?"

"My aunt, and my three cousins."

"But your uncle was a Devonshire man?"

"Yes, sir."

"Have you lived here long?"

"Seven years."

"And how d'you like it after Wales?"

"I don't know, sir."

"I suppose you don't remember?"

"Oh, yes! But it is different."

"I believe you!"

Ashurst broke in suddenly:

"How old are you?"

"Seventeen, sir."

"And what's your name?"

"Megan David."

"This is Robert Garton, and I am Frank Ashurst. We wanted to get on to Chagford."

"It is a pity your leg is hurting you."

Ashurst smiled, and when he smiled his face was rather beautiful.

Descending past the narrow wood, they came on the farm suddenly—a long, low, stone-built dwelling with casement windows, in a farmyard where pigs and fowls and an old mare were straying. A short steep-up grass hill behind was crowned with a few Scotch firs, and in front, an old orchard of apple-trees, just breaking into flower, stretched down to a stream and a long wild meadow. A little boy with oblique dark eyes was shepherding a pig, and by the house door stood a woman, who came towards them. The girl said:

"It is Mrs. Narracombe, my aunt."

"Mrs. Narracombe, my aunt," had a quick, dark eye, like a mother wild-duck's, and something of the same snaky turn about her neck.

"We met your niece on the road," said Ashurst; "she thought you might perhaps put us up for the night."

Mrs. Narracombe, taking them in from head to heel, answered:

"Well, I can, if you don't mind one room. Megan, get the spare room ready, and a bowl of cream. You'll be wanting tea, I suppose."

Passing through a sort of porch made by two yew trees and some flowering-currant bushes, the girl disappeared into the house, her peacock tam-o'-shanter bright athwart that rosy-pink and the dark green of the yews.

"Will you come into the parlor and rest your leg? You'll be from college, perhaps?"

"We were, but we've gone down now."

Mrs. Narracombe nodded sagely.

The parlor, brick-floored, with bare table and shiny chairs and sofa stuffed with horsehair, seemed never to have been used, it was so terribly clean. Ashurst sat down at once on the sofa, holding his lame knee between his hands, and Mrs. Narracombe gazed at him. He was the only son of a late professor of chemistry, but people found a certain lordliness in one who was often so sublimely unconscious of them.

"Is there a stream where we could bathe?"

"There's the strame at the bottom of the orchard, but sittin' down you'll not be covered!"

"How deep?"

"Well, 'tis about a foot and a half, maybe."

"Oh! That'll do fine. Which way?"

"Down the lane, through the second gate on the right, an' the pool's by the big apple-tree that stands by itself. There's trout there, if you can tickle them."

"They're more likely to tickle us!"

Mrs. Narracombe smiled. "There'll be the tea ready when you come back."

The pool, formed by the damming of a rock, had a sandy bottom; and the big apple-tree, lowest in the orchard, grew so close that its boughs almost overhung the water; it was in leaf, and all but in flower— its crimson buds just bursting. There was not room for more than one at a time in that narrow bath, and Ashurst waited his turn, rubbing his knee and gazing at the wild meadow, all rocks and thorn trees and field flowers, with a grove of beeches beyond, raised up on a flat mound. Every bough was swinging in the wind, every spring bird calling, and a slanting sunlight dappled the grass. He thought of Theocritus, and the river Cherwell, of the moon, and the maiden with the dewy eyes; of so many things that he seemed to think of nothing; and he felt absurdly happy.

II

During a late and sumptuous tea with eggs to it, cream and jam, and thin, fresh cakes touched with saffron, Garton descanted on the Celts. It was about the period of the Celtic awakening, and the discovery that there was Celtic blood about this family had excited one who believed that he was a Celt himself. Sprawling on a horsehair chair, with a hand-made cigarette dribbling from the corner of his curly lips, he had been plunging his cold pin-points of eyes into Ashurst's and praising the refinement of the Welsh. To come out of Wales into England was like the change from china to earthenware! Frank, as a d——d Englishman, had not of course perceived the exquisite refinement and emotional capacity of that Welsh girl! And, delicately stirring in the dark mat of his still wet hair, he explained how exactly she illustrated the writings of the Welsh bard Morgan-ap-Something in the twelfth century.

Ashurst, full length on the horsehair sofa, and jutting far beyond its end, smoked a deeply-colored pipe, and did not listen, thinking of the girl's face when she brought in a relay of cakes. It had been exactly like looking at a flower, or some other pretty sight in Nature—till, with a funny little shiver, she had lowered her glance and gone out, quiet as a mouse.

"Let's go to the kitchen," said Garton, "and see some more of her."

The kitchen was a white-washed room with rafters, to which were attached smoked hams; there were flower-pots on the window-sill, and guns hanging on nails, queer mugs, china and pewter, and portraits of Queen Victoria. A long, narrow table of plain wood was set with bowls and spoons, under a string of high-hung onions; two sheep-dogs and three cats lay here and there. On one side of the recessed fireplace sat two small boys, idle, and good as gold; on the other sat a stout, light-eyed, red-faced youth with hair and lashes the color of the tow he was running through the barrel of a gun; between them Mrs. Narracombe dreamily stirred some savory-scented stew in a large pot. Two other youths, oblique-eyed, dark-haired, rather sly-faced, like the two little boys, were talking together and lolling against the wall; and a short, elderly clean-shaven man in corduroys, seated in the window, was conning a battered journal. The girl Megan seemed the only active creature—drawing cider and passing with the jugs from cask to table. Seeing them thus about to eat, Garton said:

"Ah! If you'll let us, we'll come back when supper's over," and without waiting for an answer they withdrew again to the parlor. But the color in the kitchen, the warmth, the scents, and all those faces, heightened the bleakness of their shiny room, and they resumed their seats moodily.

"Regular gypsy type, those boys. There was only one Saxon—the fellow cleaning the gun. That girl is a very subtle study psychologically."

Ashurst's lips twitched. Garton seemed to him an ass just then. Subtle study! She was a wild flower. A creature it did you good to look at. Study!

Garton went on:

"Emotionally she would be wonderful. She wants awakening."

"Are you going to awaken her?"

Garton looked at him and smiled. 'How coarse and English you are!" that curly smile seemed saying.

And Ashurst puffed his pipe. Awaken her! This fool had the best opinion of himself! He threw up the window and leaned out. Dusk had gathered thick. The farm buildings and the wheel-house were all dim and bluish, the apple-trees but a blurred wilderness; the air smelled of wood smoke from the kitchen fire. One bird going to bed later than the others was uttering a half-hearted twitter, as though surprised at the darkness. From the stable came the snuffle and stamp of a feeding horse. And away over there was the loom of the moor, and away and away the shy stars which had not as yet full light, pricking white through the deep blue heavens. A quavering owl hooted. Ashurst drew a deep breath. What a night to wander out in! A padding of unshod hoofs came up the lane, and three dim, dark shapes passed —ponies on an evening march. Their heads, black and fuzzy, showed above the gate. At the tap of his pipe, and a shower of little sparks, they shied round and scampered. A bat went fluttering past, uttering its almost inaudible "chip, chip." Ashurst held out his hand; on the upturned palm he could feel the dew. Suddenly from overhead he heard little blurring boys' voices, little thumps of boots thrown down, and another voice, crisp and soft—the girl's putting them to bed, no doubt; and nine clear words: "No, Rick, you can't have the cat in bed"; then came a skirmish of giggles and gurgles, a soft slap, a laugh so low and pretty that it made him shiver a little. A blowing sound, and the glim of the candle which was fingering the dusk above, went out; silence reigned. Ashurst withdrew into the room and sat down; his knee pained him, and his soul felt gloomy.

"You go to the kitchen," he said; "I'm going to bed."

III

For Ashurst the wheel of slumber was wont to turn noiseless and slick and swift, but though he seemed sunk in sleep when his companion came up, he was really wide awake; and long after Garton, smothered in the other bed of that low-roofed room, was worshiping darkness with his upturned nose, he heard the owls. Barring the discomfort of his knee, it was not unpleasant—the cares of life did not loom large in night watches for this young man. In fact he had none; just enrolled a barrister, with literary aspirations, the world before him, no father or mother, and four hundred a year of his own. Did it matter where he went, what he did, or when he did it? His bed, too, was hard, and this preserved him from fever. He lay, sniffing the scent of the night which drifted into the low room through the open casement close to his head. Except for a definite irritation with his friend, natural when you have tramped with a man for three days, Ashurst's memories and visions that sleepless night were kindly and wistful and exciting. One vision, specially clear and unreasonable, for he had not even been conscious of noting it, was the face of the youth cleaning the gun; its intent, stolid, yet startled uplook at the kitchen doorway, quickly shifted to the girl carrying the cider jug. This red, blue-eyed, light-lashed, tow-haired face stuck as firmly in his memory as the girl's own face, so dewy and simple. But at last, in the square of darkness through the uncurtained casement, he saw day coming, and heard one hoarse and sleepy caw. Then followed silence, dead as ever, till the song of a blackbird, not properly awake, adventured into the hush. And, from staring at the framed brightening light, Ashurst fell asleep.

Next day his knee was badly swollen; the walking tour was obviously over. Garton, due back in London on the morrow, departed at midday with an ironical smile which left a scar of irritation—healed the moment his loping figure vanished round the corner of the steep lane. All day Ashurst rested his knee, in a green-painted wooden chair on the patch of grass by the yew-tree porch, where the sunlight distilled the scent of stocks and gilly-flowers, and a ghost of scent from the flowering-currant bushes. Beatifically, he smoked, dreamed, watched.

A farm in spring is all birth—young things coming out of bud and shell, and human beings watching over the process with faint excitement feeding and tending what has been born. So still the young man sat, that a mother-goose, with stately cross-footed waddle, brought her six yellow-necked gray-backed goslings to strop their little beaks against the grass blades at his feet. Now and again Mrs. Narracombe or the girl Megan would come and ask if he wanted anything, and he would smile and say: "Nothing, thanks. It's splendid here." Towards teatime they came out together, bearing a long poultice of some dark stuff in a bowl, and after a long and solemn scrutiny of his swollen knee, bound it on. When they were gone, he thought of the girl's soft "Oh!"—of her pitying eyes, and the little wrinkle in her brow. And again he felt that unreasoning irritation against his departed friend, who had talked such rot about her. When she brought out his tea, he said:

"How did you like my friend, Megan?"

She forced down her upper lip, as if afraid that to smile was not polite. "He was a funny gentleman; he made us laugh. I think he is very clever."

"What did he say to make you laugh?"

"He said I was a daughter of the bards. What are they?"

"Welsh poets, who lived hundreds of years ago."

"Why am I their daughter, please?"

"He meant that you were the sort of girl they sang about."

She wrinkled her brows. "I think he likes to joke. Am I?"

"Would you believe me, if I told you?"

"Oh, yes."

"Well, I think he was right."

She smiled.

And Ashurst thought: "You *are* a pretty thing!"

"He said, too, that Joe was a Saxon type. What would that be?"

"Which is Joe? With the blue eyes and red face?"

"Yes. My uncle's nephew."

"Not your cousin, then?"

"No."

"Well, he meant that Joe was like the men who came over to England about fourteen hundred years ago, and conquered it."

"Oh! I know about them; but is he?"

"Garton's crazy about that sort of thing; but I must say Joe does look a bit Early Saxon."

"Yes."

That "yes" tickled Ashurst. It was so crisp and graceful, so conclusive, and politely acquiescent in what was evidently Greek to her.

"He said that all the other boys were regular gypsies. He should not have said that. My aunt laughed, but she didn't like it, of course, and my cousins were angry. Uncle was a farmer—farmers are not gypsies. It is wrong to hurt people."

Ashurst wanted to take her hand and give it a squeeze, but he only answered:

"Quite right, Megan. By the way, I heard you putting the little ones to bed last night."

She flushed a little. "Please to drink your tea—it is getting cold. Shall I get you some fresh?"

"Do you ever have time to do anything for yourself?"

"Oh, yes."

"I've been watching, but I haven't seen it yet."

She wrinkled her brows in a puzzled frown, and her color deepened.

When she was gone, Ashurst thought: "Did she think I was chaffing her? I wouldn't for the world!" He was at that age when to some men "Beauty's a flower," as the poet says, and inspires in them the thoughts of chivalry. Never very conscious of his surroundings, it was some time before he was aware that the youth whom Garton had called "a Saxon type" was standing outside the stable door; and a fine bit of color he made in his soiled brown velvet-cords, muddy gaiters, and blue shirt; red-armed, red-faced, the sun turning his hair from tow to flax; immovably stolid, persistent, unsmiling he stood. Then, seeing Ashurst looking at him, he crossed the yard at that gait of the young countryman always ashamed not to be slow and heavy-dwelling on each leg, and disappeared round the end of the house towards the kitchen entrance. A chill came over Ashurst's mood. Clods! With all the good will in the world, how impossible to get on terms with them! And yet—see that girl! Her shoes were split, her hands rough; but—what was it? Was it really her Celtic blood, as Garton had said?—she was a lady born, a jewel, though probably she could do no more than just read and write!

The elderly, clean-shaven man he had seen last night in the kitchen had come into the yard with a dog, driving the cows to their milking. Ashurst saw that he was lame.

"You've got some good ones there!"

The lame man's face brightened. He had the upward look in his eyes which prolonged suffering often brings.

"Yeas; they'm praaper buties; gude milkers tu."

"I bet they are."

"'Ope as yure leg's better, zurr."

"Thank you, it's getting on."

The lame man touched his own: "I know what 'tes, meself; 'tes a main worritin' thing, the knee. I've a 'ad mine bad this ten year."

Ashurst made the sound of sympathy which comes so readily from those who have an independent income, and the lame man smiled again.

"Mustn't complain, though—they mighty near 'ad it off."

"Ho!"

"Yeas; an' compared with what 'twas, 'tis almost so gude as nu."

"They've put a bandage of splendid stuff on mine."

"The maid she picks et. She'm a gude maid wi' the flowers. There's folks zeem to know the healin' in things. My mother was a rare one for that. 'Ope as yu'll zune be better, zurr. Goo ahn, therr!"

Ashurst smiled. "Wi' the flowers!" A flower herself.

That evening, after his supper of cold duck, junket, and cider, the girl came in.

"Please, auntie says—will you try a piece of our Mayday cake?"

"If I may come to the kitchen for it."

"Oh, yes! You'll be missing your friend."

"Not I. But are you sure no one minds?"

"Who would mind? We shall be very pleased."

Ashurst rose too suddenly for his stiff knee, staggered and subsided. The girl gave a little gasp, and held out her hands. Ashurst took them, small, rough, brown; checked his impulse to put them to his lips, and let her pull him up. She came close beside him, offering her shoulder. And leaning on her he walked across the room. That shoulder seemed quite the pleasantest thing he had ever touched. But he had presence of mind enough to catch his stick out of the rack, and withdraw his hand before arriving at the kitchen.

That night he slept like a top, and woke with his knee of almost normal size. He again spent the morning in his chair on the grass patch, scribbling down verses; but in the afternoon he wandered about with the two little boys Nick and Rick. It was Saturday, so they were early home from school; quick, shy, dark little rascals of seven and six, soon talkative, for Ashurst had a way with children. By four o'clock they had shown him all their methods of destroying life, except the tickling of trout; and with breeches tucked up, lay on their stomachs over the trout stream, pretending they had this accomplishment also. They tickled nothing, of course, for their giggling and shouting scared every spotted thing away. Ashurst, on a rock at the edge of the beech clump, watched them, and listened to the cuckoos, till Nick, the elder and less persevering, came up and stood beside him.

"The gypsy bogle zets on that stone," he said.

"What gypsy bogle?"

"Dunno; never zeen 'e. Megan zays 'e zets there; an' old Jim zeed 'e once. 'E was zettin' there naight afore our pony kicked-in father's 'ead. 'E plays the viddle."

"What tune does he play?"

"Dunno."

"What's he like?"

" 'E's black. Old Jim zays 'e's all over 'air. 'E's a praaper bogle. 'E don' come only at naight." The little boy's oblique dark eyes slid round. "D'yu think 'e might want to take me away? Megan's feared of 'e."

"Has she seen him?"

"No. She's not afeared o' yu."

"I should think not. Why should she be?"

"She zays a prayer for yu."

"How do you know that, you little rascal?"

"When I was asleep, she said: 'God bless us all, an' Mr. Ashes.' I 'eard 'er whisperin'."

"You're a little ruffian to tell what you hear when you're not meant to hear it!"

The little boy was silent. Then he said aggressively:

"I can skin rabbits. Megan, she can't bear skinnin' 'em. I like blood."

"Oh! you do; you little monster!"

"What's that?"

"A creature that likes hurting others."

The little boy scowled. "They'm only dead rabbits, what us eats."

"Quite right, Nick. I beg your pardon."

"I can skin frogs, tu."

But Ashurst had become absent. "God bless us all, and Mr. Ashes!" And puzzled by that sudden inaccessibility, Nick ran back to the stream where the giggling and shouts again uprose at once.

When Megan brought his tea, he said:

"What's the gypsy bogle, Megan?"

She looked up, startled.

"He brings bad things."

"Surely you don't believe in ghosts?"

"I hope I will never see him."

"Of course you won't. There aren't such things. What old Jim saw was a pony."

"No! There are bogles in the rocks; they are the men who lived long ago."

"They aren't gypsies, anyway; those old men were dead long before gypsies came."

She said simply: "They are all bad."

"Why? If there are any, they're only wild, like the rabbits. The flowers aren't bad for being wild; the thorn trees were never planted—and you don't mind them. I shall go down at night and look for your bogle, and have a talk with him."

"Oh, no! Oh, no!"

"Oh, yes! I shall go and sit on his rock."

She clasped her hands together: "Oh, please!"

"Why! What does it matter if anything happens to me?"

She did not answer; and in a sort of pet he added:

"Well, I daresay I shan't see him, because I suppose I must be off soon."

"Soon?"

"Your aunt won't want to keep me here."

"Oh, yes! We always let lodgings in summer."

Fixing his eyes on her face, he asked:

"Would you like me to stay?"

"Yes."

"I'm going to say a prayer for *you* to-night!"

She flushed crimson, frowned, and went out of the room. He sat cursing himself, till his tea was stewed. It was as if he had hacked with his thick boots at a clump of bluebells. Why had he said such a silly thing? Was he just a towny college ass like Robert Garton, as far from understanding this girl?

IV

Ashurst spent the next week confirming the restoration of his leg, by exploration of the country within easy reach. Spring was a revelation to him this year. In a kind of intoxication he would watch the pink-white buds of some backward beech tree sprayed up in the sunlight against the deep blue sky, or the trunks and limbs of the few Scotch firs, tawny in violent light, or again on the moor, the gale-bent larches which had such a look of life when the wind streamed in their young green, above the rusty black underboughs. Or he would lie on the banks, gazing at the clusters of dog-violets, or up in the dead bracken, fingering the pink, transparent buds of the dewberry, while the cuckoos called and yaffles laughed, or a lark, from very high, dipped its beads of song. It was certainly different from any spring he had ever known, for spring was within him, not without. In the daytime he hardly saw the family; and when Megan brought in his meals she always seemed too busy in the house or among the young things in the yard to stay talking long. But in the evenings he installed himself in the window seat in the kitchen, smoking and chatting with the lame man Jim, or Mrs. Narracombe, while the girl sewed, or moved about, clearing the supper things away. And sometimes with the sensation a cat must feel when it purrs, he would become conscious that Megan's eyes

—those dew-gray eyes—were fixed on him with a sort of lingering soft look which was strangely flattering.

It was on Sunday week in the evening, when he was lying in the orchard listening to a blackbird and composing a love poem, that he heard the gate swing to, and saw the girl come running among the trees, with the red-cheeked, stolid Joe in swift pursuit. About twenty yards away the chase ended, and the two stood fronting each other, not noticing the stranger in the grass—the boy pressing on, the girl fending him off. Ashurst could see her face, angry, disturbed; and the youth's—who would have thought that red-faced yokel could look so distraught! And painfully affected by that sight, he jumped up. They saw him then. Megan dropped her hands, and shrank behind a tree-trunk; the boy gave an angry grunt, rushed at the bank, scrambled over and vanished. Ashurst went slowly up to her. She was standing quite still, biting her lip—very pretty, with her fine, dark hair blown loose about her face, and her eyes cast down.

"I beg your pardon," he said.

She gave him one upward look, from eyes much dilated; then, catching her breath, turned away. Ashurst followed.

"Megan!"

But she went on; and taking hold of her arm, he turned her gently round to him.

"Stop and speak to me."

"Why do you beg my pardon? It is not to me you should do that."

"Well, then, to Joe."

"How dare he come after me?"

"In love with you, I suppose."

She stamped her foot.

Ashurst uttered a short laugh. "Would you like me to punch his head?"

She cried with sudden passion:

"You laugh at me—you laugh at us!"

He caught hold of her hands, but she shrank back, till her passionate little face and loose dark hair were caught among the pink clusters of the apple blossom. Ashurst raised one of her imprisoned hands and put his lips to it. He felt how chivalrous he was, and superior to that clod Joe—just brushing that small, rough hand with his mouth! Her shrinking ceased suddenly; she seemed to tremble towards him. A sweet warmth overtook Ashurst from top to toe. This slim maiden, so simple and fine and pretty, was pleased, then, at the touch of his lips. And, yielding to a swift impulse, he put his arms round her, pressed her to him, and kissed her forehead. Then he was frightened—she went so pale, closing her eyes, so that the long, dark lashes lay on her pale cheeks; her hands, too, lay inert at her sides. The touch of her

breast sent a shiver through him. "Megan!" he sighed out, and let her go. In the utter silence a blackbird shouted. Then the girl seized his hand, put it to her cheek, her heart, her lips, kissed it passionately, and fled away among the mossy trunks of the apple-trees, till they hid her from him.

Ashurst sat down on a twisted old tree growing almost along the ground, and, all throbbing and bewildered, gazed vacantly at the blossom which had crowned her hair—those pink buds with one white open apple star. What had he done? How had he let himself be thus stampeded by beauty—or—just the spring! He felt curiously happy, all the same; happy and triumphant, with shivers running through his limbs, and a vague alarm. This was the beginning of—what? The midges bit him, the dancing gnats tried to fly into his mouth, and all the spring around him seemed to grow more lovely and alive; the songs of the cuckoos and the blackbirds, the laughter of the yaffles, the level-slanting sunlight, the apple blossom which had crowned her head—! He got up from the old trunk and strode out of the orchard, wanting space, an open sky, to get on terms with these new sensations. He made for the moor, and from an ash tree in the hedge a magpie flew out to herald him.

Of man—at any age from five years on—who can say he has never been in love? Ashurst had loved his partners at his dancing class; loved his nursery governess; girls in school-holidays; perhaps never been quite out of love, cherishing always some more or less remote admiration. But this was different, not remote at all. Quite a new sensation; terribly delightful, bringing a sense of completed manhood. To be holding in his fingers such a wild flower, to be able to put it to his lips, and feel it tremble with delight against them! What intoxication, and—embarrassment! What to do with it—how meet her next time? His first caress had been cool, pitiful: but the next could not be, now that, by her burning little kiss on his hand, by her pressure of it to her heart, he knew that she loved him. Some natures are coarsened by love bestowed on them; others, like Ashurst's, are swayed and drawn, warmed and softened, almost exalted, by what they feel to be a sort of miracle.

And up there among the tors he was racked between the passionate desire to revel in this new sensation of spring fulfilled within him, and a vague but very real uneasiness. At one moment he gave himself up completely to his pride at having captured this pretty, trustful, dewy-eyed thing! At the next he thought with factitious solemnity: "Yes, my boy! But look out what you're doing! You know what comes of it!"

Dusk dropped down without his noticing—dusk on the carved, Assyrian-looking masses of the rocks. And the voice of Nature said: "This is a new world for you!" As when a man gets up at four o'clock and goes out into a summer morning, and beasts, birds, trees stare at him and he feels as if all had been made new.

He stayed up there for hours, till it grew cold, then groped his way down the stones and heather roots to the road, back into the lane, and came again past the wild meadow to the orchard. There he struck a match and looked at his watch. Nearly twelve! It was black and unstirring in there now, very different from the lingering, bird-befriended brightness of six hours ago! And suddenly he saw this idyll of his with the eyes of the outer world—had mental vision of Mrs. Narracombe's snake-like neck turned, her quick dark glance taking it all in, her shrewd face hardening; saw the gypsy-like cousins coarsely mocking and distrustful; Joe stolid and furious; only the lame man, Jim, with the suffering eyes, seemed tolerable to his mind. And the village pub!—the gossiping matrons he passed on his walks; and then—his own friends— Robert Garton's smile when he went off that morning ten days ago; so ironical and knowing! Disgusting! For a minute he literally hated this earthly, cynical world to which one belonged, willy-nilly. The gate where he was leaning grew gray, a sort of shimmer passed before him and spread into the bluish darkness. The moon! He could just see it over the bank behind; red, nearly round—a strange moon! And turning away, he went up the lane which smelled of the night and cow-dung and young leaves. In the strawyard he could see the dark shapes of cattle, broken by the pale sickles of their horns, like so many thin moons, fallen ends-up. He unlatched the farm gate stealthily. All was dark in the house. Muffling his footsteps, he gained the porch, and, blotted against one of the yew trees, looked up at Megan's window. It was open. Was she sleeping, or lying awake perhaps disturbed—unhappy at his absence? An owl hooted while he stood there peering up, and the sound seemed to fill the whole night, so quiet was all else, save for the never-ending murmur of the stream running below the orchard. The cuckoos by day, and now the owls—how wonderful they voiced this troubled ecstasy within him! And suddenly he saw her at her window, looking out. He moved a little from the yew tree, and whispered: "Megan!" She drew back, vanished, reappeared, leaning far down. He stole forward on the grass patch, hit his shin against the green-painted chair, and held his breath at the sound. The pale blur of her stretched-down arm and face did not stir; he moved the chair, and noiselessly mounted it. By stretching up his arm he could just reach. Her hand held the huge key of the front door, and he clasped that burning hand with the cold key in it. He could just see her face, the

glint of teeth between her lips, her tumbled hair. She was still dressed—poor child, sitting up for him, no doubt! "Pretty Megan!" Her hot, roughened fingers clung to his; her face had a strange, lost look. To have been able to reach it—even with his hand! The owl hooted, a scent of sweet-briar crept into his nostrils. Then one of the farm dogs barked; her grasp relaxed, she shrank back.

"Good night, Megan!"

"Good night, sir!" She was gone! With a sigh he dropped back to earth, and, sitting on that chair, took off his boots. Nothing for it but to creep in and go to bed; yet for a long while he sat unmoving, his feet chilly in the dew, drunk on the memory of her lost, half-smiling face, and the clinging grip of her burning fingers, pressing the cold key into his hand.

V

He awoke feeling as if he had eaten heavily overnight, instead of having eaten nothing. And far off, unreal, seemed yesterday's romance! Yet it was a golden morning. Full spring had burst at last—in one night the "goldie-cups," as the little boys called them, seemed to have made the field their own, and from his window he could see apple blossoms covering the orchard as with a rose and white quilt. He went down almost dreading to see Megan; and yet, when not she but Mrs. Narracombe brought in his breakfast, he felt vexed and disappointed. The woman's quick eye and snaky neck seemed to have a new alacrity this morning. Had she noticed?

"So you an' the moon went walkin' last night, Mr. Ashurst! Did ye have your supper anywheres?"

Ashurst shook his head.

"We kept it for you, but I suppose you was too busy in your brain to think o' such a thing as that?"

Was she mocking him, in that voice of hers, which still kept some Welsh crispness against the invading burr of the West Country? If she knew! And at that moment he thought: "No, no; I'll clear out. I won't put myself in such a beastly false position."

But, after breakfast, the longing to see Megan began and increased with every minute, together with fear lest something should have been said to her which had spoiled everything. Sinister that she had not appeared, not given him even a glimpse of her! And the love poem, whose manufacture had been so important and absorbing yesterday afternoon under the apple-trees, now seemed so paltry that he tore it up and rolled it into pipe spills. What had he known of love, till she seized his hand and kissed it! And now—what did he not know? But to write of it seemed mere insipidity! He went up to his bedroom to get a book, and his heart began to beat violently, for she was in there making the bed. He stood in the doorway watching; and suddenly, with turbulent joy, he saw her stoop and kiss his pillow, just at the hollow made by his head last night. How let her know he had seen that pretty act of devotion? And yet if she heard him stealing away, it would be even worse. She took the pillow up, holding it as if reluctant to shake out the impress of his cheek, dropped it, and turned round.

"Megan!"

She put her hands up to her cheeks, but her eyes seemed to look right into him. He had never before realized the depth and purity and touching faithfulness in those dew-bright eyes, and he stammered:

"It was sweet of you to wait up for me last night."

She still said nothing, and he stammered on:

"I was wandering about on the moor; it was such a jolly night. I—I've just come up for a book."

Then, the kiss he had seen her give the pillow afflicted him with sudden headiness, and he went up to her. Touching her eyes with his lips, he thought with queer excitement: "I've done it! Yesterday all was sudden—anyhow; but now—I've done it!" The girl let her forehead rest against his lips, which moved downwards till they reached hers. That first real lover's kiss—strange, wonderful, still almost innocent —in which heart did it make the most disturbance?

"Come to the big apple-tree to-night, after they've gone to bed. Megan—promise!"

She whispered back: "I promise!"

Then, scared at her white face, scared at everything, he let her go, and went downstairs again. Yes! he had done it now! Accepted her love, declared his own! He went out to the green chair as devoid of a book as ever; and there he sat staring vacantly before him, triumphant and remorseful, while under his nose and behind his back the work of the farm went on. How long he had been sitting in that curious state of vacancy he had no notion when he saw Joe standing a little behind him to the right. The youth had evidently come from hard work in the fields, and stood shifting his feet, breathing loudly, his face colored like a setting sun, and his arms, below the rolled-up sleeves of his blue shirt, showing the hue and furry sheen of ripe peaches. His red lips were open, his blue eyes with their flaxen lashes stared fixedly at Ashurst, who said ironically:

"Well, Joe, anything I can do for you?"

"Yeas."

"What, then?"

"Yu can goo away from yere. Us don' want yu."

Ashurst's face, never too humble, assumed its most lordly look.

"Very good of you, but, do you know, I prefer the others should speak for themselves."

The youth moved a pace or two nearer, and the scent of his honest heat afflicted Ashurst's nostrils.

"What d'yu stay yere for?"

"Because it pleases me."

" 'Twon't please yu when I've bashed yure head in!"

"Indeed! When would you like to begin that?"

Joe answered only with the loudness of his breathing, but his eyes looked like those of a young and angry bull. Then a sort of spasm seemed to convulse his face.

"Megan don' want yu."

A rush of jealousy, of contempt, and anger with this thick, loud-breathing rustic got the better of Ashurst's self-possession; he jumped up and pushed back his chair.

"You can go to the devil!"

And as he said those simple words, he saw Megan in the doorway with a tiny brown spaniel puppy in her arms. She came up to him quickly:

"Its eyes are blue!" she said.

Joe turned away; the back of his neck was literally crimson.

Ashurst put his finger to the mouth of the little brown bullfrog of a creature in her arms. How cozy it looked against her!

"It's fond of you already! Ah! Megan, everything is fond of *you*."

"What was Joe saying to you, please?"

"Telling me to go away, because you didn't want me here."

She stamped her foot; then looked up at Ashurst. At that adoring look he felt his nerves quiver, just as if he had seen a moth scorching its wings.

"To-night!" he said. "Don't forget!"

"No." And smothering her face against the puppy's little fat, brown body, she slipped back into the house.

Ashurst wandered down the lane. At the gate of the wild meadow he came on the lame man and his cows.

"Beautiful day, Jim!"

"Ah! 'Tes brave weather for the grass. The ashes be later than th' oaks this year. 'When th' oak before th' ash——' "

Ashurst said idly: "Where were you standing when you saw the gypsy bogle, Jim?"

"It might be under that big apple-tree, as you might say."

"And you really do think it was there?"

The lame man answered cautiously:

"I shouldn't like to say rightly that *'twas* there. 'Twas in my mind as 'twas there."

"What do you make of it?"

The lame man lowered his voice.

"They du zay old master, Mist' Narracombe, come o' gypsy stock. But that's tellin'. They'm a wonderful people, yu know, for claimin' their own. Maybe they knu'e was goin', and sent this feller along for company. That's what I've a-thought about it."

"What was he like?"

" 'E 'ad 'air all over 'is face, an' goin' like this, he was, zame as if 'e 'ad a viddle. They zay there's no such thing as bogles, but I've a-zeen the 'air on this dog standin' up of a dark naight, when I couldn' zee nothin', meself."

"Was there a moon?"

"Yeas, very near full, but 'twas on'y just risen, gold-like be'ind them trees."

"And you think a ghost means trouble, do you?"

The lame man pushed his hat up; his aspiring eyes looked at Ashurst more earnestly than ever.

" 'Tes not for me to zay that—but 'tes they bein' so unrestin'-like. There's things us don' understand, that's zartin, for zure. There's people that zee things, tu, an' others that don't never zee nothin'. Now, our Joe—yu might putt anything under 'is eyes an' 'e'd never see it; and them other boys, tu, they'm rattlin' fellers. But you take an' putt our Megan where there's suthin', she'll zee it, an' more tu, or I'm mistaken."

"She's sensitive, that's why."

"What's that?"

"I mean, she feels everything."

"Ah! She'm very lovin'-'earted."

Ashurst, who felt color coming into his cheeks, held out his tobacco pouch.

"Have a fill, Jim?"

"Thank 'ee, sir. She'm one in an 'underd, I think."

"I expect so," said Ashurst shortly, and folding up his pouch, walked on.

"Lovin'-'earted!" Yes! And what was he doing? What were his intentions—as they say—towards this loving-hearted girl? The thought dogged him, wandering through fields bright with buttercups, where the little red calves were feeding, and the swallows flying high. Yes, the oaks were before the ashes, brown-gold already; every tree in different stage and hue. The cuckoos and a thousand birds were singing; the little streams were very bright. The ancients believed in a golden age, in the garden of the Hesperides! . . . A queen wasp settled on his sleeve. Each queen wasp killed meant two thousand fewer wasps to thieve the apples which would grow from that blossom in the orchard; but who, with love in his heart, could kill anything on a day like this? He entered a field where a young red bull was feeding. It seemed to Ashurst that he looked like Joe. But the young bull took no notice of this visitor, a little drunk himself, perhaps, on the singing and the glamour of the golden pasture, under his short legs. Ashurst crossed out unchallenged to the hillside above the stream. From that slope a tor mounted to its crown of rocks. The ground there was covered with a mist of bluebells, and nearly a score of crab-apple trees were in full bloom. He threw himself down on the grass. The change from the buttercup glory and oak-goldened glamour of the fields to this ethereal beauty under the gray tor filled him with a sort of wonder; nothing the same, save the sound of running water and the songs of the cuckoos. He lay there a long time, watching the sunlight wheel till the crab-trees threw shadows over the bluebells, his only companions a few wild bees. He was not quite sane, thinking of that morning's kiss, and of to-night under the apple-tree. In such a spot as this, fauns and dryads surely lived; nymphs, white as the crab-apple blossom, retired within those trees; fauns, brown as the dead bracken, with pointed ears, lay in wait for them. The cuckoos were still calling when he woke, there was the sound of running water; but the sun had couched behind the tor, the hillside was cool, and some rabbits had come out. "To-night!" he thought. Just as from the earth everything was pushing up, unfolding under the soft insistent fingers of an unseen hand, so were his heart and senses being pushed, unfolded. He got up and broke off a spray from a crab-apple tree. The buds were like Megan—shell-like, rose-pink, wild, and fresh; and so, too, the opening flowers, white, and wild, and touching. He put the spray into his coat. And all the rush of the spring within him escaped in a triumphant sigh. But the rabbits scurried away.

VI

It was nearly eleven that night when Ashurst put down the pocket "Odyssey" which for half an hour he had held in his hands without reading, and slipped through the yard down to the orchard. The moon had just risen, very golden, over the hill, and like a bright, powerful, watching spirit peered through the bars of an ash tree's half-naked boughs. In among the apple-trees it was still dark, and he stood making sure of his direction, feeling the rough grass with his feet. A black mass close behind him stirred with a heavy grunting sound, and three large pigs settled down again close to each other, under the wall. He listened. There was no wind, but the stream's burbling whispering chuckle had gained twice its daytime strength. One bird, he could not tell what, cried "Pip—pip," "Pip—pip," with perfect monotony; he could hear a night-jar spinning very far off; an owl hooting. Ashurst moved a step or two, and again halted, aware of a dim living whiteness all

round his head. On the dark unstirring trees in-
numerable flowers and buds all soft and blurred
were being bewitched to life by the creeping moonlight. He had the oddest feeling of actual companionship, as if a million white moths or spirits had floated
in and settled between dark sky and darker ground,
and were opening and shutting their wings on a level
with his eyes. In the bewildering, still, scentless
beauty of that moment he almost lost memory of
why he had come to the orchard. The flying glamour
which had clothed the earth all day had not gone
now that night had fallen, but only changed into this
new form. He moved on through the thicket of stems
and boughs covered with that live powdering whiteness, till he reached the big apple-tree. No mistaking
that, even in the dark, nearly twice the height and
size of any other, and leaning out towards the open
meadows and the stream. Under the thick branches
he stood still again, to listen. The same sounds exactly, and a faint grunting from the sleepy pigs. He
put his hands on the dry, almost warm tree trunk,
whose rough mossy surface gave forth a peaty scent at
his touch. Would she come—would she? And among
these quivering, haunted, moon-witched trees he was
seized with doubts of everything! All was unearthly
here, fit for no earthly lovers; fit only for god and
goddess, faun and nymph—not for him and this little
country girl. Would it not be almost a relief if she did
not come? But all the time he was listening. And still
that unknown bird went "Pip—pip," "Pip—pip," and
there rose the busy chatter of the little trout stream,
whereon the moon was flinging glances through the
bars of her tree-prison. The blossom on a level with
his eyes seemed to grow more living every moment,
seemed with its mysterious white beauty more and
more a part of his suspense. He plucked a fragment
and held it close—three blossoms. Sacrilege to pluck
fruit-tree blossom—soft, sacred, young blossom—and
throw it away! Then suddenly he heard the gate
close, the pigs stirring again and grunting; and leaning against the trunk, he pressed his hands to its
mossy sides behind him, and held his breath. She
might have been a spirit threading the trees, for all
the noise she made! Then he saw her quite close—her
dark form part of a little tree, her white face part of
its blossom; so still, and peering towards him. He
whispered: "Megan!" and held out his hands. She
ran forward, straight to his breast. When he felt her
heart beating against him, Ashurst knew to the full
the sensations of chivalry and passion. Because she
was not of his world, because she was so simple and
young and headlong, adoring and defenseless, how
could he be other than her protector in the dark! Because she was all simple Nature and beauty, as much
a part of this spring night as was the living blossom,

how should he not take all that she would give him
—how not fulfill the spring in her heart and his!
And torn between these two emotions he clasped her
close, and kissed her hair. How long they stood there
without speaking he knew not. The stream went on
chattering, the owls hooting, the moon kept stealing
up and growing whiter; the blossom all round them
and above frightened in suspense of living beauty.
Their lips had sought each other's, and they did not
speak. The moment speech began all would be unreal! Spring has no speech, nothing but rustling and
whispering. Spring has so much more than speech in
its unfolding flowers and leaves, and the coursing of
its streams, and in its sweet restless seeking! And
sometimes spring will come alive, and, like a mysterious Presence, stand, encircling lovers with its arms,
laying on them the fingers of enchantment, so that,
standing lips to lips, they forget everything but just
a kiss. While her heart beat against him, and her lips
quivered on his, Ashurst felt nothing but simple
rapture—Destiny meant her for his arms, Love could
not be flouted! But when their lips parted for breath,
division began again at once. Only, passion now was
so much the stronger, and he sighed:

"Oh! Megan! Why did you come?"

She looked up, hurt, amazed.

"Sir, you asked me to."

"Don't call me 'sir,' my pretty sweet."

"What should I be callin' you?"

"Frank."

"I could not. Oh, no!"

"But you love me—don't you?"

"I could not help lovin' you. I want to be with you
—that's all."

"All!"

So faint that he hardly heard, she whispered:

"I shall die if I can't be with you."

Ashurst took a mighty breath.

"Come and be with me, then!"

"Oh!"

Intoxicated by the awe and rapture in that "Oh!"
he went on, whispering:

"We'll go to London. I'll show you the world. And
I *will* take care of you, I promise, Megan. I'll never
be a brute to you!"

"If I can be with you—that is all."

He stroked her hair, and whispered on:

"To-morrow I'll go to Torquay and get some
money, and get you some clothes that won't be
noticed, and then we'll steal away. And when we
get to London, soon perhaps, if you love me well
enough, we'll be married."

He could feel her hair shiver with the shake of her
head.

"Oh, no! I could not. I only want to be with you!"

Drunk on his own chivalry, Ashurst went on murmuring:

"It's I who am not good enough for you. Oh! Megan, when did you begin to love me?"

"When I saw you in the road, and you looked at me. The first night I loved you; but I never thought you would want me."

She slipped down suddenly to her knees, trying to kiss his feet.

A shiver of horror went through Ashurst; he lifted her up bodily and held her fast—too upset to speak.

She whispered: "Why won't you let me?"

"It's I who will kiss your feet!"

Her smile brought tears into his eyes. The whiteness of her moonlit face so close to his, the faint pink of her opened lips, had the living, unearthly beauty of the apple blossom.

And then, suddenly, her eyes widened and stared past him painfully; she writhed out of his arms, and whispered: "Look!"

Ashurst saw nothing but the brightened stream, the furze faintly gilded, the beech trees glistening, and behind them all the wide loom of the moonlit hill. Behind him came her frozen whisper: "The gypsy bogle!"

"Where?"

"There—by the stone—under the trees!"

Exasperated, he leapt the stream, and strode towards the beech clump. Prank of the moonlight! Nothing! In and out of the bowlders and thorn trees, muttering and cursing, yet with a kind of terror, he rushed and stumbled. Absurd! Silly! Then he went back to the apple-tree. But she was gone; he could hear a rustle, the grunting of the pigs, the sound of a gate closing. Instead of her, only this old apple-tree! He flung his arms round the trunk. What a substitute for her soft body; the rough moss against his face—what a substitute for her soft cheek; only the scent, as of the woods, a little the same! And above him, and around, the blossoms, more living, more moonlit than ever, seemed to glow and breathe.

VII

Descending from the train at Torquay station, Ashurst wandered uncertainly along the front, for he did not know this particular queen of English watering-places. Having little sense of what he had on, he was quite unconscious of being remarkable among its inhabitants, and strode along in his rough Norfolk jacket, dusty boots, and battered hat, without observing that people gazed at him rather blankly. He was seeking a branch of his London bank, and having found one, found also the first obstacle to his mood.

Did he know any one in Torquay! No. In that case, if he would wire to his bank in London, they would be happy to oblige him on receipt of the reply. That suspicious breath from the matter-of-fact world somewhat tarnished the brightness of his visions. But he sent the telegram.

Nearly opposite to the post office he saw a shop full of ladies' garments, and examined the window with strange sensations. To have to undertake the clothing of his rustic love was more than a little disturbing. He went in. A young woman came forward; she had blue eyes and a faintly puzzled forehead. Ashurst stared at her in silence.

"Yes, sir?"

"I want a dress for a young lady."

The young woman smiled. Ashurst frowned—the peculiarity of his request struck him with sudden force.

The young woman added hastily:

"What style would you like—something modish?"

"No. Simple."

"What figure would the young lady be?"

"I don't know; about two inches shorter than you, I should say."

"Could you give me her waist measurement?"

Megan's waist!

"Oh! anything usual!"

"Quite!"

While she was gone he stood disconsolately eyeing the models in the window, and suddenly it seemed to him incredible that Megan—his Megan—could ever be dressed save in the rough tweed skirt, coarse blouse, and tam-o'-shanter cap he was wont to see her in. The young woman had come back with several dresses in her arms, and Ashurst eyed her laying them against her own modish figure. There was one whose color he liked, a dove-gray, but to imagine Megan clothed in it was beyond him. The young woman went away, and brought some more. But on Ashurst there had now come a feeling of paralysis. How choose? She would want a hat too, and shoes, and gloves; and, suppose, when he had got them all, they commonized her, as Sunday clothes always commonized village folk! Why should she not travel as she was? Ah? But conspicuousness would matter; this was a serious elopement. And, staring at the young woman, he thought: "I wonder if she guesses, and thinks me a blackguard?"

"Do you mind putting aside that gray one for me?" he said desperately at last. "I can't decide now; I'll come in again this afternoon."

The young woman sighed.

"Oh! certainly. It's a very tasteful costume. I don't think you'll get anything that will suit your purpose better."

"I expect not," Ashurst murmured, and went out.

Freed again from the suspicious matter-of-factness of the world, he took a long breath, and went back to visions. In fancy he saw the trustful, pretty creature who was going to join her life to his; saw himself and her stealing forth at night, walking over the moor under the moon, he with his arm around her, and carrying her new garments, till, in some far-off wood, when dawn was coming, she would slip off her old things and put on these, and an early train at a distant station would bear them away on their honeymoon journey, till London swallowed them up, and the dreams of love came true.

"Frank Ashurst! Haven't seen you since Rugby, old chap!"

Ashurst's frown dissolved; the face, close to his own, was blue-eyed, suffused with sun—one of those faces where sun from within and without join in a sort of luster. And he answered:

"Phil Halliday, by Jove!"

"What are you doing here?"

"Oh! nothing. Just looking round, and getting some money. I'm staying on the moor."

"Are you lunching anywhere? Come and lunch with us; I'm here with my young sisters. They've had measles."

Hooked in by that friendly arm Ashurst went along, up a hill, down a hill, away out of the town, while the voice of Halliday, redolent of optimism as his face was of sun, explained how "in this moldy place the only decent things were the bathing and boating," and so on, till presently they came to a crescent of houses a little above and back from the sea, and into the center one—an hotel—made their way.

"Come up to my room and have a wash. Lunch'll be ready in a jiffy."

Ashurst contemplated his visage in a looking-glass. After his farmhouse bedroom, the comb and one spare shirt *régime* of the last fortnight, this room littered with clothes and brushes was a sort of Capua; and he thought:

"Queer—one doesn't realize—" But what—he did not quite know.

When he followed Halliday into the sitting-room for lunch, three faces, very fair and blue-eyed, were turned suddenly at the words: "This is Frank Ashurst —my young sisters."

Two were indeed young, about eleven and ten. The third was perhaps seventeen, tall and fair-haired too, with pink-and-white cheeks just touched by the sun, and eyebrows, rather darker than the hair, running a little upwards from her nose to their outer points. The voices of all three were like Halliday's, high and cheerful; they stood up straight, shook hands with a quick movement, looked at Ashurst critically, away again at once, and began to talk of what they were going to do in the afternoon. A regular Diana and attendant nymphs! After the farm this crisp, slangy, eager talk, this cool, clean, offhand refinement, was queer at first, and then so natural that what he had come from became suddenly remote. The names of the two little ones seemed to be Sabina and Freda; of the eldest, Stella.

Presently the one called Sabina turned to him and said:

"I say, will you come shrimping with us?—it's awful fun!"

Surprised by this unexpected friendliness, Ashurst murmured:

"I'm afraid I've got to get back this afternoon."

"Oh!"

"Can't you put it off?"

Ashurst turned to the new speaker, Stella, shook his head, and smiled. She was very pretty! Sabina said regretfully: "You might!" Then the talk switched off to caves and swimming.

"Can you swim far?"

"About two miles."

"Oh!"

"I say!"

"How jolly!"

The three pairs of blue eyes, fixed on him, made him conscious of his new importance. The sensation was agreeable. Halliday said:

"I say, you simply must stop and have a bathe. You'd better stay the night."

"Yes, do!"

But again Ashurst smiled and shook his head. Then suddenly he found himself being catechized about his physical achievements. He had rowed—it seemed—in his college boat, played in his college football team, won his college mile, and he rose from table a sort of hero. The two little girls insisted that he must see "their" cave, and they set forth chattering like magpies, Ashurst between them, Stella and her brother a little behind. In the cave, damp and darkish like any other cave, the great feature was a pool with possibility of creatures which might be caught and put into bottles. Sabina and Freda, who wore no stockings on their shapely brown legs, exhorted Ashurst to join them in the middle of it, and help sieve the water. He too was soon bootless and sockless. Time goes fast for one who has a sense of beauty, when there are pretty children in a pool and a young Diana on the edge, to receive with wonder anything you can catch! Ashurst never had much sense of time. It was a shock when, pulling out his watch, he saw it was well past three. No cashing his check to-day—the bank would be closed before he could get there. Watching his expression, the little girls cried out at once:

"Hurrah! Now you'll have to stay!"

Ashurst did not answer. He was seeing again Megan's face, when at breakfast he had whispered: "I'm going to Torquay, darling, to get everything; I shall be back this evening. If it's fine we can go to-night. Be ready." He was seeing again how she quivered and hung on his words. What would she think? Then he pulled himself together, conscious suddenly of the calm scrutiny of this other young girl, so tall and fair and Diana-like, at the edge of the pool, of her wondering blue eyes under those brows which slanted up a little. If they knew what was in his mind—if they knew that this very night he had meant—! Well, there would be a little sound of disgust, and he would be alone in the cave. And with a curious mixture of anger, chagrin, and shame, he put his watch back into his pocket and said abruptly:

"Yes; I'm dished for to-day."

"Hurrah! Now you can bathe with us."

It was impossible not to succumb a little to the contentment of these pretty children, to the smile on Stella's lips, to Halliday's "Ripping, old chap! I can lend you things for the night!" But again a spasm of longing and remorse throbbed through Ashurst, and he said moodily:

"I must send a wire!"

The attractions of the pool palling, they went back to the hotel. Ashurst sent his wire, addressing it to Mrs. Narracombe: "Sorry, detained for the night, back to-morrow." Surely Megan would understand that he had too much to do; and his heart grew lighter. It was a lovely afternoon, warm, the sea calm and blue, and swimming his great passion; the favor of these pretty children flattered him, the pleasure of looking at them, at Stella, at Halliday's sunny face; the slight unreality, yet extreme naturalness of it all —as of a last peep at normality before he took this plunge with Megan! He got his borrowed bathing dress, and they all set forth. Halliday and he undressed behind one rock, the three girls behind another. He was first into the sea, and at once swam out with the bravado of justifying his self-given reputation. When he turned he could see Halliday swimming along shore, and the girls flopping and dipping, and riding the little waves, in the way he was accustomed to despise, but now thought pretty and sensible, since it gave him the distinction of the only deep-water fish. But drawing near, he wondered if they would like him, a stranger, to come into their splashing group; he felt shy, approaching that slim nymph. Then Sabina summoned him to teach her to float, and between them the little girls kept him so busy that he had no time even to notice whether Stella was accustomed to his presence, till suddenly he heard a startled sound from her. She was standing submerged to the waist, leaning a little forward, her slim white arms stretched out and pointing, her wet face puckered by the sun and an expression of fear.

"Look at Phil! Is he all right? Oh, look!"

Ashurst saw at once that Phil was not all right. He was splashing and struggling out of his depth, perhaps a hundred yards away; suddenly he gave a cry, threw up his arms, and went down. Ashurst saw the girl launch herself towards him, and crying out: "Go back, Stella! Go back!" he dashed out. He had never swum so fast, and reached Halliday just as he was coming up a second time. It was a case of cramp, but to get him in was not difficult, for he did not struggle. The girl, who had stopped where Ashurst told her to, helped as soon as he was in his depth, and once on the beach they sat down one on each side of him to rub his limbs, while the little ones stood by with scared faces. Halliday was soon smiling. It was—he said—rotten of him, absolutely rotten! If Frank would give him an arm, he could get to his clothes all right now. Ashurst gave him the arm, and as he did so caught sight of Stella's face, wet and flushed and tearful, all broken up out of its calm; and he thought: "I called her Stella! Wonder if she minded?"

While they were dressing, Halliday said quietly: "You saved my life, old chap!"

"Rot!"

Clothed, but not quite in their right minds, they went up all together to the hotel and sat down to tea, except Halliday, who was lying down in his room. After some slices of bread and jam, Sabina said:

"I say, you know, you *are* a brick!" And Freda chimed in:

"Rather!"

Ashurst saw Stella looking down; he got up in confusion, and went to the window. From there he heard Sabina mutter: "I say, let's swear blood bond. Where's your knife, Freda?" and out of the corner of his eye he could see each of them solemnly prick herself, squeeze out a drop of blood and dabble on a bit of paper. He turned and made for the door.

"Don't be a stoat! Come back!" His arms were seized; imprisoned between the little girls he was brought back to the table. On it lay a piece of paper with an effigy drawn in blood, and the three names Stella Halliday, Sabina Halliday, Freda Halliday— also in blood, running towards it like the rays of a star. Sabina said:

"That's you. We shall have to kiss you, you know."

And Freda echoed:

"Oh! Blow—Yes!"

Before Ashurst could escape, some wettish hair dangled against his face, something like a bite descended on his nose, he felt his left arm pinched, and other teeth softly searching his cheek. Then he was released, and Freda said:

"Now, Stella."

Ashurst, red and rigid, looked across the table at a red and rigid Stella. Sabina giggled; Freda cried:

"Buck up—it spoils everything!"

A queer, ashamed eagerness shot through Ashurst; then he said quietly:

"Shut up, you little demons!"

Again Sabina giggled.

"Well, then, she can kiss her hand, and you can put it against your nose. It *is* on one side!"

To his amazement the girl did kiss her hand and stretch it out. Solemnly he took that cool, slim hand and laid it to his cheek. The two little girls broke into clapping, and Freda said:

"Now, then, we shall have to save your life at any time; that's settled. Can I have another cup, Stella, not so beastly weak?"

Tea was resumed, and Ashurst, folding up the paper, put it in his pocket. The talk turned on the advantages of measles, tangerine oranges, honey in a spoon, no lessons, and so forth. Ashurst listened, silent, exchanging friendly looks with Stella, whose face was again of its normal sun-touched pink and white. It was soothing to be so taken to the heart of this jolly family, fascinating to watch their faces. And after tea, while the two little girls pressed seaweed, he talked to Stella in the window seat and looked at her water-color sketches. The whole thing was like a pleasurable dream; time and incident hung up, importance and reality suspended. To-morrow he would go back to Megan, with nothing of all this left save the paper with the blood of these children, in his pocket. Children! Stella was not quite that—as old as Megan! Her talk—quick, rather hard and shy, yet friendly—seemed to flourish on his silences, and about her there was something cool and virginal—a maiden in a bower. At dinner, to which Halliday, who had swallowed too much sea water, did not come, Sabina said:

"I'm going to call you Frank."

Freda echoed:

"Frank, Frank, Franky."

Ashurst grinned and bowed.

"Every time Stella calls you Mr. Ashurst, she's got to pay a forfeit. It's ridiculous."

Ashurst looked at Stella, who grew slowly red. Sabina giggled; Freda cried:

"She's 'smoking'—'smoking'!—Yah!"

Ashurst reached out to right and left, and grasped some fair hair in each hand.

"Look here," he said, "you two! Leave Stella alone, or I'll tie you together!"

Freda gurgled:

"Ouch! You *are* a beast!"

Sabina murmured cautiously:

"*You* call *her* Stella, you see!"

"Why shouldn't I? It's a jolly name!"

"All right; we give you leave to!"

Ashurst released the hair. Stella! What would she call him—after this? But she called him nothing; till at bed-time he said, deliberately:

"Good night, Stella!"

"Good night, Mr.—Good night, Frank! It *was* jolly of you, you know!"

"Oh—that! Bosh!"

Her quick, straight handshake tightened suddenly, and as suddenly, became slack.

Ashurst stood motionless in the empty sitting-room. Only last night, under the apple-tree and the living blossoms, he had held Megan to him, kissing her eyes and lips. And he gasped, swept by that rush of remembrance. To-night it should have begun—his life with her who only wanted to be with him! And now, twenty-four hours and more must pass, because—of not looking at his watch! Why had he made friends with this family of innocents just when he was saying good-by to innocence, and all the rest of it? "But I mean to marry her," he thought; "I told her so!"

He took a candle, lighted it, and went to his bedroom, which was next to Halliday's. His friend's voice called as he was passing:

"Is that you, old chap? I say, come in."

He was sitting up in bed, smoking a pipe and reading.

"Sit down a bit."

Ashurst sat down by the open window.

"I've been thinking about this afternoon, you know," said Halliday rather suddenly. "They say you go through all your past. I didn't. I suppose I wasn't far enough gone."

"What did you think of?"

Halliday was silent for a little, then said quietly:

"Well, I did think of one thing—rather odd—of a girl at Cambridge that I might have—you know; I was glad I hadn't got her on my mind. Anyhow, old chap, I owe it to you that I'm here; I should have been in the big dark by now. No more bed, or baccy; no more anything. I say, what d'you suppose happens to us?"

Ashurst murmured:

"Go out like flames, I expect."

"Phew!"

"We may flicker, and cling about a bit, perhaps."

"H'm! I think that's rather gloomy. I say, I hope my young sisters have been decent to you?"

"Awfully decent."

Halliday put his pipe down, crossed his hands behind his neck, and turned his face towards the window.

"They're not bad kids!" he said.

Watching his friend, lying there, with that smile, and the candle-light on his face, Ashurst shuddered. Quite true! He might have been lying there with no smile, with all that sunny look gone out forever! He might not have been lying there at all, but "sanded" at the bottom of the sea, waiting for resurrection on the—ninth day, was it? And that smile of Halliday's seemed to him suddenly something wonderful, as if in it were all the difference between life and death— the little flame—the all! He got up, and said softly:

"Well, you ought to sleep, I expect. Shall I blow out?"

Halliday caught his hand.

"I can't say it, you know; but it must be rotten to be dead. Good night, old boy!"

Stirred and moved, Ashurst squeezed the hand, and went downstairs. The hall door was still open, and he passed out on to the lawn before the Crescent. The stars were bright in a very dark blue sky, and by their light some lilacs had that mysterious color of flowers by night which no one can describe. Ashurst pressed his face against a spray; and before his closed eyes Megan started up, with the tiny brown spaniel pup against her breast. "I thought of a girl that I might have—you know. I was glad I hadn't got her on my mind!" He jerked his head away from the lilac, and began pacing up and down over the grass, a gray phantom coming to substance for a moment in the light from the lamp at either end. He was with her again under the living, breathing whiteness of the blossom, the stream chattering by, the moon glinting steel-blue on the bathing-pool; back in the rapture of his kisses on her upturned face of innocence and humble passion, back in the suspense and beauty of that pagan night. He stood still once more in the shadow of the lilacs. Here the sea, not the stream, was Night's voice; the sea with its sigh and rustle; no little bird, no owl, no night-jar called or spun; but a piano tinkled, and the white houses cut the sky with solid curve, and the scent from the lilacs filled the air. A window of the hotel, high up, was lighted; he saw a shadow move across the blind. And most queer sensations stirred within him, a sort of churning, and twining, and turning of a single emotion on itself, as though spring and love, bewildered and confused, seeking the way, were baffled. This girl, who had called him Frank, whose hand had given his that sudden little clutch, this girl so cool and pure—what would *she* think of such wild, unlawful loving? He sank down on the grass, sitting there cross-legged,

with his back to the house, motionless as some carved Buddha. Was he really going to break through innocence, and steal? Sniff the scent out of a wild flower, and—perhaps—throw it away? "Of a girl at Cambridge that I might have—you know!" He put his hands to the grass, one on each side, palms downwards, and pressed; it was just warm still—the grass, barely moist, soft and firm and friendly. "What am I going to do?" he thought. Perhaps Megan was at her window, looking out at the blossom, thinking of him! Poor little Megan! "Why not?" he thought. "I love her! But do I—really love her? or do I only want her because she is so pretty, and loves me? What am I going to do?" The piano tinkled on, the stars winked; and Ashurst gazed out before him at the dark sea, as if spellbound. He got up at last, cramped and rather chilly. There was no longer light in any window. And he went in to bed.

VIII

Out of a deep and dreamless sleep he was awakened by the sound of thumping on the door. A shrill voice called:

"Hi! Breakfast's ready."

He jumped up. Where was he—? Ah!

He found them already eating marmalade, and sat down in the empty place between Stella and Sabina, who, after watching him a little, said:

"I say, do buck up; we're going to start at half-past nine."

"We're going to Berry Head, old chap; you *must* come!"

Ashurst thought: "Come! Impossible. I shall be getting things and going back." He looked at Stella. She said quickly:

"Do come!"

Sabina chimed in:

"It'll be no fun without you."

Freda got up and stood behind his chair.

"You've got to come, or else I'll pull your hair!"

Ashurst thought: "Well—one day more—to think it over! One day more!" And he said:

"All right! You needn't tweak my mane!"

"Hurrah!"

At the station he wrote a second telegram to the farm, and then—tore it up; he could not have explained why. From Brixham they drove in a very little wagonette. There, squeezed between Sabina and Freda, with his knees touching Stella's, they played "Up Jenkins"; and the gloom he was feeling gave way to frolic. In this one day more to think it over, he did not want to think! They ran races, wrestled, paddled—for to-day nobody wanted to bathe—they sang catches, played games, and ate all they had brought. The little girls fell asleep against him on the way back, and his knees still touched Stella's in the wagonette. It seemed incredible that thirty hours ago he had never set eyes on any of those three flaxen heads. In the train he talked to Stella of poetry, discovering her favorites, and telling her his own with a pleasing sense of superiority; till suddenly she said, rather low:

"Phil says you don't believe in a future life, Frank. I think that's dreadful."

Disconcerted, Ashurst muttered:

"I don't either believe or not believe—I simply don't know."

She said quickly:

"I couldn't bear that. What would be the use of living?"

Watching the frown of those pretty oblique brows, Ashurst answered:

"I don't believe in believing things because one wants to."

"But why should one *wish* to live again, if one isn't going to?"

And she looked full at him.

He did not want to hurt her, but an itch to dominate pushed him on to say:

"While one's alive one naturally wants to go on living forever; that's part of being alive. But it probably isn't anything more."

"Don't you believe in the Bible at all, then?"

Ashurst thought: "Now I shall really hurt her!"

"I believe in the Sermon on the Mount, because it's beautiful and good for all time."

"But don't you believe Christ was divine?"

He shook his head.

She turned her face quickly to the window, and there sprang into his mind Megan's prayer, repeated by little Nick: "God bless us all, and Mr. Ashes!" Who else would ever say a prayer for him, like her who at this moment must be waiting—waiting to see him come down the lane? And he thought suddenly: "What a scoundrel I am!"

All that evening this thought kept coming back; but, as is not unusual, each time with less poignancy, till it seemed almost a matter of course to be a scoundrel. And—strange!—he did not know whether he was a scoundrel if he meant to go back to Megan, or if he did not mean to go back to her.

They played cards till the children were sent off to bed; then Stella went to the piano. From over on the window seat, where it was nearly dark, Ashurst watched her between the candles—that fair head on the long, white neck bending to the movement of her hands. She played fluently, without much expression; but what a picture she made, the faint golden radiance, a sort of angelic atmosphere—hovering about

her! Who could have passionate thought or wild desires in the presence of that swaying, white-clothed girl with the seraphic head? She played a thing of Schumann's called "*Warum?*" Then Halliday brought out a flute, and the spell was broken. After this they made Ashurst sing, Stella playing him accompaniments from a book of Schumann songs, till, in the middle of "*Ich grolle nicht,*" two small figures clad in blue dressing-gowns crept in and tried to conceal themselves beneath the piano. The evening broke up in confusion, and what Sabina called "a splendid rag."

That night Ashurst hardly slept at all. He was thinking, tossing and turning. The intense domestic intimacy of these last two days, the strength of this Halliday atmosphere, seemed to ring him round, and make the farm and Megan—even Megan—seem unreal. Had he really made love to her—really promised to take her away to live with him? He must have been bewitched by the spring, the night, the apple blossom! The notion that he was going to make her his mistress—that simple child not yet eighteen—now filled him with a sort of horror, even while it still stung and whipped his blood. He muttered to himself: "It's awful, what I've done—awful!" And the sound of Schumann's music throbbed and mingled with his fevered thoughts, and he saw again Stella's cool, white, fair-haired figure and bending neck, the queer, angelic radiance about her. "I must have been—I must be—mad!" he thought. "What came into me? Poor little Megan!" "God bless us all, and Mr. Ashes!" "I want to be with you—only to be with you!" And burying his face in his pillow, he smothered down a fit of sobbing. Not to go back was awful! To go back—more awful still!

Emotion, when you are young, and give real vent to it, loses its power of torture. And he fell asleep, thinking: "What was it—a few kisses—all forgotten in a month!"

Next morning he got his check cashed, but avoided the shop of the dove-gray dress like the plague; and, instead, bought himself some necessaries. He spent the whole day in a queer mood, cherishing a kind of sullenness against himself. Instead of the hankering of the last two days, he felt nothing but a blank—all passionate longing gone, as if quenched in that outburst of tears. After tea Stella put a book down beside him, and said shyly:

"Have you read that, Frank?"

It was Farrar's "Life of Christ." Ashurst smiled. Her anxiety about his beliefs seemed to him comic, but touching. Infectious, too, perhaps, for he began to have an itch to justify himself, if not to convert her. And in the evening, when the children and Halliday were mending their shrimping nets, he said:

"At the back of orthodox religion, so far as I can see, there's always the idea of reward—what you can get for being good; a kind of begging for favors. I think it all starts in fear."

She was sitting on the sofa making reefer knots with a bit of string. She looked up quickly:

"I think it's much deeper than that."

Ashurst felt again that wish to dominate.

"You think so," he said; "but wanting the *quid pro quo* is about the deepest thing in all of us! It's jolly hard to get to the bottom of it!"

She wrinkled her brows in a puzzled frown.

"I don't think I understand."

He went on obstinately:

"Well, think, and see if the most religious people aren't those who feel that this life doesn't give them all they want. I believe in being good because to be good is good in itself."

"Then you do believe in being good?"

How pretty she looked now—it was easy to be good with her! And he nodded and said:

"I say, show me how to make that knot!"

With her fingers touching his, in maneuvering the bit of string he felt soothed and happy. And when he went to bed he willfully kept his thoughts on her, wrapping himself in her fair, cool sisterly radiance, as in some garment of protection.

Next day he found they had arranged to go by train to Totness, and picnic at Berry Pomeroy Castle. Still in that resolute oblivion of the past, he took his place with them in the landau beside Halliday, back to the horses. And, then, along the sea front, nearly at the turning to the railway station, his heart almost leaped into his mouth. Megan—Megan herself!—was walking on the far pathway, in her old skirt and jacket and her tam-o'-shanter, looking up into the faces of the passers-by. Instinctively he threw his hand up for cover, then made a feint of clearing dust out of his eyes; but between his fingers he could see her still, moving, not with her free country step, but wavering, lost-looking, pitiful—like some little dog which has missed its master and does not know whether to run on, to run back—where to run. How had she come like this?—what excuse had she found to get away?—what did she hope for? But with every turn of the wheels bearing him away from her, his heart revolted and cried to him to stop them, to get out, and go to her! When the landau turned the corner to the station he could stand it no more, and opening the carriage door, muttered: "I've forgotten something! Go on—don't wait for me! I'll join you at the castle by the next train!" He jumped, stumbled, spun round, recovered his balance, and walked forward, while the carriage with the astonished Hallidays rolled on.

From the corner he could only just see Megan, a long way ahead now. He ran a few steps, checked himself, and dropped into a walk. With each step nearer to her, further from the Hallidays, he walked more and more slowly. How did it alter anything—this sight of her? How make the going to her, and that which must come of it, less ugly? For there was no hiding it—since he had met the Hallidays he had become gradually sure that he would not marry Megan. It would only be a wild love-time, a troubled, remorseful, difficult time—and then—well, then he would get tired, just because she gave him everything, was so simple, and so trustful, so dewy. And new—wears off! The little spot of faded color, her tam-o'-shanter cap, wavered on far in front of him; she was looking up into every face, and at the house windows. Had any man ever such a cruel moment to go through? Whatever he did, he felt he would be a beast. And he uttered a groan which made a nurse-maid turn and stare. He saw Megan stop and lean against the sea-wall, looking at the sea; and he too stopped. Quite likely she had never seen the sea before, and even in her distress could not resist that sight. "Yes—she's seen nothing," he thought; "everything's before her. And just for a few weeks' passion, I shall be cutting her life to ribbons. I'd better go and hang myself rather than do it!" And suddenly he seemed to see Stella's calm eyes looking into his, the wave of fluffy hair on her forehead stirred by the wind. Ah! it would be madness, would mean giving up all that he respected, and his own self-respect. He turned and walked quickly back towards the station. But memory of that poor, bewildered little figure, those anxious eyes searching the passers-by, smote him too hard again, and once more he turned towards the sea. The cap was no longer visible; that little spot of color had vanished in the stream of the noon promenaders. And impelled by the passion of longing, the dearth which comes on one when life seems to be whirling something out of reach, he hurried forward. She was nowhere to be seen; for half an hour he looked for her; then on the beach flung himself face downward in the sand. To find her again he knew he had only to go to the station and wait till she returned from her fruitless quest, to take her train home; or to take train himself and go back to the farm, so that she found him there when she returned. But he lay inert in the sand, among the indifferent groups of children with their spades and buckets. Pity at her little figure wandering, seeking, was well-nigh merged in the spring-running of his blood; for it was all wild feeling now—the chivalrous part, what there had been of it, was gone. He wanted her again, wanted her kisses, her soft, little body, her abandonment, all her quick, warm, pagan emotion;

wanted the wonderful feeling of that night under the moon-lit apple boughs; wanted it all with a horrible intensity, as the faun wants the nymph. The quick chatter of the little bright trout-stream, the dazzle of the buttercups, the rocks of the old "wild men"; the calling of the cuckoos and yaffles, the hooting of the owls; and the red moon peeping out of the velvet dark at the living whiteness of the blossom; and her face just out of reach at the window, lost in its love-look; and her heart against his, her lips answering his, under the apple-tree—all this besieged him. Yet he lay inert. What was it which struggled against pity and this feverish longing, and kept him there paralyzed in the warm sand? Three flaxen heads—a fair face with friendly blue-gray eyes, a slim hand pressing his, a quick voice speaking his name—"So you do believe in being good?" Yes, and a sort of atmosphere as of some old walled-in English garden, with pinks, and cornflowers, and roses, and scents of lavender and lilac—cool and fair, untouched, almost holy—all that he had been brought up to feel was clean and good. And suddenly he thought: "She might come along the front again and see me!" and he got up and made his way to the rock at the far end of the beach. There, with the spray biting into his face, he could think more coolly. To go back to the farm and love Megan out in the woods, among the rocks, with everything around wild and fitting— that, he knew, was impossible, utterly. To transplant her to a great town, to keep, in some little flat or rooms, one who belonged so wholly to Nature—the poet in him shrank from it. His passion would be a mere sensuous revel, soon gone; in London, her very simplicity, her lack of all intellectual quality, would make her his secret plaything—nothing else. The longer he sat on the rock, with his feet dangling over a greenish pool from which the sea was ebbing, the more clearly he saw this; but it was as if her arms and all of her were slipping slowly, slowly down from him, into the pool, to be carried away out to sea; and her face looking up, her lost face with beseeching eyes, and dark, wet hair—possessed, haunted, tortured him! He got up at last, scaled the low rock-cliff, and made his way down into a sheltered cove. Perhaps in the sea he could get back his control—lose his fever! And stripping off his clothes, he swam out. He wanted to tire himself so that nothing mattered, and swam recklessly, fast and far; then suddenly, for no reason, felt afraid. Suppose he could not reach shore again—suppose the current set him out—or he got cramps, like Halliday! He turned to swim in. The red cliffs looked a long way off. If he were drowned they would find his clothes. The Hallidays would know; but Megan perhaps never—they took no newspaper at the farm. And

Phil Halliday's words came back to him again: "A girl at Cambridge I might have— Glad I haven't got her on my mind!" And in that moment of unreasoning fear he vowed he would not have her on his mind. Then his fear left him; he swam in easily enough, dried himself in the sun, and put on his clothes. His heart felt sore, but no longer ached; his body cool and refreshed.

When one is as young as Ashurst, pity is not a violent emotion. And, back in the Hallidays' sitting-room, eating a ravenous tea, he felt much like a man recovered from fever. Everything seemed new and clear; the tea, the buttered toast, and jam tasted absurdly good; tobacco had never smelt so nice. And walking up and down the empty room, he stopped here and there to touch or look. He took up Stella's work-basket, fingered the cotton reels and a gayly colored plait of sewing silks, smelt at the little bag filled with wood-roffe she kept among them. He sat down at the piano, playing tunes with one finger, thinking: "To-night she'll play; I shall watch her while she's playing; it does me good to watch her." He took up the book, which still lay where she had placed it beside him, and tried to read. But Megan's little, sad figure began to come back at once, and he got up and leaned in the window, listening to the thrushes in the Crescent gardens, gazing at the sea, dreamy and blue below the trees. A servant came in and cleared the tea away, and he still stood, inhaling the evening air, trying not to think. Then he saw the Hallidays coming through the gate of the Crescent, Stella a little in front of Phil and the children, with their baskets, and instinctively he drew back. His heart, too sore and discomfited, shrank from this encounter, yet wanted its friendly solace—bore a grudge against this influence, yet craved its cool innocence, and the pleasure of watching Stella's face. From against the wall behind the piano he saw her come in and stand looking a little blank as though disappointed; then she saw him and smiled, a swift, brilliant smile which warmed yet irritated Ashurst.

"You never came after us, Frank."

"No; I found I couldn't."

"Look! We picked such lovely late violets!" She held out a bunch. Ashurst put his nose to them, and there stirred within him vague longings, chilled instantly by a vision of Megan's anxious face lifted to the faces of the passers-by.

He said shortly: "How jolly!" and turned away. He went up to his room, and, avoiding the children, who were coming up the stairs, threw himself on his bed, and lay there with his arms crossed over his face. Now that he felt the die really cast, and Megan given up, he hated himself, and almost hated the Hallidays and their atmosphere of healthy, happy

English homes. Why should they have chanced here, to drive away first love—to show him that he was going to be no better than a common seducer? What right had Stella, with her fair, shy beauty, to make him know for certain that he would never marry Megan; and, tarnishing it all, bring him such bitterness of regretful longing and such pity? Megan would be back by now, worn out by her miserable seeking—poor little thing!—expecting, perhaps, to find him there when she reached home. Ashurst bit at his sleeve, to stifle a groan of remorseful longing. He went to dinner glum and silent, and his mood threw a dinge even over the children. It was a melancholy, rather ill-tempered evening, for they were all tired; several times he caught Stella looking at him with a hurt, puzzled expression, and this pleased his evil mood. He slept miserably; got up quite early, and wandered out. He went down to the beach. Alone there with the serene, the blue, the sunlit sea, his heart relaxed a little. Conceited fool—to think that Megan would take it so hard! In a week or two she would almost have forgotten! And he—well, he would have the reward of virtue! A good young man! If Stella knew, she would give him her blessing for resisting that devil she believed in; and he uttered a hard laugh. But slowly the peace and beauty of sea and sky, the flight of the lonely seagulls, made him feel ashamed. He bathed, and turned homewards.

In the Crescent gardens Stella herself was sitting on a camp stool, sketching. He stole up close behind. How fair and pretty she was, bent diligently, holding up her brush, measuring, wrinkling her brows.

He said gently:

"Sorry I was such a beast last night, Stella."

She turned round, startled, flushed very pink, and said in her quick way:

"It's all right. I knew there was something. Between friends it doesn't matter, does it?"

Ashurst answered:

"Between friends—and we are, aren't we?"

She looked up at him, nodded vehemently, and her upper teeth gleamed again in that swift, brilliant smile.

Three days later he went back to London, traveling with the Hallidays. He had not written to the farm. What was there he could say?

On the last day of April in the following year he and Stella were married. . . .

Such were Ashurst's memories, sitting against the wall among the gorse, on his silver-wedding day. At this very spot, where he had laid out the lunch, Megan must have stood outlined against the sky when he had first caught sight of her. Of all queer coincidences! And there moved in him a longing to go down and see again the farm and the orchard, and the meadow of the gypsy bogle. It would not take long; Stella would be an hour yet, perhaps.

How well he remembered it all—the little crowning group of pine trees, the steep-up grass hill behind! He paused at the farm gate. The low stone house, the yew-tree porch, the flowering currants—not changed a bit; even the old green chair was out there on the grass under the window, where he had reached up to her that night to take the key. Then he turned down the lane, and stood leaning on the orchard gate—gray skeleton of a gate, as then. A black pig even was wandering in there among the trees. Was it true that twenty-six years had passed, or had he dreamed and awakened to find Megan waiting for him by the big apple-tree? Unconsciously he put up his hand to his grizzled beard and brought himself back to reality. Opening the gate, he made his way down through the docks and nettles till he came to the edge, and the old apple-tree itself. Unchanged! A little more of the gray-green lichen, a dead branch or two, and for the rest it might have been only last night that he had embraced that mossy trunk after Megan's flight and inhaled its woody savor, while above his head the moonlit blossom had seemed to breathe and live. In that early spring a few buds were showing already; the blackbirds shouting their songs, a cuckoo calling, the sunlight bright and warm. Incredibly the same—the chattering trout-stream, the narrow pool he had lain in every morning, splashing the water over his flanks and chest; and out there in the wild meadow the beech clump and the stone where the gypsy bogle was supposed to sit. And an ache for lost youth, a hankering, a sense of wasted love and sweetness, gripped Ashurst by the throat. Surely, on this earth of such wild beauty, one was meant to hold rapture to one's heart, as this earth and sky held it! And yet, one could not!

He went to the edge of the stream, and, looking down at the little pool, thought: "Youth and spring! What has become of them all, I wonder?" And then, in sudden fear of having this memory jarred by human encounter, he went back to the lane, and pensively retraced his steps to the cross-roads.

Beside the car an old, gray-bearded laborer was leaning on a stick, talking to the chauffeur. He broke off at once, as though guilty of disrespect, and, touching his hat, prepared to limp on down the lane.

Ashurst pointed to the narrow green mound. "Can you tell me what this is?"

The old fellow stopped; on his face had come a look as though he were thinking: "You've come to the right shop, mister!"

" 'Tes a grave," he said.

"But why out here?"

The old man smiled. "That's a tale, as yu may say. An' not the first time as I've a-told et—there's plenty folks asks 'bout that bit o' turf. 'Maid's Grave' us calls et, 'ereabouts."

Ashurst held out his pouch. "Have a fill?"

The old man touched his hat again, and slowly filled an old clay pipe. His eyes, looking upward out of a mass of wrinkles and hair, were still quite bright.

"If yu don' mind, zurr, I'll zet down—my leg's 'urtin' a bit to-day." And he sat down on the mound of turf.

"There's always a vlower on this grave. An' 'tain't so very lonesome, neither; brave lot o' folks goes by now, in they new motor cars an' things—not as 'twas in th' old days. She've a-got company up 'ere. 'Twas a poor soul killed 'erself."

"I see!" said Ashurst. "Cross-roads burial. I didn't know that custom was kept up."

"Ah! but 'twas a main long time ago. Us 'ad a parson as was very God-fearin' then. Let me see, I've 'ad my pension six year come Michaelmas, an' I were just on fifty when 't 'appened. There's none livin' knows more about et than what I du. She belonged close 'ere; same farm as where I used to work along o' Mrs. Narracombe—'tes Nick Narracombe's now; I dus a bit for 'im still, odd times."

Ashurst, who was leaning against the gate, lighting his pipe, left his curved hands before his face for long after the flame of the match had gone out.

"Yes?" he said, and to himself his voice sounded hoarse and queer.

"She was one in an 'underd, poor maid! I putts a vlower 'ere every time I passes. Pretty maid an' gude maid she was, though they wouldn't burry 'er up tu th' church, nor where she wanted to be burried neither." The old laborer paused, and put his hairy, twisted hand flat down on the turf beside the bluebells.

"Yes?" said Ashurst.

"In a manner of speakin'," the old man went on, "I think as 'twas a love-story—though there's no one never knu for zartin. Yu can't tell what's in a maid's 'ead—but that's wot I think about it." He drew his hand along the turf. "I was fond o' that maid—don' know as there was any one as wasn' fond of 'er. But she was tu lovin'-'earted—that's where 'twas, I think." He looked up. And Ashurst, whose lips were trembling in the cover of his beard, murmured again: "Yes?"

" 'Twas in the spring, 'bout now as 't might be, or a little later—blossom time—an' we 'ad one o' they young college gentlemen stayin' at the farm—nice feller tu, with 'is 'ead in the air. I liked 'e very well, an' I never see nothin' between 'em, but to my thinkin' 'e turned the maid's fancy." The old man took the pipe out of his mouth, spat, and went on: "Yu see, 'e went away sudden one day, an' never come back. They got 'is knapsack and bits o' things down there still. That's what stuck in my mind—'is never sendin' for 'em. 'Is name was Ashes, or somethin' like that."

"Yes?" said Ashurst once more.

The old man licked his lips.

" 'Er never said nothin', but from that day 'er went kind of dazed lukin'; didn' seem rightly therr at all. I never knu a 'uman creature so changed in me life—never. There was another young feller at the farm—Joe Biddaford 'is name wer', that was praaperly sweet on 'er, tu; I guess 'e used to plague 'er wi' 'is attentions. She got to luke quite wild. I'd zee her sometimes of an avenin' when I was bringin' up the calves; ther' she'd stand in th' orchard, under the big appletree, lukin' straight before 'er. 'Well,' I used t' think, 'I dunno what 'tes that's the matter wi' yu, but yu'm lukin' pitiful, that yu be!' "

The old man relit his pipe, and sucked at it reflectively.

"Yes?" said Ashurst.

"I remembers one day I said to 'er: 'What's the matter, Megan?'—'er name was Megan David, she come from Wales same as 'er aunt, ol' Missis Narracombe. 'Yu'm frettin' about something,' I says. 'No, Jim,' she says, 'I'm not frettin'.' 'Yes, yu be!' I says. 'No,' she says, and tu tears cam' rollin' out. 'Yu'm cryin'—what's that, then?' I says. She putts 'er 'and over 'er 'eart: 'It 'urts me,' she says; 'but 'twill sune be better,' she says. 'But if anything shude 'appen to me, Jim, I wants to be buried under this 'ere apple-tree.' I laughed. 'What's goin' to 'appen to yu?' I says: 'don' 'ee be fulish.' 'No,' she says, 'I won't be fulish.' Well, I know what maids are, an' I never thought no more about et, till tu days arter that, 'bout six in the avenin' I was comin' up wi' the calves, when I see somethin' dark lyin' in the strame, close to that big apple-tree. I says to meself: 'Is that a pig—funny place for a pig to get to!' an' I goes up to et, an' I see what 'twas."

The old man stopped: his eyes, turned upward, had a bright, suffering look.

" 'Twas the maid, in a little narrer pool ther' that's made by the stoppin' of a rock—where I see the young gentleman bathin' once or twice. 'Er was lyin' on 'er face in the watter. There was a plant o' goldie-cups growin' out o' the stone just above 'er 'ead. An' when I come to luke at 'er face, 'twas luvly, butiful, so calm's a baby's—wonderful butiful et wus. When the doctor saw 'er, 'e said: ' 'Er culdn' never a-done it in that little bit o' watter if 'er 'adn't a-been in an extarsy.' Ah! an' judgin' from 'er face, that was just 'ow she was. Et made me cry praaper—butiful et was! 'Twas June then, but she'd a-found a little bit of apple blossom left over somewheres, and stuck et in 'er 'air. That's why I thinks 'er must a-been in an extarsy, to go to et gay, like that. Why! there wasn't more than a fute and 'arf o' watter. But I tell 'ee one thing—that meadder's 'arnted; I knu et, an' she knu et; an' no one'll persuade me as 'tesn't. I told 'em what she said to me 'bout bein' buried under th' apple-tree. But I think that turned 'em—made et luke tu much 's ef she'd 'ad it in 'er mind deliberate; an' so they burried 'er up 'ere. Parson we 'ad then was very particular, 'e was."

Again the old man drew his hand over the turf.

" 'Tes wonderful, et seems," he added slowly, "what maids 'll du for love. She 'ad a lovin' 'eart; I guess 'twas broken. But us never *knu* nothin'!"

He looked up as if for approval of his story, but Ashurst had walked past him as if he were not there.

Up on the top of the hill, beyond where he had spread the lunch, over, out of sight, he lay down on his face. So had his virtue been rewarded, and "the Cyprian," goddess of love, taken her revenge! And before his eyes, dim with tears, came Megan's face with the sprig of apple blossoms in her dark, wet hair. 'What did I do that was wrong?' he thought. 'What did I do?' But he could not answer. Spring, with its rush of passion, its flowers and song—the spring in his heart and Megan's! Was it just Love seeking a victim! The Greek was right, then—the words of the "Hippolytus" as true to-day!

> *"For mad is the heart of Love,*
> *And gold the gleam of his wing;*
> *And all to the spell thereof*
> *Bend when he makes his spring.*
> *All life that is wild and young*
> *In mountain and wave and stream,*
> *All that of earth is sprung,*
> *Or breathes in the red sunbeam;*
> *Yea, and Mankind. O'er all a royal throne*
> *Cyprian, Cyprian, is thine alone!"*

The Greek was right! Megan! Poor little Megan—coming over the hill! Megan under the old apple-tree waiting and looking! Megan dead, with beauty printed on her! . . .

A voice said:

"Oh, there you are! Look."

Ashurst rose, took his wife's sketch, and stared at it in silence.

"Is the foreground right, Frank?"

"Yes."

"But there's something wanting, isn't there?"

Ashurst nodded. Wanting? The apple-tree, the singing, and the gold!

THE SECRET SHARER

JOSEPH CONRAD

JOSEPH CONRAD (1857–1924) was born Jósef Teodor Konrad Korzeniowski in Russian Poland. He went to sea before he was twenty in a French vessel, shifted to the English merchant service, learned English by reading newspapers and eventually passed the examinations for a master's command. At thirty-seven, after twenty years at sea, he retired to England, broken in health, and with the sympathetic encouragement of John Galsworthy turned to writing. Harassed by poverty, ill-health and the problem of language—it is said he thought in Polish, translated into French in his mind and then into English on paper—he nevertheless achieved a place in the very front rank of modern literature. Among his books are *Lord Jim* (1900), *Youth* (1902), *Nostromo* (1904), *Under Western Eyes* (1911), *Victory* (1915), *The Shadow Line* (1917). "Art," said Conrad in the 'Preface' to *The Nigger of the Narcissus* (1898), "may be defined as a single-minded attempt to render the highest kind of justice to the visible universe, by bringing to light the truth, manifold and one, underlying its every aspect. . . . My task which I am trying to achieve is, by the power of the written word to make you hear, to make you feel—it is, before all, to make you *see*. That—and no more, and it is everything. If I succeed, you shall find there according to your deserts: encouragement, consolation, fear, charm—all you demand—and, perhaps, also that glimpse of truth for which you have forgotten to ask."

ON my right hand there were lines of fishing-stakes resembling a mysterious system of half-submerged bamboo fences, incomprehensible in its division of the domain of tropical fishes, and crazy of aspect as if abandoned forever by some nomad tribe of fishermen now gone to the other end of the ocean; for there was no sign of human habitation as far as the eye could reach. To the left a group of barren islets, suggesting ruins of stone walls, towers, and blockhouses, had its foundations set in a blue sea that itself looked solid, so still and stable did it lie below my feet; even the track of light from the westering sun shone smoothly, without that animated glitter which tells of an imperceptible ripple. And when I turned my head to take a parting glance at the tug which had just left us anchored outside the bar, I saw the straight line of the flat shore joined to the stable sea, edge to edge, with a perfect and unmarked closeness, in one leveled floor half brown, half blue under the enormous dome of the sky. Corresponding in their insignificance to the islets of the sea, two small clumps of trees, one on each side of the only fault in the impeccable joint, marked the mouth of the river Meinam we had just left on the first preparatory stage of our homeward journey; and, far back on the inland level, a larger and loftier mass,

From *'Twixt Land and Sea* by Joseph Conrad by permission of the Trustees of the Joseph Conrad Estate and Messrs. J. M. Dent & Sons Ltd.

the grove surrounding the great Paknam pagoda, was the only thing on which the eye could rest from the vain task of exploring the monotonous sweep of the horizon. Here and there gleams as of a few scattered pieces of silver marked the windings of the great river; and on the nearest of them, just within the bar, the tug steaming right into the land became lost to my sight, hull and funnel and masts, as though the impassive earth had swallowed her up without an effort, without a tremor. My eye followed the light cloud of her smoke, now here, now there, above the plain, according to the devious curves of the stream, but always fainter and farther away, till I lost it at last behind the miter-shaped hill of the great pagoda. And then I was left alone with my ship, anchored at the head of the Gulf of Siam.

She floated at the starting-point of a long journey, very still in an immense stillness, the shadows of her spars flung far to the eastward by the setting sun. At that moment I was alone on her decks. There was not a sound in her—and around us nothing moved, nothing lived, not a canoe on the water, not a bird in the air, not a cloud in the sky. In this breathless pause at the threshold of a long passage we seemed to be measuring our fitness for a long and arduous enterprise, the appointed task of both our existences to be carried out, far from all human eyes, with only sky and sea for spectators and for judges.

There must have been some glare in the air to

interfere with one's sight, because it was only just before the sun left us that my roaming eyes made out beyond the highest ridge of the principal islet of the group something which did away with the solemnity of perfect solitude. The tide of darkness flowed on swiftly; and with tropical suddenness a swarm of stars came out above the shadowy earth, while I lingered yet, my hand resting lightly on my ship's rail as if on the shoulder of a trusted friend. But, with all that multitude of celestial bodies staring down at one, the comfort of quiet communion with her was gone for good. And there were also disturbing sounds by this time—voices, footsteps forward; the steward flitted along the main-deck, a busily ministering spirit; a hand-bell tinkled urgently under the poop-deck. . . .

I found my two officers waiting for me near the supper table, in the lighted cuddy. We sat down at once, and as I helped the chief mate, I said:

"Are you aware that there is a ship anchored inside the islands? I saw her mastheads above the ridge as the sun went down."

He raised sharply his simple face, overcharged by a terrible growth of whisker, and emitted his usual ejaculations: "Bless my soul, sir! You don't say so!"

My second mate was a round-cheeked, silent young man, grave beyond his years, I thought; but as our eyes happened to meet I detected a slight quiver on his lips. I looked down at once. It was not my part to encourage sneering on board my ship. It must be said, too, that I knew very little of my officers. In consequence of certain events of no particular significance, except to myself, I had been appointed to the command only a fortnight before. Neither did I know much of the hands forward. All these people had been together for eighteen months or so, and my position was that of the only stranger on board. I mention this because it has some bearing on what is to follow. But what I felt most was my being a stranger to the ship; and if all the truth must be told, I was somewhat of a stranger to myself. The youngest man on board (barring the second mate), and untried as yet by a position of the fullest responsibility, I was willing to take the adequacy of the others for granted. They had simply to be equal to their tasks; but I wondered how far I should turn out faithful to that ideal conception of one's own personality every man sets up for himself secretly.

Meantime the chief mate, with an almost visible effect of collaboration on the part of his round eyes and frightful whiskers, was trying to evolve a theory of the anchored ship. His dominant trait was to take all things into earnest consideration. He was of a painstaking turn of mind. As he used to say, he "liked to account to himself" for practically everything that came in his way, down to a miserable scorpion he had found in his cabin a week before. The why and the wherefore of that scorpion—how it got on board and came to select his room rather than the pantry (which was a dark place and more what a scorpion would be partial to), and how on earth it managed to drown itself in the inkwell of his writing-desk—had exercised him infinitely. The ship within the islands was much more easily accounted for; and just as we were about to rise from table he made his pronouncement. She was, he doubted not, a ship from home lately arrived. Probably she drew too much water to cross the bar except at the top of spring tides. Therefore she went into that natural harbor to wait for a few days in preference to remaining in an open roadstead.

"That's so," confirmed the second mate, suddenly, in his slightly hoarse voice. "She draws over twenty feet. She's the Liverpool ship *Sephora* with a cargo of coal. Hundred and twenty-three days from Cardiff."

We looked at him in surprise.

"The tugboat skipper told me when he came on board for your letters, sir," explained the young man. "He expects to take her up the river the day after tomorrow."

After thus overwhelming us with the extent of his information he slipped out of the cabin. The mate observed regretfully that he "could not account for that young fellow's whims." What prevented him telling us all about it at once, he wanted to know.

I detained him as he was making a move. For the last two days the crew had had plenty of hard work, and the night before they had very little sleep. I felt painfully that I—a stranger—was doing something unusual when I directed him to let all hands turn in without setting an anchor-watch. I proposed to keep on deck myself till one o'clock or thereabouts. I would get the second mate to relieve me at that hour.

"He will turn out the cook and the steward at four," I concluded, "and then give you a call. Of course at the slightest sign of any sort of wind we'll have the hands up and make a start at once."

He concealed his astonishment. "Very well, sir." Outside the cuddy he put his head in the second mate's door to inform him of my unheard-of caprice to take a five hours' anchor-watch on myself. I heard the other raise his voice incredulously—"What? The Captain himself?" Then a few more murmurs, a door closed, then another. A few moments later I went on deck.

My strangeness, which had made me sleepless, had prompted that unconventional arrangement, as if I had expected in those solitary hours of the night to get on terms with the ship of which I knew nothing, manned by men of whom I knew very little more. Fast alongside a wharf, littered like any ship in port with a tangle of unrelated things, invaded by unrelated shore people, I had hardly seen her yet properly. Now, as she lay cleared for sea, the stretch of her main-deck seemed to me very fine under the stars. Very fine, very roomy for her size, and very inviting. I descended the poop and paced the waist, my mind picturing to myself the coming passage through the Malay Archipelago, down the Indian Ocean, and up the Atlantic. All its phases were familiar enough to me, every characteristic, all the alternatives which were likely to face me on the high seas—everything! . . . except the novel responsibility of command. But I took heart from the reasonable thought that the ship was like other ships, the men like other men, and that the sea was not likely to keep any special surprises expressly for my discomfiture.

Arrived at that comforting conclusion, I bethought myself of a cigar and went below to get it. All was still down there. Everybody at the after end of the ship was sleeping profoundly. I came out again on the quarter-deck, agreeably at ease in my sleeping-suit on that warm breathless night, barefooted, a glowing cigar in my teeth, and, going forward, I was met by the profound silence of the fore end of the ship. Only as I passed the door of the forecastle I heard a deep, quiet, trustful sigh of some sleeper inside. And suddenly I rejoiced in the great security of the sea as compared with the unrest of the land, in my choice of that untempted life presenting no disquieting problems, invested with an elementary moral beauty by the absolute straightforwardness of its appeal and by the singleness of its purpose.

The riding-light in the fore-rigging burned with a clear, untroubled, as if symbolic, flame, confident and bright in the mysterious shades of the night. Passing on my way aft along the other side of the ship, I observed that the rope side-ladder, put over, no doubt, for the master of the tug when he came to fetch away our letters, had not been hauled in as it should have been. I became annoyed at this, for exactitude in small matters is the very soul of discipline. Then I reflected that I had myself peremptorily dismissed my officers from duty, and by my own act had prevented the anchor-watch being formally set and things properly attended to. I asked myself whether it was wise ever to interfere with the established routine of duties even from the kindest of motives. My action might have made me appear eccentric. Goodness only knew how that absurdly whiskered mate would "account" for my conduct,

and what the whole ship thought of that informality of their new captain. I was vexed with myself.

Not from compunction certainly, but, as it were mechanically, I proceeded to get the ladder in myself. Now a side-ladder of that sort is a light affair and comes in easily, yet my vigorous tug, which should have brought it flying on board, merely recoiled upon my body in a totally unexpected jerk. What the devil! . . . I was so astounded by the immovableness of that ladder that I remained stock-still, trying to account for it to myself like that imbecile mate of mine. In the end, of course, I put my head over the rail.

The side of the ship made an opaque belt of shadow on the darkling glassy shimmer of the sea. But I saw at once something elongated and pale floating very close to the ladder. Before I could form a guess a faint flash of phosphorescent light, which seemed to issue suddenly from the naked body of a man, flickered in the sleeping water with the elusive, silent play of summer lightning in a night sky. With a gasp I saw revealed to my stare a pair of feet, the long legs, a broad livid back immersed right up to the neck in a greenish cadaverous glow. One hand, awash, clutched the bottom rung of the ladder. He was complete but for the head. A headless corpse! The cigar dropped out of my gaping mouth with a tiny plop and a short hiss quite audible in the absolute stillness of all things under heaven. At that I suppose he raised up his face, a dimly pale oval in the shadow of the ship's side. But even then I could only barely make out down there the shape of his black-haired head. However, it was enough for the horrid, frost-bound sensation which had gripped me about the chest to pass off. The moment of vain exclamations was past, too. I only climbed on the spare spar and leaned over the rail as far as I could, to bring my eyes nearer to that mystery floating alongside.

As he hung by the ladder, like a resting swimmer, the sea-lightning played about his limbs at every stir; and he appeared in it ghastly, silvery, fish-like. He remained as mute as a fish, too. He made no motion to get out of the water, either. It was inconceivable that he should not attempt to come on board, and strangely troubling to suspect that perhaps he did not want to. And my first words were prompted by just that troubled incertitude.

"What's the matter?" I asked in my ordinary tone, speaking down to the face upturned exactly under mine.

"Cramp," it answered, no louder. Then slightly anxious, "I say, no need to call anyone."

"I was not going to," I said.

"Are you alone on deck?"

"Yes."

I had somehow the impression that he was on the point of letting go the ladder to swim away beyond my ken—mysterious as he came. But, for the moment, this being appearing as if he had risen from the bottom of the sea (it was certainly the nearest land to the ship) wanted only to know the time. I told him. And he, down there, tentatively:

"I suppose your captain's turned in?"

"I am sure he isn't," I said.

He seemed to struggle with himself, for I heard something like the low, bitter murmur of doubt. "What's the good?" His next words came out with a hesitating effort.

"Look here, my man. Could you call him out quietly?"

I thought the time had come to declare myself.

"*I* am the captain."

I heard a "By Jove!" whispered at the level of the water. The phosphorescence flashed in the swirl of the water all about his limbs, his other hand seized the ladder.

"My name's Leggatt."

The voice was calm and resolute. A good voice. The self-possession of that man had somehow induced a corresponding state in myself. It was very quietly that I remarked:

"You must be a good swimmer."

"Yes. I've been in the water practically since nine o'clock. The question for me now is whether I am to let go this ladder and go on swimming till I sink from exhaustion, or—to come on board here."

I felt this was no mere formula of desperate speech, but a real alternative in the view of a strong soul. I should have gathered from this that he was young; indeed, it is only the young who are ever confronted by such clear issues. But at the time it was pure intuition on my part. A mysterious communication was established already between us two—in the face of that silent, darkened tropical sea. I was young, too; young enough to make no comment. The man in the water began suddenly to climb up the ladder, and I hastened away from the rail to fetch some clothes.

Before entering the cabin I stood still, listening in the lobby at the foot of the stairs. A faint snore came through the closed door of the chief mate's room. The second mate's door was on the hook, but the darkness in there was absolutely soundless. He, too, was young and could sleep like a stone. Remained the steward, but he was not likely to wake up before he was called. I got a sleeping-suit out of my room and, coming back on deck, saw the naked man from the sea sitting on the main-hatch, glimmering white in the darkness, his elbows on his knees and his head in his hands. In a moment he had concealed his damp body in a sleeping-suit of the same gray-stripe pattern as the one I was wearing and followed me like my double on the poop. Together we moved right aft, barefooted, silent.

"What is it?" I asked in a deadened voice, taking the lighted lamp out of the binnacle, and raising it to his face.

"An ugly business."

He had rather regular features; a good mouth; light eyes under somewhat heavy, dark eyebrows; a smooth, square forehead; no growth on his cheeks; a small, brown mustache, and a well-shaped, round chin. His expression was concentrated, meditative, under the inspecting light of the lamp I held up to his face; such as a man thinking hard in solitude might wear. My sleeping-suit was just right for his size. A well-knit young fellow of twenty-five at most. He caught his lower lip with the edge of white, even teeth.

"Yes," I said, replacing the lamp in the binnacle. The warm, heavy tropical night closed upon his head again.

"There's a ship over there," he murmured.

"Yes, I know. The *Sephora*. Did you know of us?"

"Hadn't the slightest idea. I am the mate of her—" He paused and corrected himself. "I should say I *was*."

"Aha! Something wrong?"

"Yes. Very wrong indeed. I've killed a man."

"What do you mean? Just now?"

"No, on the passage. Weeks ago. Thirty-nine south. When I say a man—"

"Fit of temper," I suggested, confidently.

The shadowy, dark head, like mine, seemed to nod imperceptibly above the ghostly gray of my sleeping-suit. It was, in the night, as though I had been faced by my own reflection in the depths of a somber and immense mirror.

"A pretty thing to have to own up to for a Conway boy," murmured my double, distinctly.

"You're a Conway boy?"

"I am," he said, as if startled. Then, slowly . . . "Perhaps you too—"

It was so; but being a couple of years older I had left before he joined. After a quick interchange of dates a silence fell; and I thought suddenly of my absurd mate with his terrific whiskers and the "Bless my soul—you don't say so" type of intellect. My double gave me an inkling of his thoughts by saying: "My father's a parson in Norfolk. Do you see me before a judge and jury on that charge? For myself I can't see the necessity. There are fellows that an angel from heaven— And I am not that. He was one of those creatures that are just simmering all the time with a silly sort of wickedness. Miserable devils that have no business to live at all. He wouldn't do his duty and wouldn't let anybody else do theirs. But what's the good of talking! You know well enough the sort of ill-conditioned snarling cur—"

He appealed to me as if our experiences had been as identical as our clothes. And I knew well enough the pestiferous danger of such a character where there are no means of legal repression. And I knew well enough also that my double there was no homicidal ruffian. I did not think of asking him for details, and he told me the story roughly in brusque, disconnected sentences. I needed no more. I saw it all going on as though I were myself inside that other sleeping-suit.

"It happened while we were setting a reefed fore-sail, at dusk. Reefed foresail! You understand the sort of weather. The only sail we had left to keep the ship running; so you may guess what it had been like for days. Anxious sort of job, that. He gave me some of his cursed insolence at the sheet. I tell you I was overdone with this terrific weather that seemed to have no end to it. Terrific, I tell you—and a deep ship. I believe the fellow himself was half crazed with funk. It was no time for gentlemanly reproof, so I turned round and felled him like an ox. He up and at me. We closed just as an awful sea made for the ship. All hands saw it coming and took to the rigging, but I had him by the throat, and went on shaking him like a rat, the men above us yelling, 'Look out! look out!' Then a crash as if the sky had fallen on my head. They say that for over ten minutes hardly anything was to be seen of the ship—just the three masts and a bit of the forecastle head and of the poop all awash driving along in a smother of foam. It was a miracle that they found us, jammed together behind the forebitts. It's clear that I meant business, because I was holding him by the throat still when they picked us up. He was black in the face. It was too much for them. It seems they rushed us aft together, gripped as we were, screaming 'Murder!' like a lot of lunatics, and broke into the cuddy. And the ship running for her life, touch and go all the time, any minute her last in a sea fit to turn your hair gray only a-looking at it. I understand that the skipper, too, started raving like the rest of them. The man had been deprived of sleep for more than a week, and to have this sprung on him at the height of a furious gale nearly drove him out of his mind. I wonder they didn't fling me overboard after getting the carcass of their precious ship-mate out of my fingers. They had rather a job to separate us, I've been told. A sufficiently fierce story to make an old judge and a respectable jury sit up a bit. The first thing I heard when I came to myself was the maddening howling of that endless gale, and on that

the voice of the old man. He was hanging on to my bunk, staring into my face out of his sou'wester.

"'Mr. Leggatt, you have killed a man. You can act no longer as chief mate of this ship.'"

His care to subdue his voice made it sound monotonous. He rested a hand on the end of the skylight to steady himself with, and all that time did not stir a limb, so far as I could see. "Nice little tale for a quiet tea-party," he concluded in the same tone.

One of my hands, too, rested on the end of the skylight; neither did I stir a limb, so far as I knew. We stood less than a foot from each other. It occurred to me that if old "Bless my soul—you don't say so" were to put his head up the companion and catch sight of us, he would think he was seeing double, or imagine himself come upon a scene of weird witchcraft; the strange captain having a quiet confabulation by the wheel with his own gray ghost. I became very much concerned to prevent anything of the sort. I heard the other's soothing undertone.

"My father's a parson in Norfolk," it said. Evidently he had forgotten he had told me this important fact before. Truly a nice little tale.

"You had better slip down into my stateroom now," I said, moving off stealthily. My double followed my movements; our bare feet made no sound; I let him in, closed the door with care, and, after giving a call to the second mate, returned on deck for my relief.

"Not much sign of any wind yet," I remarked when he approached.

"No, sir. Not much," he assented, sleepily, in his hoarse voice, with just enough deference, no more, and barely suppressing a yawn.

"Well, that's all you have to look out for. You have got your orders."

"Yes, sir."

I paced a turn or two on the poop and saw him take up his position face forward with his elbow in the ratlines of the mizzen-rigging before I went below. The mate's faint snoring was still going on peacefully. The cuddy lamp was burning over the table on which stood a vase with flowers, a polite attention from the ship's provision merchant—the last flowers we should see for the next three months at the very least. Two bunches of bananas hung from the beam symmetrically, one on each side of the rudder-casing. Everything was as before in the ship—except that two of her captain's sleeping-suits were simultaneously in use, one motionless in the cuddy, the other keeping very still in the captain's stateroom.

It must be explained here that my cabin had the form of the capital letter L, the door being within the angle and opening into the short part of the letter. A couch was to the left, the bed-place to the right; my writing-desk and the chronometers' table faced the door. But anyone opening it, unless he stepped right inside, had no view of what I call the long (or vertical) part of the letter. It contained some lockers surmounted by a bookcase; and a few clothes, a thick jacket or two, caps, oilskin coat, and such like, hung on hooks. There was at the bottom of that part a door opening into my bath-room, which could be entered also directly from the saloon. But that way was never used.

The mysterious arrival had discovered the advantage of this particular shape. Entering my room, lighted strongly by a big bulkhead lamp swung on gimbals above my writing-desk, I did not see him anywhere till he stepped out quietly from behind the coats hung in the recessed part.

"I heard somebody moving about, and went in there at once," he whispered.

I, too, spoke under my breath.

"Nobody is likely to come in here without knocking and getting permission."

He nodded. His face was thin and the sunburn faded, as though he had been ill. And no wonder. He had been, I heard presently, kept under arrest in his cabin for nearly seven weeks. But there was nothing sickly in his eyes or in his expression. He was not a bit like me, really; yet, as we stood leaning over my bed-place, whispering side by side, with our dark heads together and our backs to the door, anybody bold enough to open it stealthily would have been treated to the uncanny sight of a double captain busy talking in whispers with his other self.

"But all this doesn't tell me how you came to hang on to our side-ladder," I inquired, in the hardly audible murmurs we used, after he had told me something more of the proceedings on board the *Sephora* once the bad weather was over.

"When we sighted Java Head I had had time to think all those matters out several times over. I had six weeks of doing nothing else, and with only an hour or so every evening for a tramp on the quarter-deck."

He whispered, his arms folded on the side of my bed-place, staring through the open port. And I could imagine perfectly the manner of this thinking out—a stubborn if not a steadfast operation; something of which I should have been perfectly incapable.

"I reckoned it would be dark before we closed with the land," he continued, so low that I had to strain my hearing, near as we were to each other, shoulder touching shoulder almost. "So I asked to speak to the old man. He always seemed very sick when he came to see me—as if he could not look me in the face. You know, that foresail saved the ship. She was

too deep to have run long under bare poles. And it was I that managed to set it for him. Anyway, he came. When I had him in my cabin—he stood by the door looking at me as if I had the halter round my neck already—I asked him right away to leave my cabin door unlocked at night while the ship was going through Sunda Straits. There would be the Java coast within two or three miles, off Angier Point. I wanted nothing more. I've had a prize for swimming my second year in the Conway."

"I can believe it," I breathed out.

"God only knows why they locked me in every night. To see some of their faces you'd have thought they were afraid I'd go about at night strangling people. Am I a murdering brute? Do I look it? By Jove! if I had been he wouldn't have trusted himself like that into my room. You'll say I might have chucked him aside and bolted out, there and then— it was dark already. Well, no. And for the same reason I wouldn't think of trying to smash the door. There would have been a rush to stop me at the noise, and I did not mean to get into a confounded scrimmage. Somebody else might have got killed— for I would not have broken out only to get chucked back, and I did not want any more of that work. **He** refused, looking more sick than ever. He was afraid of the men, and also of that old second mate of his who had been sailing with him for years—a gray-headed old humbug; and his steward, too, had been with him devil knows how long—seventeen years or more—a dogmatic sort of loafer who hated me like poison, just because I was the chief mate. No chief mate ever made more than one voyage in the *Sephora*, you know. Those two old chaps ran the ship. Devil only knows what the skipper wasn't afraid of (all his nerve went to pieces altogether in that hellish spell of bad weather we had)—of what the law would do to him—of his wife, perhaps. Oh, yes! she's on board. Though I don't think she would have meddled. She would have been only too glad to have me out of the ship in any way. The 'brand of Cain' business, don't you see. That's all right. I was ready enough to go off wandering on the face of the earth—and that was price enough to pay for an Abel of that sort. Anyhow, he wouldn't listen to me. 'This thing must take its course. I represent the law here.' He was shaking like a leaf. 'So you won't?' 'No!' 'Then I hope you will be able to sleep on that,' I said, and turned my back on him. 'I wonder that *you* can,' cries he, and locks the door.

"Well, after that, I couldn't. Not very well. That was three weeks ago. We have had a slow passage through the Java Sea; drifted about Carimata for ten days. When we anchored here they thought, I suppose, it was all right. The nearest land (and that's five miles) is the ship's destination; the consul would soon set about catching me; and there would have been no object in bolting to these islets there. I don't suppose there's a drop of water on them. I don't know how it was, but tonight that steward, after bringing me my supper, went out to let me eat it, and left the door unlocked. And I ate it—all there was, too. After I had finished I strolled out on the quarter-deck. I don't know that I meant to do anything. A breath of fresh air was all I wanted, I believe. Then a sudden temptation came over me. I kicked off my slippers and was in the water before I had made up my mind fairly. Somebody heard the splash and they raised an awful hullabaloo. 'He's gone! Lower the boats! He's committed suicide! No, he's swimming.' Certainly I was swimming. It's not so easy for a swimmer like me to commit suicide by drowning. I landed on the nearest islet before the boat left the ship's side. I heard them pulling about in the dark, hailing, and so on, but after a bit they gave up. Everything quieted down and the anchorage became as still as death. I sat down on a stone and began to think. I felt certain they would start searching for me at daylight. There was no place to hide on those stony things—and if there had been, what would have been the good? But now I was clear of that ship, I was not going back. So after a while I took off all my clothes, tied them up in a bundle with a stone inside, and dropped them in the deep water on the outer side of that islet. That was suicide enough for me. Let them think what they liked, but I didn't mean to drown myself. I meant to swim till I sank—but that's not the same thing. I struck out for another of these little islands, and it was from that one that I first saw your riding-light. Something to swim for. I went on easily, and on the way I came upon a flat rock a foot or two above water. In the daytime, I dare say, you might make it out with a glass from your poop. I scrambled up on it and rested myself for a bit. Then I made another start. That last spell must have been over a mile."

His whisper was getting fainter and fainter, and all the time he stared straight out through the porthole, in which there was not even a star to be seen. I had not interrupted him. There was something that made comment impossible in his narrative, or perhaps in himself; a sort of feeling, a quality, which I can't find a name for. And when he ceased, all I found was a futile whisper: "So you swam for our light?"

"Yes—straight for it. It was something to swim for. I couldn't see any stars low down because the coast was in the way, and I couldn't see the land, either. The water was like glass. One might have been swimming in a confounded thousand-feet-deep cistern with no place for scrambling out anywhere; but what I didn't like was the notion of swimming round and round like a crazed bullock before I gave out; and as I didn't mean to go back . . . No. Do you see me being hauled back, stark naked, off one of these little islands by the scruff of the neck and fighting like a wild beast? Somebody would have got killed for certain, and I did not want any of that. So I went on. Then your ladder—"

"Why didn't you hail the ship?" I asked, a little louder.

He touched my shoulder lightly. Lazy footsteps came right over our heads and stopped. The second mate had crossed from the other side of the poop and might have been hanging over the rail, for all we knew.

"He couldn't hear us talking—could he?" My double breathed into my very ear, anxiously.

His anxiety was an answer, a sufficient answer, to the question I had put to him. An answer containing all the difficulty of that situation. I closed the porthole quietly, to make sure. A louder word might have been overheard.

"Who's that?" he whispered then.

"My second mate. But I don't know much more of the fellow than you do."

And I told him a little about myself. I had been appointed to take charge while I least expected anything of the sort, not quite a fortnight ago. I didn't know either the ship or the people. Hadn't had the time in port to look about me or size anybody up. And as to the crew, all they knew was that I was appointed to take the ship home. For the rest, I was almost as much of a stranger on board as himself, I said. And at the moment I felt it most acutely. I felt that it would take very little to make me a suspect person in the eyes of the ship's company.

He had turned about meantime; and we, the two strangers in the ship, faced each other in identical attitudes.

"Your ladder—" he murmured, after a silence. "Who'd have thought of finding a ladder hanging over at night in a ship anchored out here! I felt just then a very unpleasant faintness. After the life I've been leading for nine weeks, anybody would have got out of condition. I wasn't capable of swimming round as far as your rudder-chains. And, lo and behold; there was a ladder to get hold of. After I gripped it I said to myself, 'What's the good?' When I saw a man's head looking over I thought I would swim away presently and leave him shouting—in whatever language it was. I didn't mind being looked at. I—I liked it. And then you speaking to me so quietly—as if you had expected me—made me hold on a little longer. It had been a confounded lonely time—I don't mean while swimming. I was glad to talk a little to somebody that didn't belong to the *Sephora*. As to asking for the captain, that was a mere impulse. It could have been no use, with all the ship knowing about me and the other people pretty certain to be round here in the morning. I don't know— I wanted to be seen, to talk with somebody, before I went on. I don't know what I would have said. . . . 'Fine night, isn't it?' or something of the sort."

"Do you think they will be round here presently?" I asked with some incredulity.

"Quite likely," he said, faintly.

He looked extremely haggard all of a sudden. His head rolled on his shoulders.

"H'm. We shall see then. Meantime get into that bed," I whispered. "Want help? There."

It was a rather high bed-place with a set of drawers underneath. This amazing swimmer really needed the lift I gave him by seizing his leg. He tumbled in, rolled over on his back, and flung one arm across his eyes. And then, with his face nearly hidden, he must have looked exactly as I used to look in that bed. I gazed upon my other self for a while before drawing across carefully the two green serge curtains which ran on a brass rod. I thought for a moment of pinning them together for greater safety, but I sat down on the couch, and once there I felt unwilling to rise and hunt for a pin. I would do it in a moment. I was extremely tired, in a peculiarly intimate way, by the strain of stealthiness, by the effort of whispering and the general secrecy of this excitement. It was three o'clock by now and I had been on my feet since nine, but I was not sleepy; I could not have gone to sleep. I sat there, fagged out, looking at the curtains, trying to clear my mind of the confused sensation of being in two places at once, and greatly bothered by an exasperating knocking in my head. It was a relief to discover suddenly that it was not in my head at all, but on the outside of the door. Before I could collect myself the words "Come in" were out of my mouth, and the steward entered with a tray, bringing in my morning coffee. I had slept, after all, and I was so frightened that I shouted, "This way! I am here, steward," as though he had been miles away. He put down the tray on the table next the couch and only then said, very quietly, "I can see you are here, sir." I felt him give me a keen look, but I dared not meet his eyes just then. He must have wondered why I had drawn the curtains of my bed before going to sleep on the couch. He went out, hooking the door open as usual.

I heard the crew washing decks above me. I knew I would have been told at once if there had been any wind. Calm, I thought, and I was doubly vexed. In-

deed, I felt dual more than ever. The steward reappeared suddenly in the doorway. I jumped up from the couch so quickly that he gave a start.

"What do you want here?"

"Close your port, sir—they are washing decks."

"It is closed," I said, reddening.

"Very well, sir." But he did not move from the doorway and returned my stare in an extraordinary, equivocal manner for a time. Then his eyes wavered, all his expression changed, and in a voice unusually gentle, almost coaxingly:

"May I come in to take the empty cup away, sir?"

"Of course!" I turned my back on him while he popped in and out. Then I unhooked and closed the door and even pushed the bolt. This sort of thing could not go on very long. The cabin was as hot as an oven, too. I took a peep at my double, and discovered that he had not moved, his arm was still over his eyes; but his chest heaved; his hair was wet; his chin glistened with perspiration. I reached over him and opened the port.

"I must show myself on deck," I reflected.

Of course, theoretically, I could do what I liked, with no one to say nay to me within the whole circle of the horizon; but to lock my cabin door and take the key away I did not dare. Directly I put my head out of the companion I saw the group of my two officers, the second mate barefooted, the chief mate in long india-rubber boots, near the break of the poop, and the steward half-way down the poop-ladder talking to them eagerly. He happened to catch sight of me and dived, the second ran down on the main-deck shouting some order or other, and the chief mate came to meet me, touching his cap.

There was a sort of curiosity in his eye that I did not like. I don't know whether the steward had told them that I was "queer" only, or downright drunk, but I know the man meant to have a good look at me. I watched him coming with a smile which, as he got into point-blank range, took effect and froze his very whiskers. I did not give him time to open his lips.

"Square the yards by lifts and braces before the hands go to breakfast."

It was the first particular order I had given on board that ship; and I stayed on deck to see it executed, too. I had felt the need of asserting myself without loss of time. That sneering young cub got taken down a peg or two on that occasion, and I also seized the opportunity of having a good look at the face of every foremast man as they filed past me to go to the after braces. At breakfast time, eating nothing myself, I presided with such frigid dignity that the two mates were only too glad to escape from the cabin as soon as decency permitted; and all the time the dual working of my mind distracted me almost to the point of insanity. I was constantly watching myself, my secret self, as dependent on my actions as my own personality, sleeping in that bed, behind that door which faced me as I sat at the head of the table. It was very much like being mad, only it was worse because one was aware of it.

I had to shake him for a solid minute, but when at last he opened his eyes it was in the full possession of his senses, with an inquiring look.

"All's well so far," I whispered. "Now you must vanish into the bath-room."

He did so, as noiseless as a ghost, and then I rang for the steward, and facing him boldly, directed him to tidy up my stateroom while I was having my bath —"and be quick about it." As my tone admitted of no excuses, he said, "Yes, sir," and ran off to fetch his dust-pan and brushes. I took a bath and did most of my dressing, splashing, and whistling softly for the steward's edification, while the secret sharer of my life stood drawn up bolt upright in that little space, his face looking very sunken in daylight, his eyelids lowered under the stern, dark line of his eyebrows drawn together by a slight frown.

When I left him there to go back to my room the steward was finishing dusting. I sent for the mate and engaged him in some insignificant conversation. It was, as it were, trifling with the terrific character of his whiskers; but my object was to give him an opportunity for a good look at my cabin. And then I could at last shut, with a clear conscience, the door of my stateroom and get my double back into the recessed part. There was nothing else for it. He had to sit still on a small folding stool, half smothered by the heavy coats hanging there. We listened to the steward going into the bath-room out of the saloon, filling the water-bottles there, scrubbing the bath, setting things to rights, whisk, bang, clatter— out again into the saloon—turn the key—click. Such was my scheme for keeping my second self invisible. Nothing better could be contrived under the circumstances. And there we sat; I at my writing-desk ready to appear busy with some papers, he behind me out of sight of the door. It would not have been prudent to talk in daytime; and I could not have stood the excitement of that queer sense of whispering to myself. Now and then, glancing over my shoulder, I saw him far back there, sitting rigidly on the low stool, his bare feet close together, his arms folded, his head hanging on his breast—and perfectly still. Anybody would have taken him for me.

I was fascinated by it myself. Every moment I had to glance over my shoulder. I was looking at him when a voice outside the door said:

"Beg pardon, sir."

"Well!" . . . I kept my eyes on him, and so when the voice outside the door announced, "There's a ship's boat coming our way, sir," I saw him give a start—the first movement he had made for hours. But he did not raise his bowed head.

"All right. Get the ladder over."

I hesitated. Should I whisper something to him? But what? His immobility seemed to have been never disturbed. What could I tell him he did not know already? . . . Finally I went on deck.

II

The skipper of the *Sephora* had a thin red whisker all round his face, and the sort of complexion that goes with hair of that color; also the particular, rather smeary shade of blue in the eyes. He was not exactly a showy figure; his shoulders were high, his stature but middling—one leg slightly more bandy than the other. He shook hands, looking vaguely around. A spiritless tenacity was his main characteristic, I judged. I behaved with a politeness which seemed to disconcert him. Perhaps he was shy. He mumbled to me as if he were ashamed of what he was saying; gave his name (it was something like Archbold—but at this distance of years I hardly am sure), his ship's name, and a few other particulars of that sort, in the manner of a criminal making a reluctant and doleful confession. He had had terrible weather on the passage out—terrible—terrible—wife aboard, too.

By this time we were seated in the cabin and the steward brought in a tray with a bottle and glasses. "Thanks! No." Never took liquor. Would have some water, though. He drank two tumblerfuls. Terrible thirsty work. Ever since daylight had been exploring the islands round his ship.

"What was that for—fun?" I asked, with an appearance of polite interest.

"No!" He sighed. "Painful duty. "

As he persisted in his mumbling and I wanted my double to hear every word, I hit upon the notion of informing him that I regretted to say I was hard of hearing.

"Such a young man, too!" he nodded, keeping his smeary blue, unintelligent eyes fastened upon me. "What was the cause of it—some disease?" he inquired, without the least sympathy and as if he thought that, if so, I'd got no more than I deserved.

"Yes; disease," I admitted in a cheerful tone which seemed to shock him. But my point was gained, because he had to raise his voice to give me his tale. It is not worth while to record that version. It was just over two months since all this had happened, and he had thought so much about it that he seemed completely muddled as to its bearings, but still immensely impressed.

"What would you think of such a thing happening on board your own ship? I've had the *Sephora* for these fifteen years. I am a well-known shipmaster."

He was densely distressed—and perhaps I should have sympathized with him if I had been able to detach my mental vision from the unsuspected sharer of my cabin as though he were my second self. There he was on the other side of the bulkhead, four or five feet from us, no more, as we sat in the saloon. I looked politely at Captain Archbold (if that was his name), but it was the other I saw, in a gray sleeping-suit, seated on a low stool, his bare feet close together, his arms folded, and every word said between us falling into the ears of his dark head bowed on his chest.

"I have been at sea now, man and boy, for seven-and-thirty years, and I've never heard of such a thing happening in an English ship. And that it should be my ship. Wife on board, too."

I was hardly listening to him.

"Don't you think," I said, "that the heavy sea which, you told me, came aboard just then might have killed the man? I have seen the sheer weight of a sea kill a man very neatly, by simply breaking his neck."

"Good God!" he uttered, impressively, fixing his smeary blue eyes on me. "The sea! No man killed by the sea ever looked like that." He seemed positively scandalized at my suggestion. And as I gazed at him, certainly not prepared for anything original on his part, he advanced his head close to mine and thrust his tongue out at me so suddenly that I couldn't help starting back.

After scoring over my calmness in this graphic way he nodded wisely. If I had seen the sight, he assured me, I would never forget it as long as I lived. The weather was too bad to give the corpse a proper sea burial. So next day at dawn they took it up on the poop, covering its face with a bit of bunting; he read a short prayer, and then, just as it was, in its oilskins and long boots, they launched it amongst those mountainous seas that seemed ready every moment to swallow up the ship herself and the terrified lives on board of her.

"That reefed foresail saved you," I threw in.

"Under God—it did," he exclaimed fervently. "It was by a special mercy, I firmly believe, that it stood some of those hurricane squalls."

"It was the setting of that sail which—" I began.

"God's own hand in it," he interrupted me. "Nothing less could have done it. I don't mind telling you that I hardly dared give the order. It seemed impossible that we could touch anything without los-

ing it, and then our last hope would have been gone."

The terror of that gale was on him yet. I let him go on for a bit, then said, casually—as if returning to a minor subject:

"You were very anxious to give up your mate to the shore people, I believe?"

He was. To the law. His obscure tenacity on that point had in it something incomprehensible and a little awful; something, as it were, mystical, quite apart from his anxiety that he should not be suspected of "countenancing any doings of that sort." Seven-and-thirty virtuous years at sea, of which over twenty of immaculate command, and the last fifteen in the *Sephora*, seemed to have laid him under some pitiless obligation.

"And you know," he went on, groping shamefacedly amongst his feelings, "I did not engage that young fellow. His people had some interest with my owners. I was in a way forced to take him on. He looked very smart, very gentlemanly, and all that. But do you know—I never liked him, somehow. I am a plain man. You see, he wasn't exactly the sort for the chief mate of a ship like the *Sephora*."

I had become so connected in thoughts and impressions with the secret sharer of my cabin that I felt as if I, personally, were being given to understand that I, too, was not the sort that would have done for the chief mate of a ship like the *Sephora*. I had no doubt of it in my mind.

"Not at all the style of man. You understand," he insisted, superfluously, looking hard at me.

I smiled urbanely. He seemed at a loss for a while.

"I suppose I must report a suicide."

"Beg pardon?"

"Sui-cide! That's what I'll have to write to my owners directly I get in."

"Unless you manage to recover him before tomorrow," I assented, dispassionately. . . . "I mean, alive."

He mumbled something which I really did not catch, and I turned my ear to him in a puzzled manner. He fairly bawled:

"The land—I say, the mainland is at least seven miles off my anchorage."

"About that."

My lack of excitement, of curiosity, of surprise, of any sort of pronounced interest, began to arouse his distrust. But except for the felicitous pretense of deafness I had not tried to pretend anything. I had felt utterly incapable of playing the part of ignorance properly, and therefore was afraid to try. It is also certain that he had brought some ready-made suspicions with him, and that he viewed my politeness as a strange and unnatural phenomenon. And yet how else could I have received him? Not heartily! That was impossible for psychological reasons, which I need not state here. My only object was to keep off his inquiries. Surlily? Yes, but surliness might have provoked a point-blank question. From its novelty to him and from its nature, punctilious courtesy was the manner best calculated to restrain the man. But there was the danger of his breaking through my defense bluntly. I could not, I think, have met him by a direct lie, also for psychological (not moral) reasons. If he had only known how afraid I was of his putting my feeling of identity with the other to the test! But, strangely enough—(I thought of it only afterwards)—I believe that he was not a little disconcerted by the reverse side of that weird situation, by something in me that reminded him of the man he was seeking—suggested a mysterious similitude to the young fellow he had distrusted and disliked from the first.

However that might have been, the silence was not very prolonged. He took another oblique step.

"I reckon I had no more than a two-mile pull to your ship. Not a bit more."

"And quite enough, too, in this awful heat," I said.

Another pause full of mistrust followed. Necessity, they say, is mother of invention, but fear, too, is not barren of ingenious suggestions. And I was afraid he would ask me point-blank for news of my other self.

"Nice little saloon, isn't it?" I remarked, as if noticing for the first time the way his eyes roamed from one closed door to the other. "And very well fitted out, too. Here, for instance," I continued, reaching over the back of my seat negligently and flinging the door open, "is my bath-room."

He made an eager movement, but hardly gave it a glance. I got up, shut the door of the bath-room, and invited him to have a look round, as if I were very proud of my accommodation. He had to rise and be shown round, but he went through the business without any raptures whatever.

"And now we'll have a look at my stateroom," I declared, in a voice as loud as I dared to make it, crossing the cabin to the starboard side with purposely heavy steps.

He followed me in and gazed around. My intelligent double had vanished. I played my part.

"Very convenient—isn't it?"

"Very nice. Very comf . . ." He didn't finish and went out brusquely as if to escape from some unrighteous wiles of mine. But it was not to be. I had been too frightened not to feel vengeful; I felt I had him on the run, and I meant to keep him on the run. My polite insistence must have had something menacing in it, because he gave in suddenly. And I did not let him off a single item; mate's room, pantry,

storerooms, the very sail-locker which was also under the poop—he had to look into them all. When at last I showed him out on the quarter-deck he drew a long, spiritless sigh, and mumbled dismally that he must really be going back to his ship now. I desired my mate, who had joined us, to see to the captain's boat.

The man of whiskers gave a blast on the whistle which he used to wear hanging round his neck, and yelled, "*Sephora's* away!" My double down there in my cabin must have heard, and certainly could not feel more relieved than I. Four fellows came running out from somewhere forward and went over the side, while my own men, appearing on deck too, lined the rail. I escorted my visitor to the gangway ceremoniously, and nearly overdid it. He was a tenacious beast. On the very ladder he lingered, and in that unique, guiltily conscientious manner of sticking to the point:

"I say . . . you . . . you don't think that—"

I covered his voice loudly:

"Certainly not. . . . I am delighted. Good-by."

I had an idea of what he meant to say, and just saved myself by the privilege of defective hearing. He was too shaken generally to insist, but my mate, close witness of that parting, looked mystified and his face took a thoughtful cast. As I did not want to appear as if I wished to avoid all communication with my officers, he had the opportunity to address me.

"Seems a very nice man. His boat's crew told our chaps a very extraordinary story, if what I am told by the steward is true. I suppose you had it from the captain, sir?"

"Yes. I had a story from the captain."

"A very horrible affair—isn't it, sir?"

"It is."

"Beats all these tales we hear about murders in Yankee ships."

"I don't think it beats them. I don't think it resembled them in the least."

"Bless my soul—you don't say so! But of course I've no acquaintance whatever with American ships, not I, so I couldn't go against your knowledge. It's horrible enough for me. . . . But the queerest part is that those fellows seemed to have some idea the man was hidden aboard here. They had really. Did you ever hear of such a thing?"

"Preposterous—isn't it?"

We were walking to and fro athwart the quarter-deck. No one of the crew forward could be seen (the day was Sunday), and the mate pursued:

"There was some little dispute about it. Our chaps took offense. 'As if we would harbor a thing like that,' they said. 'Wouldn't you like to look for him in our coal-hole?' Quite a tiff. But they made it up in the end. I suppose he did drown himself. Don't you, sir?"

"I don't suppose anything."

"You have no doubt in the matter, sir?"

"None whatever."

I left him suddenly. I felt I was producing a bad impression, but with my double down there it was most trying to be on deck. And it was almost as trying to be below. Altogether a nerve-trying situation. But on the whole I felt less torn in two when I was with him. There was no one in the whole ship whom I dared take into my confidence. Since the hands had got to know his story, it would have been impossible to pass him off for anyone else, and an accidental discovery was to be dreaded now more than ever. . . .

The steward being engaged in laying the table for dinner, we could talk only with our eyes when I first went down. Later in the afternoon we had a cautious try at whispering. The Sunday quietness of the ship was against us; the stillness of air and water around her was against us; the elements, the men were against us—everything was against us in our secret partnership; time itself—for this could not go on forever. The very trust in Providence was, I suppose, denied to his guilt. Shall I confess that this thought cast me down very much? And as to the chapter of accidents which counts for so much in the book of success, I could only hope that it was closed. For what favorable accident could be expected?

"Did you hear everything?" were my first words as soon as we took up our position side by side, leaning over my bed-place.

He had. And the proof of it was his earnest whisper, "The man told you he hardly dared to give the order."

I understood the reference to be to that saving foresail.

"Yes. He was afraid of it being lost in the setting."

"I assure you he never gave the order. He may think he did, but he never gave it. He stood there with me on the break of the poop after the maintopsail blew away, and whimpered about our last hope—positively whimpered about it and nothing else—and the night coming on! To hear one's skipper go on like that in such weather was enough to drive any fellow out of his mind. It worked me up into a sort of desperation. I just took it into my own hands and went away from him, boiling, and— But what's the use telling you? *You* know! . . . Do you think that if I had not been pretty fierce with them I should have got the men to do anything? Not it! The bo's'n perhaps? Perhaps! It wasn't a heavy sea—it was a sea

gone mad! I suppose the end of the world will be something like that; and a man may have the heart to see it coming once and be done with it—but to have to face it day after day— I don't blame anybody. I was precious little better than the rest. Only—I was an officer of that old coal-wagon, anyhow—"

"I quite understand," I conveyed that sincere assurance into his ear. He was out of breath with whispering; I could hear him pant slightly. It was all very simple. The same strung-up force which had given twenty-four men a chance, at least, for their lives, had, in a sort of recoil, crushed an unworthy mutinous existence.

But I had no leisure to weigh the merits of the matter—footsteps in the saloon, a heavy knock. "There's enough wind to get under way with, sir." Here was the call of a new claim upon my thoughts and even upon my feelings.

"Turn the hands up," I cried through the door. "I'll be on deck directly."

I was going out to make the acquaintance of my ship. Before I left the cabin our eyes met—the eyes of the only two strangers on board. I pointed to the recessed part where the little camp-stool awaited him and laid my finger on my lips. He made a gesture—somewhat vague—a little mysterious, accompanied by a faint smile, as if of regret.

This is not the place to enlarge upon the sensations of a man who feels for the first time a ship move under his feet to his own independent word. In my case they were not unalloyed. I was not wholly alone with my command; for there was that stranger in my cabin. Or rather, I was not completely and wholly with her. Part of me was absent. That mental feeling of being in two places at once affected me physically as if the mood of secrecy had penetrated my very soul. Before an hour had elapsed since the ship had begun to move, having occasion to ask the mate (he stood by my side) to take a compass bearing of the Pagoda, I caught myself reaching up to his ear in whispers. I say I caught myself, but enough had escaped to startle the man. I can't describe it otherwise than by saying that he shied. A grave, preoccupied manner, as though he were in possession of some perplexing intelligence, did not leave him henceforth. A little later I moved away from the rail to look at the compass with such a stealthy gait that the helmsman noticed it—and I could not help noticing the unusual roundness of his eyes. These are trifling instances, though it's to no commander's advantage to be suspected of ludicrous eccentricities. But I was also more seriously affected. There are to a seamen certain words, gestures, that should in given conditions come as naturally, as instinctively as the winking of a menaced eye. A cer-

tain order should spring onto his lips without thinking; a certain sign should get itself made, so to speak,
without reflection. But all unconscious alertness had
abandoned me. I had to make an effort of will to
recall myself back (from the cabin) to the conditions
of the moment. I felt that I was appearing an irresolute commander to those people who were watching
me more or less critically.

And, besides, there were the scares. On the second
day out, for instance, coming off the deck in the
afternoon (I had straw slippers on my bare feet) I
stopped at the open pantry door and spoke to the
steward. He was doing something there with his
back to me. At the sound of my voice he nearly
jumped out of his skin, as the saying is, and inciden-
tally broke a cup.

"What on earth's the matter with you?" I asked,
astonished.

He was extremely confused. "Beg your pardon, sir.
I made sure you were in your cabin."

"You see I wasn't."

"No, sir. I could have sworn I had heard you moving in there not a moment ago. It's most extraordinary . . . very sorry, sir."

I passed on with an inward shudder. I was so
identified with my secret double that I did not even
mention the fact in those scanty, fearful whispers we
exchanged. I suppose he had made some slight noise
of some kind or other. It would have been miraculous
if he hadn't at one time or another. And yet, haggard
as he appeared, he looked always perfectly self-
controlled, more than calm—almost invulnerable. On
my suggestion he remained almost entirely in the
bath-room, which, upon the whole, was the safest
place. There could be really no shadow of an excuse
for anyone ever wanting to go in there, once the
steward had done with it. It was a very tiny place.
Sometimes he reclined on the floor, his legs bent, his
head sustained on one elbow. At others I would find
him on the camp-stool, sitting in his gray sleeping-
suit and with his cropped dark hair like a patient,
unmoved convict. At night I would smuggle him
into my bed-place, and we would whisper together,
with the regular foot-falls of the officer of the watch
passing and repassing over our heads. It was an infinitely miserable time. It was lucky that some tins
of fine preserves were stowed in a locker in my stateroom; hard bread I could always get hold of; and so
he lived on stewed chicken, pâté de foie gras, aspar-
agus, cooked oysters, sardines—on all sorts of abomi-
nable sham delicacies out of tins. My early morning
coffee he always drank; and it was all I dared do for
him in that respect.

Every day there was the horrible maneuvering to
go through so that my room and then the bath-room

should be done in the usual way. I came to hate the
sight of the steward, to abhor the voice of that harmless man. I felt that it was he who would bring on
the disaster of discovery. It hung like a sword over
our heads.

The fourth day out, I think (we were then working down the east side of the Gulf of Siam, tack for
tack, in light winds and smooth water)—the fourth
day, I say, of this miserable juggling with the un-
avoidable, as we sat at our evening meal, that man,
whose slightest movement I dreaded, after putting
down the dishes ran up on deck busily. This could
not be dangerous. Presently he came down again;
and then it appeared that he had remembered a coat
of mine which I had thrown over a rail to dry after
having been wetted in a shower which had passed
over the ship in the afternoon. Sitting stolidly at the
head of the table I became terrified at the sight of
the garment on his arm. Of course he made for my
door. There was no time to lose.

"Steward," I thundered. My nerves were so shaken
that I could not govern my voice and conceal my
agitation. This was the sort of thing that made my
terrifically whiskered mate tap his forehead with his
forefinger. I had detected him using that gesture
while talking on deck with a confidential air to the
carpenter. It was too far to hear a word, but I had
no doubt that this pantomime could only refer to the
strange new captain.

"Yes, sir," the pale-faced steward turned resignedly to me. It was this maddening course of being
shouted at, checked without rhyme or reason, arbi-
trarily chased out of my cabin, suddenly called into
it, sent flying out of his pantry on incomprehensible
errands, that accounted for the growing wretchedness of his expression.

"Where are you going with that coat?"

"To your room, sir."

"Is there another shower coming?"

"I'm sure I don't know, sir. Shall I go up again and
see, sir?"

"No! never mind."

My object was attained, as of course my other
self in there would have heard everything that
passed. During this interlude my two officers never
raised their eyes off their respective plates; but the
lip of that confounded cub, the second mate, quivered visibly.

I expected the steward to hook my coat on and
come out at once. He was very slow about it; but
I dominated my nervousness sufficiently not to shout
after him. Suddenly I became aware (it could be
heard plainly enough) that the fellow for some reason or other was opening the door of the bath-room.
It was the end. The place was literally not big

enough to swing a cat in. My voice died in my throat and I went stony all over. I expected to hear a yell of surprise and terror, and made a movement, but had not the strength to get on my legs. Everything remained still. Had my second self taken the poor wretch by the throat? I don't know what I could have done next moment if I had not seen the steward come out of my room, close the door, and then stand quietly by the sideboard.

"Saved," I thought. "But, no! Lost! Gone! He was gone!"

I laid my knife and fork down and leaned back in my chair. My head swam. After a while, when sufficiently recovered to speak in a steady voice, I instructed my mate to put the ship round at eight o'clock himself.

"I won't come on deck," I went on. "I think I'll turn in, and unless the wind shifts I don't want to be disturbed before midnight. I feel a bit seedy."

"You did look middling bad a little while ago," the chief mate remarked without showing any great concern.

They both went out, and I stared at the steward clearing the table. There was nothing to be read on that wretched man's face. But why did he avoid my eyes I asked myself. Then I thought I should like to hear the sound of his voice.

"Steward!"

"Sir!" Startled as usual.

"Where did you hang up that coat?"

"In the bath-room, sir." The usual anxious tone. "It's not quite dry yet, sir."

For some time longer I sat in the cuddy. Had my double vanished as he had come? But of his coming there was an explanation, whereas his disappearance would be inexplicable. . . . I went slowly into my dark room, shut the door, lighted the lamp, and for a time dared not turn round. When at last I did I saw him standing bolt-upright in the narrow recessed part. It would not be true to say I had a shock, but an irresistible doubt of his bodily existence flitted through my mind. Can it be, I asked myself, that he is not visible to other eyes than mine? It was like being haunted. Motionless, with a grave face, he raised his hands slightly at me in a gesture which meant clearly, "Heavens! what a narrow escape!" Narrow indeed. I think I had come creeping quietly as near insanity as any man who has not actually gone over the border. That gesture restrained me, so to speak.

The mate with the terrific whiskers was now putting the ship on the other tack. In the moment of profound silence which follows upon the hands going to their stations I heard on the poop his raised voice: "Hard alee!" and the distant shout of the order repeated on the main-deck. The sails, in that light breeze, made but a faint fluttering noise. It ceased. The ship was coming round slowly; I held my breath in the renewed stillness of expectation; one wouldn't have thought that there was a single living soul on her decks. A sudden brisk shout, "Mainsail haul!" broke the spell, and in the noisy cries and rush overhead of the men running away with the main-brace we two, down in my cabin, came together in our usual position by the bed-place.

He did not wait for my question. "I heard him fumbling here and just managed to squat myself down in the bath," he whispered to me. "The fellow only opened the door and put his arm in to hang the coat up. All the same—"

"I never thought of that," I whispered back, even more appalled than before at the closeness of the shave, and marveling at that something unyielding in his character which was carrying him through so finely. There was no agitation in his whisper. Whoever was being driven distracted, it was not he. He was sane. And the proof of his sanity was continued when he took up the whispering again.

"It would never do for me to come to life again."

It was something that a ghost might have said. But what he was alluding to was his old captain's reluctant admission of the theory of suicide. It would obviously serve his turn—if I had understood at all the view which seemed to govern the unalterable purpose of his action.

"You must maroon me as soon as ever you can get amongst these islands off the Cambodge shore," he went on.

"Maroon you! We are not living in a boy's adventure tale," I protested. His scornful whispering took me up.

"We aren't indeed! There's nothing of a boy's tale in this. But there's nothing else for it. I want no more. You don't suppose I am afraid of what can be done to me? Prison or gallows or whatever they may please. But you don't see me coming back to explain such things to an old fellow in a wig and twelve respectable tradesmen, do you? What can they know whether I am guilty or not—or of *what* I am guilty, either? That's my affair. What does the Bible say? 'Driven off the face of the earth.' Very well. I am off the face of the earth now. As I came at night so I shall go."

"Impossible!" I murmured. "You can't."

"Can't? . . . Not naked like a soul on the Day of Judgment. I shall freeze on to this sleeping-suit. The Last Day is not yet—and . . . you have understood thoroughly. Didn't you?"

I felt suddenly ashamed of myself. I may say truly that I understood—and my hesitation in letting that man swim away from my ship's side had been a mere sham sentiment, a sort of cowardice.

"It can't be done now till next night," I breathed out. "The ship is on the offshore tack and the wind may fail us."

"As long as I know that you understand," he whispered. "But of course you do. It's a great satisfaction to have got somebody to understand. You seem to have been there on purpose." And in the same whisper, as if we two whenever we talked had to say things to each other which were not fit for the world to hear, he added, "It's very wonderful."

We remained side by side talking in our secret way—but sometimes silent or just exchanging a whispered word or two at long intervals. And as usual he stared through the port. A breath of wind came now and again into our faces. The ship might have been moored in dock, so gently and on an even keel she slipped through the water, that did not murmur even at our passage, shadowy and silent like a phantom sea.

At midnight I went on deck, and to my mate's great surprise put the ship round on the other tack. His terrible whiskers flitted round me in silent criticism. I certainly should not have done it if it had been only a question of getting out of that sleepy gulf as quickly as possible. I believe he told the second mate, who relieved him, that it was a great want of judgment. The other only yawned. That intolerable cub shuffled about so sleepily and lolled against the rails in such a slack, improper fashion that I came down on him sharply.

"Aren't you properly awake yet?"

"Yes, sir! I am awake."

"Well, then, be good enough to hold yourself as if you were. And keep a look-out. If there's any current we'll be closing with some islands before daylight."

The east side of the gulf is fringed with islands, some solitary, others in groups. On the blue background of the high coast they seem to float on silvery patches of calm water, arid and gray, or dark green and rounded like clumps of evergreen bushes, with the larger ones, a mile or two long, showing the outlines of ridges, ribs of gray rock under the dank mantle of matted leafage. Unknown to trade, to travel, almost to geography, the manner of life they harbor is an unsolved secret. There must be villages —settlements of fishermen at least—on the largest of them, and some communication with the world is probably kept up by native craft. But all that forenoon, as we headed for them, fanned along by the faintest of breezes, I saw no sign of man or canoe in the field of the telescope I kept on pointing at the scattered group.

At noon I gave no orders for a change of course, and the mate's whiskers became much concerned and seemed to be offering themselves unduly to my notice. At last I said:

"I am going to stand right in. Quite in—as far as I can take her."

The stare of extreme surprise imparted an air of ferocity also to his eyes, and he looked truly terrific for a moment.

"We're not doing well in the middle of the gulf," I continued, casually. "I am going to look for the land breezes tonight."

"Bless my soul! Do you mean, sir, in the dark amongst the lot of all them islands and reefs and shoals?"

"Well—if there are any regular land breezes at all on this coast one must get close inshore to find them, mustn't one?"

"Bless my soul!" he exclaimed again under his breath. All that afternoon he wore a dreamy, contemplative appearance which in him was a mark of perplexity. After dinner I went into my stateroom as if I meant to take some rest. There we two bent our dark heads over a half-unrolled chart lying on my bed.

"There," I said. "It's got to be Koh-ring. I've been looking at it ever since sunrise. It has got two hills and a low point. It must be inhabited. And on the coast opposite there is what looks like the mouth of a biggish river—with some town, no doubt, not far up. It's the best chance for you that I can see."

"Anything. Koh-ring let it be."

He looked thoughtfully at the chart as if surveying chances and distances from a lofty height—and following with his eyes his own figure wandering on the blank land of Cochin-China, and then passing off that piece of paper clean out of sight into uncharted regions. And it was as if the ship had two captains to plan her course for her. I had been so worried and restless running up and down that I had not had the patience to dress that day. I had remained in my sleeping-suit, with straw slippers and a soft floppy hat. The closeness of the heat in the gulf had been most oppressive, and the crew were used to see me wandering in that airy attire.

"She will clear the south point as she heads now," I whispered into his ear. "Goodness only knows when, though, but certainly after dark. I'll edge her in to half a mile, as far as I may be able to judge in the dark—"

"Be careful," he murmured, warningly—and I realized suddenly that all my future, the only future for which I was fit, would perhaps go irretrievably to pieces in any mishap to my first command.

I could not stop a moment longer in the room. I

motioned him to get out of sight and made my way on the poop. That unplayful cub had the watch. I walked up and down for a while thinking things out, then beckoned him over.

"Send a couple of hands to open the two quarter-deck ports," I said, mildly.

He actually had the impudence, or else so forgot himself in his wonder at such an incomprehensible order, as to repeat:

"Open the quarter-deck ports! What for, sir?"

"The only reason you need concern yourself about is because I tell you to do so. Have them opened wide and fastened properly."

He reddened and went off, but I believe made some jeering remark to the carpenter as to the sensible practice of ventilating a ship's quarter-deck. I know he popped into the mate's cabin to impart the fact to him because the whiskers came on deck, as it were by chance, and stole glances at me from below—for signs of lunacy or drunkenness, I suppose.

A little before supper, feeling more restless than ever, I rejoined, for a moment, my second self. And to find him sitting so quietly was surprising, like something against nature, inhuman.

I developed my plan in a hurried whisper.

"I shall stand in as close as I dare and then put her round. I will presently find means to smuggle you out of here into the sail-locker, which communicates with the lobby. But there is an opening, a sort of square for hauling the sails out, which gives straight on the quarter-deck and which is never closed in fine weather, so as to give air to the sails. When the ship's way is deadened in stays and all the hands are at the main-braces you will have a clear road to slip out and get overboard through the open quarter-deck port. I've had them both fastened up. Use a rope's end to lower yourself into the water so as to avoid a splash—you know. It could be heard and cause some beastly complication."

He kept silent for a while, then whispered, "I understand."

"I won't be there to see you go," I began with an effort. "The rest . . . I only hope I have understood, too."

"You have. From first to last"—and for the first time there seemed to be a faltering, something strained in his whisper. He caught hold of my arm, but the ringing of the supper bell made me start. He didn't, though; he only released his grip.

After supper I didn't come below again till well past eight o'clock. The faint, steady breeze was loaded with dew; and the wet, darkened sails held all there was of propelling power in it. The night, clear and starry, sparkled darkly, and the opaque, lightless patches shifting slowly against the low stars were the drifting islets. On the port bow there was a big one more distant and shadowily imposing by the great space of sky it eclipsed.

On opening the door I had a back view of my very own self looking at a chart. He had come out of the recess and was standing near the table.

"Quite dark enough," I whispered.

He stepped back and leaned against my bed with a level, quiet glance. I sat on the couch. We had nothing to say to each other. Over our heads the officer of the watch moved here and there. Then I heard him move quickly. I knew what that meant. He was making for the companion; and presently his voice was outside my door.

"We are drawing in pretty fast, sir. Land looks rather close."

"Very well," I answered. "I am coming on deck directly."

I waited till he was gone out of the cuddy, then rose. My double moved too. The time had come to exchange our last whispers, for neither of us was ever to hear each other's natural voice.

"Look here!" I opened a drawer and took out three sovereigns. "Take this anyhow. I've got six and I'd give you the lot, only I must keep a little money to buy some fruit and vegetables for the crew from native boats as we go through Sunda Straits."

He shook his head.

"Take it," I urged him, whispering desperately. "No one can tell what—"

He smiled and slapped meaningly the only pocket of the sleeping-jacket. It was not safe, certainly. But I produced a large old silk handkerchief of mine, and tying the three pieces of gold in a corner, pressed it on him. He was touched, I suppose, because he took it at last and tied it quickly round his waist under the jacket, on his bare skin.

Our eyes met; several seconds elapsed, till, our glances still mingled, I extended my hand and turned the lamp out. Then I passed through the cuddy, leaving the door of my room wide open. . . . "Steward!"

He was still lingering in the pantry in the greatness of his zeal, giving a rub-up to a plated cruet stand the last thing before going to bed. Being careful not to wake up the mate, whose room was opposite, I spoke in an undertone.

He looked round anxiously. "Sir!"

"Can you get me a little hot water from the galley?"

"I am afraid, sir, the galley fire's been out for some time now."

"Go and see."

He flew up the stairs.

"Now," I whispered, loudly, into the saloon—too

loudly, perhaps, but I was afraid I couldn't make a sound. He was by my side in an instant—the double captain slipped past the stairs—through a tiny dark passage . . . a sliding door. We were in the sail-locker, scrambling on our knees over the sails. A sudden thought struck me. I saw myself wandering barefooted, bareheaded, the sun beating on my dark poll. I snatched off my floppy hat and tried hurriedly in the dark to ram it on my other self. He dodged and fended off silently. I wonder what he thought had come to me before he understood and suddenly desisted. Our hands met gropingly, lingered, united in a steady, motionless clasp for a second. . . . No word was breathed by either of us when they separated.

I was standing quietly by the pantry door when the steward returned.

"Sorry, sir. Kettle barely warm. Shall I light the spirit-lamp?"

"Never mind."

I came out on deck slowly. It was now a matter of conscience to shave the land as close as possible—for now he must go overboard whenever the ship was put in stays. Must! There could be no going back for him. After a moment I walked over to leeward and my heart flew into my mouth at the nearness of the land on the bow. Under any other circumstances I would not have held on a minute longer. The second mate had followed me anxiously.

I looked on till I felt I could command my voice.

"She will weather," I said then in a quiet tone.

"Are you going to try that, sir?" he stammered out incredulously.

I took no notice of him and raised my tone just enough to be heard by the helmsman.

"Keep her good full."

"Good full, sir."

The wind fanned my cheek, the sails slept, the world was silent. The strain of watching the dark loom of the land grow bigger and denser was too much for me. I had shut my eyes—because the ship must go closer. She must! The stillness was intolerable. Were we standing still?

When I opened my eyes the second view started my heart with a thump. The black southern hill of Koh-ring seemed to hang right over the ship like a towering fragment of the everlasting night. On that enormous mass of blackness there was not a gleam to be seen, not a sound to be heard. It was gliding irresistibly towards us and yet seemed already within reach of the hand. I saw the vague figures of the watch grouped in the waist, gazing in awed silence.

"Are you going on, sir?" inquired an unsteady voice at my elbow.

I ignored it. I had to go on.

"Keep her full. Don't check her way. That won't do now," I said, warningly.

"I can't see the sails very well," the helmsman answered me, in strange, quavering tones.

Was she close enough? Already she was, I won't say in the shadow of the land, but in the very blackness of it, already swallowed up as it were, gone too close to be recalled, gone from me altogether.

"Give the mate a call," I said to the young man who stood at my elbow as still as death. "And turn all hands up."

My tone had a borrowed loudness reverberated from the height of the land. Several voices cried out together: "We are all on deck, sir."

Then stillness again, with the great shadow gliding closer, towering higher, without a light, without a sound. Such a hush had fallen on the ship that she might have been a bark of the dead floating in slowly under the very gate of Erebus.

"My God! Where are we?"

It was the mate moaning at my elbow. He was thunderstruck, and as it were deprived of the moral support of his whiskers. He clapped his hands and absolutely cried out, "Lost!"

"Be quiet," I said, sternly.

He lowered his tone, but I saw the shadowy gesture of his despair. "What are we doing here?"

"Looking for the land wind."

He made as if to tear his hair, and addressed me recklessly.

"She will never get out. You have done it, sir. I knew it'd end in something like this. She will never weather, and you are too close now to stay. She'll drift ashore before she's round. O my God!"

I caught his arm as he was raising it to batter his poor devoted head, and shook it violently.

"She's ashore already," he wailed, trying to tear himself away.

"Is she? . . . Keep good full there!"

"Good full, sir," cried the helmsman in a frightened, thin, child-like voice.

I hadn't let go the mate's arm and went on shaking it. "Ready about, do you hear? You go forward"—shake—"and stop there"—shake—"and hold your noise"—shake—"and see these head-sheets properly overhauled"—shake, shake—shake.

And all the time I dared not look towards the land lest my heart should fail me. I released my grip at last and he ran forward as if fleeing for dear life.

I wondered what my double there in the sail-locker thought of this commotion. He was able to hear everything—and perhaps he was able to understand why, on my conscience, it had to be thus close —no less. My first order "Hard alee!" re-echoed ominously under the towering shadow of Koh-ring as if I had shouted in a mountain gorge. And then I watched the land intently. In that smooth water and light wind it was impossible to feel the ship coming-to. No! I could not feel her. And my second self was making now ready to slip out and lower himself overboard. Perhaps he was gone already . . . ?

The great black mass brooding over our very mastheads began to pivot away from the ship's side silently. And now I forgot the secret stranger ready to depart, and remembered only that I was a total stranger to the ship. I did not know her. Would she do it? How was she to be handled?

I swung the mainyard and waited helplessly. She was perhaps stopped, and her very fate hung in the balance, with the black mass of Koh-ring like the gate of the everlasting night towering over her taffrail. What would she do now? Had she way on her yet? I stepped to the side swiftly, and on the shadowy water I could see nothing except a faint phosphorescent flash revealing the glassy smoothness of the sleeping surface. It was impossible to tell—and I had not learned yet the feel of my ship. Was she moving? What I needed was something easily seen, a piece of paper, which I could throw overboard and watch. I had nothing on me. To run down for it I didn't dare. There was no time. All at once my strained, yearning stare distinguished a white object floating within a yard of the ship's side. White on the black water. A phosphorescent flash passed under it. What was that thing? . . . I recognized my own floppy hat. It must have fallen off his head . . . and he didn't bother. Now I had what I wanted—the saving mark for my eyes. But I hardly thought of my other self, now gone from the ship, to be hidden forever from all friendly faces, to be a fugitive and a vagabond on the earth, with no brand of the curse on his sane forehead to stay a slaying hand . . . too proud to explain.

And I watched the hat—the expression of my sudden pity for his mere flesh. It had been meant to save his homeless head from the dangers of the sun. And now—behold—it was saving the ship, by serving me for a mark to help out the ignorance of my strangeness. Ha! It was drifting forward, warning me just in time that the ship had gathered sternway.

"Shift the helm," I said in a low voice to the seaman standing still like a statue.

The man's eyes glistened wildly in the binnacle light as he jumped round to the other side and spun round the wheel.

I walked to the break of the poop. On the overshadowed deck all hands stood by the forebraces waiting for my order. The stars ahead seemed to be gliding from right to left. And all was so still in the world that I heard the quiet remark, "She's round," passed in a tone of intense relief between two seamen.

"Let go and haul."

The foreyards ran round with a great noise, amidst cheery cries. And now the frightful whiskers made themselves heard giving various orders. Already the ship was drawing ahead. And I was alone with her. Nothing! no one in the world should stand now between us, throwing a shadow on the way of silent knowledge and mute affection, the perfect communion of a seaman with his first command.

Walking to the taffrail, I was in time to make out, on the very edge of a darkness thrown by a towering black mass like the very gateway of Erebus—yes, I was in time to catch an evanescent glimpse of my white hat left behind to mark the spot where the secret sharer of my cabin and of my thoughts, as though he were my second self, had lowered himself into the water to take his punishment: a free man, a proud swimmer striking out for a new destiny.

THE BLUE HOTEL

STEPHEN CRANE

STEPHEN CRANE (1871–1900) was born in Newark, New Jersey, attended Lafayette College and Syracuse University, worked in New York as a reporter and later as a war correspondent in Cuba and Greece, and eventually settled in England. His most distinguished work is probably the novel, *The Red Badge of Courage* (1895).

THE Palace Hotel at Fort Romper was painted a light blue, a shade that is on the legs of a kind of heron, causing the bird to declare its position against any background. The Palace Hotel, then, was always screaming and howling in a way that made the dazzling winter landscape of Nebraska seem only a gray swampish hush. It stood alone on the prairie, and when the snow was falling the town two hundred yards away was not visible. But when the traveler alighted at the railway station he was obliged to pass the Palace Hotel before he could come upon the company of low clapboard houses which composed Fort Romper, and it was not to be thought that any traveler could pass the Palace Hotel without looking at it. Pat Scully, the proprietor, had proved himself a master of strategy when he chose his paints. It is true that on clear days, when the great transcontinental expresses, long lines of swaying Pullmans, swept through Fort Romper, passengers were overcome at the sight, and the cult that knows the brown-reds and the subdivisions of the dark greens of the East expressed shame, pity, horror, in a laugh. But to the citizens of this prairie town and to the people who would naturally stop there, Pat Scully had performed a feat. With this opulence and splendor, these creeds, classes, egotisms, that streamed through Romper on the rails day after day, they had no color in common.

As if the displayed delights of such a blue hotel were not sufficiently enticing, it was Scully's habit to go every morning and evening to meet the leisurely trains that stopped at Romper and work his seductions upon any man that he might see wavering, gripsack in hand.

One morning, when a snow-crusted engine dragged its long string of freight cars and its one passenger coach to the station, Scully performed the marvel of catching three men. One was a shaky and quick-eyed Swede, with a great shining cheap valise; one was a

Published 1930, 1952 by Alfred A. Knopf, Inc. Reprinted from *Stephen Crane: An Omnibus*, by Stephen Crane by permission of Alfred A. Knopf, Inc.

tall bronzed cowboy, who was on his way to a ranch near the Dakota line; one was a little silent man from the East, who didn't look it, and didn't announce it. Scully practically made them prisoners. He was so nimble and merry and kindly that each probably felt it would be the height of brutality to try to escape. They trudged off over the creaking board sidewalks in the wake of the eager little Irishman. He wore a heavy fur cap squeezed tightly down on his head. It caused his two red ears to stick out stiffly, as if they were made of tin.

At last, Scully, elaborately, with boisterous hospitality, conducted them through the portals of the blue hotel. The room which they entered was small. It seemed to be merely a proper temple for an enormous stove, which, in the center, was humming with godlike violence. At various points on its surface the iron had become luminous and glowed yellow from the heat. Beside the stove Scully's son Johnnie was playing High-Five with an old farmer who had whiskers both gray and sandy. They were quarreling. Frequently the old farmer turned his face toward a box of sawdust—colored brown from tobacco juice —that was behind the stove, and spat with an air of great impatience and irritation. With a loud flourish of words Scully destroyed the game of cards, and bustled his son upstairs with part of the baggage of the new guests. He himself conducted them to three basins of the coldest water in the world. The cowboy and the Easterner burnished themselves fiery red with this water, until it seemed to be some kind of metal-polish. The Swede, however, merely dipped his fingers gingerly and with trepidation. It was notable that throughout this series of small ceremonies the three travelers were made to feel that Scully was very benevolent. He was conferring great favors upon them. He handed the towel from one to another with an air of philanthropic impulse.

Afterward they went to the first room, and, sitting about the stove, listened to Scully's officious clamor at his daughters, who were preparing the midday meal. They reflected in the silence of experienced men who tread carefully amid new people. Nevertheless, the old farmer, stationary, invincible in his chair near the warmest part of the stove, turned his face from the sawdust-box frequently and addressed a glowing commonplace to the strangers. Usually he was answered in short but adequate sentences by either the cowboy or the Easterner. The Swede said nothing. He seemed to be occupied in making furtive estimates of each man in the room. One might have thought that he had the sense of silly suspicion which comes to guilt. He resembled a badly frightened man.

Later, at dinner, he spoke a little, addressing his conversation entirely to Scully. He volunteered that he had come from New York, where for ten years he had worked as a tailor. These facts seemed to strike Scully as fascinating, and afterward he volunteered that he had lived at Romper for fourteen years. The Swede asked about the crops and the price of labor. He seemed barely to listen to Scully's extended replies. His eyes continued to rove from man to man.

Finally, with a laugh and a wink, he said that some of these Western communities were very dangerous; and after his statement he straightened his legs under the table, tilted his head, and laughed again, loudly. It was plain that the demonstration had no meaning to the others. They looked at him wondering and in silence.

II

As the men trooped heavily back into the front room, the two little windows presented views of a turmoiling sea of snow. The huge arms of the wind were making attempts—mighty, circular, futile—to embrace the flakes as they sped. A gate-post like a still man with a blanched face stood aghast amid this profligate fury. In a hearty voice Scully announced the presence of a blizzard. The guests of the blue hotel, lighting their pipes, assented with grunts of lazy masculine contentment. No island of the sea could be exempt in the degree of this little room with its humming stove. Johnnie, son of Scully, in a tone which defined his opinion of his ability as a card-player, challenged the old farmer of both gray and sandy whiskers to a game of High-Five. The farmer agreed with a contemptuous and bitter scoff. They sat close to the stove, and squared their knees under a wide board. The cowboy and the Easterner watched the game with interest. The Swede remained near the window, aloof, but with a countenance that showed signs of an inexplicable excitement.

The play of Johnnie and the gray-beard was suddenly ended by another quarrel. The old man arose while casting a look of heated scorn at his adversary.

He slowly buttoned his coat, and then stalked with fabulous dignity from the room. In the discreet silence of all other men the Swede laughed. His laughter rang somehow childish. Men by this time had begun to look at him askance, as if they wished to inquire what ailed him.

A new game was formed jocosely. The cowboy volunteered to become the partner of Johnnie, and they all then turned to ask the Swede to throw in his lot with the little Easterner. He asked some questions about the game, and, learning that it wore many names, and that he had played it when it was under an alias, he accepted the invitation. He strode toward the men nervously, as if he expected to be assaulted. Finally, seated, he gazed from face to face and laughed shrilly. This laugh was so strange that the Easterner looked up quickly, the cowboy sat intent and with his mouth open, and Johnnie paused, holding the cards with still fingers.

Afterward there was a short silence. Then Johnnie said, "Well, let's get at it. Come on now!" They pulled their chairs forward until their knees were bunched under the board. They began to play, and their interest in the game caused the others to forget the manner of the Swede.

The cowboy was a board-whacker. Each time that he held superior cards he whanged them, one by one, with exceeding force, down upon the improvised table, and took the tricks with a glowing air of prowess and pride that sent thrills of indignation into the hearts of his opponents. A game with a board-whacker in it is sure to become intense. The countenances of the Easterner and the Swede were miserable whenever the cowboy thundered down his aces and kings, while Johnnie, his eyes gleaming with joy, chuckled and chuckled.

Because of the absorbing play none considered the strange ways of the Swede. They paid strict heed to the game. Finally, during a lull caused by a new deal, the Swede suddenly addressed Johnnie: "I suppose there have been a good many men killed in this room." The jaws of the others dropped and they looked at him.

"What in hell are you talking about?" said Johnnie.

The Swede laughed again his blatant laugh, full of a kind of false courage and defiance. "Oh, you know what I mean all right," he answered.

"I'm a liar if I do!" Johnnie protested. The card game was halted, and the men stared at the Swede. Johnnie evidently felt that as the son of the proprietor he should make a direct inquiry. "Now, what might you be drivin' at, mister?" he asked. The Swede winked at him. It was a wink full of cunning. His fingers shook on the edge of the board. "Oh, maybe you think I have been to nowheres. Maybe you think I'm a tenderfoot?"

"I don't know nothin' about you," answered Johnnie, "and I don't give a damn where you've been. All I got to say is that I don't know what you're driving at. There hain't never been nobody killed in this room."

The cowboy, who had been steadily gazing at the Swede, then spoke: "What's wrong with you, mister?"

Apparently it seemed to the Swede that he was formidably menaced. He shivered and turned white near the corners of his mouth. He sent an appealing glance in the direction of the little Easterner. During these moments he did not forget to wear his air of advanced potvalor. "They say they don't know what I mean," he remarked mockingly to the Easterner.

The latter answered after prolonged and cautious reflection. "I don't understand you," he said, impassively.

The Swede made a movement then which announced that he thought he had encountered treachery from the only quarter where he had expected sympathy, if not help. "Oh, I see you are all against me, I see——"

The cowboy was in a state of deep stupefaction. "Say," he cried, as he tumbled the deck violently down upon the board, "say, what are you gittin' at, hey?"

The Swede sprang up with the celerity of a man escaping from a snake on the floor. "I don't want to fight!" he shouted. "I don't want to fight!"

The cowboy stretched his long legs indolently and deliberately. His hands were in his pockets. He spat into the sawdust-box. "Well, who the hell thought you did?" he inquired.

The Swede backed rapidly toward a corner of the room. His hands were out protectingly in front of his chest, but he was making an obvious struggle to control his fright. "Gentlemen," he quavered, "I suppose I am going to be killed before I can leave this house! I suppose I am going to be killed before I can leave this house!" In his eyes was the dying-swan look. Through the windows could be seen the snow turning blue in the shadow of dusk. The wind tore at the house, and some loose thing beat regularly against the clapboards like a spirit tapping.

A door opened, and Scully himself entered. He paused in surprise as he noted the tragic attitude of the Swede. Then he said, "What's the matter here?"

The Swede answered him swiftly and eagerly: "These men are going to kill me."

"Kill you!" ejaculated Scully. "Kill you! What are you talkin'?"

The Swede made the gesture of a martyr.

Scully wheeled sternly upon his son. "What is this, Johnnie?"

The lad had grown sullen. "Damned if I know," he answered. "I can't make no sense to it." He began to shuffle the cards, fluttering them together with an angry snap. "He says a good many men have been killed in this room, or something like that. And he says he's goin' to be killed here too. I don't know what ails him. He's crazy, I shouldn't wonder."

Scully then looked for explanation to the cowboy, but the cowboy simply shrugged his shoulders.

"Kill you?" said Scully again to the Swede. "Kill you? Man, you're off your nut."

"Oh, I know," burst out the Swede. "I know what will happen. Yes, I'm crazy—yes. Yes, of course, I'm crazy—yes. But I know one thing—" There was a sort of sweat of misery and terror upon his face. "I know I won't get out of here alive."

The cowboy drew a deep breath, as if his mind was passing into the last stages of dissolution. "Well, I'm doggoned," he whispered to himself.

Scully wheeled suddenly and faced his son. "You've been troublin' this man!"

Johnnie's voice was loud with its burden of grievance. "Why, good Gawd, I ain't done nothin' to 'im."

The Swede broke in. "Gentlemen, do not disturb yourselves. I will leave this house. I will go away, because"—he accused them dramatically with his glance —"because I do not want to be killed."

Scully was furious with his son. "Will you tell me what is the matter, you young divil? What's the matter, anyhow? Speak out!"

"Blame it!" cried Johnnie in despair, "don't I tell you I don't know? He—he says we want to kill him, and that's all I know. I can't tell what ails him."

The Swede continued to repeat: "Never mind, Mr. Scully; never mind. I will leave this house. I will go away, because I do not wish to be killed. Yes, of course, I am crazy—yes. But I know one thing! I will go away. I will leave this house. Never mind, Mr. Scully; never mind. I will go away."

"You will not go 'way," said Scully. "You will not go 'way until I hear the reason of this business. If anybody has troubled you I will take care of him. This is my house. You are under my roof, and I will not allow any peaceable man to be troubled here." He cast a terrible eye upon Johnnie, the cowboy, and the Easterner.

"Never mind, Mr. Scully; never mind. I will go away. I do not wish to be killed." The Swede moved toward the door which opened upon the stairs. It was evidently his intention to go at once for his baggage.

"No, no," shouted Scully peremptorily; but the white-faced man slid by him and disappeared.

"Now," said Scully severely, "what does this mane?"

Johnnie and the cowboy cried together: "Why, we didn't do nothin' to 'im!"

Scully's eyes were cold. "No," he said, "you didn't?"

Johnnie swore a deep oath. "Why, this is the wildest loon I ever see. We didn't do nothin' at all. We were jest sittin' here playin' cards, and he——"

The father suddenly spoke to the Easterner, "Mr. Blanc," he asked, "what has these boys been doin'?"

The Easterner reflected again. "I didn't see anything wrong at all," he said at last, slowly.

Scully began to howl. "But what does it mane?" He stared ferociously at his son. "I have a mind to lather you for this, me boy."

Johnnie was frantic. "Well, what have I done?" he bawled at his father.

III

"I think you are tongue-tied," said Scully finally to his son, the cowboy, and the Easterner; and at the end of this scornful sentence he left the room.

Upstairs the Swede was swiftly fastening the straps of his great valise. Once his back happened to be half turned toward the door, and, hearing a noise there, he wheeled and sprang up, uttering a loud cry. Scully's wrinkled visage showed grimly in the light of the small lamp he carried. This yellow effulgence, streaming upward, colored only his prominent features, and left his eyes, for instance, in mysterious shadow. He resembled a murderer.

"Man! man!" he exclaimed, "have you gone daffy?"

"Oh, no! Oh, no!" rejoined the other. "There are people in this world who know pretty nearly as much as you do—understand?"

For a moment they stood gazing at each other. Upon the Swede's deathly pale cheeks were two spots brightly crimson and sharply edged, as if they had been carefully painted. Scully placed the light on the table and sat himself on the edge of the bed. He spoke ruminatively. "By cracky, I never heard of such a thing in my life. It's a complete muddle. I can't, for the soul of me, think how you ever got this idea into your head." Presently he lifted his eyes and asked: "And did you sure think they were going to kill you?"

The Swede scanned the old man as if he wished to see into his mind. "I did," he said at last. He obviously suspected that this answer might precipitate an outbreak. As he pulled on a strap his whole arm shook, the elbow wavering like a bit of paper.

Scully banged his hand impressively on the foot-board of the bed. "Why, man, we're goin' to have a line of ilictric street-cars in this town next spring."

"'A line of electric street-cars,'" repeated the Swede, stupidly.

"And," said Scully, "there's a new railroad goin' to be built down from Broken Arm to here. Not to mintion the four churches and the smashin' big brick schoolhouse. Then there's the big factory, too. Why, in two years Romper'll be a met-tro-*pol*-is."

Having finished the preparation of his baggage, the Swede straightened himself. "Mr. Scully," he said, with sudden hardihood, "how much do I owe you?"

"You don't owe me anythin'," said the old man, angrily.

"Yes, I do," retorted the Swede. He took seventy-five cents from his pocket and tendered it to Scully; but the latter snapped his fingers in disdainful refusal. However, it happened that they both stood gazing in a strange fashion at three silver pieces on the Swede's open palm.

"I'll not take your money," said Scully at last. "Not after what's been goin' on here." Then a plan seemed to strike him. "Here," he cried, picking up his lamp and moving toward the door. "Here! Come with me a minute."

"No," said the Swede, in overwhelming alarm.

"Yes," urged the old man. "Come on! I want you to come and see a picter—just across the hall—in my room."

The Swede must have concluded that his hour was come. His jaw dropped and his teeth showed like a dead man's. He ultimately followed Scully across the corridor, but he had the step of one hung in chains.

Scully flashed the light high on the wall of his own chamber. There was revealed a ridiculous photograph of a little girl. She was leaning against a balustrade of gorgeous decoration, and the formidable bang to her hair was prominent. The figure was as graceful as an upright sled-stake, and, withal, it was of the hue of lead. "There," said Scully, tenderly, "that's the picter of my little girl that died. Her name was Carrie. She had the purtiest hair you ever saw! I was that fond of her, she——"

Turning then, he saw that the Swede was not contemplating the picture at all, but, instead, was keeping keen watch on the gloom in the rear.

"Look, man!" cried Scully, heartily. "That's the picter of my little gal that died. Her name was Carrie. And then here's the picter of my oldest boy, Michael. He's a lawyer in Lincoln, an' doin' well. I gave that boy a grand eddication, and I'm glad for it now. He's a fine boy. Look at 'im now. Ain't he bold as blazes, him there in Lincoln, an honored an' respicted gintleman! An honored and respicted gintleman," concluded Scully with a flourish. And, so saying, he smote the Swede jovially on the back.

The Swede faintly smiled.

"Now," said the old man, "there's only one more thing." He dropped suddenly to the floor and thrust his head beneath the bed. The Swede could hear his muffled voice. "I'd keep it under me piller if it wasn't for that boy Johnnie. Then there's the old woman— Where is it now? I never put it twice in the same place. Ah, now come out with you!"

Presently he backed clumsily from under the bed, dragging with him an old coat rolled into a bundle. "I've fetched him," he muttered. Kneeling on the floor, he unrolled the coat and extracted from its heart a large yellow-brown whisky-bottle.

His first maneuver was to hold the bottle up to the light. Reassured, apparently, that nobody had been tampering with it, he thrust it with a generous movement toward the Swede.

The weak-kneed Swede was about to eagerly clutch this element of strength, but he suddenly jerked his hand away and cast a look of horror upon Scully.

"Drink," said the old man affectionately. He had risen to his feet, and now stood facing the Swede.

There was a silence. Then again Scully said: "Drink!"

The Swede laughed wildly. He grabbed the bottle, put it to his mouth; and as his lips curled absurdly around the opening and his throat worked, he kept his glance, burning with hatred, upon the old man's face.

IV

After the departure of Scully the three men, with the cardboard still upon their knees, preserved for a long time an astounded silence. Then Johnnie said: "That's the doddangedest Swede I ever see."

"He ain't no Swede," said the cowboy, scornfully.

"Well, what is he then?" cried Johnnie. "What is he then?"

"It's my opinion," replied the cowboy deliberately, "he's some kind of a Dutchman." It was a venerable custom of the country to entitle as Swedes all light-haired men who spoke with a heavy tongue. In consequence the idea of the cowboy was not without its daring. "Yes, sir," he repeated. "It's my opinion this feller is some kind of a Dutchman."

"Well, he says he's a Swede, anyhow," muttered Johnnie, sulkily. He turned to the Easterner: "What do you think, Mr. Blanc?"

"Oh, I don't know," replied the Easterner.

"Well, what do you think makes him act that way?" asked the cowboy.

"Why, he's frightened." The Easterner knocked his pipe against a rim of the stove. "He's clear frightened out of his boots."

"What at?" cried Johnnie and the cowboy together.

The Easterner reflected over his answer.

"Oh, I don't know, but it seems to me this man has been reading dime novels, and he thinks he's right out in the middle of it—the shootin' and stabbin' and all."

"But," said the cowboy, deeply scandalized, "this ain't Wyoming, ner none of them places. This is Nebrasker."

"Yes," added Johnnie, "an' why don't he wait till he gits *out West*?"

The traveled Easterner laughed. "It isn't different there even—not in these days. But he thinks he's right in the middle of hell."

Johnnie and the cowboy mused long.

"It's awful funny," remarked Johnnie at last.

"Yes," said the cowboy. "This is a queer game. I hope we don't git snowed in, because then we'd have to stand this here man bein' around with us all the time. That wouldn't be no good."

"I wish pop would throw him out," said Johnnie.

Presently they heard a loud stamping on the stairs, accompanied by ringing jokes in the voice of old Scully, and laughter, evidently from the Swede. The men around the stove stared vacantly at each other. "Gosh!" said the cowboy. The door flew open, and old Scully, flushed and anecdotal, came into the room. He was jabbering at the Swede, who followed him, laughing bravely. It was the entry of two roisterers from a banquet hall.

"Come now," said Scully sharply to the three seated men, "move up and give us a chance at the stove." The cowboy and the Easterner obediently sidled their chairs to make room for the new-comers. Johnnie, however, simply arranged himself in a more indolent attitude, and then remained motionless.

"Come! Git over, there," said Scully.

"Plenty of room on the other side of the stove," said Johnnie.

"Do you think we want to sit in the draught?" roared the father.

But the Swede here interposed with a grandeur of confidence. "No, no. Let the boy sit where he likes," he cried in a bullying voice to the father.

"All right! All right!" said Scully, deferentially. The cowboy and the Easterner exchanged glances of wonder.

The five chairs were formed in a crescent about one side of the stove. The Swede began to talk; he talked arrogantly, profanely, angrily. Johnnie, the cowboy, and the Easterner maintained a morose silence, while old Scully appeared to be receptive and eager, breaking in constantly with sympathetic ejaculations.

Finally the Swede announced that he was thirsty. He moved in his chair, and said that he would go for a drink of water.

"I'll git it for you," cried Scully at once.

"No," said the Swede, contemptuously. "I'll get it for myself." He arose and stalked with the air of an owner off into the executive parts of the hotel.

As soon as the Swede was out of hearing Scully sprang to his feet and whispered intensely to the others: "Upstairs he thought I was tryin' to poison 'im."

"Say," said Johnnie, "this makes me sick. Why don't you throw 'im out in the snow?"

"Why, he's all right now," declared Scully. "It was only that he was from the East, and he thought this was a tough place. That's all. He's all right now."

The cowboy looked with admiration upon the Easterner. "You were straight," he said. "You were on to that there Dutchman."

"Well," said Johnnie to his father, "he may be all right now, but I don't see it. Other time he was scared, but now he's too fresh."

Scully's speech was always a combination of Irish brogue and idiom, Western twang and idiom, and scraps of curiously formal diction taken from the storybooks and newspapers. He now hurled a strange mass of language at the head of his son. "What do I keep? What do I keep? What do I keep?" he demanded, in a voice of thunder. He slapped his knee impressively, to indicate that he himself was going to make reply, and that all should heed. "I keep a hotel," he shouted. "A hotel, do you mind? A guest under my roof has sacred privileges. He is to be intimidated by none. Not one word shall he hear that would prijudice him in favor of goin' away. I'll not have it. There's no place in this here town where they can say they iver took in a guest of mine because he was afraid to stay here." He wheeled suddenly upon the cowboy and the Easterner. "Am I right?"

"Yes, Mr. Scully," said the cowboy, "I think you're right."

"Yes, Mr. Scully," said the Easterner, "I think you're right."

V

At six-o'clock supper, the Swede fizzed like a fire-wheel. He sometimes seemed on the point of bursting into riotous song, and in all his madness he was encouraged by old Scully. The Easterner was encased in reserve; the cowboy sat in wide-mouthed amazement, forgetting to eat, while Johnnie wrathily de-molished great plates of food. The daughters of the house, when they were obliged to replenish the biscuits, approached as warily as Indians, and, having succeeded in their purpose, fled with ill-concealed trepidation. The Swede domineered the whole feast, and he gave it the appearance of a cruel bacchanal. He seemed to have grown suddenly taller; he gazed, brutally disdainful, into every face. His voice rang through the room. Once when he jabbed out harpoon-fashion with his fork to pinion a biscuit, the weapon nearly impaled the hand of the Easterner, which had been stretched quietly out for the same biscuit.

After supper, as the men filed toward the other room, the Swede smote Scully ruthlessly on the shoulder. "Well, old boy, that was a good, square meal." Johnnie looked hopefully at his father; he knew that shoulder was tender from an old fall; and, indeed, it appeared for a moment as if Scully was going to flame out over the matter, but in the end he smiled a sickly smile and remained silent. The others understood from his manner that he was admitting his responsibility for the Swede's new view-point.

Johnnie, however, addressed his parent in an aside. "Why don't you license somebody to kick you downstairs?" Scully scowled darkly by way of reply.

When they were gathered about the stove, the Swede insisted on another game of High-Five. Scully gently deprecated the plan at first, but the Swede turned a wolfish glare upon him. The old man subsided, and the Swede canvassed the others. In his tone there was always a great threat. The cowboy and the Easterner both remarked indifferently that they would play. Scully said that he would presently have to go to meet the 6.58 train, and so the Swede turned menacingly upon Johnnie. For a moment their glances crossed like blades, and then Johnnie smiled and said, "Yes, I'll play."

They formed a square, with the little board on their knees. The Easterner and the Swede were again partners. As the play went on, it was noticeable that the cowboy was not board-whacking as usual. Meanwhile, Scully, near the lamp, had put on his spectacles and, with an appearance curiously like an old priest, was reading a newspaper. In time he went out to meet the 6.58 train, and, despite his precautions, a gust of polar wind whirled into the room as he opened the door. Besides scattering the cards, it chilled the players to the marrow. The Swede cursed frightfully. When Scully returned, his entrance disturbed a cozy and friendly scene. The Swede again cursed. But presently they were once more intent, their heads bent forward and their hands moving swiftly. The Swede had adopted the fashion of board-whacking.

Scully took up his paper and for a long time remained immersed in matters which were extraordinarily remote from him. The lamp burned badly, and once he stopped to adjust the wick. The newspaper, as he turned from page to page, rustled with a slow and comfortable sound. Then suddenly he heard three terrible words: "You are cheatin'!"

Such scenes often prove that there can be little of dramatic import in environment. Any room can present a tragic front; any room can be comic. This little den was now hideous as a torture-chamber. The new faces of the men themselves had changed it upon the instant. The Swede held a huge fist in front of Johnnie's face, while the latter looked steadily over it into the blazing orbs of his accuser. The Easterner had grown pallid; the cowboy's jaw had dropped in that expression of bovine amazement which was one of his important mannerisms. After the three words, the first sound in the room was made by Scully's paper as it floated forgotten to his feet. His spectacles had also fallen from his nose, but by a clutch he had saved them in air. His hand, grasping the spectacles, now remained poised awkwardly and near his shoulder. He stared at the card-players.

Probably the silence was while a second elapsed. Then, if the floor had been suddenly twitched out from under the men they could not have moved quicker. The five had projected themselves headlong toward a common point. It happened that Johnnie, in rising to hurl himself upon the Swede, had stumbled slightly because of his curiously instinctive care for the cards and the board. The loss of the moment allowed time for the arrival of Scully, and also allowed the cowboy time to give the Swede a great push which sent him staggering back. The men found tongue together, and hoarse shouts of rage, appeal, or fear burst from every throat. The cowboy pushed and jostled feverishly at the Swede, and the Easterner and Scully clung wildly to Johnnie; but through the smoky air, above the swaying bodies of the peace-compellers, the eyes of the two warriors ever sought each other in glances of challenge that were at once hot and steely.

Of course the board had been overturned, and now the whole company of cards was scattered over the floor, where the boots of the men trampled the fat and painted kings and queens as they gazed with their silly eyes at the war that was waging above them.

Scully's voice was dominating the yells. "Stop now! Stop, I say! Stop, now——"

Johnnie, as he struggled to burst through the rank formed by Scully and the Easterner, was crying, "Well, he says I cheated! He says I cheated! I won't allow no man to say I cheated! If he says I cheated, he's a——!"

The cowboy was telling the Swede, "Quit, now! Quit, d'ye hear——"

The screams of the Swede never ceased: "He did cheat! I saw him! I saw him——"

As for the Easterner, he was importuning in a voice that was not heeded: "Wait a moment, can't you? Oh, wait a moment. What's the good of a fight over a game of cards? Wait a moment——"

In this tumult no complete sentences were clear. "Cheat"—"Quit"—"He says"—these fragments pierced the uproar and rang out sharply. It was remarkable that, whereas Scully undoubtedly made the most noise, he was the least heard of any of the riotous band.

Then suddenly there was a great cessation. It was as if each man had paused for breath; and although the room was still lighted with the anger of men, it could be seen that there was no danger of immediate conflict, and at once Johnnie, shouldering his way forward, almost succeeded in confronting the Swede. "What did you say I cheated for? What did you say I cheated for? I don't cheat, and I won't let no man say I do!"

The Swede said, "I saw you! I saw you!"

"Well," cried Johnnie, "I'll fight any man what says I cheat!"

"No, you won't," said the cowboy. "Not here."

"Ah, be still, can't you?" said Scully, coming between them.

The quiet was sufficient to allow the Easterner's voice to be heard. He was repeating, "Oh, wait a moment, can't you? What's the good of a fight over a game of cards? Wait a moment!"

Johnnie, his red face appearing above his father's shoulder, hailed the Swede again. "Did you say I cheated?"

The Swede showed his teeth. "Yes."

"Then," said Johnnie, "we must fight."

"Yes, fight," roared the Swede. He was like a demoniac. "Yes, fight! I'll show you what kind of a man I am! I'll show you who you want to fight! Maybe you think I can't fight! Maybe you think I can't! I'll show you, you skin, you card-sharp! Yes, you cheated! You cheated! You cheated!"

"Well, let's go at it, then, mister," said Johnnie, coolly.

The cowboy's brow was beaded with sweat from his efforts in intercepting all sorts of raids. He turned in despair to Scully. "What are you goin' to do now?"

A change had come over the Celtic visage of the old man. He now seemed all eagerness; his eyes glowed.

"We'll let them fight," he answered, stalwartly. "I

can't put up with it any longer. I've stood this damned Swede till I'm sick. We'll let them fight."

VI

The men prepared to go out of doors. The Easterner was so nervous that he had great difficulty in getting his arms into the sleeves of his new leather coat. As the cowboy drew his fur cap down over his ears his hands trembled. In fact, Johnnie and old Scully were the only ones who displayed no agitation. These preliminaries were conducted without words.

Scully threw open the door. "Well, come on," he said. Instantly a terrific wind caused the flame of the lamp to struggle at its wick, while a puff of black smoke sprang from the chimney-top. The stove was in mid-current of the blast, and its voice swelled to equal the roar of the storm. Some of the scarred and bedabbled cards were caught up from the floor and dashed helplessly against the farther wall. The men lowered their heads and plunged into the tempest as into a sea.

No snow was falling, but great whirls and clouds of flakes, swept up from the ground by the frantic winds, were streaming southward with the speed of bullets. The covered land was blue with the sheen of an unearthly satin, and there was no other hue save where, at the low, black railway station—which seemed incredibly distant—one light gleamed like a tiny jewel. As the men floundered into a thigh-deep drift, it was known that the Swede was bawling out something. Scully went to him, put a hand on his shoulder, and projected an ear. "What's that you say?" he shouted.

"I say," bawled the Swede again, "I won't stand much show against this gang. I know you'll all pitch on me."

Scully smote him reproachfully on the arm. "Tut, man!" he yelled. The wind tore the words from Scully's lips and scattered them far alee.

"You are all a gang of—" boomed the Swede, but the storm also seized the remainder of this sentence.

Immediately turning their backs upon the wind, the men had swung around a corner to the sheltered side of the hotel. It was the function of the little house to preserve here, amid this great devastation of snow, an irregular V-shape of heavily encrusted grass, which crackled beneath the feet. One could imagine the great drifts piled against the windward side. When the party reached the comparative peace of this spot it was found that the Swede was still bellowing.

"Oh, I know what kind of a thing this is! I know you'll all pitch on me. I can't lick you all!"

Scully turned upon him panther-fashion. "You'll not have to whip all of us. You'll have to whip my son Johnnie. An' the man what troubles you durin' that time will have me to dale with."

The arrangements were swiftly made. The two men faced each other, obedient to the harsh commands of Scully, whose face, in the subtly luminous gloom, could be seen set in the austere impersonal lines that are pictured on the countenances of the Roman veterans. The Easterner's teeth were chattering, and he was hopping up and down like a mechanical toy. The cowboy stood rock-like.

The contestants had not stripped off any clothing. Each was in his ordinary attire. Their fists were up, and they eyed each other in a calm that had the elements of leonine cruelty in it.

During this pause, the Easterner's mind, like a film, took lasting impressions of three men—the iron-nerved master of the ceremony; the Swede, pale, motionless, terrible; and Johnnie, serene yet ferocious, brutish yet heroic. The entire prelude had in it a tragedy greater than the tragedy of action, and this aspect was accentuated by the long, mellow cry of the blizzard, as it sped the tumbling and wailing flakes into the black abyss of the south.

"Now!" said Scully.

The two combatants leaped forward and crashed together like bullocks. There was heard the cushioned sound of blows, and of a curse squeezing out from between the tight teeth of one.

As for the spectators, the Easterner's pent-up breath exploded from him with a pop of relief, absolute relief from the tension of the preliminaries. The cowboy bounded into the air with a yowl. Scully was immovable as from supreme amazement and fear at the fury of the fight which he himself had permitted and arranged.

For a time the encounter in the darkness was such a perplexity of flying arms that it presented no more detail than would a swiftly revolving wheel. Occasionally a face, as if illumined by a flash of light, would shine out, ghastly and marked with pink spots. A moment later, the men might have been known as shadows, if it were not for the involuntary utterance of oaths that came from them in whispers.

Suddenly a holocaust of warlike desire caught the cowboy, and he bolted forward with the speed of a broncho. "Go it, Johnnie! go it! Kill him! Kill him!"

Scully confronted him. "Kape back," he said; and by his glance the cowboy could tell that this man was Johnnie's father.

To the Easterner there was a monotony of unchangeable fighting that was an abomination. This confused mingling was eternal to his sense, which was concentrated in a longing for the end, the priceless end. Once the fighters lurched near him, and as he scrambled hastily backward he heard them breathe like men on the rack.

"Kill him, Johnnie! Kill him! Kill him! Kill him!" The cowboy's face was contorted like one of those agony masks in museums.

"Keep still," said Scully, icily.

Then there was a sudden loud grunt, incomplete, cut short, and Johnnie's body swung away from the Swede and fell with sickening heaviness to the grass. The cowboy was barely in time to prevent the mad Swede from flinging himself upon his prone adversary. "No, you don't," said the cowboy, interposing an arm. "Wait a second."

Scully was at his son's side. "Johnnie! Johnnie, me boy!" His voice had a quality of melancholy tenderness. "Johnnie! Can you go on with it?" He looked anxiously down into the bloody, pulpy face of his son.

There was a moment of silence, and then Johnnie answered in his ordinary voice, "Yes, I—it—yes."

Assisted by his father he struggled to his feet. "Wait a bit now till you git your wind," said the old man.

A few paces away the cowboy was lecturing the Swede. "No, you don't! Wait a second!"

The Easterner was plucking at Scully's sleeve. "Oh, this is enough," he pleaded. "This is enough! Let it go as it stands. This is enough!"

"Bill," said Scully, "git out of the road." The cowboy stepped aside. "Now." The combatants were actuated by a new caution as they advanced toward collision. They glared at each other, and then the Swede aimed a lightning blow that carried with it his entire weight. Johnnie was evidently half stupid from weakness, but he miraculously dodged, and his fist sent the over-balanced Swede sprawling.

The cowboy, Scully, and the Easterner burst into a cheer that was like a chorus of triumphant soldiery, but before its conclusion the Swede had scuffled agilely to his feet and come in berserk abandon at his foe. There was another perplexity of flying arms, and Johnnie's body again swung away and fell, even as a bundle might fall from a roof. The Swede instantly staggered to a little wind-waved tree and leaned upon it, breathing like an engine, while his savage and flame-lit eyes roamed from face to face as the men bent over Johnnie. There was a splendor of isolation in his situation at this time which the Easterner felt once when, lifting his eyes from the man on the ground, he beheld that mysterious and lonely figure, waiting.

"Are you any good yet, Johnnie?" asked Scully in a broken voice.

The son gasped and opened his eyes languidly. After a moment he answered, "No—I ain't—any good

—any—more." Then, from shame and bodily ill, he began to weep, the tears furrowing down through the bloodstains on his face. "He was too—too—too heavy for me."

Scully straightened and addressed the waiting figure. "Stranger," he said, evenly, "it's all up with our side." Then his voice changed into that vibrant huskiness which is commonly the tone of the most simple and deadly announcements. "Johnnie is whipped."

Without replying, the victor moved off on the route to the front door of the hotel.

The cowboy was formulating new and unspellable blasphemies. The Easterner was startled to find that they were out in a wind that seemed to come direct from the shadowed arctic floes. He heard again the wail of the snow as it was flung to its grave in the south. He knew now that all this time the cold had been sinking into him deeper and deeper, and he wondered that he had not perished. He felt indifferent to the condition of the vanquished man.

"Johnnie, can you walk?" asked Scully.

"Did I hurt—hurt him any?" asked the son.

"Can you walk, boy? Can you walk?"

Johnnie's voice was suddenly strong. There was a robust impatience in it. "I asked you whether I hurt him any!"

"Yes, yes, Johnnie," answered the cowboy, consolingly; "he's hurt a good deal."

They raised him from the ground, and as soon as he was on his feet he went tottering off, rebuffing all attempts at assistance. When the party rounded the corner they were fairly blinded by the pelting of the snow. It burned their faces like fire. The cowboy carried Johnnie through the drift to the door. As they entered, some cards again rose from the floor and beat against the wall.

The Easterner rushed to the stove. He was so profoundly chilled that he almost dared to embrace the glowing iron. The Swede was not in the room. Johnnie sank into a chair and, folding his arms on his knees, buried his face in them. Scully, warming one foot and then the other at a rim of the stove, muttered to himself with Celtic mournfulness. The cowboy had removed his fur cap, and with a dazed and rueful air he was running one hand through his tousled locks. From overhead they could hear the creaking of boards, as the Swede tramped here and there in his room.

The sad quiet was broken by the sudden flinging open of a door that led toward the kitchen. It was instantly followed by an inrush of women. They precipitated themselves upon Johnnie amid a chorus of lamentation. Before they carried their prey off to the kitchen, there to be bathed and harangued with that mixture of sympathy and abuse which is a feat of their sex, the mother straightened herself and fixed old Scully with an eye of stern reproach. "Shame be upon you, Patrick Scully!" she cried. "Your own son, too. Shame be upon you!"

"There, now! Be quiet, now!" said the old man, weakly.

"Shame be upon you, Patrick Scully!" The girls, rallying to this slogan, sniffed disdainfully in the direction of those trembling accomplices, the cowboy and the Easterner. Presently they bore Johnnie away, and left the three men to dismal reflection.

VII

"I'd like to fight this here Dutchman myself," said the cowboy, breaking a long silence.

Scully wagged his head sadly. "No, that wouldn't do. It wouldn't be right. It wouldn't be right."

"Well, why wouldn't it?" argued the cowboy. "I don't see no harm in it."

"No," answered Scully, with mournful heroism. "It wouldn't be right. It was Johnnie's fight, and now we mustn't whip the man just because he whipped Johnnie."

"Yes, that's true enough," said the cowboy; "but—he better not get fresh with me, because I couldn't stand no more of it."

"You'll not say a word to him," commanded Scully, and even then they heard the tread of the Swede on the stairs. His entrance was made theatric. He swept the door back with a bang and swaggered to the middle of the room. No one looked at him. "Well," he cried, insolently, at Scully, "I s'pose you'll tell me now how much I owe you?"

The old man remained stolid. "You don't owe me nothin'."

"Huh!" said the Swede, "huh! Don't owe 'im nothin'."

The cowboy addressed the Swede. "Stranger, I don't see how you come to be so gay around here."

Old Scully was instantly alert. "Stop!" he shouted, holding his hand forth, fingers upward. "Bill, you shut up!"

The cowboy spat carelessly into the sawdust-box. "I didn't say a word, did I?" he asked.

"Mr. Scully," called the Swede, "how much do I owe you?" It was seen that he was attired for departure, and that he had his valise in his hand.

"You don't owe me nothin'," repeated Scully in the same imperturbable way.

"Huh!" said the Swede. "I guess you're right. I guess if it was any way at all, you'd owe me somethin'. That's what I guess." He turned to the cowboy. "'Kill him! Kill him! Kill him!'" he mimicked, and

then guffawed victoriously. "'Kill him!'" He was convulsed with ironical humor.

But he might have been jeering the dead. The three men were immovable and silent, staring with glassy eyes at the stove.

The Swede opened the door and passed into the storm, giving one derisive glance backward at the still group.

As soon as the door was closed, Scully and the cowboy leaped to their feet and began to curse. They trampled to and fro, waving their arms and smashing into the air with their fists. "Oh, but that was a hard minute!" wailed Scully. "That was a hard minute! Him there leerin' and scoffin'! One bang at his nose was worth forty dollars to me that minute! How did you stand it, Bill?"

"How did I stand it?" cried the cowboy in a quivering voice. "How did I stand it? Oh!"

The old man burst into sudden brogue. "I'd loike to take that Swade," he wailed, "and hould 'im down on a shtone flure and bate 'im to a jelly wid a shtick!"

The cowboy groaned in sympathy. "I'd like to git him by the neck and ha-ammer him"—he brought his hand down on a chair with a noise like a pistol-shot—"hammer that there Dutchman until he couldn't tell himself from a dead coyote!"

"I'd bate 'im until he——"

"I'd show *him* some things——"

And then together they raised a yearning, fanatic cry—"Oh-o-oh! if we only could——"

"Yes!"

"Yes!"

"And then I'd——"

"O-o-oh!"

VIII

The Swede, tightly gripping his valise, tacked across the face of the storm as if he carried sails. He was following a line of little naked, gasping trees which, he knew, must mark the way of the road. His face, fresh from the pounding of Johnnie's fists, felt more pleasure than pain in the wind and the driving snow. A number of square shapes loomed upon him finally, and he knew them as the houses of the main body of the town. He found a street and made travel along it, leaning heavily upon the wind whenever, at a corner, a terrific blast caught him.

He might have been in a deserted village. We picture the world as thick with conquering and elate humanity, but here, with the bugles of the tempest pealing, it was hard to imagine a peopled earth. One viewed the existence of man then as a marvel, and conceded a glamour of wonder to these lice which were caused to cling to a whirling, fire-smitten, ice-locked, disease-stricken, space-lost bulb. The conceit of man was explained by this storm to be the very engine of life. One was a coxcomb not to die in it. However, the Swede found a saloon.

In front of it an indomitable red light was burning, and the snowflakes were made blood-color as they flew through the circumscribed territory of the lamp's shining. The Swede pushed open the door of the saloon and entered. A sanded expanse was before him, and at the end of it four men sat about a table drinking. Down one side of the room extended a radiant bar, and its guardian was leaning upon his elbows listening to the talk of the men at the table. The Swede dropped his valise upon the floor and, smiling fraternally upon the barkeeper, said, "Gimme some whisky, will you?" The man placed a bottle, a whisky-glass, and a glass of ice-thick water upon the bar. The Swede poured himself an abnormal portion of whisky and drank it in three gulps. "Pretty bad night," remarked the bartender, indifferently. He was making the pretension of blindness which is usually a distinction of his class; but it could have been seen that he was furtively studying the half-erased blood-stains on the face of the Swede. "Bad night," he said again.

"Oh, it's good enough for me," replied the Swede, hardily, as he poured himself some more whisky. The barkeeper took his coin and maneuvered it through its reception by the highly nickeled cash-machine. A bell rang; a card labeled "20 cts." had appeared.

"No," continued the Swede, "this isn't too bad weather. It's good enough for me."

"So?" murmured the barkeeper, languidly.

The copious drams made the Swede's eyes swim, and he breathed a trifle heavier. "Yes, I like this weather. I like it. It suits me." It was apparently his design to impart a deep significance to these words.

"So?" murmured the bartender again. He turned to gaze dreamily at the scroll-like birds and bird-like scrolls which had been drawn with soap upon the mirrors in back of the bar.

"Well, I guess I'll take another drink," said the Swede, presently. "Have something?"

"No, thanks; I'm not drinking'," answered the bartender. Afterward he asked, "How did you hurt your face?"

The Swede immediately began to boast loudly. "Why, in a fight. I thumped the soul out of a man down here at Scully's hotel."

The interest of the four men at the table was at last aroused.

"Who was it?" said one.

"Johnnie Scully," blustered the Swede. "Son of the man what runs it. He will be pretty near dead for some weeks, I can tell you. I made a nice thing of him, I did. He couldn't get up. They carried him in the house. Have a drink?"

Instantly the men in some subtle way encased themselves in reserve. "No, thanks," said one. The group was of curious formation. Two were prominent local business men; one was the district attorney; and one was a professional gambler of the kind known as "square." But a scrutiny of the group would not have enabled an observer to pick the gambler from the men of more reputable pursuits. He was, in fact, a man so delicate in manner, when among people of fair class, and so judicious in his choice of victims, that in the strictly masculine part of the town's life he had come to be explicitly trusted and admired. People called him a thoroughbred. The fear and contempt with which his craft was regarded were undoubtedly the reason why his quiet dignity shone conspicuous above the quiet dignity of men who might be merely hatters, billiard-markers, or grocery clerks. Beyond an occasional unwary traveler who came by rail, this gambler was supposed to prey solely upon reckless and senile farmers, who, when flush with good crops, drove into town in all the pride and confidence of an absolutely invulnerable stupidity. Hearing at times in circuitous fashion of the despoilment of such a farmer, the important men of Romper invariably laughed in contempt of the victim, and if they thought of the wolf at all, it was with a kind of pride at the knowledge that he would never dare think of attacking their wisdom and courage. Besides, it was popular that this gambler had a real wife and two real children in a neat cottage in a suburb, where he led an exemplary home life; and when anyone even suggested a discrepancy in his character, the crowd immediately vociferated descriptions of this virtuous family circle. Then men who led exemplary home lives, and men who did not lead exemplary home lives, all subsided in a bunch, remarking that there was nothing more to be said.

However, when a restriction was placed upon him —as, for instance, when a strong clique of members of the new Pollywog Club refused to permit him, even as a spectator, to appear in the rooms of the organization—the candor and gentleness with which he accepted the judgment disarmed many of his foes and made his friends more desperately partisan. He invariably distinguished between himself and a respectable Romper man so quickly and frankly that his manner actually appeared to be a continual broadcast compliment.

And one must not forget to declare the fundamental fact of his entire position in Romper. It is irrefutable that in all affairs outside his business, in all matters that occur eternally and commonly between man and man, this thieving card-player was so generous, so just, so moral, that, in a contest, he could have put to flight the consciences of nine tenths of the citizens of Romper.

And so it happened that he was seated in this saloon with the two prominent local merchants and the district attorney.

The Swede continued to drink raw whisky, meanwhile babbling at the barkeeper and trying to induce him to indulge in potations. "Come on. Have a drink. Come on. What—no? Well, have a little one, then. By gawd, I've whipped a man tonight, and I want to celebrate. I whipped him good, too. Gentlemen," the Swede cried to the men at the table, "have a drink?"

"Ssh!" said the barkeeper.

The group at the table, although furtively attentive, had been pretending to be deep in talk, but now a man lifted his eyes toward the Swede and said, shortly, "Thanks. We don't want any more."

At this reply the Swede ruffled out his chest like a rooster. "Well," he exploded, "it seems I can't get anybody to drink with me in this town. Seems so, don't it? Well!"

"Ssh!" said the barkeeper.

"Say," snarled the Swede, "don't you try to shut me up. I won't have it. I'm a gentleman, and I want people to drink with me. And I want 'em to drink with me now. *Now*—do you understand?" He rapped the bar with his knuckles.

Years of experience had calloused the bartender. He merely grew sulky. "I hear you," he answered.

"Well," cried the Swede, "listen hard then. See those men over there? Well, they're going to drink with me, and don't you forget it. Now you watch."

"Hi!" yelled the barkeeper, "this won't do!"

"Why won't it?" demanded the Swede. He stalked over to the table, and by chance laid his hand upon the shoulder of the gambler. "How about this?" he asked wrathfully. "I asked you to drink with me."

The gambler simply twisted his head and spoke over his shoulder. "My friend, I don't know you."

"Oh, hell!" answered the Swede, "come and have a drink."

"Now, my boy," advised the gambler, kindly, "take your hand off my shoulder and go 'way and mind your own business." He was a little, slim man, and it seemed strange to hear him use this tone of heroic patronage to the burly Swede. The other men at the table said nothing.

"What! You won't drink with me, you little dude? I'll make you, then! I'll make you!" The Swede had grasped the gambler frenziedly at the throat, and was dragging him from his chair. The other men sprang up. The barkeeper dashed around the corner of his bar. There was a great tumult, and then was

seen a long blade in the hand of the gambler. It shot forward, and a human body, this citadel of virtue, wisdom, power, was pierced as easily as if it had been a melon. The Swede fell with a cry of supreme astonishment.

The prominent merchants and the district attorney must have at once tumbled out of the place backward. The bartender found himself hanging limply to the arm of a chair and gazing into the eyes of a murderer.

"Henry," said the latter, as he wiped his knife on one of the towels that hung beneath the bar rail, "you tell 'em where to find me. I'll be home, waiting for 'em." Then he vanished. A moment afterward the barkeeper was in the street dinning through the storm for help and, moreover, companionship.

The corpse of the Swede, alone in the saloon, had its eyes fixed upon a dreadful legend that dwelt atop of the cash-machine: "This registers the amount of your purchase."

IX

Months later, the cowboy was frying pork over the stove of a little ranch near the Dakota line, when there was a quick thud of hoofs outside, and presently the Easterner entered with the letters and the papers.

"Well," said the Easterner at once, "the chap that killed the Swede has got three years. Wasn't much, was it?"

"He has? Three years?" The cowboy poised his pan of pork, while he ruminated upon the news. "Three years. That ain't much."

"No. It was a light sentence," replied the Easterner as he unbuckled his spurs. "Seems there was a good deal of sympathy for him in Romper."

"If the bartender had been any good," observed the cowboy, thoughtfully, "he would have gone in and cracked that there Dutchman on the head with a bottle in the beginnin' of it and stopped all this here murderin'."

"Yes, a thousand things might have happened," said the Easterner, tartly.

The cowboy returned his pan of pork to the fire, but his philosophy continued. "It's funny, ain't it? If he hadn't said Johnnie was cheatin' he'd be alive this minute. He was an awful fool. Game played for fun, too. Not for money. I believe he was crazy."

"I feel sorry for that gambler," said the Easterner.

"Oh, so do I," said the cowboy. "He don't deserve none of it for killin' who he did."

"The Swede might not have been killed if everything had been square."

"Might not have been killed?" exclaimed the cowboy. "Everythin' square? Why, when he said that Johnnie was cheatin' and acted like such a jackass? And then in the saloon he fairly walked up to git hurt?" With these arguments the cowboy browbeat the Easterner and reduced him to rage.

"You're a fool!" cried the Easterner, viciously. "You're a bigger jackass than the Swede by a million majority. Now let me tell you one thing. Let me tell you something. Listen! Johnnie *was* cheating!"

"'Johnnie,'" said the cowboy, blankly. There was a minute of silence, and then he said, robustly, "Why, no. The game was only for fun."

"Fun or not," said the Easterner, "Johnnie was cheating. I saw him. I know it. I saw him. And I refused to stand up and be a man. I let the Swede fight it out alone. And you—you were simply puffing around the place and wanting to fight. And then old Scully himself! We are all in it! This poor gambler isn't even a noun. He is kind of an adverb. Every sin is the result of a collaboration. We, five of us, have collaborated in the murder of this Swede. Usually there are from a dozen to forty women really involved in every murder, but in this case it seems to be only five men—you, I, Johnnie, old Scully; and that fool of an unfortunate gambler came merely as a culmination, the apex of a human movement, and gets all the punishment."

The cowboy, injured and rebellious, cried out blindly into this fog of mysterious theory: "Well, I didn't do anythin', did I?"

NEIGHBOUR ROSICKY

WILLA CATHER

WILLA CATHER (1876–1947) was born in Virginia but moved at an early age to Nebraska. She said later that her first two years among the pioneering settlers of that region were, to her as a writer, the most important of her life. Educated at home before high school, she graduated from the University of Nebraska in 1895, did journalistic work and teaching in Pittsburgh, editorial work in New York, and traveled widely in this country and Europe. After 1911 she turned wholly to writing. Among her books are *O Pioneers!* (1913), *My Ántonia* (1918), *A Lost Lady* (1923), *My Mortal Enemy* (1926), *Death Comes for the Archbishop* (1927) and *Shadows on the Rock* (1931). "The higher processes of art," she said, "are all processes of simplification. . . . What I always want to do is to make the writing count for less and less and the people for more and more. I'd like the writing to be so lost in the object that it doesn't exist for the reader. . . . If [the writer] achieves anything noble, anything enduring, it must be by giving himself absolutely to his material. And this gift of sympathy is his great gift; is the fine thing in him that alone can make his work fine."

I

WHEN Doctor Burleigh told neighbour Rosicky he had a bad heart, Rosicky protested.

"So? No, I guess my heart was always pretty good. I got a little asthma, maybe. Just a awful short breath when I was pitchin' hay last summer, dat's all."

"Well, now, Rosicky, if you know more about it than I do, what did you come to me for? It's your heart that makes you short of breath, I tell you. You're sixty-five years old, and you've always worked hard, and your heart's tired. You've got to be careful from now on, and you can't do heavy work any more. You've got five boys at home to do it for you."

The old farmer looked up at the doctor with a gleam of amusement in his queer, triangular-shaped eyes. His eyes were large and lively, but the lids were caught up in the middle in a curious way, so that they formed a triangle. He did not look like a sick man. His brown face was creased but not wrinkled, he had a ruddy colour in his smooth-shaven cheeks and in his lips, under his long brown moustache. His hair was thin and ragged around his ears, but very little grey. His forehead, naturally high and crossed by deep parallel lines, now ran all the way up to his pointed crown. Rosicky's face had the habit of looking interested—suggested a contented disposition and a reflective quality that was gay rather than grave. This gave him a certain detachment, the easy manner of an onlooker and observer.

"Well, I guess you ain't got no pills fur a bad

heart, Doctor Ed. I guess the only thing is fur me to git me a new one."

Doctor Burleigh swung round in his desk chair and frowned at the old farmer.

"I think if I were you I'd take a little care of the old one, Rosicky."

Rosicky shrugged. "Maybe I don't know how. I expect you mean fur me not to drink my coffee no more."

"I wouldn't, in your place. But you will do as you choose about that. I've never yet been able to separate a Bohemian from his coffee or his pipe. I've quit trying. But the sure thing is you've got to cut out farm work. You can feed the stock and do chores about the barn, but you can't do anything in the fields that makes you short of breath."

"How about shelling corn?"

"Of course not!"

Rosicky considered with puckered brows.

"I can't make my heart go no longer'n it wants to, can I, Doctor Ed?"

"I think it's good for five or six years yet, maybe more, if you'll take the strain off it. Sit around the house and help Mary. If I had a good wife like yours, I'd want to stay around the house."

His patient chuckled. "It ain't no place fur a man. I don't like no old man hanging round the kitchen too much. An' my wife, she's awful hard worker her own self."

"That's it; you can help her a little. My Lord, Rosicky, you are one of the few men I know who has a family he can get some comfort out of; happy dispositions, never quarrel among themselves, and they treat you right. I want to see you live a few years and enjoy them."

"Oh, they're good kids, all right," Rosicky assented.

The doctor wrote him a prescription and asked him how his oldest son, Rudolph, who had married in the spring, was getting on. Rudolph had struck out for himself, on rented land. "And how's Polly? I was afraid Mary mightn't like an American daughter-in-law, but it seems to be working out all right."

"Yes, she's a fine girl. Dat widder woman bring her daughters up very nice. Polly got lots of spunk, an' she got some style, too. Da's nice, for young folks to have some style." Rosicky inclined his head gallantly. His voice and his twinkly smile were an affectionate compliment to his daughter-in-law.

"It looks like a storm, and you'd better be getting home before it comes. In town in the car?" Doctor Burleigh rose.

"No, I'm in de wagon. When you got five boys, you ain't got much chance to ride round in de Ford. I ain't much for cars, noway."

"Well, it's a good road out to your place; but I don't want you bumping around in a wagon much. And never again on a hay-rake, remember!"

Rosicky placed the doctor's fee delicately behind the desk-telephone, looking the other way, as if this were an absent-minded gesture. He put on his plush cap and his corduroy jacket with a sheepskin collar, and went out.

The doctor picked up his stethoscope and frowned at it as if he were seriously annoyed with the instrument. He wished it had been telling tales about some other man's heart, some old man who didn't look the doctor in the eye so knowingly, or hold out such a warm brown hand when he said goodbye. Doctor Burleigh had been a poor boy in the country before he went away to medical school; he had known Rosicky almost ever since he could remember, and he had a deep affection for Mrs. Rosicky.

Only last winter he had had such a good breakfast at Rosicky's, and that when he needed it. He had been out all night on a long, hard confinement case at Tom Marshall's—a big rich farm where there was plenty of stock and plenty of feed and a great deal of expensive farm machinery of the newest model, and no comfort whatever. The woman had too many children and too much work, and she was no manager. When the baby was born at last, and handed over to the assisting neighbour woman, and the mother was properly attended to, Burleigh refused any breakfast in that slovenly house, and drove his buggy—the snow was too deep for a car—eight miles to Anton Rosicky's place. He didn't know another farm-house where a man could get such a warm welcome, and such good strong coffee with rich cream. No wonder the old chap didn't want to give up his coffee!

He had driven in just when the boys had come back from the barn and were washing up for breakfast. The long table, covered with a bright oilcloth, was set out with dishes waiting for them, and the warm kitchen was full of the smell of coffee and hot biscuit and sausage. Five big handsome boys, running from twenty to twelve, all with what Burleigh called natural good manners—they hadn't a bit of the painful self-consciousness he himself had to struggle with when he was a lad. One ran to put his horse away, another helped him off with his fur coat and hung it up, and Josephine, the youngest child and the only daughter, quickly set another place under her mother's direction.

With Mary, to feed creatures was the natural expression of affection—her chickens, the calves, her big hungry boys. It was a rare pleasure to feed a young man whom she seldom saw and of whom she was as proud as if he belonged to her. Some country housekeepers would have stopped to spread a white cloth over the oilcloth, to change the thick cups and plates for their best china, and the wooden-handled knives for plated ones. But not Mary.

"You must take us as you find us, Doctor Ed. I'd be glad to put out my good things for you if you was expected, but I'm glad to get you anyway at all."

He knew she was glad—she threw back her head and spoke out as if she were announcing him to the whole prairie. Rosicky hadn't said anything at all; he merely smiled his twinkling smile, put some more coal on the fire, and went into his own room to pour the doctor a little drink in a medicine glass. When they were all seated, he watched his wife's face from his end of the table and spoke to her in Czech. Then, with the instinct of politeness which seldom failed him, he turned to the doctor and said slyly: "I was just tellin' her not to ask you no questions about Mrs. Marshall till you eat some breakfast. My wife, she's terrible fur to ask questions."

The boys laughed, and so did Mary. She watched the doctor devour her biscuit and sausage, too much excited to eat anything herself. She drank her coffee and sat taking in everything about her visitor. She had known him when he was a poor country boy, and was boastfully proud of his success, always saying: "What do people go to Omaha for, to see a doctor, when we got the best one in the State right here?" If Mary liked people at all, she felt physical pleasure in the sight of them, personal exultation in any good fortune that came to them. Burleigh didn't know many women like that, but he knew she was like that.

When his hunger was satisfied, he did, of course, have to tell them about Mrs. Marshall, and he noticed what a friendly interest the boys took in the matter.

Rudolph, the oldest one (he was still living at home then), said: "The last time I was over there, she was lifting them big heavy milk-cans, and I knew she ought not to be doing it."

"Yes, Rudolph told me about that when he come home, and I said it wasn't right," Mary put in warmly. "It was all right for me to do them things up to the last, for I was terrible strong, but that woman's weakly. And do you think she'll be able to nurse it, Ed?" She sometimes forgot to give him the title she was so proud of. "And to think of your being up all night and then not able to get a decent breakfast! I don't know what's the matter with such people."

"Why, mother," said one of the boys, "if Doctor Ed had got breakfast there, we wouldn't have him here. So you ought to be glad."

"He knows I'm glad to have him, John, any time. But I'm sorry for that poor woman, how bad she'll feel the doctor had to go away in the cold without his breakfast."

"I wish I had been in practice when these were getting born." The doctor looked down the row of close-clipped heads. "I missed some good breakfasts by not being."

The boys began to laugh at their mother because she flushed so red, but she stood her ground and threw up her head. "I don't care, you wouldn't have got away from this house without breakfast. No doctor ever did. I'd have had something ready fixed that Anton could warm up for you."

The boys laughed harder than ever, and exclaimed at her: "I'll bet you would!" "She would, that!"

"Father, did you get breakfast for the doctor when we were born?"

"Yes, and he used to bring me my breakfast, too, mighty nice. I was always awful hungry!" Mary admitted with a guilty laugh.

While the boys were getting the doctor's horse, he went to the window to examine the house plants.

"What do you do to your geraniums to keep them blooming all winter, Mary? I never pass this house that from the road I don't see your windows full of flowers."

She snapped off a dark red one, and a ruffled new green leaf, and put them in his buttonhole. "There, that looks better. You look too solemn for a young man, Ed. Why don't you git married? I'm worried about you. Settin' at breakfast, I looked at you real hard, and I seen you've got some grey hairs already."

"Oh, yes! They're coming. Maybe they'd come faster if I married."

"Don't talk so. You'll ruin your health eating at the hotel. I could send your wife a nice loaf of nut bread, if you only had one. I don't like to see a young man getting grey. I'll tell you something, Ed; you make some strong black tea and keep it handy in a bowl, and every morning just brush it into your hair, an' it'll keep the grey from showin' much. That's the way I do!"

Sometimes the doctor heard gossipers in the drug-store wondering why Rosicky didn't get on faster. He was industrious, and so were his boys, but they were rather free and easy, weren't pushers, and they didn't always show good judgment. They were comfortable, they were out of debt, but they didn't get much ahead. Maybe, Doctor Burleigh reflected, people as generous and warm-hearted and affectionate as the Rosickys never got ahead much; maybe you could not enjoy your life and put it into the bank, too.

II

When Rosicky left Doctor Burleigh's office, he went into the farm-implement store to light his pipe and put on his glasses and read over the list Mary had given him. Then he went into the general merchandise place next door and stood about until the pretty girl with the plucked eyebrows, who always waited on him, was free. Those eyebrows, two thin India-ink strokes, amused him, because he remembered how they used to be. Rosicky always prolonged his shopping by a little joking; the girl knew the old fellow admired her, and she liked to chaff with him.

"Seems to me about every other week you buy ticking, Mr. Rosicky, and always the best quality," she remarked as she measured off the heavy bolt with red stripes.

"You see, my wife is always makin' goose-fedder pillows, an' de thin stuff don't hold in dem little down-fedders."

"You must have lots of pillows at your house."

"Sure. She makes quilts of dem, too. We sleeps easy. Now she's makin' a fedder quilt for my son's wife. You know Polly, that married my Rudolph. How much my bill, Miss Pearl?"

"Eight eighty-five."

"Chust make it nine, and put in some candy fur de women."

"As usual. I never did see a man buy so much candy for his wife. First thing you know, she'll be getting too fat."

"I'd like dat. I ain't much fur all dem slim women like what de style is now."

"That's one for me, I suppose, Mr. Bohunk!" Pearl sniffed and elevated her India-ink strokes.

When Rosicky went out to his wagon, it was beginning to snow—the first snow of the season, and he was glad to see it. He rattled out of town and along the highway through a wonderfully rich stretch of country, the finest farms in the county. He admired this High Prairie, as it was called, and always liked to drive through it. His own place lay in a rougher territory, where there was some clay in the soil and it was not so productive. When he bought his land, he hadn't the money to buy on High Prairie; so he told his boys, when they grumbled, that if their land hadn't some clay in it, they wouldn't own it at all. All the same, he enjoyed looking at these fine farms, as he enjoyed looking at a prize bull.

After he had gone eight miles, he came to the graveyard, which lay just at the edge of his own hay-land. There he stopped his horses and sat still on his wagon seat, looking about at the snowfall.

Over yonder on the hill he could see his own house, crouching low, with the clump of orchard behind and the windmill before, and all down the gentle hill-slope the rows of pale gold cornstalks stood out against the white field. The snow was falling over the cornfield and the pasture and the hay-land, steadily, with very little wind—a nice dry snow. The graveyard had only a light wire fence about it and was all overgrown with long red grass. The fine snow, settling into this red grass and upon the few little evergreens and the headstones, looked very pretty.

It was a nice graveyard, Rosicky reflected, sort of snug and homelike, not cramped or mournful—a big sweep all round it. A man could lie down in the long grass and see the complete arch of the sky over him, hear the wagons go by; in summer the mowing-machine rattled right up to the wire fence. And it was so near home. Over there across the cornstalks his own roof and windmill looked so good to him that he promised himself to mind the doctor and take care of himself. He was awful fond of his place, he admitted. He wasn't anxious to leave it. And it was a comfort to think that he would never have to go farther than the edge of his own hayfield. The snow, falling over his barnyard and the graveyard, seemed to draw things together like. And they were all old neighbours in the graveyard, most of them friends; there was nothing to feel awkward or embarrassed about. Embarrassment was the most disagreeable feeling Rosicky knew. He didn't often have it—only with certain people whom he didn't understand at all.

Well, it was a nice snowstorm; a fine sight to see the snow falling so quietly and graciously over so much open country. On his cap and shoulders, on the horses' backs and manes, light, delicate, mysterious it fell; and with it a dry cool fragrance was released into the air. It meant rest for vegetation and men and beast, for the ground itself; a season of long nights for sleep, leisurely breakfasts, peace by the fire. This and much more went through Rosicky's mind, but he merely told himself that winter was coming, clucked to his horses, and drove on.

When he reached home, John, the youngest boy, ran out to put away his team for him, and he met Mary coming up from the outside cellar with her apron full of carrots. They went into the house together. On the table, covered with oilcloth figured with clusters of blue grapes, a place was set, and he smelled hot coffee-cake of some kind. Anton never lunched in town; he thought that extravagant, and anyhow he didn't like the food. So Mary always had something ready for him when he got home.

After he was settled in his chair, stirring his coffee

in a big cup, Mary took out of the oven a pan of *kolache* stuffed with apricots, examined them anxiously to see whether they had got too dry, put them beside his plate, and then sat down opposite him.

Rosicky asked her in Czech if she wasn't going to have any coffee.

She replied in English, as being somehow the right language for transacting business: "Now what did Doctor Ed say, Anton? You tell me just what."

"He said I was to tell you some compliments, but I forgot 'em." Rosicky's eyes twinkled.

"About you, I mean. What did he say about your asthma?"

"He says I ain't got no asthma." Rosicky took one of the little rolls in his broad brown fingers. The thickened nail of his right thumb told the story of his past.

"Well, what is the matter? And don't try to put me off."

"He don't say nothing much, only I'm a little older, and my heart ain't so good like it used to be."

Mary started and brushed her hair back from her temples with both hands as if she were a little out of her mind. From the way she glared, she might have been in a rage with him.

"He says there's something the matter with your heart? Doctor Ed says so?"

"Now don't yell at me like I was a hog in de garden, Mary. You know I always did like to hear a woman talk soft. He didn't say anything de matter wid my heart, only it ain't so young like it used to be, an' he tell me not to pitch hay or run de corn-sheller."

Mary wanted to jump up, but she sat still. She admired the way he never under any circumstances raised his voice or spoke roughly. He was city-bred, and she was country-bred; she often said she wanted her boys to have their papa's nice ways.

"You never have no pain there, do you? It's your breathing and your stomach that's been wrong. I wouldn't believe nobody but Doctor Ed about it. I guess I'll go see him myself. Didn't he give you no advice?"

"Chust to take it easy like, an' stay round de house dis winter. I guess you got some carpenter work for me to do. I kin make some new shelves for you, and I want dis long time to build a closet in de boys' room and make dem two little fellers keep dere clo'es hung up."

Rosicky drank his coffee from time to time, while he considered. His moustache was of the soft long variety and came down over his mouth like the teeth of a buggy rake over a bundle of hay. Each time he put down his cup, he ran his blue handkerchief over his lips. When he took a drink of water, he managed very neatly with the back of his hand.

Mary sat watching him intently, trying to find any change in his face. It is hard to see anyone who has become like your own body to you. Yes, his hair had got thin, and his high forehead had deep lines running from left to right. But his neck, always clean-shaved except in the busiest seasons, was not loose or baggy. It was burned a dark reddish brown, and there were deep creases in it, but it looked firm and full of blood. His cheeks had a good colour. On either side of his mouth there was a half-moon down the length of his cheek, not wrinkles, but two lines that had come there from his habitual expression. He was shorter and broader than when she married him; his back had grown broad and curved, a good deal like the shell of an old turtle, and his arms and legs were short.

He was fifteen years older than Mary, but she had hardly ever thought about it before. He was her man, and the kind of man she liked. She was rough, and he was gentle—city-bred, as she always said. They had been shipmates on a rough voyage and had stood by each other in trying times. Life had gone well with them because, at bottom, they had the same ideas about life. They agreed, without discussion, as to what was most important and what was secondary. They didn't often exchange opinions, even in Czech —it was as if they had thought the same thought together. A good deal had to be sacrificed and thrown overboard in a hard life like theirs, and they had never disagreed as to the things that could go. It had been a hard life, and a soft life, too. There wasn't anything brutal in the short, broad-backed man with the three-cornered eyes and the forehead that went on to the top of his skull. He was a city man, a gentle man, and though he had married a rough farm girl, he had never touched her without gentleness.

They had been at one accord not to hurry through life, not to be always skimping and saving. They saw their neighbours buy more land and feed more stock than they did, without discontent. Once when the creamery agent came to the Rosickys to persuade them to sell him their cream, he told them how much money the Fasslers, their nearest neighbours, had made on their cream last year.

"Yes," said Mary, "and look at them Fassler children! Pale, pinched little things, they look like skimmed milk. I had rather put some colour into my children's faces than put money into the bank."

The agent shrugged and turned to Anton.

"I guess we'll do like she says," said Rosicky.

III

Mary very soon got into town to see Doctor Ed, and then she had a talk with her boys and set a guard over Rosicky. Even John, the youngest, had his father on his mind. If Rosicky went to throw hay down from the loft, one of the boys ran up the ladder and took the fork from him. He sometimes complained that though he was getting to be an old man, he wasn't an old woman yet.

That winter he stayed in the house in the afternoons and carpentered, or sat in the chair between the window full of plants and the wooden bench where the two pails of drinking-water stood. This spot was called "Father's corner," though it was not a corner at all. He had a shelf there, where he kept his Bohemian papers and his pipes and tobacco, and his shears and needles and thread and tailor's thimble. Having been a tailor in his youth, he couldn't bear to see a woman patching at his clothes, or at the boys'. He liked tailoring, and always patched all the overalls and jackets and work shirts. Occasionally he made over a pair of pants one of the older boys had outgrown, for the little fellow.

While he sewed, he let his mind run back over his life. He had a good deal to remember, really; life in three countries. The only part of his youth he didn't like to remember was the two years he had spent in London, in Cheapside, working for a German tailor who was wretchedly poor. Those days, when he was nearly always hungry, when his clothes were dropping off him for dirt, and the sound of a strange language kept him in continual bewilderment, had left a sore spot in his mind that wouldn't bear touching.

He was twenty when he landed at Castle Garden in New York, and he had a protector who got him work in a tailor shop in Vesey Street, down near the Washington Market. He looked upon that part of his life as very happy. He became a good workman, he was industrious, and his wages were increased from time to time. He minded his own business and envied nobody's good fortune. He went to night school and learned to read English. He often did overtime work and was well paid for it, but somehow he never saved anything. He couldn't refuse a loan to a friend, and he was self-indulgent. He liked a good dinner, and a little went for beer, a little for tobacco; a good deal went to the girls. He often stood through an opera on Saturday nights; he could get standing-room for a dollar. Those were the great days of opera in New York, and it gave a fellow something to think about for the rest of the week. Rosicky had a quick ear, and a childish love of all the stage splendour; the scenery, the costumes, the ballet. He usually went with a chum, and after the performance they had beer, and maybe some oysters, somewhere. It was a fine life; for the first five years or so it satisfied him completely. He was never hungry or cold or dirty, and everything amused him: a fire, a dog fight, a parade, a storm, a ferry ride. He thought New York the finest, richest, friendliest city in the world.

Moreover, he had what he called a happy home life. Very near the tailor shop was a small furniture factory, where an old Austrian, Loeffler, employed a few skilled men and made unusual furniture, most of it to order, for the rich German housewives uptown. The top floor of Loeffler's five-story factory was a loft, where he kept his choice lumber and stored the odd pieces of furniture left on his hands. One of the young workmen he employed was a Czech, and he and Rosicky became fast friends. They persuaded Loeffler to let them have a sleeping-room in one corner of the loft. They bought good beds and bedding and had their pick of the furniture kept up there. The loft was low-pitched, but light and airy, full of windows, and good-smelling by reason of the fine lumber put up there to season. Old Loeffler used to go down to the docks and buy wood from South America and the East from the sea captains. The young men were as foolish about their house as a bridal pair. Zichec, the young cabinet-maker, devised every sort of convenience, and Rosicky kept their clothes in order. At night and on Sundays, when the quiver of machinery underneath was still, it was the quietest place in the world, and on summer nights all the sea winds blew in. Zichec often practised on his flute in the evening. They were both fond of music and went to the opera together. Rosicky thought he wanted to live like that forever.

But as the years passed, all alike, he began to get a little restless. When spring came round, he would begin to feel fretted, and he got to drinking. He was likely to drink too much of a Saturday night. On Sunday he was languid and heavy, getting over his spree. On Monday he plunged into work again. So he never had time to figure out what ailed him, although he knew something did. When the grass turned green in Park Place, and the lilac hedge at the back of Trinity church-yard put out its blossoms, he was tormented by a longing to run away. That was why he drank too much; to get a temporary illusion of freedom and wide horizons.

Rosicky, the old Rosicky, could remember as if it were yesterday the day when the young Rosicky found out what was the matter with him. It was on a Fourth-of-July afternoon, and he was sitting in Park Place in the sun. The lower part of New York was empty. Wall Street, Liberty Street, Broadway, all empty. So much stone and asphalt with nothing going on, so many empty windows. The emptiness was intense, like the stillness in a great factory when the machinery stops and the belts and bands cease running. It was too great a change, it took all the strength out of one. Those blank buildings, without the stream of life pouring through them, were like empty jails. It struck young Rosicky that this was the trouble with big cities; they built you in from the earth itself, cemented you away from any contact with the ground. You lived in an unnatural world, like the fish in an aquarium, who were probably much more comfortable than they ever were in the sea.

On that very day he began to think seriously about the articles he had read in the Bohemian papers, describing prosperous Czech farming communities in the West. He believed he would like to go out there as a farm-hand; it was hardly possible that he could ever have land of his own. His people had always been workmen; his father and grandfather had worked in shops. His mother's parents had lived in the country, but they rented their farm and had a hard time to get along. Nobody in his family had ever owned any land—that belonged to a different station of life altogether. Anton's mother died when he was little, and he was sent into the country to her parents. He stayed with them until he was twelve, and formed those ties with the earth and the farm animals and growing things which are never made at all unless they are made early. After his grandfather died, he went back to live with his father and stepmother, but she was very hard on him, and his father helped him to get passage to London.

After that Fourth-of-July day in Park Place, the desire to return to the country never left him. To work on another man's farm would be all he asked; to see the sun rise and set and to plant things and watch them grow. He was a very simple man. He was like a tree that has not many roots, but one tap-root that goes down deep. He subscribed for a Bohemian paper printed in Chicago, then for one printed in Omaha. His mind got farther and farther west. He began to save a little money to buy his liberty. When he was thirty-five, there was a great meeting in New York of Bohemian athletic societies, and Rosicky left the tailor shop and went home with the Omaha delegates to try his fortune in another part of the world.

IV

Perhaps the fact that his own youth was well over before he began to have a family was one reason why Rosicky was so fond of his boys. He had almost a grandfather's indulgence for them. He had never had to worry about any of them—except, just now, a little about Rudolph.

On Saturday night the boys always piled into the Ford, took little Josephine, and went to town to the moving-picture show. One Saturday morning they were talking at the breakfast table about starting early that evening, so that they would have an hour or so to see the Christmas things in the stores before the show began. Rosicky looked down the table.

"I hope you boys ain't disappointed, but I want you to let me have de car tonight. Maybe some of you can go in with de neighbours."

Their faces fell. They worked hard all the week, and they were still children. A new jack-knife or a box of candy pleased the older ones as much as the little fellow.

"If you and mother are going to town," Frank said, "maybe you could take a couple of us along with you, anyway."

"No, I want to take de car down to Rudolph's, and let him an' Polly go in to de show. She don't git into town enough, an' I'm afraid she's gittin' lonesome, an' he can't afford no car yet."

That settled it. The boys were a good deal dashed. Their father took another piece of apple-cake and went on: "Maybe next Saturday night de two little fellers can go along wid dem."

"Oh, is Rudolph going to have the car every Saturday night?"

Rosicky did not reply at once; then he began to speak seriously: "Listen, boys; Polly ain't lookin' so good. I don't like to see nobody lookin' sad. It comes hard fur a town girl to be a farmer's wife. I don't want no trouble to start in Rudolph's family. When it starts, it ain't so easy to stop. An American girl don't git used to our ways all at once. I like to tell Polly she and Rudolph can have the car every Saturday night till after New Year's, if it's all right with you boys."

"Sure it's all right, papa," Mary cut in. "And it's good you thought about that. Town girls is used to more than country girls. I lay awake nights, scared she'll make Rudolph discontented with the farm."

The boys put as good a face on it as they could. They surely looked forward to their Saturday nights in town. That evening Rosicky drove the car the half mile down to Rudolph's new, bare little house.

Polly was in a short-sleeved gingham dress, clearing away the supper dishes. She was a trim, slim little thing, with blue eyes and shingled yellow hair, and her eyebrows were reduced to a mere brush-stroke, like Miss Pearl's.

"Good-evening, Mr. Rosicky. Rudolph's at the barn, I guess." She never called him father, or Mary mother. She was sensitive about having married a foreigner. She never in the world would have done it if Rudolph hadn't been such a handsome, persuasive fellow and such a gallant lover. He had graduated in her class in the high school in town, and their friendship began in the ninth grade.

Rosicky went in, though he wasn't exactly asked. "My boys ain't goin' to town tonight, an' I brought de car over fur you two to go in to de picture show."

Polly, carrying dishes to the sink, looked over her shoulder at him. "Thank you. But I'm late with my work tonight, and pretty tired. Maybe Rudolph would like to go in with you."

"Oh, I don't go to de shows! I'm too old-fashioned. You won't feel so tired after you ride in de air a ways. It's a nice clear night, an' it ain't cold. You go an' fix yourself up, Polly, an' I'll wash de dishes an' leave everything nice fur you."

Polly blushed and tossed her bob. "I couldn't let you do that, Mr. Rosicky. I wouldn't think of it."

Rosicky said nothing. He found a bib apron on a nail behind the kitchen door. He slipped it over his head and then took Polly by her two elbows and pushed her gently toward the door of her own room. "I washed up de kitchen many times for my wife, when de babies was sick or somethin'. You go an' make yourself look nice. I like you to look prettier'n any of dem town girls when you go in. De young folks must have some fun, an' I'm goin' to look out fur you, Polly."

That kind, reassuring grip on her elbows, the old man's funny bright eyes, made Polly want to drop her head on his shoulder for a second. She restrained herself, but she lingered in his grasp at the door of her room, murmuring tearfully: "You always lived in the city when you were young, didn't you? Don't you ever get lonesome out here?"

As she turned round to him, her hand fell naturally into his, and he stood holding it and smiling into her face with his peculiar, knowing, indulgent smile without a shadow of reproach in it. "Dem big cities is all right fur de rich, but dey is terrible hard for de poor."

"I don't know. Sometimes I think I'd like to take a chance. You lived in New York, didn't you?"

"An' London. Da's bigger still. I learned my trade dere. Here's Rudolph comin', you better hurry."

"Will you tell me about London sometime?"

"Maybe. Only I ain't no talker, Polly. Run an' dress yourself up."

The bedroom door closed behind her, and Rudolph came in from the outside, looking anxious. He had seen the car and was sorry any of his family should come just then. Supper hadn't been a very pleasant occasion. Halting in the doorway, he saw his father in a kitchen apron, carrying dishes to the sink. He flushed crimson and something flashed in his eye. Rosicky held up a warning finger.

"I brought de car over fur you an' Polly to go to de picture show, an' I made her let me finish here so you won't be late. You go put on a clean shirt, quick!"

"But don't the boys want the car, father?"

"Not tonight dey don't." Rosicky fumbled under his apron and found his pants pocket. He took out a silver dollar and said in a hurried whisper: "You go an' buy dat girl some ice cream an' candy tonight, like you was courtin'. She's awful good friends wid me."

Rudolph was very short of cash, but he took the money as if it hurt him. There had been a crop failure all over the county. He had more than once been sorry he'd married this year.

In a few minutes the young people came out, looking clean and a little stiff. Rosicky hurried them off, and then he took his own time with the dishes. He scoured the pots and pans and put away the milk and swept the kitchen. He put some coal in the stove and shut off the draughts, so the place would be warm for them when they got home late at night. Then he sat down and had a pipe and listened to the clock tick.

Generally speaking, marrying an American girl was certainly a risk. A Czech should marry a Czech. It was lucky that Polly was the daughter of a poor widow woman; Rudolph was proud, and if she had a prosperous family to throw up at him, they could never make it go. Polly was one of four sisters, and they all worked; one was bookkeeper in the bank, one taught music, and Polly and her younger sister had been clerks, like Miss Pearl. All four of them were musical, had pretty voices, and sang in the Methodist choir, which the eldest sister directed.

Polly missed the sociability of a store position. She missed the choir, and the company of her sisters. She didn't dislike housework, but she disliked so much of it. Rosicky was a little anxious about this pair. He was afraid Polly would grow so discontented that Rudy would quit the farm and take a factory job in Omaha. He had worked for a winter up there, two years ago, to get money to marry on. He had done very well, and they would always take him back at the stockyards. But to Rosicky that meant the end of everything for his son. To be a landless man was to be a wage-earner, a slave, all your life; to have nothing, to be nothing.

Rosicky thought he would come over and do a little carpentering for Polly after the New Year. He guessed she needed jollying. Rudolph was a serious sort of chap, serious in love and serious about his work.

Rosicky shook out his pipe and walked home across the fields. Ahead of him the lamplight shone from his kitchen windows. Suppose he were still in a tailor shop on Vesey Street, with a bunch of pale, narrow-chested sons working on machines, all coming home tired and sullen to eat supper in a kitchen that was a parlour also; with another crowded, angry family quarrelling just across the dumb-waiter shaft, and squeaking pulleys at the windows where dirty washings hung on dirty lines above a court full of old brooms and mops and ash-cans . . .

He stopped by the windmill to look up at the frosty winter stars and draw a long breath before he went inside. That kitchen with the shining windows was dear to him; but the sleeping fields and bright stars and the noble darkness were dearer still.

V

On the day before Christmas the weather set in very cold; no snow, but a bitter, biting wind that whistled and sang over the flat land and lashed one's face like fine wires. There was baking going on in the Rosicky kitchen all day, and Rosicky sat inside, making over a coat that Albert had outgrown into an overcoat for John. Mary had a big red geranium in bloom for Christmas, and a row of Jerusalem cherry trees, full of berries. It was the first year she had ever grown these; Doctor Ed brought her the seeds from Omaha when he went to some medical convention. They reminded Rosicky of plants he had seen in England; and all afternoon, as he stitched, he sat thinking about those two years in London, which his mind usually shrank from even after all this while.

He was a lad of eighteen when he dropped down into London, with no money and no connexions except the address of a cousin who was supposed to be working at a confectioner's. When he went to the pastry shop, however, he found that the cousin had gone to America. Anton tramped the streets for several days, sleeping in doorways and on the Embankment, until he was in utter despair. He knew no English, and the sound of the strange language all about him confused him. By chance he met a poor German tailor who had learned his trade in Vienna, and could speak a little Czech. This tailor, Lifschnitz, kept a repair shop in a Cheapside basement, underneath a cobbler. He didn't much need an apprentice, but he was sorry for the boy and took him in for no wages but his keep and what he could pick up. The pickings were supposed to be coppers given you when you took work home to a customer. But most of the customers called for their clothes themselves, and the coppers that came Anton's way were very few. He had, however, a place to sleep. The tailor's family lived upstairs in three rooms; a kitchen, a bedroom, where Lifschnitz and his wife and five children slept, and a living-room. Two corners of this living-room were curtained off for lodgers; in one Rosicky slept on an old horsehair sofa, with a feather quilt to wrap himself in. The other corner was rented to a wretched, dirty boy, who was studying the violin. He actually practised there. Rosicky was dirty, too. There was no way to be anything else. Mrs. Lifschnitz got the water she cooked and washed with from a pump in a brick court, four flights down. There were bugs in the place, and multitudes of fleas, though the poor woman did the best she could. Rosicky knew she often went empty to give another potato or a spoonful of dripping to the two hungry, sad-eyed boys who lodged with her. He used to think he would never get out of there, never get a clean shirt to his back again. What would he do, he wondered, when his clothes actually dropped to pieces and the worn cloth wouldn't hold patches any longer?

It was still early when the old farmer put aside his sewing and his recollections. The sky had been a dark grey all day, with not a gleam of sun, and the light failed at four o'clock. He went to shave and change his shirt while the turkey was roasting. Rudolph and Polly were coming over for supper.

After supper they sat round in the kitchen, and the younger boys were saying how sorry they were it hadn't snowed. Everybody was sorry. They wanted a deep snow that would lie long and keep the wheat warm, and leave the ground soaked when it melted.

"Yes, sir!" Rudolph broke out fiercely; "if we have another dry year like last year, there's going to be hard times in this country."

Rosicky filled his pipe. "You boys don't know what hard times is. You don't owe nobody, you got plenty to eat an' keep warm, an' plenty water to keep clean. When you got them, you can't have it very hard."

Rudolph frowned, opened and shut his big right hand, and dropped it clenched upon his knee. "I've got to have a good deal more than that, father, or I'll quit this farming gamble. I can always make good wages railroading, or at the packing-house, and be sure of my money."

"Maybe so," his father answered dryly.

Mary, who had just come in from the pantry and was wiping her hands on the roller towel, thought Rudy and his father were getting too serious. She brought her darning-basket and sat down in the middle of the group.

"I ain't much afraid of hard times, Rudy," she said heartily. "We've had a plenty, but we've always come through. Your father wouldn't never take nothing very hard, not even hard times. I got a mind to tell you a story on him. Maybe you boys can't hardly remember the year we had that terrible hot wind, that burned everything up on the Fourth of July? All the corn an' the gardens. An' that was in the days when we didn't have alfalfa yet—I guess it wasn't invented.

"Well, that very day your father was out cultivatin'

corn, and I was here in the kitchen makin' plum preserves. We had bushels of plums that year. I noticed
it was terrible hot, but it's always hot in the kitchen
when you're preservin', an' I was too busy with my
plums to mind. Anton come in from the field about
three o'clock, an' I asked him what was the matter.

"'Nothin',' he says, 'but it's pretty hot, an' I think
I won't work no more today.' He stood round for a
few minutes an' then he says: 'Ain't you near
through? I want you should git up a nice supper for
us tonight. It's Fourth of July.'

"I told him to git along, that I was right in the
middle of preservin', but the plums would taste good
on a hot biscuit. 'I'm goin' to have fried chicken, too,'
he says, and he went off an' killed a couple. You
three oldest boys was little fellers, playin' round outside, real hot an' sweaty, an' your father took you to
the horse tank down by the windmill an' took off
your clothes an' put you in. Them two box-elder trees
was little then, but they made shade over the tank.
Then he took off all his own clothes, an' got in with
you. While he was playin' in the water with you, the
Methodist preacher drove into our place to say how
all the neighbours was goin' to meet at the schoolhouse that night, to pray for rain. He drove right to
the windmill, of course, and there was your father
and you three with no clothes on. I was in the
kitchen door, an' I had to laugh, for the preacher
acted like he ain't never seen a naked man before.
He surely was embarrassed, an' your father couldn't
git to his clothes; they was all hangin' up on the windmill to let the sweat dry out of 'em. So he laid in the
tank where he was, an' put one of you boys on top of
him to cover him up a little, an' talked to the
preacher.

"When you got through playin' in the water, he
put clean clothes on you and a clean shirt on himself,
and by that time I'd begun to get supper. He says:
'It's too hot in here to eat comfortable. Let's have a
picnic in the orchard. We'll eat our supper behind
the mulberry hedge, under them linden trees.'

"So he carried our supper down, an' a bottle of my
wild-grape wine, an' everything tasted good, I can
tell you. The wind got cooler as the sun was goin'
down, and it turned out pleasant, only I noticed how
the leaves was curled up on the linden trees. That
made me think, an' I asked your father if that hot
wind all day hadn't been terrible hard on the
gardens an' the corn.

"'Corn,' he says, 'there ain't no corn.'

"'What you talkin' about?' I said. 'Ain't we got
forty acres?'

"'We ain't got an ear,' he says, 'nor nobody else
ain't got none. All the corn in this country was

cooked by three o'clock today, like you'd roasted it in
an oven.'

"'You mean you won't get no crop at all?' I asked
him. I couldn't believe it, after he'd worked so hard.

"'No crop this year,' he says. 'That's why we're
havin' a picnic. We might as well enjoy what we got.'

"An' that's how your father behaved, when all the
neighbours was so discouraged they couldn't look
you in the face. An' we enjoyed ourselves that year,
poor as we was, an' our neighbours wasn't a bit better off for bein' miserable. Some of 'em grieved till
they got poor digestions and couldn't relish what
they did have."

The younger boys said they thought their father
had the best of it. But Rudolph was thinking that, all
the same, the neighbours had managed to get ahead
more, in the fifteen years since that time. There must
be something wrong about his father's way of doing
things. He wished he knew what was going on in the
back of Polly's mind. He knew she liked his father,
but he knew, too, that she was afraid of something.
When his mother sent over coffee-cake or prune tarts
or a loaf of fresh bread, Polly seemed to regard them
with a certain suspicion. When she observed to him
that his brothers had nice manners, her tone implied
that it was remarkable they should have. With his
mother she was stiff and on her guard. Mary's hearty
frankness and gusts of good humour irritated her.
Polly was afraid of being unusual or conspicuous in
any way, of being "ordinary," as she said!

When Mary had finished her story, Rosicky laid
aside his pipe. "You boys like me to tell you about
some of dem hard times I been through in London?"
Warmly encouraged, he sat rubbing his forehead
along the deep creases. It was bothersome to tell a
long story in English (he nearly always talked to the
boys in Czech), but he wanted Polly to hear this one.

"Well, you know about dat tailor shop I worked in
in London? I had one Christmas dere I ain't never
forgot. Times was awful bad before Christmas; de
boss ain't got much work, an' have it awful hard to
pay his rent. It ain't so much fun, bein' poor in a big
city like London, I'll say! All de windows is full of
good t'ings to eat, an' all de pushcarts in de streets is
full, an' you smell 'em all de time, an' you ain't got
no money—not a damn bit. I didn't mind de cold so
much, though I didn't have no overcoat, chust a short
jacket I'd outgrowed so it wouldn't meet on me, an'
my hands was chapped raw. But I always had a good
appetite, like you all know, an' de sight of dem pork
pies in de windows was awful fur me!

"Day before Christmas was terrible foggy dat year,
an' dat fog gits into your bones and makes you all
damp like. Mrs. Lifschnitz didn't give us nothin' but
a little bread an' drippin' for supper, because she was

savin' to try for to give us a good dinner on Christmas Day. After supper de boss say I can go an' enjoy myself, so I went into de streets to listen to de Christmas singers. Dey sing old songs an' make very nice music, an' I run round after dem a goodways, till I got awful hungry. I t'ink maybe if I go home, I can sleep till morning an' forget my belly.

"I went into my corner real quiet, and roll up in my fedder quilt. But I ain't got my head down, till I smell somet'ing good. Seem like it git stronger an' stronger, an' I can't git to sleep noway. I can't understand dat smell. Dere was a gas light in a hall across de court, dat always shine in at my window a little. I got up an' look round. I got a little wooden box in my corner fur a stool, 'cause I ain't got no chair. I picks up dat box, and under it dere is a roast goose on a platter! I can't believe my eyes. I carry it to de window where de light comes in, an' touch it and smell it to find out, an' den I taste it to be sure. I say, I will eat chust one little bite of dat goose, so I can go to sleep, and tomorrow I won't eat none at all. But I tell you, boys, when I stop, one half of dat goose was gone!"

The narrator bowed his head, and the boys shouted. But little Josephine slipped behind his chair and kissed him on the neck beneath his ear.

"Poor little papa, I don't want him to be hungry!"

"Da's long ago, child. I ain't never been hungry since I had your mudder to cook fur me."

"Go on and tell us the rest, please," said Polly.

"Well, when I come to realize what I done, of course, I felt terrible. I felt better in de stomach, but very bad in de heart. I set on my bed wid dat platter on my knees, an' it all come to me; how hard dat poor woman save to buy dat goose, and how she get some neighbour to cook it dat got more fire, an' how she put it in my corner to keep it away from dem hungry children. Dere was a old carpet hung up to shut my corner off, an' de children wasn't allowed to go in dere. An' I know she put it in my corner because she trust me more'n she did de violin boy. I can't stand it to face her after I spoil de Christmas. So I put on my shoes and go out into de city. I tell myself I better throw myself in de river; but I guess I ain't dat kind of a boy.

"It was after twelve o'clock, an' terrible cold, an' I start out to walk about London all night. I walk along de river awhile, but dey was lots of drunks all along; men, and women too. I chust move along to keep away from de police. I git onto de Strand, an' den over to New Oxford Street, where dere was a big German restaurant on de ground floor, wid big windows all fixed up fine, an' I could see de people havin' parties inside. While I was lookin' in, two men and two ladies come out, laughin' and talkin' and feelin' happy about all dey been eatin' an' drinkin', and dey was speakin' Czech—not like de Austrians, but like de home folks talk it.

"I guess I went crazy, an' I done what I ain't never done before nor since. I went right up to dem gay people an' begun to beg dem: 'Fellow countrymen, for God's sake give me money enough to buy a goose!'

"Dey laugh, of course, but de ladies speak awful kind to me, an' dey take me back into de restaurant and give me hot coffee and cakes, an' make me tell all about how I happened to come to London, an' what I was doin' dere. Dey take my name and where I work down on paper, an' both of dem ladies give me ten shillings.

"De big market at Covent Garden ain't very far away, an' by dat time it was open. I go dere an' buy a big goose an' some pork pies, an' potatoes and onions, an' cakes an' oranges fur de children—all I could carry! When I git home, everybody is still asleep. I pile all I bought on de kitchen table, an' go in an' lay down on my bed, an' I ain't waken up till I hear dat woman scream when she come out into her kitchen. My goodness, but she was surprise'! She laugh an' cry at de same time, an' hug me and waken all de children. She ain't stop fur no breakfast; she git de Christmas dinner ready dat morning, and we all sit down an' eat all we can hold. I ain't never seen dat violin boy have all he can hold before.

"Two-t'ree days after dat, de two men come to hunt me up, an' dey ask my boss, and he give me a good report an' tell dem I was steady boy all right. One of dem Bohemians was very smart an' run a Bohemian newspaper in New York, an de' odder was a rich man, in de importing business, an' dey been travelling togedder. Dey told me how t'ings was easier in New York, an' offered to pay my passage when dey was goin' home soon on a boat. My boss say to me: 'You go. You ain't got no chance here, an' I like to see you git ahead, fur you always been a good boy to my woman, and fur dat fine Christmas dinner you give us all.' An' da's how I got to New York."

That night when Rudolph and Polly, arm in arm, were running home across the fields with the bitter wind at their backs, his heart leaped for joy when she said she thought they might have his family come over for supper on New Year's Eve. "Let's get up a nice supper, and not let your mother help at all; make her be company for once."

"That would be lovely of you, Polly," he said humbly. He was a very simple, modest boy, and he, too, felt vaguely that Polly and her sisters were more experienced and worldly than his people.

VI

The winter turned out badly for farmers. It was bitterly cold, and after the first light snows before Christmas there was no snow at all—and no rain. March was as bitter as February. On those days when the wind fairly punished the country, Rosicky sat by his window. In the fall he and the boys had put in a big wheat planting, and now the seed had frozen in the ground. All that land would have to be ploughed up and planted over again, planted in corn. It had happened before, but he was younger then, and he never worried about what had to be. He was sure of himself and of Mary; he knew they could bear what they had to bear, that they would always pull through somehow. But he was not so sure about the young ones, and he felt troubled because Rudolph and Polly were having such a hard start.

Sitting beside his flowering window while the panes rattled and the wind blew in under the door, Rosicky gave himself to reflection as he had not done since those Sundays in the loft of the furniture factory in New York, long ago. Then he was trying to find what he wanted in life for himself; now he was trying to find what he wanted for his boys, and why it was he so hungered to feel sure they would be here, working this very land, after he was gone.

They would have to work hard on the farm, and probably they would never do much more than make a living. But if he could think of them as staying here on the land, he wouldn't have to fear any great unkindness for them. Hardships, certainly; it was a hardship to have the wheat freeze in the ground when seed was so high; and to have to sell your stock because you had no feed. But there would be other years when everything came along right, and you caught up. And what you had was your own. You didn't have to choose between bosses and strikers, and go wrong either way. You didn't have to do with dishonest and cruel people. They were the only things in his experience he had found terrifying and horrible; the look in the eyes of a dishonest and crafty man, of a scheming and rapacious woman.

In the country, if you had a mean neighbour, you could keep off his land and make him keep off yours. But in the city, all the foulness and misery and brutality of your neighbours was part of your life. The worst things he had come upon in his journey through the world were human—depraved and poisonous specimens of man. To this day he could recall certain terrible faces in the London streets. There were mean people everywhere, to be sure, even in their own country town here. But they weren't tempered, hardened, sharpened, like the treacherous people in cities who live by grinding or cheating or poisoning their fellowmen. He had helped to bury two of his fellow workmen in the tailoring trade, and he was distrustful of the organized industries that see one out of the world in big cities. Here, if you were sick, you had Doctor Ed to look after you; and if you died, fat Mr. Haycock, the kindest man in the world, buried you.

It seemed to Rosicky that for good, honest boys like his, the worst they could do on the farm was better than the best they would be likely to do in the city. If he'd had a mean boy, now, one who was crooked and sharp and tried to put anything over on his brothers, then town would be the place for him. But he had no such boy. As for Rudolph, the discontented one, he would give the shirt off his back to anyone who touched his heart. What Rosicky really hoped for his boys was that they could get through the world without ever knowing much about the cruelty of human beings. "Their mother and me ain't prepared them for that," he sometimes said to himself.

These thoughts brought him back to a grateful consideration of his own case. What an escape he had had, to be sure! He, too, in his time, had had to take money for repair work from the hand of a hungry child who let it go so wistfully; because it was money due his boss. And now, in all these years, he had never had to take a cent from anyone in bitter need—never had to look at the face of a woman become like a wolf's from struggle and famine. When he thought of these things, Rosicky would put on his cap and jacket and slip down to the barn and give his work-horses a little extra oats, letting them eat it out of his hand in their slobbery fashion. It was his way of expressing what he felt, and made him chuckle with pleasure.

The spring came warm, with blue skies—but dry, dry as a bone. The boys began ploughing up the wheat-fields to plant them over in corn. Rosicky would stand at the fence corner and watch them, and the earth was so dry it blew up in clouds of brown dust that hid the horses and the sulky plough and the driver. It was a bad outlook.

The big alfalfa-field that lay between the home place and Rudolph's came up green, but Rosicky was worried because during that open windy winter a great many Russian thistle plants had blown in there and lodged. He kept asking the boys to rake them out; he was afraid their seed would root and "take the alfalfa." Rudolph said that was nonsense. The boys were working so hard planting corn, their father felt he couldn't insist about the thistles, but he set great store by that big alfalfa-field. It was a feed you could depend on—and there was some deeper reason, vague, but strong. The peculiar green of that clover woke early memories in old Rosicky, went back to something in his childhood in the Old World. When he was a little boy, he had played in fields of that strong blue-green colour.

One morning, when Rudolph had gone to town in the car, leaving a work-team idle in his barn, Rosicky went over to his son's place, put the horses to the buggy rake, and set about quietly raking up those thistles. He behaved with guilty caution, and rather enjoyed stealing a march on Doctor Ed, who was just then taking his first vacation in seven years of practice and was attending a clinic in Chicago. Rosicky got the thistles raked up, but did not stop to burn them. That would take some time, and his breath was pretty short, so he thought he had better get the horses back to the barn.

He got them into the barn and to their stalls, but the pain had come on so sharp in his chest that he didn't try to take the harness off. He started for the house, bending lower with every step. The cramp in his chest was shutting him up like a jack-knife. When he reached the windmill, he swayed and caught at the ladder. He saw Polly coming down the hill, running with the swiftness of a slim greyhound. In a flash she had her shoulder under his armpit.

"Lean on me, father, hard! Don't be afraid. We can get to the house all right."

Somehow they did, though Rosicky became blind with pain; he could keep on his legs, but he couldn't steer his course. The next thing he was conscious of was lying on Polly's bed, and Polly bending over him wringing out bath-towels in hot water and putting them on his chest. She stopped only to throw coal into the stove, and she kept the tea-kettle and the black pot going. She put these hot applications on him for nearly an hour, she told him afterward, and all that time he was drawn up stiff and blue, with the sweat pouring off him.

As the pain gradually loosed its grip, the stiffness went out of his jaws, the black circles round his eyes disappeared, and a little of his natural colour came back. When his daughter-in-law buttoned his shirt over his chest at last, he sighed.

"Da's fine, de way I feel now, Polly. It was a awful bad spell, an' I was so sorry it all come on you like it did."

Polly was flushed and excited. "Is the pain really gone? Can I leave you long enough to telephone over to your place?"

Rosicky's eyelids fluttered. "Don't telephone, Polly. It ain't no use to scare my wife. It's nice and quiet here, an' if I ain't too much trouble to you, just let me lay still till I feel like myself. I ain't got no pain now. It's nice here."

Polly bent over him and wiped the moisture from his face. "Oh, I'm so glad it's over!" she broke out impulsively. "It just broke my heart to see you suffer so, father."

Rosicky motioned her to sit down on the chair where the tea-kettle had been, and looked up at her with that lively affectionate gleam in his eyes. "You was awful good to me, I won't never forget dat. I hate it to be sick on you like dis. Down at de barn I say to myself, dat young girl ain't had much experience in sickness, I don't want to scare her, an' maybe she's got a baby comin' or somet'ing."

Polly took his hand. He was looking at her so intently and affectionately and confidingly; his eyes seemed to caress her face, to regard it with pleasure. She frowned with her funny streaks of eyebrows, and then smiled back at him.

"I guess maybe there is something of that kind going to happen. But I haven't told anyone yet, not my mother or Rudolph. You'll be the first to know."

His hand pressed hers. She noticed that it was warm again. The twinkle in his yellow-brown eyes seemed to come nearer.

"I like mighty well to see dat little child, Polly," was all he said. Then he closed his eyes and lay half-smiling. But Polly sat still, thinking hard. She had a sudden feeling that nobody in the world, not her mother, not Rudolph, or anyone, really loved her as much as old Rosicky did. It perplexed her. She sat frowning and trying to puzzle it out. It was as if Rosicky had a special gift for loving people, something that was like an ear for music or an eye for colour. It was quiet, unobtrusive; it was merely there. You saw it in his eyes—perhaps that was why they were merry. You felt it in his hands, too. After he dropped off to sleep, she sat holding his warm, broad, flexible brown hand. She had never seen another in the least like it. She wondered if it wasn't a kind of gipsy hand, it was so alive and quick and light in its communications—very strange in a farmer. Nearly all the farmers she knew had huge lumps of fists, like mauls, or they were knotty and bony and uncomfortable-looking, with stiff fingers. But Rosicky's hand was like quick-silver, flexible, muscular, about the colour of a pale cigar, with deep, deep creases across the palm. It wasn't nervous, it wasn't a stupid lump; it was a warm brown human hand, with some cleverness in it, a great deal of generosity, and something else which Polly could only call "gipsy-like"—something nimble and lively and sure, in the way that animals are.

Polly remembered that hour long afterward; it had been like an awakening to her. It seemed to her that she had never learned so much about life from any-thing as from old Rosicky's hand. It brought her to herself; it communicated some direct and untranslat-able message.

When she heard Rudolph coming in the car, she ran out to meet him.

"Oh, Rudy, your father's been awful sick! He raked up those thistles he's been worrying about, and afterward he could hardly get to the house. He suffered so I was afraid he was going to die."

Rudolph jumped to the ground. "Where is he now?"

"On the bed. He's asleep. I was terribly scared, because, you know, I'm so fond of your father." She slipped her arm through his and they went into the house.

That afternoon they took Rosicky home and put him to bed, though he protested that he was quite well again.

The next morning he got up and dressed and sat down to breakfast with his family. He told Mary that his coffee tasted better than usual to him, and he warned the boys not to bear any tales to Doctor Ed when he got home. After breakfast he sat down by his window to do some patching and asked Mary to thread several needles for him before she went to feed her chickens—her eyes were better than his, and her hands steadier. He lit his pipe and took up John's overalls. Mary had been watching him anxiously all morning, and as she went out of the door with her bucket of scraps, she saw that he was smiling. He was thinking, indeed, about Polly, and how he might never have known what a tender heart she had if he hadn't got sick over there. Girls nowadays didn't wear their hearts on their sleeves. But now he knew Polly would make a fine woman after the foolishness wore off. Either a woman had that sweetness at her heart or she hadn't. You couldn't always tell by the look of them; but if they had that, everything came out right in the end.

After he had taken a few stitches, the cramp began in his chest, like yesterday. He put his pipe cau-tiously down on the window-sill and bent over to ease the pull. No use—he had better try to get to his bed if he could. He rose and groped his way across the familiar floor, which was rising and falling like the deck of a ship. At the door he fell. When Mary came in, she found him lying there, and the moment she touched him she knew that he was gone.

Doctor Ed was away when Rosicky died, and for the first few weeks after he got home he was hard-driven. Every day he said to himself that he must get out to see that family that had lost their father. One soft, warm moonlight night in early summer he started for the farm. His mind was on other things, and not until his road ran by the graveyard did he realize that Rosicky wasn't over there on the hill where the red lamp-light shone, but here, in the moonlight. He stopped his car, shut off the engine, and sat there for a while.

A sudden hush had fallen on his soul. Everything here seemed strangely moving and significant, though signifying what, he did not know. Close by the wire fence stood Rosicky's mowing-machine, where one of the boys had been cutting hay that afternoon; his own work-horses had been going up and down there. The new-cut hay perfumed all the night air. The moonlight silvered the long, billowy grass that grew over the graves and hid the fence; the few little ever-greens stood out black in it, like shadows in a pool. The sky was very blue and soft, the stars rather faint because the moon was full.

For the first time it struck Doctor Ed that this was really a beautiful graveyard. He thought of city cemeteries; acres of shrubbery and heavy stone, so arranged and lonely and unlike anything in the living world. Cities of the dead, indeed; cities of the for-gotten, of the "put away." But this was open and free, this little square of long grass which the wind forever stirred. Nothing but the sky overhead, and the many-coloured fields running on until they met that sky. The horses worked here in summer; the neighbours passed on their way to town; and over yonder, in the cornfield, Rosicky's own cattle would be eating fodder as winter came on. Nothing could be more undeathlike than this place; nothing could be more right for a man who had helped to do the work of great cities and had always longed for the open country and had got to it at last. Rosicky's life seemed to him complete and beautiful.

COUNTERPARTS

JAMES JOYCE

JAMES JOYCE (1882–1941) was born and educated in Dublin. In 1904 he left Ireland and spent the remainder of his life on the Continent, chiefly in Zurich, Trieste and Paris. His books include *Dubliners* (1914), *A Portrait of the Artist as a Young Man* (1916), *Ulysses* (1922) and *Finnegans Wake* (1939). In these works he moves from short fiction in the naturalistic manner to a "stream-of-consciousness" technique in which the action is entirely inward. His books have had great influence on the younger writers of our time.

THE bell rang furiously and, when Miss Parker went to the tube, a furious voice called out in a piercing North of Ireland accent:

"Send Farrington here!"

Miss Parker returned to her machine, saying to a man who was writing at a desk:

"Mr. Alleyne wants you upstairs."

The man muttered *"Blast* him!" under his breath and pushed back his chair to stand up. When he stood up he was tall and of great bulk. He had a hanging face, dark wine-coloured, with fair eyebrows and moustache: his eyes bulged forward slightly and the whites of them were dirty. He lifted up the counter and, passing by the clients, went out of the office with a heavy step.

He went heavily upstairs until he came to the second landing, where a door bore a brass plate with the inscription *Mr. Alleyne.* Here he halted, puffing with labour and vexation, and knocked. The shrill voice cried:

"Come in!"

The man entered Mr. Alleyne's room. Simultaneously Mr. Alleyne, a little man wearing gold-rimmed glasses on a clean-shaven face, shot his head up over a pile of documents. The head itself was so pink and hairless it seemed like a large egg reposing on the papers. Mr. Alleyne did not lose a moment:

"Farrington? What is the meaning of this? Why have I always to complain of you? May I ask you why you haven't made a copy of that contract between Bodley and Kirwan? I told you it must be ready by four o'clock."

"But Mr. Shelley said, sir——"

"*Mr. Shelley said, sir.* . . . Kindly attend to what I say and not to what *Mr. Shelley says, sir.* You have always some excuse or another for shirking work. Let

me tell you that if the contract is not copied before this evening I'll lay the matter before Mr. Crosbie. . . . Do you hear me now?"

"Yes, sir."

"Do you hear me now? . . . Ay and another little matter! I might as well be talking to the wall as talking to you. Understand once for all that you get a half an hour for your lunch and not an hour and a half. How many courses do you want, I'd like to know. . . . Do you mind me now?"

"Yes, sir."

Mr. Alleyne bent his head again upon his pile of papers. The man stared fixedly at the polished skull which directed the affairs of Crosbie & Alleyne, gauging its fragility. A spasm of rage gripped his throat for a few moments and then passed, leaving after it a sharp sensation of thirst. The man recognised the sensation and felt that he must have a good night's drinking. The middle of the month was passed and, if he could get the copy done in time, Mr. Alleyne might give him an order on the cashier. He stood still, gazing fixedly at the head upon the pile of papers. Suddenly Mr. Alleyne began to upset all the papers, searching for something. Then, as if he had been unaware of the man's presence till that moment, he shot up his head again, saying:

"Eh? Are you going to stand there all day? Upon my word, Farrington, you take things easy!"

"I was waiting to see . . ."

"Very good, you needn't wait to see. Go downstairs and do your work."

The man walked heavily towards the door and, as he went out of the room, he heard Mr. Alleyne cry after him that if the contract was not copied by evening Mr. Crosbie would hear of the matter.

He returned to his desk in the lower office and counted the sheets which remained to be copied. He took up his pen and dipped it in the ink but he continued to stare stupidly at the last words he had written: *In no case shall the said Bernard Bodley be . . .*

The evening was falling and in a few minutes they would be lighting the gas: then he could write. He felt that he must slake the thirst in his throat. He stood up from his desk and, lifting the counter as before, passed out of the office. As he was passing out the chief clerk looked at him inquiringly.

"It's all right, Mr. Shelley," said the man, pointing with his finger to indicate the objective of his journey.

The chief clerk glanced at the hat-rack, but, seeing the row complete, offered no remark. As soon as he was on the landing the man pulled a shepherd's plaid cap out of his pocket, put it on his head and ran quickly down the rickety stairs. From the street door he walked on furtively on the inner side of the path towards the corner and all at once dived into a doorway. He was now safe in the dark snug of O'Neill's shop, and, filling up the little window that looked into the bar with his inflamed face, the colour of dark wine or dark meat, he called out:

"Here, Pat, give us a g.p., like a good fellow."

The curate brought him a glass of plain porter. The man drank it at a gulp and asked for a caraway seed. He put his penny on the counter and, leaving the curate to grope for it in the gloom, retreated out of the snug as furtively as he had entered it.

Darkness, accompanied by a thick fog, was gaining upon the dusk of February and the lamps in Eustace Street had been lit. The man went up by the houses until he reached the door of the office, wondering whether he could finish his copy in time. On the stairs a moist pungent odour of perfumes saluted his nose: evidently Miss Delacour had come while he was out in O'Neill's. He crammed his cap back again into his pocket and re-entered the office, assuming an air of absent-mindedness.

"Mr. Alleyne has been calling for you," said the chief clerk severely. "Where were you?"

The man glanced at the two clients who were standing at the counter as if to intimate that their presence prevented him from answering. As the clients were both male the chief clerk allowed himself a laugh.

"I know that game," he said. "Five times in one day is a little bit. . . . Well, you better look sharp and get a copy of our correspondence in the Delacour case for Mr. Alleyne."

This address in the presence of the public, his run upstairs and the porter he had gulped down so hastily confused the man and, as he sat down at his desk to get what was required, he realised how hopeless was the task of finishing his copy of the contract before half past five. The dark damp night was coming and he longed to spend it in the bars, drinking with his friends amid the glare of gas and the clatter of glasses. He got out the Delacour correspondence and passed out of the office. He hoped Mr. Alleyne would not discover that the last two letters were missing.

The moist pungent perfume lay all the way up to Mr. Alleyne's room. Miss Delacour was a middle-aged woman of Jewish appearance. Mr. Alleyne was said to be sweet on her or on her money. She came to the office often and stayed a long time when she came. She was sitting beside his desk now in an aroma of perfumes, smoothing the handle of her umbrella and nodding the great black feather in her hat. Mr. Alleyne had swivelled his chair round to face her and thrown his right foot jauntily upon his left knee. The man put the correspondence on the desk and bowed respectfully but neither Mr. Alleyne nor Miss Delacour took any notice of his bow. Mr. Alleyne tapped a finger on the correspondence and then flicked it towards him as if to say: *"That's all right: you can go."*

The man returned to the lower office and sat down again at his desk. He stared intently at the incomplete phrase: *In no case shall the said Bernard Bodley be . . .* and thought how strange it was that the last three words began with the same letter. The chief clerk began to hurry Miss Parker, saying she would never have the letters typed in time for post. The man listened to the clicking of the machine for a few minutes and then set to work to finish his copy. But his head was not clear and his mind wandered away to the glare and rattle of the public-house. It was a night for hot punches. He struggled on with his copy, but when the clock struck five he had still fourteen pages to write. Blast it! He couldn't finish it in time. He longed to execrate aloud, to bring his fist down on something violently. He was so enraged that he wrote *Bernard Bernard* instead of *Bernard Bodley* and had to begin again on a clean sheet.

He felt strong enough to clear out the whole office single-handed. His body ached to do something, to rush out and revel in violence. All the indignities of his life enraged him. . . . Could he ask the cashier privately for an advance? No, the cashier was no good, no damn good: he wouldn't give an advance. . . . He knew where he would meet the boys: Leonard and O'Halloran and Nosey Flynn. The barometer of his emotional nature was set for a spell of riot.

His imagination had so abstracted him that his name was called twice before he answered. Mr. Alleyne and Miss Delacour were standing outside the counter and all the clerks had turned round in anticipation of something. The man got up from his desk. Mr. Alleyne began a tirade of abuse, saying that two letters were missing. The man answered that he knew nothing about them, that he had made a faithful copy. The tirade continued: it was so bitter and violent that the man could hardly restrain his fist from descending upon the head of the manikin before him.

"I know nothing about any other two letters," he said stupidly.

"*You—know—nothing.* Of course you know nothing," said Mr. Alleyne. "Tell me," he added, glancing first for approval to the lady beside him, "do you take me for a fool? Do you think me an utter fool?"

The man glanced from the lady's face to the little egg-shaped head and back again; and, almost before he was aware of it, his tongue had found a felicitous moment:

"I don't think, sir," he said, "that that's a fair question to put to me."

There was a pause in the very breathing of the clerks. Everyone was astounded (the author of the witticism no less than his neighbours) and Miss Delacour, who was a stout amiable person, began to smile broadly. Mr. Alleyne flushed to the hue of a wild rose and his mouth twitched with a dwarf's passion. He shook his fist in the man's face till it seemed to vibrate like the knob of some electric machine:

"You impertinent ruffian! You impertinent ruffian! I'll make short work of you! Wait till you see! You'll apologise to me for your impertinence or you'll quit the office instanter! You'll quit this, I'm telling you, or you'll apologise to me!"

.   .   .   .

He stood in a doorway opposite the office watching to see if the cashier would come out alone. All the clerks passed out and finally the cashier came out with the chief clerk. It was no use trying to say a word to him when he was with the chief clerk. The man felt that his position was bad enough. He had been obliged to offer an abject apology to Mr. Alleyne for his impertinence but he knew what a hornet's nest the office would be for him. He could remember the way in which Mr. Alleyne had hounded little Peake out of the office in order to make room for his own nephew. He felt savage and thirsty and revengeful, annoyed with himself and with everyone else. Mr. Alleyne would never give him an hour's rest; his life would be a hell to him. He had made a proper fool of himself this time. Could he not keep his tongue in his cheek? But they had never pulled together from the first, he and Mr. Alleyne, ever since the day Mr. Alleyne had overheard him mimicking his North of Ireland accent to amuse Higgins and Miss Parker: that had been the beginning of it. He might have tried Higgins for the money, but sure Higgins never had anything for himself. A man with two establishments to keep up, of course he couldn't. . . .

He felt his great body again aching for the comfort of the public-house. The fog had begun to chill him and he wondered could he touch Pat in O'Neill's. He could not touch him for more than a bob—and a bob was no use. Yet he must get money somewhere or other: he had spent his last penny for the g.p. and soon it would be too late for getting money anywhere. Suddenly, as he was fingering his watch-chain, he thought of Terry Kelly's pawn-office in Fleet Street. That was the dart! Why didn't he think of it sooner?

He went through the narrow alley of Temple Bar quickly, muttering to himself that they could all go to hell because he was going to have a good night of it. The clerk in Terry Kelly's said *A crown!* but the consignor held out for six shillings; and in the end the six shillings was allowed him literally. He came out of the pawn-office joyfully, making a little cylinder of the coins between his thumb and fingers. In Westmoreland Street the footpaths were crowded with young men and women returning from business and ragged urchins ran here and there yelling out the names of the evening editions. The man passed through the crowd, looking on the spectacle generally with proud satisfaction and staring masterfully at the office-girls. His head was full of the noises of tram-gongs and swishing trolleys and his nose already sniffed the curling fumes of punch. As he walked on he preconsidered the terms in which he would narrate the incident to the boys:

"So, I just looked at him—coolly, you know, and looked at her. Then I looked back at him again—taking my time, you know. 'I don't think that that's a fair question to put to me,' says I."

Nosey Flynn was sitting up in his usual corner of Davy Byrne's and, when he heard the story, he stood Farrington a half-one, saying it was as smart a thing as ever he heard. Farrington stood a drink in his turn. After a while O'Halloran and Paddy Leonard came in and the story was repeated to them. O'Halloran stood tailors of malt, hot, all round and told the story of the retort he had made to the chief clerk when he was in Callan's of Frownes's Street; but, as the retort was after the manner of the liberal shepherds in the eclogues, he had to admit that it was not as clever as Farrington's retort. At this Farrington told the boys to polish off that and have another.

Just as they were naming their poisons who should come in but Higgins! Of course he had to join in with the others. The men asked him to give his version of it, and he did so with great vivacity for the sight of five small hot whiskies was very exhilarating. Everyone roared laughing when he showed the way in which Mr. Alleyne shook his fist in Farrington's face. Then he imitated Farrington, saying, "*And here was my nabs, as cool as you please,"* while Farrington looked at the company out of his heavy dirty eyes, smiling and at times drawing forth stray drops of liquor from his moustache with the aid of his lower lip.

When that round was over there was a pause. O'Halloran had money but neither of the other two seemed to have any; so the whole party left the shop somewhat regretfully. At the corner of Duke Street Higgins and Nosey Flynn bevelled off to the left while the other three turned back towards the city. Rain was drizzling down on the cold streets and, when they reached the Ballast Office, Farrington suggested the Scotch House. The bar was full of men and loud with the noise of tongues and glasses. The three men pushed past the whining match-sellers at the door and formed a little party at the corner of the counter. They began to exchange stories. Leonard introduced them to a young fellow named Weathers who was performing at the Tivoli as an acrobat and knockabout *artiste.* Farrington stood a drink all round. Weathers said he would take a small Irish and Apollinaris. Farrington, who had definite notions of what was what, asked the boys would they have an Apollinaris too; but the boys told Tim to make theirs hot. The talk became theatrical. O'Halloran stood a round and then Farrington stood another round, Weathers protesting that the hospitality was too Irish. He promised to get them in behind the scenes and introduce them to some nice girls. O'Halloran said that he and Leonard would go, but that Farrington wouldn't go because he was a married man; and Farrington's heavy dirty eyes leered at the company in token that he understood he was being chaffed. Weathers made them all have just one little tincture at his expense and promised to meet them later on at Mulligan's in Poolbeg Street.

When the Scotch House closed they went round to Mulligan's. They went into the parlour at the back and O'Halloran ordered small hot specials all round. They were all beginning to feel mellow. Farrington was just standing another round when Weathers came back. Much to Farrington's relief he drank a glass of bitter this time. Funds were getting low but they had enough to keep them going. Presently two young women with big hats and a young man in a check suit came in and sat at a table close by. Weathers saluted them and told the company that they were out of the Tivoli. Farrington's eyes wandered at every moment in the direction of one of the young women. There was something striking in her appearance. An immense scarf of peacock-blue muslin was wound round her hat and knotted in a great bow under her chin; and she wore bright yellow gloves, reaching to the elbow. Farrington gazed admiringly at the plump arm which she moved very

often and with much grace; and when, after a little time, she answered his gaze he admired still more her large dark brown eyes. The oblique staring expression in them fascinated him. She glanced at him once or twice and, when the party was leaving the room, she brushed against his chair and said *"O, pardon!"* in a London accent. He watched her leave the room in the hope that she would look back at him, but he was disappointed. He cursed his want of money and cursed all the rounds he had stood, particularly all the whiskies and Apollinaris which he had stood to Weathers. If there was one thing that he hated it was a sponge. He was so angry that he lost count of the conversation of his friends.

When Paddy Leonard called him he found that they were talking about feats of strength. Weathers was showing his biceps muscle to the company and boasting so much that the other two had called on Farrington to uphold the national honour. Farrington pulled up his sleeve accordingly and showed his biceps muscle to the company. The two arms were examined and compared and finally it was agreed to have a trial of strength. The table was cleared and the two men rested their elbows on it, clasping hands. When Paddy Leonard said *"Go!"* each was to try to bring down the other's hand on to the table. Farrington looked very serious and determined.

The trial began. After about thirty seconds Weathers brought his opponent's hand slowly down on to the table. Farrington's dark wine-coloured face flushed darker still with anger and humiliation at having been defeated by such a stripling.

"You're not to put the weight of your body behind it. Play fair," he said.

"Who's not playing fair?" said the other.

"Come on again. The two best out of three."

The trial began again. The veins stood out on Farrington's forehead, and the pallor of Weathers' complexion changed to peony. Their hands and arms trembled under the stress. After a long struggle Weathers again brought his opponent's hand slowly on to the table. There was a murmur of applause from the spectators. The curate, who was standing beside the table, nodded his red head towards the victor and said with stupid familiarity:

"Ah! that's the knack!"

"What the hell do you know about it?" said Farrington fiercely, turning on the man. "What do you put in your gab for?"

"Sh, sh!" said O'Halloran, observing the violent expression of Farrington's face. "Pony up, boys. We'll have just one little smahan more and then we'll be off."

A very sullen-faced man stood at the corner of

O'Connell Bridge waiting for the little Sandymount tram to take him home. He was full of smouldering anger and revengefulness. He felt humiliated and discontented; he did not even feel drunk; and he had only twopence in his pocket. He cursed everything. He had done for himself in the office, pawned his watch, spent all his money; and he had not even got drunk. He began to feel thirsty again and he longed to be back again in the hot reeking public-house. He had lost his reputation as a strong man, having been defeated twice by a mere boy. His heart swelled with fury and, when he thought of the woman in the big hat who had brushed against him and said *Pardon!* his fury nearly choked him.

His tram let him down at Shelbourne Road and he steered his great body along in the shadow of the wall of the barracks. He loathed returning to his home. When he went in by the side-door he found the kitchen empty and the kitchen fire nearly out. He bawled upstairs:

"Ada! Ada!"

His wife was a little sharp-faced woman who bullied her husband when he was sober and was bullied by him when he was drunk. They had five children. A little boy came running down the stairs.

"Who is that?" said the man, peering through the darkness.

"Me, pa."

"Who are you? Charlie?"

"No, pa. Tom."

"Where's your mother?"

"She's out at the chapel."

"That's right. . . . Did she think of leaving any dinner for me?"

"Yes, pa. I——"

"Light the lamp. What do you mean by having the place in darkness? Are the other children in bed?"

The man sat down heavily on one of the chairs while the little boy lit the lamp. He began to mimic his son's flat accent, saying half to himself: *"At the chapel. At the chapel, if you please!"* When the lamp was lit he banged his fist on the table and shouted:

"What's for my dinner?"

"I'm going . . . to cook it, pa," said the little boy.

The man jumped up furiously and pointed to the fire.

"On that fire! You let the fire out! By God, I'll teach you to do that again!"

He took a step to the door and seized the walking-stick which was standing behind it.

"I'll teach you to let the fire out!" he said, rolling up his sleeve in order to give his arm free play.

The little boy cried "O, pa!" and ran whimpering round the table, but the man followed him and caught him by the coat. The little boy looked about him wildly but, seeing no way of escape, fell upon his knees.

"Now, you'll let the fire out the next time!" said the man, striking at him vigorously with the stick. "Take that, you little whelp!"

The boy uttered a squeal of pain as the stick cut his thigh. He clasped his hands together in the air and his voice shook with fright.

"O, pa!" he cried. "Don't beat me, pa! And I'll . . . I'll say a *Hail Mary* for you. . . . I'll say a *Hail Mary* for you, pa, if you don't beat me. . . . I'll say a *Hail Mary*. . . ."

DEATH IN THE WOODS

SHERWOOD ANDERSON

SHERWOOD ANDERSON (1876–1941) was born in Camden, Ohio. He had little formal schooling after he was fourteen. He fought in the Spanish-American War, managed a paint factory, ultimately deserted it for writing. Among his books are *Winesburg, Ohio* (1919), *Poor White* (1920), *The Triumph of the Egg* (1921), *A Story Teller's Story* (1924), *Dark Laughter* (1925), and *Memoirs* (1942).

SHE was an old woman and lived on a farm near the town in which I lived. All country and small-town people have seen such old women, but no one

knows much about them. Such an old woman comes into town driving an old worn-out horse or she comes afoot carrying a basket. She may own a few hens and have eggs to sell. She brings them in a basket and takes them to a grocer. There she trades them in. She gets some salt pork and some beans.

Then she gets a pound or two of sugar and some flour.

Afterwards she goes to the butcher's and asks for some dog-meat. She may spend ten or fifteen cents, but when she does she asks for something. Formerly the butchers gave liver to any one who wanted to carry it away. In our family we were always having it. Once one of my brothers got a whole cow's liver at the slaughter-house near the fairgrounds in our town. We had it until we were sick of it. It never cost a cent. I have hated the thought of it ever since.

The old farm woman got some liver and a soup-bone. She never visited with any one, and as soon as she got what she wanted she lit out for home. It made quite a load for such an old body. No one gave her a lift. People drive right down a road and never notice an old woman like that.

There was such an old woman who used to come into town past our house one Summer and Fall when I was a young boy and was sick with what was called inflammatory rheumatism. She went home later carrying a heavy pack on her back. Two or three large gaunt-looking dogs followed at her heels.

The old woman was nothing special. She was one of the nameless ones that hardly any one knows, but she got into my thoughts. I have just suddenly now, after all these years, remembered her and what happened. It is a story. Her name was Grimes, and she lived with her husband and son in a small unpainted house on the bank of a small creek four miles from town.

The husband and son were a tough lot. Although the son was but twenty-one, he had already served a term in jail. It was whispered about that the woman's husband stole horses and ran them off to some other county. Now and then, when a horse turned up missing, the man had also disappeared. No one ever caught him. Once, when I was loafing at Tom Whitehead's livery-barn, the man came there and sat on the bench in front. Two or three other men were there, but no one spoke to him. He sat for a few minutes and then got up and went away. When he was leaving he turned around and stared at the men. There was a look of defiance in his eyes. "Well, I have tried to be friendly. You don't want to talk to me. It has been so wherever I have gone in this town. If, some day, one of your fine horses turns up missing, well, then what?" He did not say anything actually. "I'd like to bust one of you on the jaw," was about what his eyes said. I remember how the look in his eyes made me shiver.

The old man belonged to a family that had had money once. His name was Jake Grimes. It all comes back clearly now. His father, John Grimes, had owned a sawmill when the country was new, and had made money. Then he got to drinking and running after women. When he died there wasn't much left.

Jake blew in the rest. Pretty soon there wasn't any more lumber to cut and his land was nearly all gone.

He got his wife off a German farmer, for whom he went to work one June day in the wheat harvest. She was a young thing then and scared to death. You see, the farmer was up to something with the girl—she was, I think, a bound girl and his wife had her suspicions. She took it out on the girl when the man wasn't around. Then, when the wife had to go off to town for supplies, the farmer got after her. She told young Jake that nothing really ever happened, but he didn't know whether to believe it or not.

He got her pretty easy himself, the first time he was out with her. He wouldn't have married her if the German farmer hadn't tried to tell him where to get off. He got her to go riding with him in his buggy one night when he was threshing on the place, and then he came for her the next Sunday night.

She managed to get out of the house without her employer's seeing, but when she was getting into the buggy he showed up. It was almost dark, and he just popped up suddenly at the horse's head. He grabbed the horse by the bridle and Jack got out his buggy-whip.

They had it out all right! The German was a tough one. Maybe he didn't care whether his wife knew or not. Jake hit him over the face and shoulders with the buggy-whip, but the horse got to acting up and he had to get out.

Then the two men went for it. The girl didn't see it. The horse started to run away and went nearly a mile down the road before the girl got him stopped. Then she managed to tie him to a tree beside the road. (I wonder how I know all this. It must have stuck in my mind from small-town tales when I was a boy.) Jake found her there after he got through with the German. She was huddled up in the buggy seat, crying, scared to death. She told Jake a lot of stuff, how the German had tried to get her, how he chased her once into the barn, how another time, when they happened to be alone in the house together, he tore her dress open clear down the front. The German, she said, might have got her that time if he hadn't heard his old woman drive in at the gate. She had been off to town for supplies. Well, she would be putting the horse in the barn. The German managed to sneak off to the fields without his wife seeing. He told the girl he would kill her if she told. What could she do? She told a lie about ripping her dress in the barn when she was feeding the stock. I remember now that she was a bound girl and did not know where her father and mother were. Maybe she did not have any father. You know what I mean.

Such bound children were often enough cruelly treated. They were children who had no parents, slaves really. There were very few orphan homes then. They were legally bound into some home. It was a matter of pure luck how it came out.

II

She married Jake and had a son and daughter, but the daughter died.

Then she settled down to feed stock. That was her job. At the German's place she had cooked the food for the German and his wife. The wife was a strong woman with big hips and worked most of the time in the fields with her husband. She fed them and fed the cows in the barn, fed the pigs, the horses and the chickens. Every moment of every day, as a young girl, was spent feeding something.

Then she married Jake Grimes and he had to be fed. She was a slight thing, and when she had been married for three or four years, and after the two children were born, her slender shoulders became stooped.

Jake always had a lot of big dogs around the house, that stood near the unused sawmill near the creek. He was always trading horses when he wasn't stealing something and had a lot of poor bony ones about. Also he kept three or four pigs and a cow. They were all pastured in the few acres left of the Grimes place and Jake did little enough work.

He went into debt for a threshing outfit and ran it for several years, but it did not pay. People did not trust him. They were afraid he would steal the grain at night. He had to go a long way off to get work and it cost too much to get there. In the Winter he hunted and cut a little firewood, to be sold in some nearby town. When the son grew up he was just like the father. They got drunk together. If there wasn't anything to eat in the house when they came home the old man gave his old woman a cut over the head. She had a few chickens of her own and had to kill one of them in a hurry. When they were all killed she wouldn't have any eggs to sell when she went to town, and then what would she do?

She had to scheme all her life about getting things fed, getting the pigs fed so they would grow fat and could be butchered in the Fall. When they were butchered her husband took most of the meat off to town and sold it. If he did not do it first the boy did. They fought sometimes and when they fought the old woman stood aside trembling.

She had got the habit of silence anyway—that was fixed. Sometimes, when she began to look old—she wasn't forty yet—and when the husband and son were both off, trading horses or drinking or hunting or stealing, she went around the house and the barnyard muttering to herself.

How was she going to get everything fed?—that was her problem. The dogs had to be fed. There wasn't enough hay in the barn for the horses and the cow. If she didn't feed the chickens how could they lay eggs? Without eggs to sell how could she get things in town, things she had to have to keep the life of the farm going? Thank heaven, she did not have to feed her husband—in a certain way. That hadn't lasted long after their marriage and after the babies came. Where he went on his long trips she did not know. Sometimes he was gone from home for weeks, and after the boy grew up they went off together.

They left everything at home for her to manage and she had no money. She knew no one. No one ever talked to her in town. When it was Winter she had to gather sticks of wood for her fire, had to try to keep the stock fed with very little grain.

The stock in the barn cried to her hungrily, the dogs followed her about. In the Winter the hens laid few enough eggs. They huddled in the corners of the barn and she kept watching them. If a hen lays an egg in the barn in the Winter and you do not find it, it freezes and breaks.

One day in Winter the old woman went off to town with a few eggs and the dogs followed her. She did not get started until nearly three o'clock and the snow was heavy. She hadn't been feeling very well for several days and so she went muttering along, scantily clad, her shoulders stooped. She had an old grain bag in which she carried her eggs, tucked away down in the bottom. There weren't many of them, but in Winter the price of eggs is up. She would get a little meat in exchange for the eggs, some salt pork, a little sugar, and some coffee perhaps. It might be the butcher would give her a piece of liver.

When she had got to town and was trading in her eggs the dogs lay by the door outside. She did pretty well, got the things she needed, more than she had hoped. Then she went to the butcher and he gave her some liver and some dog-meat.

It was the first time any one had spoken to her in a friendly way for a long time. The butcher was alone in his shop when she came in and was annoyed by the thought of such a sick-looking old woman out on such a day. It was bitter cold and the snow, that had let up during the afternoon, was falling again. The butcher said something about her husband and her son, swore at them, and the old woman stared at him, a look of mild surprise in her eyes as he talked. He said that if either the husband or the son were going to get any of the liver or the heavy bones with scraps of meat hanging to them that he had put into the grain bag, he'd see him starve first.

Starve, eh? Well, things had to be fed. Men had to

be fed, and the horses that weren't any good but maybe could be traded off, and the poor thin cow that hadn't given any milk for three months.

Horses, cows, pigs, dogs, men.

III

The old woman had to get back before darkness came if she could. The dogs followed at her heels, sniffing at the heavy grain bag she had fastened on her back. When she got to the edge of town she stopped by a fence and tied the bag on her back with a piece of rope she had carried in her dress-pocket for just that purpose. It was hard when she had to crawl over fences and once she fell over and landed in the snow. The dogs went frisking about. She had to struggle to get to her feet again, but she made it. The point of climbing over the fences was that there was a short cut over a hill and through a woods. She might have gone around by the road, but it was a mile farther that way. She was afraid she couldn't make it. And then, besides, the stock had to be fed. There was a little hay left and a little corn. Perhaps her husband and son would bring some home when they came. They had driven off in the only buggy the Grimes family had, a rickety thing, a rickety horse hitched to the buggy, two other rickety horses led by halters. They were going to trade horses, get a little money if they could. They might come home drunk. It would be well to have something in the house when they came back.

The son had an affair on with a woman at the county seat, fifteen miles away. She was a rough enough woman, a tough one. Once, in the Summer, the son had brought her to the house. Both she and the son had been drinking. Jake Grimes was away and the son and his woman ordered the old woman about like a servant. She didn't mind much; she was used to it. Whatever happened she never said anything. That was her way of getting along. She had managed that way when she was a young girl at the German's and ever since she had married Jake. That time her son brought his woman to the house they stayed all night, sleeping together just as though they were married. It hadn't shocked the old woman, not much. She had got past being shocked early in life.

With the pack on her back she went painfully along across an open field, wading in the deep snow, and got into the woods.

There was a path, but it was hard to follow. Just beyond the top of the hill, where the woods was thickest, there was a small clearing. Had some one once thought of building a house there? The clearing was as large as a building lot in town, large enough for a house and a garden. The path ran along the side of the clearing, and when she got there the old woman sat down to rest at the foot of a tree.

It was a foolish thing to do. When she got herself placed, the pack against the tree's trunk, it was nice, but what about getting up again? She worried about that for a moment and then quietly closed her eyes.

She must have slept for a time. When you are about so cold you can't get any colder. The afternoon grew a little warmer and the snow came thicker than ever. Then after a time the weather cleared. The moon even came out.

There were four Grimes dogs that had followed Mrs. Grimes into town, all tall gaunt fellows. Such men as Jake Grimes and his son always keep just such dogs. They kick and abuse them, but they stay. The Grimes dogs, in order to keep from starving, had to do a lot of foraging for themselves, and they had been at it while the old woman slept with her back to the tree at the side of the clearing. They had been chasing rabbits in the woods and in adjoining fields and in their ranging had picked up three other farm dogs.

After a time all the dogs came back to the clearing. They were excited about something. Such nights, cold and clear and with a moon, do things to dogs. It may be that some old instinct, come down from the time when they were wolves and ranged the woods in packs on Winter nights, comes back into them.

The dogs in the clearing, before the old woman, had caught two or three rabbits and their immediate hunger had been satisfied. They began to play, running in circles in the clearing. Round and round they ran, each dog's nose at the tail of the next dog. In the clearing, under the snow-laden trees and under the wintry moon they made a strange picture, running thus silently, in a circle their running had beaten in the soft snow. The dogs made no sound. They ran around and around in the circle.

It may have been that the old woman saw them doing that before she died. She may have awakened once or twice and looked at the strange sight with dim old eyes.

She wouldn't be very cold now, just drowsy. Life hangs on a long time. Perhaps the old woman was out of her head. She may have dreamed of her girlhood at the German's, and before that, when she was a child and before her mother lit out and left her.

Her dreams couldn't have been very pleasant. Not many pleasant things had happened to her. Now and then one of the Grimes dogs left the running circle and came to stand before her. The dog thrust his face to her face. His red tongue was hanging out.

The running of the dogs may have been a kind of death ceremony. It may have been that the primitive instinct of the wolf, having been aroused in the dogs by the night and the running, made them somehow, afraid.

"Now we are no longer wolves. We are dogs, the servants of men. Keep alive, man! When man dies we become wolves again."

When one of the dogs came to where the old woman sat with her back against the tree and thrust his nose close to her face he seemed satisfied and went back to run with the pack. All the Grimes dogs did it at some time during the evening, before she died. I knew all about it afterward, when I grew to be a man, because once in a woods in Illinois, on another Winter night, I saw a pack of dogs act just like that. The dogs were waiting for me to die as they had waited for the old woman that night when I was a child, but when it happened to me I was a young man and had no intention whatever of dying.

The old woman died softly and quietly. When she was dead and when one of the Grimes dogs had come to her and had found her dead all the dogs stopped running.

They gathered about her.

Well, she was dead now. She had fed the Grimes dogs when she was alive, what about now?

There was the pack on her back, the grain bag containing the piece of salt pork, the liver the butcher had given her, the dog-meat, the soup bones. The butcher in town, having been suddenly overcome with a feeling of pity, had loaded her grain bag heavily. It had been a big haul for the old woman.

It was a big haul for the dogs now.

IV

One of the Grimes dogs sprang suddenly out from among the others and began worrying the pack on the old woman's back. Had the dogs really been wolves that one would have been the leader of the pack. What he did, all the others did.

All of them sank their teeth into the grain bag the old woman had fastened with ropes to her back.

They dragged the old woman's body out into the open clearing. The worn-out dress was quickly torn from her shoulders. When she was found, a day or two later, the dress had been torn from her body clear to the hips, but the dogs had not touched her body. They had got the meat out of the grain bag, that was all. Her body was frozen stiff when it was found, and the shoulders were so narrow and the body so slight that in death it looked like the body of some charming young girl.

Such things happened in towns of the Middle West, on farms near town, when I was a boy. A hunter out after rabbits found the old woman's body

and did not touch it. Something, the beaten round path in the little snow-covered clearing, the silence of the place, the place where the dogs had worried the body trying to pull the grain bag away or tear it open—something startled the man and he hurried off to town.

I was in Main Street with one of my brothers who was town newsboy and who was taking the afternoon papers to the stores. It was almost night.

The hunter came into a grocery and told his story. Then he went into a hardware-shop and into a drug-store. Men began to gather on the sidewalks. Then they started out along the road to the place in the woods.

My brother should have gone on about his business of distributing papers but he didn't. Every one was going to the woods. The undertaker went and the town marshal. Several men got on a dray and rode out to where the path left the road and went into the woods, but the horses weren't very sharply shod and slid about on the slippery roads. They made no better time than those of us who walked.

The town marshal was a large man whose leg had been injured in the Civil War. He carried a heavy cane and limped rapidly along the road. My brother and I followed at his heels, and as we went other men and boys joined the crowd.

It had grown dark by the time we got to where the old woman had left the road but the moon had come out. The marshal was thinking there might have been a murder. He kept asking the hunter questions. The hunter went along with his gun across his shoulders, a dog following at his heels. It isn't often a rabbit hunter has a chance to be so conspicuous. He was taking full advantage of it, leading the procession with the town marshal. "I didn't see any wounds. She was a beautiful young girl. Her face was buried in the snow. No, I didn't know her." As a matter of fact, the hunter had not looked closely at the body. He had been frightened. She might have been murdered and some one might spring out from behind a tree and murder him. In a woods, in the late afternoon, when the trees are all bare and there is white snow on the ground, when all is silent, something creepy steals over the mind and body. If something strange or uncanny has happened in the neighborhood all you think about is getting away from there as fast as you can.

The crowd of men and boys had got to where the old woman had crossed the field and went, following the marshal and the hunter, up the slight incline and into the woods.

My brother and I were silent. He had his bundle of papers in a bag slung across his shoulder. When he got back to town he would have to go on distributing his papers before he went home to supper. If I went along, as he had no doubt already determined I should, we would both be late. Either mother or our older sister would have to warm our supper.

Well, we would have something to tell. A boy did not get such a chance very often. It was lucky we just happened to go into the grocery when the hunter came in. The hunter was a country fellow. Neither of us had ever seen him before.

Now the crowd of men and boys had got to the clearing. Darkness comes quickly on such Winter nights, but the full moon made everything clear. My brother and I stood near the tree, beneath which the old woman had died.

She did not look old, lying there in that light, frozen and still. One of the men turned her over in the snow and I saw everything. My body trembled with some strange mystical feeling and so did my brother's. It might have been the cold.

Neither of us had ever seen a woman's body before. It may have been the snow, clinging to the frozen flesh, that made it look so white and lovely, so like marble. No woman had come with the party from town; but one of the men, he was the town blacksmith, took off his overcoat and spread it over her. Then he gathered her into his arms and started off to town, all the others following silently. At that time no one knew who she was.

V

I had seen everything, had seen the oval in the snow, like a miniature race-track, where the dogs had run, had seen how the men were mystified, had seen the white bare young-looking shoulders, had heard the whispered comments of the men.

The men were simply mystified. They took the body to the undertaker's, and when the blacksmith, the hunter, the marshal and several others had got inside they closed the door. If father had been there perhaps he could have got in, but we boys couldn't.

I went with my brother to distribute the rest of his papers and when we got home it was my brother who told the story.

I kept silent and went to bed early. It may have been I was not satisfied with the way he told it.

Later, in the town, I must have heard other fragments of the old woman's story. She was recognized the next day and there was an investigation.

The husband and son were found somewhere and brought to town and there was an attempt to connect them with the woman's death, but it did not work. They had perfect enough alibis.

However, the town was against them. They had to get out. Where they went I never heard.

I remember only the picture there in the forest, the men standing about, the naked girlish-looking figure, face down in the snow, the tracks made by the running dogs and the clear cold Winter sky above. White fragments of clouds were drifting across the sky. They went racing across the little open space among the trees.

The scene in the forest had become for me, without my knowing it, the foundation for the real story I am now trying to tell. The fragments, you see, had to be picked up slowly, long afterwards.

Things happened. When I was a young man I worked on the farm of a German. The hired-girl was afraid of her employer. The farmer's wife hated her.

I saw things at that place. Once later, I had a half-uncanny, mystical adventure with dogs in an Illinois forest on a clear, moon-lit Winter night. When I was a schoolboy, and on a Summer day, I went with a boy friend out along a creek some miles from town and came to the house where the old woman had lived. No one had lived in the house since her death. The doors were broken from the hinges; the window lights were all broken. As the boy and I stood in the road outside, two dogs, just roving farm dogs no doubt, came running around the corner of the house. The dogs were tall, gaunt fellows and came down to the fence and glared through at us, standing in the road.

The whole thing, the story of the old woman's death, was to me as I grew older like music heard from far off. The notes had to be picked up slowly one at a time. Something had to be understood.

The woman who died was one destined to feed animal life. Anyway, that is all she ever did. She was feeding animal life before she was born, as a child, as a young woman working on the farm of the German, after she married, when she grew old and when she died. She fed animal life in cows, in chickens, in pigs, in horses, in dogs, in men. Her daughter had died in childhood and with her one son she had no articulate relations. On the night when she died she was hurrying homeward, bearing on her body food for animal life.

She died in the clearing in the woods and even after her death continued feeding animal life.

You see it is likely that, when my brother told the story, that night when we got home and my mother and sister sat listening, I did not think he got the point. He was too young and so was I. A thing so complete has its own beauty.

I shall not try to emphasize the point. I am only explaining why I was dissatisfied then and have been ever since. I speak of that only that you may understand why I have been impelled to try to tell the simple story over again.

WHY I LIVE AT THE P.O.

EUDORA WELTY

EUDORA WELTY (1909–   ) was born in Jackson, Mississippi. She has spent most of her life in her native state, and material for much of her writing has been drawn from small-town Mississippi life. Her first short story collection, *A Curtain of Green* (1941), was acclaimed by critics, and her succeeding books have continued to draw praise. They include *The Golden Apples* (1949), a short story collection; *The Robber Bridegroom* (1942), a novelette; *Delta Wedding* (1946) and *The Ponder Heart* (1954), novels.

I WAS getting along fine with Mama, Papa-Daddy and Uncle Rondo until my sister Stella-Rondo just separated from her husband and came back home again. Mr. Whitaker! Of course I went with Mr. Whitaker first, when he first appeared here in China Grove, taking "Pose Yourself" photos, and Stella-Rondo broke us up. Told him I was one-sided. Bigger on one side than the other, which is a deliberate, calculated falsehood: I'm the same. Stella-Rondo is exactly twelve months to the day younger than I am and for that reason she's spoiled.

She's always had anything in the world she wanted and then she'd throw it away. Papa-Daddy gave her this gorgeous Add-a-Pearl necklace when she was eight years old and she threw it away playing baseball when she was nine, with only two pearls.

So as soon as she got married and moved away from home the first thing she did was separate! From Mr. Whitaker! This photographer with the popeyes she said she trusted. Came home from one of those towns up in Illinois and to our complete surprise brought this child of two.

Mama said she'd like to make her drop dead for a second. "Here you had this marvelous blonde child and never so much as wrote your mother a word about it," says Mama. "I'm thoroughly ashamed of you." But of course she wasn't.

Stella-Rondo just calmly takes off this *hat*, I wish you could see it. She says, "Why, Mama, Shirley-T.'s adopted, I can prove it."

"How?" says Mama, but all I says was, "H'm!" There I was over the hot stove, trying to stretch two chickens over five people and a completely unexpected child into the bargain, without one moment's notice.

"What do you mean—'H'm!'?" says Stella-Rondo, and Mama says, "I heard that, Sister."

I said that oh, I didn't mean a thing, only that whoever Shirley-T. was, she was the spit-image of Papa-Daddy if he'd cut off his beard, which of course he'd never do in the world. Papa-Daddy's Mama's papa and sulks.

Stella-Rondo got furious! She said, "Sister, I don't need to tell you you got a lot of nerve and always did have and I'll thank you to make no future reference to my adopted child whatsoever!"

"Very well," I said. "Very well, very well. Of course I noticed at once she looks like Mr. Whitaker's side too. That frown. She looks like a cross between Mr. Whitaker and Papa-Daddy."

"Well, all I can say is she isn't."

"She looks exactly like Shirley Temple to me," says Mama, but Shirley-T. just ran away from her.

So the first thing Stella-Rondo did at the table was turn Papa-Daddy against me.

"Papa-Daddy," she says. He was trying to cut up his meat. "Papa-Daddy!" I was taken completely by surprise. Papa-Daddy is about a million years old and's got this long-long beard. "Papa-Daddy, Sister says she fails to understand why you don't cut off your beard."

So Papa-Daddy l-a-y-s down his knife and fork! He's real rich. Mama says he is, he says he isn't. So he says, "Have I heard correctly? You don't understand why I don't cut off my beard?"

"Why," I says, "Papa-Daddy, of course I understand. I did not say any such of a thing, the idea!"

He says, "Hussy!"

I says, "Papa-Daddy, you know I wouldn't any more want you to cut off your beard than the man in the moon. It was the farthest thing from my mind! Stella-Rondo sat there and made that up while she was eating breast of chicken."

But he says, "So the postmistress fails to understand why I don't cut off my beard. Which job I got you through my influence with the government. 'Bird's nest'—is that what you call it?"

Not that it isn't the next to smallest P.O. in the entire state of Mississippi.

I says, "Oh, Papa-Daddy," I says, "I didn't say any such of a thing. I never dreamed it was a bird's nest, I have always been grateful though this is the next to smallest P.O. in the state of Mississippi, and I do not enjoy being referred to as a hussy by my own grandfather."

But Stella-Rondo says, "Yes, you did say it too. Anybody in the world could of heard you, that had ears."

"Stop right there," says Mama, looking at *me*.

So I pulled my napkin straight back through the napkin ring and left the table.

As soon as I was out of the room Mama says, "Call her back, or she'll starve to death," but Papa-Daddy says, "This is the beard I started growing on the Coast when I was fifteen years old." He would of gone on till nightfall if Shirley-T. hadn't lost the Milky Way she ate in Cairo.

So Papa-Daddy says, "I am going out and lie in the hammock, and you can all sit here and remember my words: I'll never cut off my beard as long as I live, even one inch, and I don't appreciate it in you at all." Passed right by me in the hall and went straight out and got in the hammock.

It would be a holiday. It wasn't five minutes before Uncle Rondo suddenly appeared in the hall in one of Stella-Rondo's flesh-colored kimonos, all cut on the bias, like something Mr. Whitaker probably thought was gorgeous.

"Uncle Rondo!" I says. "I didn't know who that was! Where are you going?"

"Sister," he says, "get out of my way, I'm poisoned."

"If you're poisoned stay away from Papa-Daddy," I says. "Keep out of the hammock. Papa-Daddy will certainly beat you on the head if you come within forty miles of him. He thinks I deliberately said he ought to cut off his beard after he got me the P.O., and I've told him and told him and told him, and he acts like he just don't hear me. Papa-Daddy must of gone stone deaf."

"He picked a fine day to do it then," says Uncle Rondo, and before you could say "Jack Robinson" flew out in the yard.

What he'd really done, he'd drunk another bottle of that prescription. He does it every single Fourth of July as sure as shooting, and it's horribly expensive. Then he falls over in the hammock and snores. So he insisted on zigzagging right on out to the hammock, looking like a half-wit.

Papa-Daddy woke up with this horrible yell and right there without moving an inch he tried to turn Uncle Rondo against me. I heard every word he said. Oh, he told Uncle Rondo I didn't learn to read till I was eight years old and he didn't see how in the world I ever got the mail put up at the P.O., much less read it all, and he said if Uncle Rondo could only fathom the lengths he had gone to to get me that job! And he said on the other hand he thought Stella-Rondo had a brilliant mind and deserved credit for getting out of town. All the time he was just lying there swinging as pretty as you please and looping out his beard, and poor Uncle Rondo was *pleading* with him to slow down the hammock, it was making him as dizzy as a witch to watch it. But that's what Papa-Daddy likes about a hammock. So Uncle Rondo was too dizzy to get turned against me for the time being. He's Mama's only brother and is a good case of a one-track mind. Ask anybody. A certified pharmacist.

Just then I heard Stella-Rondo raising the upstairs window. While she was married she got this peculiar idea that it's cooler with the window shut and locked. So she has to raise the window before she can make a soul hear her outdoors.

So she raises the window and says, "*Oh!*" You would have thought she was mortally wounded.

Uncle Rondo and Papa-Daddy didn't even look up, but kept right on with what they were doing. I had to laugh.

I flew up the stairs and threw the door open! I says, "What in the wide world's the matter, Stella-Rondo? You mortally wounded?"

"No," she says, "I am not mortally wounded but I wish you would do me the favor of looking out the window there and telling me what you see."

So I shade my eyes and look out the window.

"I see the front yard," I says.

"Don't you see any human beings?" she says.

"I see Uncle Rondo trying to run Papa-Daddy out of the hammock," I says. "Nothing more. Naturally, it's so suffocating-hot in the house, with all the windows shut and locked, everybody who cares to stay in their right mind will have to go out and get in the hammock before the Fourth of July is over."

"Don't you notice anything different about Uncle Rondo?" asks Stella-Rondo.

"Why, no, except he's got on some terrible-looking flesh-colored contraption I wouldn't be found dead in, is all I can see," I says.

"Never mind, you won't be found dead in it, because it happens to be part of my trousseau, and Mr. Whitaker took several dozen photographs of me in it," says Stella-Rondo. "What on earth could Uncle Rondo *mean* by wearing part of my trousseau out in the broad open daylight without saying so much as 'Kiss my foot,' *knowing* I only got home this morning after my separation and hung my negligee up on the bathroom door, just as nervous as I could be?"

"I'm sure I don't know, and what do you expect me to do about it?" I says. "Jump out the window?"

"No, I expect nothing of the kind. I simply declare that Uncle Rondo looks like a fool in it, that's all," she says. "It makes me sick to my stomach."

"Well, he looks as good as he can," I says. "As good as anybody in reason could." I stood up for Uncle Rondo, please remember. And I said to Stella-Rondo, "I think I would do well not to criticize so freely if I were you and came home with a two-year-old child I had never said a word about, and no explanation whatever about my separation."

"I asked you the instant I entered this house not to refer one more time to my adopted child, and you gave me your word of honor you would not," was all Stella-Rondo would say, and started pulling out every one of her eyebrows with some cheap Kress tweezers.

So I merely slammed the door behind me and went down and made some green-tomato pickle. Somebody had to do it. Of course Mama had turned both the niggers loose; she always said no earthly power could hold one anyway on the Fourth of July, so she wouldn't even try. It turned out that Jaypan fell in the lake and came within a very narrow limit of drowning.

So Mama trots in. Lifts up the lid and says, "H'm! Not very good for your Uncle Rondo in his precarious condition, I must say. Or poor little adopted Shirley-T. Shame on you!"

That made me tired. I says, "Well, Stella-Rondo had better thank her lucky stars it was her instead of me came trotting in with that very peculiar-looking child. Now if it had been me that trotted in from Illinois and brought a peculiar-looking child of two, I shudder to think of the reception I'd of got, much less controlled the diet of an entire family."

"But you must remember, Sister, that you were never married to Mr. Whitaker in the first place and didn't go up to Illinois to live," says Mama, shaking a spoon in my face. "If you had I would of been just as overjoyed to see you and your little adopted girl as I was to see Stella-Rondo, when you wound up with your separation and came on back home."

"You would not," I says.

"Don't contradict me, I would," says Mama.

But I said she couldn't convince me though she talked till she was blue in the face. Then I said, "Besides, you know as well as I do that that child is not adopted."

"She most certainly is adopted," says Mama, stiff as a poker.

I says, "Why, Mama, Stella-Rondo had her just as sure as anything in this world, and just too stuck up to admit it."

"Why, Sister," said Mama. "Here I thought we were going to have a pleasant Fourth of July, and you start right out not believing a word your own baby sister tells you!"

"Just like Cousin Annie Flo. Went to her grave denying the facts of life," I remind Mama.

"I told you if you ever mentioned Auntie Flo's name I'd slap your face," says Mama, and slaps my face.

"All right, you wait and see," I says.

"I," says Mama, "I prefer to take my children's word for anything when it's humanly possible." You ought to see Mama, she weighs two hundred pounds and has real tiny feet.

Just then something perfectly horrible occurred to me.

"Mama," I says, "can that child talk?" I simply had to whisper! "Mama, I wonder if that child can be—you know—in any way? Do you realize," I says, "that she hasn't spoken one single, solitary word to a human being up to the minute? This is the way she looks," I says, and I looked like this.

Well, Mama and I just stood there and stared at each other. It was horrible!

"I remember well that Joe Whitaker frequently drank like a fish," says Mama. "I believed to my soul he drank *chemicals*." And without another word she marches to the foot of the stairs and calls Stella-Rondo.

"Stella-Rondo? O-o-o-o-o! Stella-Rondo!"

"What?" says Stella-Rondo from upstairs. Not even the grace to get up off the bed.

"Can that child of yours talk?" asks Mama.

Stella-Rondo says, "Can she what?"

"Talk! Talk!" says Mama. "Burdyburdyburdyburdy!"

So Stella-Rondo yells back, "Who says she can't talk?"

"Sister says so," says Mama.

"You didn't have to tell me, I know whose word of honor don't mean a thing in this house," says Stella-Rondo.

And in a minute the loudest Yankee voice I ever heard in my life yells out, "OE'm Pop-OE the Sailor-r-r-r Ma-a-n!" and then somebody jumps up and down in the upstairs hall. In another second the house would of fallen down.

"Not only talks, she can tap-dance!" calls Stella-Rondo. "Which is more than some people I won't name can do."

"Why, the little precious darling thing!" Mama says, so surprised. "Just as smart as she can be!" Starts talking baby talk right there. Then she turns on me. "Sister, you ought to be thoroughly ashamed!

Run upstairs this instant and apologize to Stella-Rondo and Shirley-T."

"Apologize for what?" I says. "I merely wondered if the child was normal, that's all. Now that she's proved she is, why, I have nothing further to say."

But Mama just turned on her heel and flew out, furious. She ran right upstairs and hugged the baby. She believed it was adopted. Stella-Rondo hadn't done a thing but turn her against me from upstairs while I stood there helpless over the hot stove. So that made Mama, Papa-Daddy and the baby all on Stella-Rondo's side.

Next, Uncle Rondo.

I must say that Uncle Rondo had been marvelous to me at various times in the past and I was completely unprepared to be made to jump out of my skin, the way it turned out. Once Stella-Rondo did something perfectly horrible to him—broke a chain letter from Flanders Field—and he took the radio back he had given her and gave it to me. Stella-Rondo was furious! For six months we all had to call her Stella instead of Stella-Rondo, or she wouldn't answer. I always thought Uncle Rondo had all the brains of the entire family. Another time he sent me to Mammoth Cave, with all expenses paid.

But this would be the day he was drinking that prescription, the Fourth of July.

So at supper Stella-Rondo speaks up and says she thinks Uncle Rondo ought to try to eat a little something. So finally Uncle Rondo said he would try a little cold biscuits and ketchup, but that was all. So *she* brought it to him.

"Do you think it wise to disport with ketchup in Stella-Rondo's flesh-colored kimono?" I says. Trying to be considerate! If Stella-Rondo couldn't watch out for her trousseau, somebody had to.

"Any objections?" asks Uncle Rondo, just about to pour out all the ketchup.

"Don't mind what she says, Uncle Rondo," says Stella-Rondo. "Sister has been devoting this solid afternoon to sneering out my bedroom window at the way you look."

"What's that?" says Uncle Rondo. Uncle Rondo has got the most terrible temper in the world. Anything is liable to make him tear the house down if it comes at the wrong time.

So Stella-Rondo says, "Sister says, 'Uncle Rondo certainly does look like a fool in that pink kimono!'"

Do you remember who it was really said that?

Uncle Rondo spills out all the ketchup and jumps out of his chair and tears off the kimono and throws it down on the dirty floor and puts his foot on it. It had to be sent all the way to Jackson to the cleaners and re-pleated.

"So that's your opinion of your Uncle Rondo, is it?" he says. "I look like a fool, do I? Well, that's the last straw. A whole day in this house with nothing to do, and then to hear you come out with a remark like that behind my back!"

"I didn't say any such of a thing, Uncle Rondo," I says, "and I'm not saying who did, either. Why, I think you look all right. Just try to take care of yourself and not talk and eat at the same time," I says. "I think you better go lie down."

"Lie down my foot," says Uncle Rondo. I ought to of known by that he was fixing to do something perfectly horrible.

So he didn't do anything that night in the precarious state he was in—just played Casino with Mama and Stella-Rondo, and Shirley-T. and gave Shirley-T. a nickel with a head on both sides. It tickled her nearly to death, and she called him "Papa." But at 6:30 A.M. the next morning, he threw a whole five-cent package of some unused one-inch firecrackers from the store as hard as he could into my bedroom and they every one went off. Not one bad one in the string. Anybody else, there'd be one that wouldn't go off.

Well, I'm just terribly susceptible to noise of any kind, the doctor has always told me I was the most sensitive person he had ever seen in his whole life, and I was simply prostrated. I couldn't eat! People tell me they heard it as far as the cemetery, and old Aunt Jep Patterson, that had been holding her own so good, thought it was Judgment Day and she was going to meet her whole family. It's usually so quiet here.

And I'll tell you it didn't take me any longer than a minute to make up my mind what to do. There I was with the whole entire house on Stella-Rondo's side and turned against me. If I have anything at all I have pride.

So I just decided I'd go straight down to the P.O. There's plenty of room there in the back, I says to myself.

Well! I made no bones about letting the family catch on to what I was up to. I didn't try to conceal it.

The first thing they knew, I marched in where they were all playing Old Maid and pulled the electric oscillating fan out by the plug, and everything got real hot. Next I snatched the pillow I'd done the needlepoint on right off the davenport from behind Papa-Daddy. He went "Ugh!" I beat Stella-Rondo up the stairs and finally found my charm bracelet in her bureau drawer under a picture of Nelson Eddy.

"So that's the way the land lies," says Uncle Rondo. There he was, piecing on the ham. "Well, Sister, I'll be glad to donate my army cot if you got any place to set it up, providing you'll leave right this minute and let me get some peace." Uncle Rondo was in France.

"Thank you kindly for the cot and 'peace' is hardly the word I would select if I had to resort to fire-crackers at 6:30 A.M. in a young girl's bedroom," I says back to him. "And as to where I intend to go, you seem to forget my position as postmistress of China Grove, Mississippi," I says, "I've always got the P.O."

Well, that made them all sit up and take notice.

I went out front and started digging up some four-o'clocks to plant around the P.O.

"Ah-ah-ah!" says Mama, raising the window. "Those happen to be my four-o'clocks. Everything planted in that star is mine. I've never known you to make anything grow in your life."

"Very well," I says. "But I take the fern. Even you, Mama, can't stand there and deny that I'm the one watered that fern. And I happen to know where I can send in a box top and get a packet of one thousand mixed seeds, no two the same kind, free."

"Oh, where?" Mama wants to know.

But I says, "Too late. You 'tend to your house, and I'll 'tend to mine. You hear things like that all the time if you know how to listen to the radio. Perfectly marvelous offers. Get anything you want free."

So I hope to tell you I marched in and got that radio, and they could of all bit a nail in two, especially Stella-Rondo, that it used to belong to, and she well knew she couldn't get it back, I'd sue for it like a shot. And I very politely took the sewing-machine motor I helped pay the most on to give Mama for Christmas back in 1929, and a good big calendar, with the first-aid remedies on it. The thermometer and the Hawaiian ukulele certainly were rightfully mine, and I stood on the step-ladder and got all my watermelon-rind preserves and every fruit and vegetable I'd put up, every jar. Then I began to pull the tacks out of the bluebird wall vases on the archway to the dining room.

"Who told you you could have those, Miss Priss?" says Mama, fanning as hard as she could.

"I bought 'em and I'll keep track of 'em," I says. "I'll tack 'em up one on each side the post-office window, and you can see 'em when you come to ask me for your mail, if you're so dead to see 'em."

"Not I! I'll never darken the door to that post office again if I live to be a hundred," Mama says. "Ungrateful child! After all the money we spent on you at the Normal."

"Me either," says Stella-Rondo. "You can just let my mail lie there and *rot*, for all I care. I'll never come and relieve you of a single, solitary piece."

"I should worry," I says. "And who you think's going to sit down and write you all those big fat letters and postcards, by the way? Mr. Whitaker? Just because he was the only man ever dropped down in China Grove and you got him—unfairly—is he going to sit down and write you a lengthy correspondence after you come home giving no rhyme nor reason whatsoever for your separation and no explanation for the presence of that child? I may not have your brilliant mind, but I fail to see it."

So Mama says, "Sister, I've told you a thousand times that Stella-Rondo simply got homesick, and this child is far too big to be hers," and she says, "Now, why don't you all just sit down and play Casino?"

Then Shirley-T. sticks out her tongue at me in this perfectly horrible way. She has no more manners than the man in the moon. I told her she was going to cross her eyes like that some day and they'd stick.

"It's too late to stop me now," I says. "You should have tried that yesterday. I'm going to the P.O. and the only way you can possibly see me is to visit me there."

So Papa-Daddy says, "You'll never catch me setting foot in that post office, even if I should take a notion into my head to write a letter some place." He says, "I won't have you reachin' out of that little old window with a pair of shears and cuttin' off any beard of mine. I'm too smart for you!"

"We all are," says Stella-Rondo.

But I said, "If you're so smart, where's Mr. Whit-aker?"

So then Uncle Rondo says, "I'll thank you from now on to stop reading all the orders I get on post-cards and telling everybody in China Grove what you think is the matter with them," but I says, "I draw my own conclusions and will continue in the future to draw them." I says, "If people want to write their inmost secrets on penny postcards, there's nothing in the wide world you can do about it, Uncle Rondo."

"And if you think we'll ever *write* another post-card you're sadly mistaken," says Mama.

"Cutting off your nose to spite your face then," I says. "But if you're all determined to have no more to do with the U. S. mail, think of this: What will Stella-Rondo do now, if she wants to tell Mr. Whit-aker to come after her?"

"Wah!" says Stella-Rondo. I knew she'd cry. She had a conniption fit right there in the kitchen.

"It will be interesting to see how long she holds out," I says. "And now—I am leaving."

"Good-bye," says Uncle Rondo.

"Oh, I declare," says Mama, "to think that a family of mine should quarrel on the Fourth of July, or the day after, over Stella-Rondo leaving old Mr. Whit-aker and having the sweetest little adopted child! It looks like we'd all be glad!"

"Wah!" says Stella-Rondo, and has a fresh con-niption fit.

"*He* left *her*—you mark my words," I says. "That's Mr. Whitaker. I know Mr. Whitaker. After all, I knew him first. I said from the beginning he'd up and leave her. I foretold every single thing that's happened."

"Where did he go?" asks Mama.

"Probably to the North Pole, if he knows what's good for him," I says.

But Stella-Rondo just bawled and wouldn't say another word. She flew to her room and slammed the door.

"Now look what you've gone and done, Sister," says Mama. "You go apologize."

"I haven't got time, I'm leaving," I says.

"Well, what are you waiting around for?" asks Uncle Rondo.

So I just picked up the kitchen clock and started off, without saying "Kiss my foot" or anything, and never did tell Stella-Rondo good-bye.

There was a nigger girl going along on a little wagon, right in front.

"Nigger girl," I says, "come help me haul these things down the hill. I'm going to live in the post office."

Took her nine trips in her express wagon. Uncle Rondo came out on the porch and threw her a nickel.

And that's the last I've laid eyes on any of my family or my family laid eyes on me for five solid days and nights. Stella-Rondo may be telling the most horrible tales in the world about Mr. Whitaker, but I haven't heard them. As I tell everybody, I draw my own conclusions.

But oh, I like it here. It's ideal, as I've been saying. You see, I've got everything cater-cornered, the way I like it. Hear the radio? All the war news. Radio, sewing machine, book ends, ironing board and that great big piano lamp—peace, that's what I like. Butter-bean vines planted all along the front where the strings are.

Of course, there's not much mail. My family are naturally the main people in China Grove, and if they prefer to vanish from the face of the earth, for all the mail they get or the mail they write, why, I'm not going to open my mouth. Some of the folks here in town are taking up for me and some turned against me. I know which is which. There are always people who will quit buying stamps just to get on the right side of Papa-Daddy.

But here I am, and here I'll stay. I want the world to know I'm happy.

And if Stella-Rondo should come to me this minute, on bended knees, and *attempt* to explain the incidents of her life with Mr. Whitaker, I'd simply put my fingers in both my ears and refuse to listen.

THE SHORT HAPPY LIFE
OF FRANCIS MACOMBER

ERNEST HEMINGWAY

ERNEST HEMINGWAY (1899–1961) was born in Oak Park, Illinois, served with a volunteer American ambulance unit in the First World War, and was wounded on the Italian front. After the war he was identified with the literary expatriates on the Continent. During his life he traveled widely. For a time he lived in Key West, Florida, then in Cuba, and finally in Ketchum, Idaho. Among his books are *The Sun Also Rises* (1926), *A Farewell to Arms* (1929), *Death in the Afternoon* (1932), *The Fifth Column and the First Forty-Nine Stories* (1938), *For Whom the Bell Tolls* (1940), and *The Old Man and the Sea* (1952), which was cited specifically when he was awarded the Nobel Prize for Literature in 1954.

IT WAS now lunch time and they were all sitting under the double green fly of the dining tent pretending that nothing had happened.

"Will you have lime juice or lemon squash?" Macomber asked.

"I'll have a gimlet," Robert Wilson told him.

"I'll have a gimlet too. I need something," Macomber's wife said.

"I suppose it's the thing to do," Macomber agreed. "Tell him to make three gimlets."

The mess boy had started them already, lifting the bottles out of the canvas cooling bags that sweated wet in the wind that blew through the trees that shaded the tents.

"What had I ought to give them?" Macomber asked.

"A quid would be plenty," Wilson told him. "You don't want to spoil them."

"Will the headman distribute it?"

"Absolutely."

Francis Macomber had, half an hour before, been carried to his tent from the edge of the camp in triumph on the arms and shoulders of the cook, the personal boys, the skinner and the porters. The gunbearers had taken no part in the demonstration. When the native boys put him down at the door of his tent, he had shaken all their hands, received their congratulations, and then gone into the tent and sat on the bed until his wife came in. She did not speak to him when she came in and he left the tent at once to wash his face and hands in the portable wash basin outside and go over to the dining tent to sit in a comfortable canvas chair in the breeze and the shade.

"You've got your lion," Robert Wilson said to him, "and a damned fine one too."

Mrs. Macomber looked at Wilson quickly. She was an extremely handsome and well-kept woman of the beauty and social position which had, five years before, commanded five thousand dollars as the price of endorsing, with photographs, a beauty product which she had never used. She had been married to Francis Macomber for eleven years.

"He is a good lion, isn't he?" Macomber said. His wife looked at him now. She looked at both these men as though she had never seen them before.

One, Wilson, the white hunter, she knew she had never truly seen before. He was about middle height with sandy hair, a stubby mustache, a very red face and extremely cold blue eyes with faint white wrinkles at the corners that grooved merrily when he smiled. He smiled at her now and she looked away from his face at the way his shoulders sloped in the loose tunic he wore with the four big cartridges held in loops where the left breast pocket should have been, at his big brown hands, his old slacks, his very dirty boots and back to his red face again. She noticed where the baked red of his face stopped in a white line that marked the circle left by his Stetson hat that hung now from one of the pegs of the tent pole.

"Well, here's to the lion," Robert Wilson said. He smiled at her again and, not smiling, she looked curiously at her husband.

Francis Macomber was very tall, very well built if you did not mind that length of bone, dark, his hair cropped like an oarsman, rather thin-lipped, and was considered handsome. He was dressed in the same sort of safari clothes that Wilson wore except that his were new, he was thirty-five years old, kept himself very fit, was good at court games, had a number of big-game fishing records, and had just shown himself, very publicly, to be a coward.

"Here's to the lion," he said. "I can't ever thank you for what you did."

Margaret, his wife, looked away from him and back to Wilson.

"Let's not talk about the lion," she said.

Wilson looked over at her without smiling and now she smiled at him.

"It's been a very strange day," she said. "Hadn't you ought to put your hat on even under the canvas at noon? You told me that, you know."

"Might put it on," said Wilson.

"You know you have a very red face, Mr. Wilson," she told him and smiled again.

"Drink," said Wilson.

"I don't think so," she said. "Francis drinks a great deal, but his face is never red."

"It's red today," Macomber tried a joke.

"No," said Margaret. "It's mine that's red today. But Mr. Wilson's is always red."

"Must be racial," said Wilson. "I say, you wouldn't like to drop my beauty as a topic, would you?"

"I've just started on it."

"Let's chuck it," said Wilson.

"Conversation is going to be so difficult," Margaret said.

"Don't be silly, Margot," her husband said.

"No difficulty," Wilson said. "Got a damn fine lion."

Margot looked at them both and they both saw that she was going to cry. Wilson had seen it coming for a long time and he dreaded it. Macomber was past dreading it.

"I wish it hadn't happened. Oh, I wish it hadn't happened," she said and started for her tent. She made no noise of crying but they could see that her shoulders were shaking under the rose-colored, sunproofed shirt she wore.

"Women upset," said Wilson to the tall man. "Amounts to nothing. Strain on the nerves and one thing'n another."

"No," said Macomber. "I suppose that I rate that for the rest of my life now."

"Nonsense. Let's have a spot of the giant killer," said Wilson. "Forget the whole thing. Nothing to it anyway."

"We might try," said Macomber. "I won't forget what you did for me though."

"Nothing," said Wilson. "All nonsense."

So they sat there in the shade where the camp was pitched under some wide-topped acacia trees with a boulder-strewn cliff behind them, and a stretch of grass that ran to the bank of a boulder-filled stream in front with forest beyond it, and drank their just-cool lime drinks and avoided one another's eyes while the boys set the table for lunch. Wilson could tell that the boys all knew about it now and when he saw Macomber's personal boy looking curiously at his master while he was putting dishes on the table he snapped at him in Swahili. The boy turned away with his face blank.

"What were you telling him?" Macomber asked.

"Nothing. Told him to look alive or I'd see he got about fifteen of the best."

"What's that? Lashes?"

"It's quite illegal," Wilson said. "You're supposed to fine them."

"Do you still have them whipped?"

"Oh, yes. They could raise a row if they chose to complain. But they don't. They prefer it to the fines."

"How strange!" said Macomber.

"Not strange, really," Wilson said. "Which would you rather do? Take a good birching or lose your pay?"

Then he felt embarrassed at asking it and before Macomber could answer he went on, "We all take a beating every day, you know, one way or another."

This was no better. "Good God," he thought. "I am a diplomat, aren't I?"

"Yes, we take a beating," said Macomber, still not looking at him. "I'm awfully sorry about that lion business. It doesn't have to go any further, does it? I mean no one will hear about it, will they?"

"You mean will I tell it at the Mathaiga Club?" Wilson looked at him now coldly. He had not expected this. So he's a bloody four-letter man as well as a bloody coward, he thought. I rather liked him too until today. But how is one to know about an American?

"No," said Wilson. "I'm a professional hunter. We never talk about our clients. You can be quite easy on that. It's supposed to be bad form to ask us not to talk though."

He had decided now that to break would be much easier. He would eat, then, by himself and could read a book with his meals. They would eat by themselves. He would see them through the safari on a very formal basis—what was it the French called it? Distinguished consideration—and it would be a damn sight easier than having to go through this emotional trash. He'd insult him and make a good clean break. Then he could read a book with his meals and he'd still be drinking their whisky. That was the phrase for it when a safari went bad. You ran into another white hunter and you asked, "How is everything going?" and he answered, "Oh, I'm still drinking their whisky," and you knew everything had gone to pot.

"I'm sorry," Macomber said and looked at him with his American face that would stay adolescent until it became middle-aged, and Wilson noted his crew-cropped hair, fine eyes only faintly shifty, good nose, thin lips and handsome jaw. "I'm sorry I didn't realize that. There are lots of things I don't know."

So what could he do, Wilson thought. He was all ready to break it off quickly and neatly and here the beggar was apologizing after he had just insulted him. He made one more attempt. "Don't worry about me talking," he said. "I have a living to make. You know in Africa no woman ever misses her lion and no white man ever bolts."

"I bolted like a rabbit," Macomber said.

Now what in hell were you going to do about a man who talked like that, Wilson wondered.

Wilson looked at Macomber with his flat, blue, machine-gunner's eyes and the other smiled back at him. He had a pleasant smile if you did not notice how his eyes showed when he was hurt.

"Maybe I can fix it up on buffalo," he said. "We're after them next, aren't we?"

"In the morning if you like," Wilson told him. Perhaps he had been wrong. This was certainly the way to take it. You most certainly could not tell a damned thing about an American. He was all for Macomber again. If you could forget the morning. But, of course, you couldn't. The morning had been about as bad as they come.

"Here comes the Memsahib," he said. She was walking over from her tent looking refreshed and cheerful and quite lovely. She had a very perfect oval face, so perfect that you expected her to be stupid. But she wasn't stupid, Wilson thought, no, not stupid.

"How is the beautiful red-faced Mr. Wilson? Are you feeling better, Francis, my pearl?"

"Oh, much," said Macomber.

"I've dropped the whole thing," she said, sitting down at the table. "What importance is there to whether Francis is any good at killing lions? That's not his trade. That's Mr. Wilson's trade. Mr. Wilson is really very impressive killing anything. You do kill anything, don't you?"

"Oh, anything," said Wilson. "Simply anything." They are, he thought, the hardest in the world; the hardest, the cruelest, the most predatory and the most attractive and their men have softened or gone to pieces nervously as they have hardened. Or is it that they pick men they can handle? They can't know that much at the age they marry, he thought. He was grateful that he had gone through his education on American women before now because this was a very attractive one.

"We're going after buff in the morning," he told her.

"I'm coming," she said.

"No, you're not."

"Oh, yes, I am. Mayn't I, Francis?"

"Why not stay in camp?"

"Not for anything," she said. "I wouldn't miss something like today for anything."

When she left, Wilson was thinking, when she went off to cry, she seemed a hell of a fine woman. She seemed to understand, to realize, to be hurt for him and for herself and to know how things really stood. She is away for twenty minutes and now she is back, simply enamelled in that American female cruelty. They are the damnedest women. Really the damnedest.

"We'll put on another show for you tomorrow," Francis Macomber said.

"You're not coming," Wilson said.

"You're very mistaken," she told him. "And I want *so* to see you perform again. You were lovely this morning. That is if blowing things' heads off is lovely."

"Here's the lunch," said Wilson. "You're very merry, aren't you?"

"Why not? I didn't come out here to be dull."

"Well, it hasn't been dull," Wilson said. He could see the boulders in the river and the high bank beyond with the trees and he remembered the morning.

"Oh, no," she said. "It's been charming. And tomorrow. You don't know how I look forward to tomorrow."

"That's eland he's offering you," Wilson said.

"They're the big cowy things that jump like hares, aren't they?"

"I suppose that describes them," Wilson said.

"It's very good meat," Macomber said.

"Did you shoot it, Francis?" she asked.

"Yes."

"They're not dangerous, are they?"

"Only if they fall on you," Wilson told her.

"I'm so glad."

"Why not let up on the bitchery just a little, Margot," Macomber said, cutting the eland steak and putting some mashed potato, gravy and carrot on the down-turned fork that tined through the piece of meat.

"I suppose I could," she said, "since you put it so prettily."

"Tonight we'll have champagne for the lion," Wilson said. "It's a bit too hot at noon."

"Oh, the lion," Margot said. "I'd forgotten the lion!"

So, Robert Wilson thought to himself, she *is* giving him a ride, isn't she? Or do you suppose that's her idea of putting up a good show? How should a woman act when she discovers her husband is a bloody coward? She's damn cruel but they're all cruel. They govern, of course, and to govern one has to be cruel sometimes. Still, I've seen enough of their damn terrorism.

"Have some more eland," he said to her politely.

That afternoon, late, Wilson and Macomber went out in the motor car with the native driver and the two gun-bearers. Mrs. Macomber stayed in the camp. It was too hot to go out, she said, and she was going with them in the early morning. As they drove off Wilson saw her standing under the big tree, looking pretty rather than beautiful in her faintly rosy khaki, her dark hair drawn back off her forehead and gathered in a knot low on her neck, her face as fresh, he thought, as though she were in England. She waved to them as the car went off through the swale of high grass and curved around through the trees into the small hills of orchard bush.

In the orchard bush they found a herd of impala, and leaving the car they stalked one old ram with long, wide-spread horns and Macomber killed it with a very creditable shot that knocked the buck down at a good two hundred yards and sent the herd off bounding wildly and leaping over one another's back in long, leg-drawn-up leaps as unbelievable and as floating as those one makes sometimes in dreams.

"That was a good shot," Wilson said. "They're a small target."

"Is it a worth-while head?" Macomber asked.

"It's excellent," Wilson told him. "You shoot like that and you'll have no trouble."

"Do you think we'll find buffalo tomorrow?"

"There's a good chance of it. They feed out early in the morning and with luck we may catch them in the open."

"I'd like to clear away that lion business," Macomber said. "It's not very pleasant to have your wife see you do something like that."

I should think it would be even more unpleasant to do it, Wilson thought, wife or no wife, or to talk about it having done it. But he said, "I wouldn't think about that any more. Any one could be upset by his first lion. That's all over."

But that night after dinner and a whisky and soda by the fire before going to bed, as Francis Macomber lay on his cot with the mosquito bar over him and listened to the night noises it was not all over. It was neither all over nor was it beginning. It was there exactly as it happened with some parts of it indelibly emphasized and he was miserably ashamed at it. But more than shame he felt cold, hollow fear in him. The fear was still there like a cold slimy hollow in all the emptiness where once his confidence had been and it made him feel sick. It was still there with him now.

It had started the night before when he had wakened and heard the lion roaring somewhere up along the river. It was a deep sound and at the end there were sort of coughing grunts that made him seem just outside the tent, and when Francis Macomber woke in the night to hear it he was afraid. He could hear his wife breathing quietly, asleep. There was no one to tell he was afraid, nor to be afraid with him, and, lying alone, he did not know the Somali proverb that says a brave man is always frightened three times by a lion; when he first sees his track, when he first hears him roar and when he first confronts him. Then while they were eating breakfast by lantern lights out in the dining tent, before the sun was up, the lion roared again and Francis thought he was just at the edge of camp.

"Sounds like an old-timer," Robert Wilson said, looking up from his kippers and coffee. "Listen to him cough."

"Is he very close?"

"A mile or so up the stream."

"Will we see him?"

"We'll have a look."

"Does his roaring carry that far? It sounds as though he were right in camp."

"Carries a hell of a long way," said Robert Wilson. "It's strange the way it carries. Hope he's a shootable cat. The boys said there was a very big one about here."

"If I get a shot, where should I hit him," Macomber asked, "to stop him?"

"In the shoulders," Wilson said. "In the neck if you can make it. Shoot for bone. Break him down."

"I hope I can place it properly," Macomber said.

"You shoot very well," Wilson told him. "Take your time. Make sure of him. The first one in is the one that counts."

"What range will it be?"

"Can't tell. Lion has something to say about that. Won't shoot unless it's close enough so you can make sure."

"At under a hundred yards?" Macomber asked.

Wilson looked at him quickly.

"Hundred's about right. Might have to take him a bit under. Shouldn't chance a shot at much over that. A hundred's a decent range. You can hit him wherever you want at that. Here comes the Memsahib."

"Good morning," she said. "Are we going after that lion?"

"As soon as you deal with your breakfast," Wilson said. "How are you feeling?"

"Marvellous," she said. "I'm very excited."

"I'll just go and see that everything is ready," Wilson went off. As he left the lion roared again.

"Noisy beggar," Wilson said. "We'll put a stop to that."

"What's the matter, Francis?" his wife asked him.

"Nothing," Macomber said.

"Yes, there is," she said. "What are you upset about?"

"Nothing," he said.

"Tell me," she looked at him. "Don't you feel well?"

"It's that damned roaring," he said. "It's been going on all night, you know."

"Why didn't you wake me," she said. "I'd love to have heard it."

"I've got to kill the damned thing," Macomber said, miserably.

"Well, that's what you're out here for, isn't it?"

"Yes. But I'm nervous. Hearing the thing roar gets on my nerves."

"Well then, as Wilson said, kill him and stop his roaring."

"Yes, darling," said Francis Macomber. "It sounds easy, doesn't it?"

"You're not afraid, are you?"

"Of course not. But I'm nervous from hearing him roar all night."

"You'll kill him marvellously," she said. "I know you will. I'm awfully anxious to see it."

"Finish your breakfast and we'll be starting."

"It's not light yet," she said. "This is a ridiculous hour."

Just then the lion roared in a deep-chested moaning, suddenly guttural, ascending vibration that seemed to shake the air and ended in a sigh and a heavy, deep-chested grunt.

"He sounds almost here," Macomber's wife said.

"My God," said Macomber. "I hate that damned noise."

"It's very impressive."

"Impressive. It's frightful."

Robert Wilson came up then carrying his short, ugly, shockingly big-bored .505 Gibbs and grinning.

"Come on," he said. "Your gun-bearer has your Springfield and the big gun. Everything's in the car. Have your solids?"

"Yes."

"I'm ready," Mrs. Macomber said.

"Must make him stop that racket," Wilson said. "You get in front. The Memsahib can sit back here with me."

They climbed into the motor car and, in the gray first daylight, moved off up the river through the trees. Macomber opened the breech of his rifle and saw he had metal-cased bullets, shut the bolt and put the rifle on safety. He saw his hand was trembling. He felt in his pocket for more cartridges and moved his fingers over the cartridges in the loops of his tunic front. He turned back to where Wilson sat in the rear seat of the doorless, box-bodied motor car beside his wife, them both grinning with excitement, and Wilson leaned forward and whispered.

"See the birds dropping. Means the old boy has left his kill."

On the far bank of the stream Macomber could see, above the trees, vultures circling and plummeting down.

"Chances are he'll come to drink along here," Wilson whispered. "Before he goes to lay up. Keep an eye out."

They were driving slowly along the high bank of the stream which here cut deeply to its boulder-filled bed, and they wound in and out through big trees as they drove. Macomber was watching the opposite bank when he felt Wilson take hold of his arm. The car stopped.

"There he is," he heard the whisper. "Ahead and to the right. Get out and take him. He's a marvellous lion."

Macomber saw the lion now. He was standing almost broadside, his great head up and turned toward them. The early morning breeze that blew toward them was just stirring his dark mane, and the lion looked huge, silhouetted on the rise of bank in the gray morning light, his shoulders heavy, his barrel of a body bulking smoothly.

"How far is he?" asked Macomber, raising his rifle.

"About seventy-five. Get out and take him."

"Why not shoot from where I am?"

"You don't shoot them from cars," he heard Wilson saying in his ear. "Get out. He's not going to stay there all day."

Macomber stepped out of the curved opening at the side of the front seat, onto the step and down onto the ground. The lion still stood looking majestically and cooly toward this object that his eyes only showed in silhouette, bulking like some super-rhino. There was no man smell carried toward him and he watched the object, moving his great head a little from side to side. Then watching the object, not afraid, but hesitating before going down the bank to drink with such a thing opposite him, he saw a man figure detach himself from it and he turned his heavy head and swung away toward the cover of the trees as he heard a cracking crash and felt the slam of a .30—06 220-grain solid bullet that bit his flank and ripped in sudden hot scalding nausea through his stomach. He trotted, heavy, big-footed, swinging wounded full-bellied, through the trees toward the tall grass and cover, and the crash came again to go past him ripping the air apart. Then it crashed again and he left the blow as it hit his lower ribs and ripped on through, blood sudden hot and frothy in his mouth, and he galloped toward the high grass where he could crouch and not be seen and make them bring the crashing thing close enough so he could make a rush and get the man that held it.

Macomber had not thought how the lion felt as he got out of the car. He only knew his hands were shaking and as he walked away from the car it was almost impossible for him to make his legs move. They were stiff in the thighs, but he could feel the muscles fluttering. He raised the rifle, sighted on the junction of the lion's head and shoulders and pulled the trigger. Nothing happened though he pulled until he thought his finger would break. Then he knew he had the safety on and as he lowered the rifle to move the safety over he moved another frozen pace forward, and the lion seeing his silhouette now clear of the silhouette of the car, turned and started off at a trot, and, as Macomber fired, he heard a whunk that meant that the bullet was home; but the lion kept on going. Macomber shot again and every one saw the bullet throw a spout of dirt beyond the trotting lion. He shot again, remembering to lower his aim, and they all heard the bullet hit, and the lion went into a gallop and was in the tall grass before he had the bolt pushed forward.

Macomber stood there feeling sick at his stomach, his hands that held the Springfield still cocked, shaking, and his wife and Robert Wilson were standing by him. Beside him too were the two gun-bearers chattering in Wakamba.

"I hit him," Macomber said. "I hit him twice."

"You gut-shot him and you hit him somewhere forward," Wilson said without enthusiasm. The gunbearers looked very grave. They were silent now.

"You may have killed him," Wilson went on. "We'll have to wait a while before we go in to find out."

"What do you mean?"

"Let him get sick before we follow him up."

"Oh," said Macomber.

"He's a hell of a fine lion," Wilson said cheerfully. "He's gotten into a bad place though."

"Why is it bad?"

"Can't see him until you're on him."

"Oh," said Macomber.

"Come on," said Wilson. "The Memsahib can stay here in the car. We'll go to have a look at the blood spoor."

"Stay here, Margot," Macomber said to his wife. His mouth was very dry and it was hard for him to talk.

"Why?" she asked.

"Wilson says to."

"We're going to have a look," Wilson said. "You stay here. You can see even better from here."

"All right."

Wilson spoke in Swahili to the driver. He nodded and said, "Yes, Bwana."

Then they went down the steep bank and across the stream, climbing over and around the boulders and up the other bank, pulling up by some projecting roots, and along it until they found where the lion had been trotting when Macomber first shot. There was dark blood on the short grass that the gun-bearers pointed out with grass stems, and that ran away behind the river bank trees.

"What do we do?" asked Macomber.

"Not much choice," said Wilson. "We can't bring the car over. Bank's too steep. We'll let him stiffen up a bit and then you and I'll go in and have a look for him."

"Can't we set the grass on fire?" Macomber asked.

"Too green."

"Can't we send beaters?"

Wilson looked at him appraisingly. "Of course we can," he said. "But it's just a touch murderous. You see we know the lion's wounded. You can drive an unwounded lion—he'll move on ahead of a noise—but a wounded lion's going to charge. You can't see him until you're right on him. He'll make himself perfectly flat in cover you wouldn't think would hide a hare. You can't very well send boys in there to that sort of a show. Somebody bound to get mauled."

"What about the gun-bearers?"

"Oh, they'll go with us. It's their *shauri*. You see, they signed on for it. They don't look too happy though, do they?"

"I don't want to go in there," said Macomber. It was out before he knew he'd said it.

"Neither do I," said Wilson very cheerily. "Really no choice though." Then, as an afterthought, he glanced at Macomber and saw suddenly how he was trembling and the pitiful look on his face.

"You don't have to go in, of course," he said. "That's what I'm hired for, you know. That's why I'm so expensive."

"You mean you'd go in by yourself? Why not leave him there?"

Robert Wilson, whose entire occupation had been with the lion and the problem he presented, and who had not been thinking about Macomber except to note that he was rather windy, suddenly felt as though he had opened the wrong door in a hotel and seen something shameful.

"What do you mean?"

"Why not just leave him?"

"You mean pretend to ourselves he hasn't been hit?"

"No. Just drop it."

"It isn't done."

"Why not?"

"For one thing, he's certain to be suffering. For another, some one else might run onto him."

"I see."

"But you don't have to have anything to do with it."

"I'd like to," Macomber said. "I'm just scared, you know."

"I'll go ahead when we go in," Wilson said, "with Kongoni tracking. You keep behind me and a little to one side. Chances are we'll hear him growl. If we see him we'll both shoot. Don't worry about anything. I'll keep you backed up. As a matter of fact, you know, perhaps you'd better not go. It might be much better. Why don't you go over and join the Memsahib while I just get it over with?"

"No, I want to go."

"All right," said Wilson. "But don't go in if you don't want to. This is my *shauri* now, you know."

"I want to go," said Macomber.

They sat under a tree and smoked.

"Want to go back and speak to the Memsahib while we're waiting?" Wilson asked.

"No."

"I'll just step back and tell her to be patient."

"Good," said Macomber. He sat there, sweating under his arms, his mouth dry, his stomach hollow feeling, wanting to find courage to tell Wilson to go on and finish off the lion without him. He could not know that Wilson was furious because he had not noticed the state he was in earlier and sent him back to his wife. While he sat there Wilson came up. "I have your big gun," he said. "Take it. We've given him time, I think. Come on."

Macomber took the big gun and Wilson said:

"Keep behind me and about five yards to the right and do exactly as I tell you." Then he spoke in Swahili to the two gun-bearers who looked the picture of gloom.

"Let's go," he said.

"Could I have a drink of water?" Macomber asked. Wilson spoke to the older gun-bearer, who wore a canteen on his belt, and the man unbuckled, unscrewed the top and handed it to Macomber, who took it noticing how heavy it seemed and how hairy and shoddy the felt covering was in his hand. He raised it to drink and looked ahead at the high grass with the flat-topped trees behind it. A breeze was blowing toward them and the grass rippled gently in the wind. He looked at the gun-bearer and he could see the gun-bearer was suffering too with fear.

Thirty-five yards into the grass the big lion lay flattened out along the ground. His ears were back and his only movement was a slight twitching up and down of his long, black-tufted tail. He had turned at bay as soon as he had reached this cover and he was sick with the wound through his full belly, and weakening with the wound through his lungs that brought a thin foamy red to his mouth each time he breathed. His flanks were wet and hot and flies were on the little openings the solid bullets had made in his tawny hide, and his big yellow eyes, narrowed with hate, looked straight ahead, only blinking when the pain came as he breathed, and his claws dug in the soft baked earth. All of him, pain, sickness, hatred and all of his remaining strength, was tightening into an absolute concentration for a rush. He could hear the men talking and he waited, gathering all of himself into this preparation for a charge as soon as the men would come into the grass. As he heard their voices his tail stiffened to twitch up and down, and, as they came into the edge of the grass, he made a coughing grunt and charged.

Kongoni, the old gun-bearer, in the lead watching the blood spoor, Wilson watching the grass for any movement, his big gun ready, the second gun-bearer looking ahead and listening, Macomber close to Wilson, his rifle cocked, they had just moved into the grass when Macomber heard the blood-choked coughing grunt, and saw the swishing rush in the grass. The next thing he knew was running; running wildly, in panic in the open, running toward the stream.

He heard the *ca-ra-wong!* of Wilson's big rifle, and again in a second a crashing *carawong!* and turning saw the lion, horrible-looking now, with half his head seeming to be gone, crawling toward Wilson in the edge of the tall grass while the red-faced man worked the bolt on the short ugly rifle and aimed carefully as another blasting *carawong!* came from the muzzle, and the crawling, heavy, yellow bulk of the lion stiffened and the huge, mutilated head slid forward and Macomber, standing by himself in the clearing where he had run, holding a loaded rifle, while two black men and a white man looked back at him in contempt, knew the lion was dead. He came toward Wilson, his tallness all seeming a naked reproach, and Wilson looked at him and said:

"Want to take pictures?"

"No," he said.

That was all any one had said until they reached the motor car. Then Wilson had said:

"Hell of a fine lion. Boys will skin him out. We might as well stay here in the shade."

Macomber's wife had not looked at him nor he at her and he had sat by her in the back seat with Wilson sitting in the front seat. Once he had reached over and taken his wife's hand without looking at her and she had removed her hand from his. Looking across the stream to where the gun-bearers were skinning out the lion he could see that she had been able to see the whole thing. While they sat there his wife had reached forward and put her hand on Wilson's shoulder. He turned and she had leaned forward over the low seat and kissed him on the mouth.

"Oh, I say," said Wilson, going redder than his natural baked color.

"Mr. Robert Wilson," she said. "The beautiful red-faced Mr. Robert Wilson."

Then she sat down beside Macomber again and looked away across the stream to where the lion lay, with uplifted, white-muscled, tendon-marked naked forearms, and white bloating belly, as the black men fleshed away the skin. Finally the gun-bearers brought the skin over, wet and heavy, and climbed in behind with it, rolling it up before they got in, and the motor car started. No one had said anything more until they were back in camp.

That was the story of the lion. Macomber did not know how the lion had felt before he started his rush, nor during it when the unbelievable smash of the .505 with a muzzle velocity of two tons had hit him in the mouth, nor what kept him coming after that, when the second ripping crash had smashed his hind quarters and he had come crawling on toward the crashing, blasting thing that had destroyed him. Wilson knew something about it and only expressed it by saying, "Damned fine lion," but Macomber did not know how Wilson felt about things either. He did not know how his wife felt except that she was through with him.

His wife had been through with him before but it never lasted. He was very wealthy, and would be much wealthier, and he knew she would not leave him ever now. That was one of the few things that he really knew. He knew about that, about motor cycles—that was earliest—about motor cars, about duck-shooting, about fishing, trout, salmon and big-sea, about sex in books, many books, too many books, about all court games, about dogs, not much about horses, about hanging on to his money, about most of the other things his world dealt in, and about his wife not leaving him. His wife had been a great beauty and she was still a great beauty in Africa, but she was not a great enough beauty any more at home to be able to leave him and better herself and she knew it and he knew it. She had missed the chance to leave him and he knew it. If he had been better with women she would probably have started to worry about him getting another new, beautiful wife; but she knew too much about him to worry about him either. Also, he had always had a great tolerance which seemed the nicest thing about him if it were not the most sinister.

All in all they were known as a comparatively happily married couple, one of those whose disruption is often rumored but never occurs, and as the society columnist put it, they were adding more than a spice of *adventure* to their much envied and ever-enduring *Romance* by a *Safari* in what was known as *Darkest Africa* until the Martin Johnsons lighted it on so many silver screens where they were pursuing *Old Simba* the lion, the buffalo, *Tembo* and the elephant and as well collecting specimens for the Museum of Natural History. This same columnist had reported them *on the verge* at least three times in the past and they had been. But they always made it up. They had a sound basis of union. Margot was too beautiful for Macomber to divorce her and Macomber had too much money for Margot ever to leave him.

It was now about three o'clock in the morning and Francis Macomber, who had been asleep a little while after he had stopped thinking about the lion, wakened and then slept again, woke suddenly, frightened in a dream of the bloody-headed lion standing over him, and listening while his heart pounded, he realized that his wife was not in the other cot in the tent. He lay awake with that knowledge for two hours.

At the end of that time his wife came into the tent, lifted her mosquito bar and crawled cozily into bed.

"Where have you been?" Macomber asked in the darkness.

"Hello," she said. "Are you awake?"

"Where have you been?"

"I just went out to get a breath of air."

"You did, like hell."

"What do you want me to say, darling?"

"Where have you been?"

"Out to get a breath of air."

"That's a new name for it. You *are* a bitch."

"Well, you're a coward."

"All right," he said. "What of it?"

"Nothing as far as I'm concerned. But please let's not talk, darling, because I'm very sleepy."

"You think that I'll take anything."

"I know you will, sweet."

"Well, I won't."

"Please, darling, let's not talk. I'm so very sleepy."

"There wasn't going to be any of that. You promised there wouldn't be."

"Well, there is now," she said sweetly.

"You said if we made this trip that there would be none of that. You promised."

"Yes, darling. That's the way I meant it to be. But the trip was spoiled yesterday. We don't have to talk about it, do we?"

"You don't wait long when you have an **advanta**ge, do you?"

"Please let's not talk. I'm so **sleepy**, darling."

"I'm going to talk."

"Don't mind me then, because I'm going to sleep." And she did.

At breakfast they were all three at the table before daylight and Francis Macomber found that, of all the many men that he had hated, he hated Robert Wilson the most.

"Sleep well?" Wilson asked in his throaty voice, filling a pipe.

"Did you?"

"Topping," the white hunter told him.

You bastard, thought Macomber, you insolent bastard.

So she woke him when she came in, Wilson thought, looking at them both with his flat, cold eyes. Well, why doesn't he keep his wife where she belongs? What does he think I am, a bloody plaster saint? Let him keep her where she belongs. It's his own fault.

"Do you think we'll find buffalo?" Margot asked, pushing away a dish of apricots.

"Chance of it," Wilson said and smiled at her. "Why don't you stay in camp?"

"Not for anything," she told him.

"Why not order her to stay in camp?" Wilson said to Macomber.

"You order her," said Macomber coldly.

"Let's not have any ordering, nor," turning to Macomber, "any silliness, Francis," Margot said quite pleasantly.

"Are you ready to start?" Macomber asked.

"Any time," Wilson told him. "Do you want the Memsahib to go?"

"Does it make any difference whether I do or not?"

The hell with it, thought Robert Wilson. The utter complete hell with it. So this is what it's going to be like. Well, this is what it's going to be like, then.

"Makes no difference," he said.

"You sure you wouldn't like to stay in camp with her yourself and let me go out and hunt the buffalo?" Macomber asked.

"Can't do that," said Wilson. "Wouldn't talk rot if I were you."

"I'm not talking rot. I'm disgusted."

"Bad word, disgusted."

"Francis, will you please try to speak sensibly?" his wife said.

"I speak too damned sensibly," Macomber said. "Did you ever eat such filthy food?"

"Something wrong with the food?" asked Wilson quietly.

"No more than with everything else."

"I'd pull yourself together, laddybuck," Wilson said very quietly. "There's a boy waits at table that understands a little English."

"The hell with him."

Wilson stood up and puffing on his pipe strolled away, speaking a few words in Swahili to one of the gun-bearers who was standing waiting for him. Macomber and his wife sat on at the table. He was staring at his coffee cup.

"If you make a scene I'll leave you, darling," Margot said quietly.

"No, you won't."

"You can try it and see."

"You won't leave me."

"No," she said. "I won't leave you and you'll behave yourself."

"Behave myself? That's a way to talk. Behave myself."

"Yes. Behave yourself."

"Why don't *you* try behaving?"

"I've tried it so long. So very long."

"I hate that red-faced swine," Macomber said. "I loathe the sight of him."

"He's really *very* nice."

"Oh, *shut* up," Macomber almost shouted. Just then the car came up and stopped in front of the dining tent and the driver and the two gun-bearers got out. Wilson walked over and looked at the husband and wife sitting there at the table.

"Going shooting?" he asked.

"Yes," said Macomber, standing up. "Yes."

"Better bring a woolly. It will be cool in the car," Wilson said.

"I'll get my leather jacket," Margot said.

"The boy has it," Wilson told her. He climbed into the front with the driver and Francis Macomber and his wife sat, not speaking, in the back seat.

Hope the silly beggar doesn't take a notion to blow the back of my head off, Wilson thought to himself. Women *are* a nuisance on safari.

The car was grinding down to cross the river at a pebbly ford in the gray daylight and then climbed, angling up the steep bank, where Wilson had ordered a way shovelled out the day before so they could reach the parklike wooded rolling country on the far side.

It was a good morning, Wilson thought. There was a heavy dew and as the wheels went through the grass and low bushes he could smell the odor of the crushed fronds. It was an odor like verbena and he liked this early morning smell of the dew, the crushed bracken and the look of the tree trunks showing black through the early morning mist, as the car made its way through the untracked, parklike country. He had put the two in the back seat out of his mind now and was thinking about buffalo. The buffalo that he was after stayed in the daytime in a thick swamp where it was impossible to get a shot, but in the night they fed out into an open stretch of country and if he could come between them and their swamp with the car, Macomber would have a good chance at them in the open. He did not want to hunt buff with Macomber in thick cover. He did not want to hunt buff or anything else with Macomber at all, but he was a professional hunter and he had hunted with some rare ones in his time. If they got buff today there would only be rhino to come and the poor man would have gone through his dangerous game and things might pick up. He'd have nothing more to do with the woman and Macomber would get over that too. He must have gone through plenty of that before by the look of things. Poor beggar. He must have a way of getting over it. Well, it was the poor sod's own bloody fault.

He, Robert Wilson, carried a double size cot on safari to accommodate any windfalls he might receive. He had hunted for a certain clientele, the international, fast, sporting set, where the women did not feel they were getting their money's worth unless they had shared that cot with the white hunter. He despised them when he was away from them although he liked some of them well enough at the time, but he made his living by them; and their standards were his standards as long as they were hiring him.

They were his standards in all except the shooting. He had his own standards about the killing and they could live up to them or get some one else to hunt them. He knew, too, that they all respected him for this. This Macomber was an odd one though. Damned if he wasn't. Now the wife. Well, the wife. Yes, the wife. Hm, the wife. Well he'd dropped all that. He looked around at them. Macomber sat grim and furious. Margot smiled at him. She looked younger today, more innocent and fresher and not so professionally beautiful. What's in her heart God knows, Wilson thought. She hadn't talked much last night. At that it was a pleasure to see her.

The motor car climbed up a slight rise and went on through the trees and then out into a grassy prairie-like opening and kept in the shelter of the trees along the edge, the driver going slowly and Wilson looking carefully out across the prairie and all along its far side. He stopped the car and studied the opening with his field glasses. Then he motioned to the driver to go on and the car moved slowly along, the driver avoiding wart-hog holes and driving around the mud castles ants had built. Then, looking across the opening, Wilson suddenly turned and said,

"By God, there they are!"

And looking where he pointed, while the car

jumped forward and Wilson spoke in rapid Swahili to the driver, Macomber saw three huge, black animals looking almost cylindrical in their long heaviness, like big black tank cars, moving at a gallop across the far edge of the open prairie. They moved at a stiff-necked, stiff-bodied gallop and he could see the up-swept wide black horns on their heads as they galloped heads out; the heads not moving.

"They're three old bulls," Wilson said. "We'll cut them off before they get to the swamp."

The car was going a wild forty-five miles an hour across the open and as Macomber watched, the buffalo got bigger and bigger until he could see the gray, hairless, scabby look of one huge bull and how his neck was a part of his shoulders and the shiny black of his horns as he galloped a little behind the others that were strung out in that steady plunging gait; and then, the car swaying as though it had just jumped a road, they drew up close and he could see the plunging hugeness of the bull, and the dust in his sparsely haired hide, the wide boss of horn and his out-stretched, wide-nostrilled muzzle, and he was raising his rifle when Wilson shouted, "Not from the car, you fool!" and he had no fear, only hatred of Wilson, while the brakes clamped on and the car skidded, plowing sideways to an almost stop and Wilson was out on one side and he on the other, stumbling as his feet hit the still speeding-by of the earth, and then he was shooting at the bull as he moved away, hearing the bullets whunk into him, emptying his rifle at him as he moved steadily away, finally remembering to get his shots forward into the shoulder, and as he fumbled to re-load, he saw the bull was down. Down on his knees, his big head tossing, and seeing the other two still galloping he shot at the leader and hit him. He shot again and missed and he heard the *carawonging* roar as Wilson shot and saw the leading bull slide forward onto his nose.

"Get that other," Wilson said. "Now you're shooting!"

But the other bull was moving steadily at the same gallop and he missed, throwing a spout of dirt, and Wilson missed and the dust rose in a cloud and Wilson shouted, "Come on. He's too far!" and grabbed his arm and they were in the car again, Macomber and Wilson hanging on the sides and rocketing swayingly over the uneven ground, drawing up on the steady, plunging, heavy-necked, straight-moving gallop of the bull.

They were behind him and Macomber was filling his rifle, dropping shells onto the ground, jamming it, clearing the jam, then they were almost up with the bull when Wilson yelled "Stop," and the car skidded so that it almost swung over and Macomber fell forward onto his feet, slammed his bolt forward and fired as far forward as he could aim into the galloping, rounded black back, aimed and shot again, then again, then again, and the bullets, all of them hitting, had no effect on the buffalo that he could see. Then Wilson shot, the roar deafening him, and he could see the bull stagger. Macomber shot again, aiming carefully, and down he came, onto his knees.

"All right," Wilson said. "Nice work. That's three."

Macomber felt a drunken elation.

"How many times did you shoot?" he asked.

"Just three," Wilson said. "You killed the first bull. The biggest one. I helped you finish the other two. Afraid they might have got into cover. You had them killed. I was just mopping up a little. You shot damn well."

"Let's go to the car," said Macomber. "I want a drink."

"Got to finish off that buff first," Wilson told him. The buffalo was on his knees and he jerked his head furiously and bellowed in pig-eyed, roaring rage as they came toward him.

"Watch he doesn't get up," Wilson said. Then, "Get a little broadside and take him in the neck just behind the ear."

Macomber aimed carefully at the center of the huge, jerking, rage-driven neck and shot. At the shot the head dropped forward.

"That does it," said Wilson. "Got the spine. They're a hell of a looking thing, aren't they?"

"Let's get the drink," said Macomber. In his life he had never felt so good.

In the car Macomber's wife sat very white faced. "You were marvellous, darling," she said to Macomber. "What a ride."

"Was it rough?" Wilson asked.

"It was frightful. I've never been more frightened in my life."

"Let's all have a drink," Macomber said.

"By all means," said Wilson. "Give it to the Memsahib." She drank the neat whisky from the flask and shuddered a little when she swallowed. She handed the flask to Macomber who handed it to Wilson.

"It was frightfully exciting," she said. "It's given me a dreadful headache. I didn't know you were allowed to shoot them from cars though."

"No one shot from cars," said Wilson coldly.

"I mean chase them from cars."

"Wouldn't ordinarily," Wilson said. "Seemed sporting enough to me though while we were doing it. Taking more chance driving that way across the plain full of holes and one thing and another than hunting on foot. Buffalo could have charged us each time we shot if he liked. Gave him every chance. Wouldn't mention it to any one though. It's illegal if that's what you mean."

"It seemed very unfair to me," Margot said, "chasing those big helpless things in a motor car."

"Did it?" said Wilson.

"What would happen if they heard about it in Nairobi?"

"I'd lose my licence for one thing. Other unpleasantnesses," Wilson said, taking a drink from the flask. "I'd be out of business."

"Really?"

"Yes, really."

"Well," said Macomber, and he smiled for the first time all day. "Now she has something on you."

"You have such a pretty way of putting things, Francis," Margot Macomber said. Wilson looked at them both. If a four-letter man marries a five-letter woman, he was thinking, what number of letters would their children be? What he said was, "We lost a gun-bearer. Did you notice it?"

"My God, no," Macomber said.

"Here he comes," Wilson said. "He's all right. He must have fallen off when we left the first bull."

Approaching them was the middle-aged gun-bearer, limping along in his knitted cap, khaki tunic, shorts and rubber sandals, gloomy-faced and disgusted looking. As he came up he called out to Wilson in Swahili and they all saw the change in the white hunter's face.

"What does he say?" asked Margot.

"He says the first bull got up and went into the bush," Wilson said with no expression in his voice.

"Oh," said Macomber blankly.

"Then it's going to be just like the lion," said Margot, full of anticipation.

"It's not going to be a damned bit like the lion," Wilson told her. "Did you want another drink, Macomber?"

"Thanks, yes," Macomber said. He expected the feeling he had had about the lion to come back but it did not. For the first time in his life he really felt wholly without fear. Instead of fear he had a feeling of definite elation.

"We'll go and have a look at the second bull," Wilson said. "I'll tell the driver to put the car in the shade."

"What are you going to do?" asked Margaret Macomber.

"Take a look at the buff," Wilson said.

"I'll come."

"Come along."

The three of them walked over to where the second buffalo bulked blackly in the open, head forward on the grass, the massive horns swung wide.

"He's a very good head," Wilson said. "That's close to a fifty-inch spread."

Macomber was looking at him with delight.

"He's hateful looking," said Margot. "Can't we go into the shade?"

"Of course," Wilson said. "Look," he said to Macomber, and pointed. "See that patch of bush?"

"Yes."

"That's where the first bull went in. The gun-bearer said when he fell off the bull was down. He was watching us helling along and the other two buff galloping. When he looked up there was the bull up and looking at him. Gun-bearer ran like hell and the bull went off slowly into that bush."

"Can we go in after him now?" asked Macomber eagerly.

Wilson looked at him appraisingly. Damned if this isn't a strange one, he thought. Yesterday he's scared sick and today he's a ruddy fire eater.

"No, we'll give him a while."

"Let's please go into the shade," Margot said. Her face was white and she looked ill.

They made their way to the car where it stood under a single, wide-spreading tree and all climbed in.

"Chances are he's dead in there," Wilson remarked. "After a little we'll have a look."

Macomber felt a wild unreasonable happiness that he had never known before.

"By God, that was a chase," he said. "I've never felt any such feeling. Wasn't it marvellous, Margot?"

"I hated it."

"Why?"

"I hated it," she said bitterly. "I loathed it."

"You know I don't think I'd be afraid of anything again," Macomber said to Wilson. "Something happened in me after we first saw the buff and started after him. Like a dam bursting. It was pure excitement."

"Cleans out your liver," said Wilson. "Damn funny things happen to people."

Macomber's face was shining. "You know something did happen to me," he said. "I feel absolutely different."

His wife said nothing and eyed him strangely. She was sitting far back in the seat and Macomber was sitting forward talking to Wilson who turned sideways talking over the back of the front seat.

"You know, I'd like to try another lion," Macomber said. "I'm really not afraid of them now. After all, what can they do to you?"

"That's it," said Wilson. "Worst one can do is kill you. How does it go? Shakespeare. Damned good. See if I can remember. Oh, damned good. Used to quote it to myself at one time. Let's see. 'By my troth, I care not; a man can die but once; we owe God a death and let it go which way it will, he that dies this year is quit for the next.' Damned fine, eh?"

He was very embarrased, having brought out this thing he had lived by, but he had seen men come of age before and it always moved him. It was not a matter of their twenty-first birthday.

It had taken a strange chance of hunting, a sudden precipitation into action without opportunity for worrying beforehand, to bring this about with Macomber, but regardless of how it had happened it had most certainly happened. Look at the beggar now, Wilson thought. It's that some of them stay little boys so long, Wilson thought. Sometimes all their lives. Their figures stay boyish when they're fifty. The great American boy-men. Damned strange people. But he liked this Macomber now. Damned strange fellow. Probably meant the end of cuckoldry too. Well, that would be a damned good thing. Damned good thing. Beggar had probably been afraid all his life. Don't know what started it. But over now. Hadn't had time to be afraid with the buff. That and being angry too. Motor car too. Motor cars made it familiar. Be a damn fire eater now. He'd seen it in the war work the same way. More of a change than any loss of virginity. Fear gone like an operation. Something else grew in its place. Main thing a man had. Made him into a man. Women knew it too. No bloody fear.

From the far corner of the seat Margaret Macomber looked at the two of them. There was no change in Wilson. She saw Wilson as she had seen him the day before when she had first realized what his great talent was. But she saw the change in Francis Macomber now.

"Do you have that feeling of happiness about what's going to happen?" Macomber asked, still exploring his new wealth.

"You're not supposed to mention it," Wilson said, looking in the other's face. "Much more fashionable to say you're scared. Mind you, you'll be scared too, plenty of times."

"But you *have* a feeling of happiness about action to come?"

"Yes," said Wilson. "There's that. Doesn't do to talk too much about all this. Talk the whole thing away. No pleasure in anything if you mouth it up too much."

"You're both talking rot," said Margot. "Just because you've chased some helpless animals in a motor car you talk like heroes."

"Sorry," said Wilson. "I have been gassing too much." She's worried about it already, he thought.

"If you don't know what we're talking about why not keep out of it?" Macomber asked his wife.

"You've gotten awfully brave, awfully suddenly,"

his wife said contemptuously, but her contempt was not secure. She was very afraid of something.

Macomber laughed, a very natural hearty laugh. "You know I *have*," he said. "I really have."

"Isn't it sort of late?" Margot said bitterly. Because she had done the best she could for many years back and the way they were together now was no one person's fault.

"Not for me," said Macomber.

Margot said nothing but sat back in the corner of the seat."

"Do you think we've given him time enough?" Macomber asked Wilson cheerfully.

"We might have a look," Wilson said. "Have you any solids left?"

"The gun-bearer has some."

Wilson called in Swahili and the older gun-bearer, who was skinning out one of the heads, straightened up, pulled a box of solids out of his pocket and brought them over to Macomber, who filled his magazine and put the remaining shells in his pocket.

"You might as well shoot the Springfield," Wilson said. "You're used to it. We'll leave the Mannlicher in the car with the Memsahib. Your gun-bearer can carry your heavy gun. I've this damned cannon. Now let me tell you about them." He had saved this until the last because he did not want to worry Macomber. "When a buff comes he comes with his head high and thrust straight out. The boss of the horns covers any sort of a brain shot. The only shot is straight into the nose. The only other shot is into his chest or, if you're to one side, into the neck or the shoulders. After they've been hit once they take a hell of a lot of killing. Don't try anything fancy. Take the easiest shot there is. They've finished skinning out that head now. Should we get started?"

He called to the gun-bearers, who came up wiping their hands, and the older one got into the back.

"I'll only take Kongoni," Wilson said. "The other can watch to keep the birds away."

As the car moved slowly across the open space toward the island of brushy trees that ran in a tongue of foliage along a dry water course that cut the open swale, Macomber felt his heart pounding and his mouth was dry again, but it was excitement, not fear.

"Here's where he went in," Wilson said. Then to the gun-bearer in Swahili, "Take the blood spoor."

The car was parallel to the patch of bush. Macomber, Wilson and the gun-bearer got down. Macomber, looking back, saw his wife, with the rifle by her side, looking at him. He waved to her and she did not wave back.

The brush was very thick ahead and the ground was dry. The middle-aged gun-bearer was sweating heavily and Wilson had his hat down over his eyes and his red neck showed just ahead of Macomber. Suddenly the gun-bearer said something in Swahili to Wilson and ran forward.

"He's dead in there," Wilson said. "Good work," and he turned to grip Macomber's hand and as they shook hands, grinning at each other, the gun-bearer shouted wildly and they saw him coming out of the bush sideways, fast as a crab, and the bull coming, nose out, mouth tight closed, blood dripping, massive head straight out, coming in a charge, his little pig eyes bloodshot as he looked at them. Wilson, who was ahead, was kneeling shooting, and Macomber, as he fired, unhearing his shot in the roaring of Wilson's gun, saw fragments like slate burst from the huge boss of the horns, and the head jerked, he shot again at the wide nostrils and saw the horns jolt again and fragments fly, and he did not see Wilson now and, aiming carefully, shot again with the buffalo's huge bulk almost on him and his rifle almost level with the oncoming head, nose out, and he could see the little wicked eyes and the head started to lower and he felt a sudden white-hot, blinding flash explode inside his head and that was all he ever felt.

Wilson had ducked to one side to get in a shoulder shot. Macomber had stood solid and shot for the nose, shooting a touch high each time and hitting the heavy horns, splintering and chipping them like hitting a slate roof, and Mrs. Macomber, in the car, had shot at the buffalo with the 6.5 Mannlicher as it seemed about to gore Macomber and had hit her husband about two inches up and a little to one side of the base of his skull.

Francis Macomber lay now, face down, not two yards from where the buffalo lay on his side and his wife knelt over him with Wilson beside her.

"I wouldn't turn him over," Wilson said.

The woman was crying hysterically.

"I'd get back in the car," Wilson said. "Where's the rifle?"

She shook her head, her face contorted. The gun-bearer picked up the rifle.

"Leave it as it is," said Wilson. Then, "Go get Abdulla so that he may witness the manner of the accident."

He knelt down, took a handkerchief from his pocket, and spread it over Francis Macomber's crew-cropped head where it lay. The blood sank into the dry, loose earth.

Wilson stood up and saw the buffalo on his side, his legs out, his thinly-haired belly crawling with ticks. "Hell of a good bull," his brain registered automatically. "A good fifty inches, or better. Better." He called to the driver and told him to spread a blanket over the body and stay by it. Then he walked over to the motor car where the woman sat crying in the corner.

"That was a pretty thing to do," he said in a toneless voice. "He *would* have left you too."

"Stop it," she said.

"Of course it's an accident," he said. "I know that."

"Stop it," she said.

"Don't worry," he said. "There will be a certain amount of unpleasantness but I will have some photographs taken that will be very useful at the inquest. There's the testimony of the gun-bearers and the driver too. You're perfectly all right."

"Stop it," she said.

"There's a hell of a lot to be done," he said. "And I'll have to send a truck off to the lake to wireless for a plane to take the three of us into Nairobi. Why didn't you poison him? That's what they do in England."

"Stop it. Stop it. Stop it," the woman cried.

Wilson looked at her with his flat blue eyes.

"I'm through now," he said. "I was a little angry. I'd begun to like your husband."

"Oh, please stop it," she said. "Please, please stop it."

"That's better," Wilson said. "Please is much better. Now I'll stop."

THE BEAR

WILLIAM FAULKNER

WILLIAM FAULKNER (1897–1962) was born in New Albany, Mississippi. The novelist lived most of his life in Oxford, Mississippi, the center of the region which he has immortalized in his imaginative saga of Yoknapatawpha County, whose decadent gentlemen and "poor whites" are the subject of almost all of his fiction. His books include *The Sound and the Fury* (1929), *Sanctuary* (1931), *Light in August* (1932), *Absalom, Absalom!* (1936), *Go Down, Moses* (1942), and *Requiem for a Nun* (1951). *A Fable* (1954) and *The Reivers* (1962) were both awarded Pulitzer Prizes. In 1949 Faulkner was awarded the Nobel Prize for Literature.

HE was ten. But it had already begun, long before that day when at last he wrote his age in two figures and he saw for the first time the camp where his father and Major de Spain and old General Compson and the others spent two weeks each November and two weeks again each June. He had already inherited then, without ever having seen it, the tremendous bear with one trap-ruined foot which, in an area almost a hundred miles deep, had earned itself a name, a definite designation like a living man.

He had listened to it for years: the long legend of corncribs rifled, of shotes and grown pigs and even calves carried bodily into the woods and devoured, of traps and deadfalls overthrown and dogs mangled and slain, and shotgun and even rifle charges delivered at point-blank range and with no more effect than so many peas blown through a tube by a boy—a corridor of wreckage and destruction beginning back before he was born, through which sped, not fast but rather with the ruthless and irresistible deliberation of a locomotive, the shaggy tremendous shape.

It ran in his knowledge before he ever saw it. It looked and towered in his dreams before he even saw the unaxed woods where it left its crooked print, shaggy, huge, red-eyed, not malevolent but just big—too big for the dogs which tried to bay it, for the horses which tried to ride it down, for the men and the bullets they fired into it, too big for the very country which was its constricting scope. He seemed to see it entire with a child's complete divination before he ever laid eyes on either—the doomed wilderness whose edges were being constantly and punily

gnawed at by men with axes and plows who feared it because it was wilderness, men myriad and nameless even to one another in the land where the old bear had earned a name, through which ran not even a mortal animal but an anachronism, indomitable and invincible, out of an old dead time, a phantom, epitome and apotheosis of the old wild life at which the puny humans swarmed and hacked in a fury of abhorrence and fear, like pygmies about the ankles of a drowsing elephant: the old bear solitary, indomitable and alone, widowered, childless, and absolved of mortality—old Priam reft of his old wife and having outlived all his sons.

Until he was ten, each November he would watch the wagon containing the dogs and the bedding and food and guns and his father and Tennie's Jim, the Negro, and Sam Fathers, the Indian, son of a slave woman and a Chickasaw chief, depart on the road to town, to Jefferson, where Major de Spain and the others would join them. To the boy, at seven, eight, and nine, they were not going into the Big Bottom to hunt bear and deer, but to keep yearly rendezvous with the bear which they did not even intend to kill. Two weeks later they would return, with no trophy, no head and skin. He had not expected it. He had not even been afraid it would be in the wagon. He believed that even after he was ten and his father would let him go too, for those two weeks in November, he would merely make another one, along with his father and Major de Spain and General Compson and the others, the dogs which feared to bay at it and the rifles and shotguns which failed even to bleed it, in the yearly pageant of the old bear's furious immortality.

Then he heard the dogs. It was in the second week of his first time in the camp. He stood with Sam Fathers against a big oak beside the faint crossing where they had stood each dawn for nine days now, hearing the dogs. He had heard them once before, one morning last week—a murmur, sourceless, echoing through the wet woods, swelling presently into separate voices which he could recognize and call by name. He had raised and cocked the gun as Sam told him and stood motionless again while the uproar, the invisible course, swept up and past and faded; it seemed to him that he could actually see the deer, the buck, blond, smoke-colored, elongated with speed, fleeing, vanishing, the woods, the gray solitude, still ringing even when the cries of the dogs had died away.

"Now let the hammers down," Sam said.

"You knew they were not coming here too," he said.

"Yes," Sam said. "I want you to learn how to do when you didn't shoot. It's after the chance for the bear or the deer has done already come and gone that men and dogs get killed."

"Anyway," he said, "it was just a deer."

Then on the tenth morning he heard the dogs again. And he readied the too-long, too-heavy gun as Sam had taught him, before Sam even spoke. But this time it was no deer, no ringing chorus of dogs running strong on a free scent, but a moiling yapping an octave too high, with something more than indecision and even abjectness in it, not even moving very fast, taking a long time to pass completely out of hearing, leaving then somewhere in the air that echo, thin, slightly hysterical, abject, almost grieving, with no sense of a fleeing, unseen, smoke-colored, grass-eating shape ahead of it, and Sam, who had taught him first of all to cock the gun and take position where he could see everywhere and then never move again, had himself moved up beside him; he could hear Sam breathing at his shoulder, and he could see the arched curve of the old man's inhaling nostrils.

"Hah," Sam said. "Not even running. Walking."

"Old Ben!" the boy said. "But up here!" he cried. "Way up here!"

"He do it every year," Sam said. "Once. Maybe to see who in camp this time, if he can shoot or not. Whether we got the dog yet that can bay and hold him. He'll take them to the river, then he'll send them back home. We may as well go back too; see how they look when they come back to camp."

When they reached the camp the hounds were already there, ten of them crouching back under the kitchen, the boy and Sam squatting to peer back into the obscurity where they had huddled, quiet, the eyes luminous, glowing at them and vanishing, and no sound, only that effluvium of something more than dog, stronger than dog and not just animal, just beast, because still there had been nothing in front of that abject and almost painful yapping save the solitude, the wilderness, so that when the eleventh hound came in at noon and with all the others watching—even old Uncle Ash, who called himself first a cook—Sam daubed the tattered ear and the raked shoulder with turpentine and axle grease, to the boy it was still no living creature, but the wilderness which, leaning for the moment down, had patted lightly once the hound's temerity.

"Just like a man," Sam said. "Just like folks. Put off as long as she could having to be brave, knowing all the time that sooner or later she would have to be brave to keep on living with herself, and knowing all the time beforehand what was going to happen to her when she done it."

That afternoon, himself on the one-eyed wagon mule which did not mind the smell of blood nor, as they told him, of bear, and with Sam on the other one, they rode for more than three hours through the rapid, shortening winter day. They followed no path, no trail even that he could see; almost at once they were in a country which he had never seen before. Then he knew why Sam had made him ride the mule which would not spook. The sound one stopped short and tried to whirl and bolt even as Sam got down, blowing its breath, jerking and wrenching at the rein, while Sam held it, coaxing it forward with his voice, since he could not risk tying it, drawing it forward while the boy got down from the marred one.

Then, standing beside Sam in the gloom of the dying afternoon, he looked down at the rotted overturned log, gutted and scored with claw marks and, in the wet earth beside it, the print of the enormous warped two-toed foot. He knew now what he had smelled when he peered under the kitchen where the dogs huddled. He realized for the first time that the bear which had run in his listening and loomed in his dreams since before he could remember to the contrary, and which, therefore, must have existed in the listening and dreams of his father and Major de Spain and even old General Compson, too, before they began to remember in their turn, was a mortal animal, and that if they had departed for the camp each November without any actual hope of bringing its trophy back, it was not because it could not be slain, but because so far they had had no actual hope to.

"Tomorrow," he said.

"We'll try tomorrow," Sam said. "We ain't got the dog yet."

"We've got eleven. They ran him this morning."

"It won't need but one," Sam said. "He ain't here. Maybe he ain't nowhere. The only other way will be for him to run by accident over somebody that has a gun."

"That wouldn't be me," the boy said. "It will be Walter or Major or—"

"It might," Sam said. "You watch close in the morning. Because he's smart. That's how come he has lived this long. If he gets hemmed up and has to pick out somebody to run over, he will pick out you."

"How?" the boy said. "How will he know—" He ceased. "You mean he already knows me, that I ain't never been here before, ain't had time to find out yet whether I—" He ceased again, looking at Sam, the old man whose face revealed nothing until it smiled. He said humbly, not even amazed, "It was me he was watching. I don't reckon he did need to come but once."

The next morning they left the camp three hours before daylight. They rode this time because it was too far to walk, even the dogs in the wagon; again the first gray light found him in a place which he had never seen before, where Sam had placed him and told him to stay and then departed. With the gun which was too big for him, which did not even belong to him, but to Major de Spain, and which he had fired only once—at a stump on the first day, to learn the recoil and how to reload it—he stood against a gum tree beside a little bayou whose black still water crept without movement out of a canebrake and crossed a small clearing and into cane again, where, invisible, a bird—the big woodpecker called Lord-to-God by Negroes—clattered at a dead limb.

It was a stand like any other, dissimilar only in incidentals to the one where he had stood each morning for ten days; a territory new to him, yet no less familiar than that other one which, after almost two weeks, he had come to believe he knew a little—the same solitude, the same loneliness through which human beings had merely passed without altering it, leaving no mark, no scar, which looked exactly as it must have looked when the first ancestor of Sam Fathers' Chickasaw predecessors crept into it and looked about, club or stone ax or bone arrow drawn and poised; different only because, squatting at the edge of the kitchen, he smelled the hounds huddled and cringing beneath it and saw the raked ear and shoulder of the one who, Sam said, had had to be brave once in order to live with herself, and saw yesterday in the earth beside the gutted log the print of the living foot.

He heard no dogs at all. He never did hear them. He only heard the drumming of the woodpecker stop short off and knew that the bear was looking at him. He never saw it. He did not know whether it was in front of him or behind him. He did not move, holding the useless gun, which he had not even had warning to cock and which even now he did not cock, tasting in his saliva that taint as of brass which he knew now because he had smelled it when he peered under the kitchen at the huddled dogs.

Then it was gone. As abruptly as it had ceased, the woodpecker's dry, monotonous clatter set up again, and after a while he even believed he could hear the dogs—a murmur, scarce a sound even, which he had probably been hearing for some time before he even remarked it, drifting into hearing and then out again, dying away. They came nowhere near him. If it was a bear they ran, it was another bear. It was Sam himself who came out of the cane and crossed the bayou, followed by the injured bitch of yesterday. She was almost at heel, like a bird dog, making no sound. She came and crouched against his leg, trembling, staring off into the cane.

"I didn't see him," he said. "I didn't, Sam!"

"I know it," Sam said. "He done the looking. You didn't hear him neither, did you?"

"No," the boy said. "I—"

"He's smart," Sam said. "Too smart." He looked down at the hound, trembling faintly and steadily against the boy's knee. From the raked shoulder a few drops of fresh blood oozed and clung. "Too big. We ain't got the dog yet. But maybe someday. Maybe not next time. But someday."

So I must see him, he thought. *I must look at him.* Otherwise, it seemed to him that it would go on like this forever, as it had gone on with his father and Major de Spain, who was older than his father, and even with old General Compson, who had been old enough to be a brigade commander in 1865. Otherwise, it would go on so forever, next time and next time, after and after and after. It seemed to him that he could never see the two of them, himself and the bear, shadowy in the limbo from which time emerged, becoming time; the old bear absolved of mortality and himself partaking, sharing a little of it, enough of it. And he knew now what he had smelled in the huddled dogs and tasted in his saliva. He recognized fear. *So I will have to see him,* he thought, without dread or even hope. *I will have to look at him.*

It was in June of the next year. He was eleven. They were in camp again, celebrating Major de Spain's and General Compson's birthdays. Although the one had been born in September and the other in the depth of winter and in another decade, they had met for two weeks to fish and shoot squirrels and turkey and run coons and wildcats with the dogs at night. That is, he and Boon Hoggenback and the Negroes fished and shot squirrels and ran the coons and cats, because the proved hunters, not only Major de Spain and old General Compson, who spent those two weeks sitting in a rocking chair before a tremendous iron pot of Brunswick stew, stirring and tasting, with old Ash to quarrel with about how he was making it and Tennie's Jim to pour whiskey from the demijohn into the tin dipper from which he drank it, but even the boy's father and Walter Ewell, who were still young enough, scorned such, other than shooting the wild gobblers with pistols for wagers on their marksmanship.

Or, that is, his father and the others believed he was hunting squirrels. Until the third day, he thought that Sam Fathers believed that too. Each morning he would leave the camp right after breakfast. He had his own gun now, a Christmas present. He went back to the tree beside the bayou where he had stood that morning. Using the compass which old General Compson had given him, he ranged from that point; he was teaching himself to be a better-than-fair woodsman without knowing he was doing it. On the second day he even found the gutted log where he had first seen the crooked print. It was almost completely crumbled now, healing with unbelievable speed, a passionate and almost visible relinquishment, back into the earth from which the tree had grown.

He ranged the summer woods now, green with gloom; if anything, actually dimmer than in November's gray dissolution, where, even at noon, the sun fell only in intermittent dappling upon the earth, which never completely dried out and which crawled with snakes—moccasins and water snakes and rattlers, themselves the color of the dappling gloom, so that he would not always see them until they moved, returning later and later, first day, second day, passing in the twilight of the third evening the little log pen enclosing the log stable where Sam was putting up the horses for the night.

"You ain't looked right yet," Sam said.

He stopped. For a moment he didn't answer. Then he said peacefully, in a peaceful rushing burst as when a boy's miniature dam in a little brook gives way, "All right. But how? I went to the bayou. I even found that log again. I—"

"I reckon that was all right. Likely he's been watching you. You never saw his foot?"

"I," the boy said—"I didn't—I never thought—"

"It's the gun," Sam said. He stood beside the fence, motionless—the old man, the Indian, in the battered faded overalls and the five-cent straw hat which in the Negro's race had been the badge of his enslavement and was now the regalia of his freedom. The camp—the clearing, the house, the barn and its tiny lot with which Major de Spain in his turn had scratched punily and evanescently at the wilderness

—faded in the dusk, back into the immemorial darkness of the woods. *The gun,* the boy thought. *The gun.*

"Be scared," Sam said. "You can't help that. But don't be afraid. Ain't nothing in the woods going to hurt you unless you corner it, or it smells that you are afraid. A bear or a deer, too, has got to be scared of a coward the same as a brave man has got to be."

The gun, the boy thought.

"You will have to choose," Sam said.

He left the camp before daylight, long before Uncle Ash would wake in his quilts on the kitchen floor and start the fire for breakfast. He had only the compass and a stick for snakes. He could go almost a mile before he would begin to need the compass. He sat on a log, the invisible compass in his invisible hand, while the secret night sounds, fallen still at his movements, scurried again and then ceased for good, and the owls ceased and gave over to the waking of day birds, and he could see the compass. Then he went fast yet still quietly; he was becoming better and better as a woodsman, still without having yet realized it.

He jumped a doe and a fawn at sunrise, walked them out of the bed, close enough to see them—the crash of undergrowth, the white scut, the fawn scudding behind her faster than he had believed it could run. He was hunting right, upwind, as Sam had taught him; not that it mattered now. He had left the gun; of his own will and relinquishment he had accepted not a gambit, not a choice, but a condition in which not only the bear's heretofore inviolable anonymity but all the old rules and balances of hunter and hunted had been abrogated. He would not even be afraid, not even in the moment when the fear would take him completely—blood, skin, bowels, bones, memory from the long time before it became his memory—all save that thin, clear, immortal lucidity which alone differed him from this bear and from all the other bear and deer he would ever kill in the humility and pride of his skill and endurance, to which Sam had spoken when he leaned in the twilight on the lot fence yesterday.

By noon he was far beyond the little bayou, farther into the new and alien country than he had ever been. He was traveling now not only by the old, heavy, biscuit-thick silver watch which had belonged to his grandfather. When he stopped at last, it was for the first time since he had risen from the log at dawn when he could see the compass. It was far enough. He had left the camp nine hours ago; nine hours from now, dark would have already been an hour old. But he didn't think that. He thought, *All right. Yes. But what?* and stood for a moment, alien and small in the green and topless solitude, answering his own question before it had formed and ceased. It was the watch, the compass, the stick— the three lifeless mechanicals with which for nine hours he had fended the wilderness off; he hung the watch and compass carefully on a bush and leaned the stick beside them and relinquished completely to it.

He had not been going very fast for the last two or three hours. He went no faster now, since distance would not matter even if he could have gone fast. And he was trying to keep a bearing on the tree where he had left the compass, trying to complete a circle which would bring him back to it or at least intersect itself, since direction would not matter now either. But the tree was not there, and he did as Sam had schooled him—made the next circle in the opposite direction, so that the two patterns would bisect somewhere, but crossing no print of his own feet, finding the tree at last, but in the wrong place—no bush, no compass, no watch—and the tree not even the tree, because there was a down log beside it and he did what Sam Fathers had told him was the next thing and the last.

As he sat down on the log he saw the crooked print—the warped, tremendous, two-toed indentation which, even as he watched it, filled with water. As he looked up, the wilderness coalesced, solidified—the glade, the tree he sought, the bush, the watch and the compass glinting where a ray of sunshine touched them. Then he saw the bear. It did not emerge, appear; it was just there, immobile, solid, fixed in the hot dappling of the green and windless noon, not as big as he had dreamed it, but as big as he had expected it, bigger, dimensionless, against the dappled obscurity, looking at him where he sat quietly on the log and looked back at it.

Then it moved. It made no sound. It did not hurry. It crossed the glade, walking for an instant into the full glare of the sun; when it reached the other side it stopped again and looked back at him across one shoulder while his quiet breathing inhaled and exhaled three times.

Then it was gone. It didn't walk into the woods, the undergrowth. It faded, sank back into the wilderness as he had watched a fish, a huge old bass, sink and vanish into the dark depths of its pool without even any movement of its fins.

He thought, *It will be next fall.* But it was not next fall, nor the next nor the next. He was fourteen then. He had killed his buck, and Sam Fathers had marked his face with the hot blood, and in the next year he killed a bear. But even before that accolade he had become as competent in the woods as many grown men with the same experience; by his fourteenth year he was a better woodsman than most grown men with more. There was no territory within thirty miles of the camp that he did not know— bayou, ridge, brake, landmark, tree and path. He could have led anyone to any point in it without deviation, and brought them out again. He knew the game trails that even Sam Fathers did not know; in his thirteenth year he found a buck's bedding place, and unbeknown to his father he borrowed Walter Ewell's rifle and lay in wait at dawn and killed the buck when it walked back to the bed, as Sam had told him how the old Chickasaw fathers did.

But not the old bear, although by now he knew its footprints better than he did his own, and not only the crooked one. He could see any one of the three sound ones and distinguish it from any other, and not only by its size. There were other bears within these thirty miles which left tracks almost as large, but this was more than that. If Sam Fathers had been his mentor and the back-yard rabbits and squirrels at home his kindergarten, then the wilderness the old bear ran was his college, the old male bear itself, so long unwifed and childless as to have become its own ungendered progenitor, was his alma mater. But he never saw it.

He could find the crooked print now almost whenever he liked, fifteen or ten or five miles, or sometimes nearer the camp than that. Twice while on stand during the three years he heard the dogs strike its trail by accident; on the second time they jumped it seemingly, the voices high, abject, almost human in hysteria, as on that first morning two years ago. But not the bear itself. He would remember that noon three years ago, the glade, himself and the bear fixed during that moment in the windless and dappled blaze, and it would seem to him that it had never happened, that he had dreamed that too. But it had happened. They had looked at each other, they had emerged from the wilderness old as earth, synchronized to the instant by something more than the blood that moved the flesh and bones which bore them, and touched, pledged something, affirmed, something more lasting than the frail web of bones and flesh which any accident could obliterate.

Then he saw it again. Because of the very fact that he thought of nothing else, he had forgotten to look for it. He was still hunting with Walter Ewell's rifle. He saw it cross the end of a long blow-down, a corridor where a tornado had swept, rushing through rather than over the tangle of trunks and branches as a locomotive would have, faster than he had ever believed it could move, almost as fast as a deer even, because a deer would have spent most of that time in the air, faster than he could bring the rifle sights up with it. And now he knew what had been wrong during all the three years. He sat on a log, shaking and trembling as if he had never seen the woods before nor anything that ran them, wondering with incredulous amazement how he could have forgotten the very thing which Sam Fathers had told him and which the bear itself had proved the next day and had now returned after three years to reaffirm.

And now he knew what Sam Fathers had meant about the right dog, a dog in which size would mean less than nothing. So when he returned alone in April—school was out then, so that the sons of farmers could help with the land's planting, and at last his father had granted him permission, on his promise to be back in four days—he had the dog. It was his own, a mongrel of the sort called by Negroes a fyce, a ratter, itself not much bigger than a rat and possessing that bravery which had long since stopped being courage and had become foolhardiness.

It did not take four days. Alone again, he found the trail on the first morning. It was not a stalk; it was an ambush. He timed the meeting almost as if it were an appointment with a human being. Himself holding the fyce muffled in a feed sack and Sam Fathers with two of the hounds on a piece of a plow-line rope, they lay down wind of the trail at dawn of the second morning. They were so close that the bear turned without even running, as if in surprised amazement at the shrill and frantic uproar of the released fyce, turning at bay against the trunk of a tree, on its hind feet; it seemed to the boy that it would never stop rising, taller and taller, and even the two hounds seemed to take a desperate and despairing courage from the fyce, following it as it went in.

Then he realized that the fyce was actually not going to stop. He flung, threw the gun away, and ran; when he overtook and grasped the frantically pin-wheeling little dog, it seemed to him that he was directly under the bear.

He could smell it, strong and hot and rank. Sprawling, he looked up to where it loomed and towered over him like a cloudburst and colored like a thunderclap, quite familiar, peacefully and even lucidly familiar, until he remembered: This was the way he had used to dream about it. Then it was gone. He didn't see it go. He knelt, holding the frantic fyce with both hands, hearing the abashed wailing of the hounds drawing farther and farther away, until Sam came up. He carried the gun. He laid it down quietly beside the boy and stood looking down at him.

"You've done seed him twice now with a gun in your hands," he said. "This time you couldn't have missed him."

The boy rose. He still held the fyce. Even in his arms and clear of the ground, it yapped frantically, straining and surging after the fading uproar of the two hounds like a tangle of wire springs. He was panting a little, but he was neither shaking nor trembling now.

"Neither could you!" he said. "You had the gun! Neither did you!"

"And you didn't shoot," his father said. "How close were you?"

"I don't know, sir," he said. "There was a big wood tick inside his right hind leg. I saw that. But I didn't have the gun then."

"But you didn't shoot when you had the gun," his father said. "Why?"

But he didn't answer, and his father didn't wait for him to, rising and crossing the room, across the pelt of the bear which the boy had killed two years ago and the larger one which his father had killed before he was born, to the bookcase beneath the mounted head of the boy's first buck. It was the room which his father called the office, from which all the plantation business was transacted; in it for the fourteen years of his life he had heard the best of all talking. Major de Spain would be there and sometimes old General Compson, and Walter Ewell and Boon Hoggenback and Sam Fathers and Tennie's Jim, too, were hunters, knew the woods and what ran them.

He would hear it, not talking himself but listening —the wilderness, the big woods, bigger and older than any recorded document of white man fatuous enough to believe he had bought any fragment of it or Indian ruthless enough to pretend that any fragment of it had been his to convey. It was of the men, not white nor black nor red, but men, hunters with the will and hardihood to endure and the humility and skill to survive, and the dogs and the bear and deer juxtaposed and reliefed against it, ordered and compelled by and within the wilderness in the ancient and unremitting contest by the ancient and immitigable rules which voided all regrets and brooked no quarter, the voices quiet and weighty and deliberate for retrospection and recollection and exact remembering, while he squatted in the blazing firelight as Tennie's Jim squatted, who stirred only to put more wood on the fire and to pass the bottle from one glass to another. Because the bottle was always present, so that after a while it seemed to him that those fierce instants of heart and brain and courage and wiliness and speed were concentrated and distilled into that brown liquor which not women, not boys and children, but only hunters drank, drinking not of the blood they had spilled but some condensation of the wild immortal spirit, drinking it moderately, humbly even, not with the pagan's base hope of acquiring the virtues of cunning and strength and speed, but in salute to them.

His father returned with the book and sat down again and opened it. "Listen," he said. He read the five stanzas aloud, his voice quiet and deliberate in the room where there was no fire now because it was already spring. Then he looked up. The boy watched him. "All right," his father said. "Listen." He read again, but only the second stanza this time, to the end of it, the last two lines, and closed the book and put it on the table beside him. "She cannot fade, though thou hast not thy bliss, for ever wilt thou love, and she be fair," he said.

"He's talking about a girl," the boy said.

"He had to talk about something," his father said. Then he said, "He was talking about truth. Truth doesn't change. Truth is one thing. It covers all things which touch the heart—honor and pride and pity and justice and courage and love. Do you see now?"

He didn't know. Somehow it was simpler than that. There was an old bear, fierce and ruthless, not merely just to stay alive, but with the fierce pride of liberty and freedom, proud enough of the liberty and freedom to see it threatened without fear or even alarm; nay, who at times even seemed deliberately to put that freedom and liberty in jeopardy in order to savor them, to remind his old strong bones and flesh to keep supple and quick to defend and preserve them. There was an old man, son of a Negro slave and an Indian king, inheritor on the one side of the long chronicle of a people who had learned humility through suffering, and pride through the endurance which survived the suffering and injustice, and on the other side, the chronicle of a people even longer in the land than the first, yet who no longer existed in the land at all save in the solitary brotherhood of an old Negro's alien blood and the wild and invincible spirit of an old bear. There was a boy who wished to learn humility and pride in order to become skillful and worthy in the woods, who suddenly found himself becoming so skillful so rapidly that he feared he would never become worthy because he

had not learned humility and pride, although he had tried to, until one day and as suddenly he discovered that an old man who could not have defined either had led him, as though by the hand, to that point where an old bear and a little mongrel of a dog showed him that, by possessing one thing other, he would possess them both.

And a little dog, nameless and mongrel and many-fathered, grown, yet weighing less than six pounds, saying as if to itself, "I can't be dangerous, because there's nothing much smaller than I am; I can't be fierce, because they would call it just a noise; I can't be humble, because I'm already too close to the ground to genuflect; I can't be proud, because I wouldn't be near enough to it for anyone to know who was casting the shadow, and I don't even know that I'm not going to heaven, because they have already decided that I don't possess an immortal soul. So all I can be is brave. But it's all right. I can be that, even if they still call it just noise."

That was all. It was simple, much simpler than somebody talking in a book about youth and a girl he would never need to grieve over, because he could never approach any nearer her and would never have to get any farther away. He had heard about a bear, and finally got big enough to trail it, and he trailed it four years and at last met it with a gun in his hands and he didn't shoot. Because a little dog—But he could have shot long before the little dog covered the twenty yards to where the bear waited, and Sam Fathers could have shot at any time during that interminable minute while Old Ben stood on his hind feet over them. He stopped. His father was watching him gravely across the spring-rife twilight of the room; when he spoke, his words were as quiet as the twilight, too, not loud, because they did not need to be because they would last, "Courage, and honor, and pride," his father said, "and pity, and love of justice and of liberty. They all touch the heart, and what the heart holds to becomes truth, as far as we know the truth. Do you see now?"

Sam, and Old Ben, and Nip, he thought. And himself too. He had been all right too. His father had said so. "Yes, sir," he said.

METAMORPHOSIS

FRANZ KAFKA

FRANZ KAFKA (1883–1924) was born in Prague, educated for the law at the University of Prague and worked in the workmen's compensation division of the Austrian government. This controversial figure in modern literature has described in a famous letter to his father the sense of oppression, engendered by his father's authoritarian personality, under which he lived and wrote; he suffered from tuberculosis and spent several years in sanitoriums; and on two occasions rejected marriage because of a sense of self-inadequacy. Most of his work was edited and published posthumously against his wishes by his friend Max Brod, who sees in it centrally the theme of loneliness. One of Kafka's aphorisms, however, in behalf of the justification of life, offers us another perspective: "One must not cheat anybody, not even the world of its triumph." Among Kafka's books are *The Trial, The Castle, Amerika,* two volumes of diaries, and several collections of short stories, notably *The Great Wall of China.*

AS Gregor Samsa awoke one morning from a troubled dream, he found himself changed in his bed to some monstrous kind of vermin.

He lay on his back, which was as hard as armor plate, and, raising his head a little, he could see the arch of his great, brown belly, divided by bowed corrugations. The bedcover was slipping helplessly off the summit of the curve, and Gregor's legs, pitiably thin compared with their former size, fluttered helplessly before his eyes.

"What has happened?" he thought. It was no dream. His room, a real man's room—though rather small—lay quiet within its four familiar walls. Over the table, where a collection of cloth samples was scattered—Samsa was a commercial traveler—hung the picture that he had recently cut from an illustrated paper and had put in a pretty gilded frame. This picture showed a lady sitting very upright, wearing a small fur hat and a fur boa; she offered to the gaze a heavy muff into which her arm was thrust up to the elbow.

Gregor looked toward the window; rain could be heard falling on the panes; the foggy weather made him sad. "How would it be if I go to sleep again for awhile and forget all this stupidity?" he thought; but it was absolutely impossible, for he was used to sleeping on the right side and in his present plight he could not get into that position. However hard he tried to throw himself violently on his side, he always turned over on his back with a little swinging movement. He tried a hundred times, closing his eyes so that he should not see the trembling of his legs, and he did not give up until he felt in his side a slight but deep pain, never before experienced.

"God!" he thought, "What a job I've chosen.

Traveling day in, day out. A much more worrying occupation than working in the office! And apart from business itself, this plague of traveling: the anxieties of changing trains, the irregular, inferior meals, the ever changing faces, never to be seen again, people with whom one has no chance to be friendly. To hell with it all!" He felt a little itch above his stomach and wriggled nearer to the bedpost, dragging himself slowly on his back so that he might more easily raise his head; and he saw, just where he was itching, a few little white points, whose purpose he could not guess at; he tried to scratch the place with one of his feet but he had to draw it back quickly, for the contact made him shudder coldly.

He returned to his former position. He said to himself: "Nothing is more degrading than always to have to rise so early. A man must have his sleep. Other travelers can live like harem women. When I return to the hotel in the morning to enter my orders, I find these gentlemen still at breakfast. I'd like to see what my boss would say if I tried it; I should be sacked immediately. Who knows if that wouldn't be a good thing, after all! If I didn't hold back because of my parents, I would have given notice long ago; I would have gone to the boss and I wouldn't have minced matters. He would have fallen from his desk. That's a funny thing; to sit on a desk so as to speak to one's employees from such a height, especially when one is hard of hearing and people must come close! Still, all hope is not lost; once I have got together the money my parents owe him—that will be in about five or six years—I shall certainly do it. Then I'll take the big step! Meanwhile, I must get up, for my train goes at five."

He looked at the alarm clock which was ticking on

the chest. "My God!" he thought; it was half-past six; quarter to seven was not far off. Hadn't the alarm gone? From the bed it could be seen that the little hand was set at four, right enough; the alarm had sounded. But had he been able to sleep calmly through that furniture-shattering din? Calmly, no; his sleep had not been calm; but he had slept only the sounder for that. What should he do now?

The next train went at seven; to catch it he must hurry madly, and his collection of samples was not packed; besides, he himself did not feel at all rested nor inclined to move. And even if he did catch the train, his employer's anger was inevitable, since the firm's errand boy would have been waiting at the five o'clock train and would have notified the firm of his lapse. He was just a toady to his boss, a stupid and servile boy. Supposing Gregor pretended to be ill? But that would be very tiresome, and suspicious, too, for during the four years he had been with the firm he had never had the slightest illness. The manager would come with the Health Insurance doctor; he would reproach his parents for their son's idleness and would cut short any objections by giving the doctor's arguments that no people are sick, only idle. And would he be so far wrong, in such a case? Gregor felt in very good fettle, apart from his unnecessary need for more sleep after such a long night; he even had an unusually keen appetite.

Just as he was quickly turning these thoughts over in his mind without being able to decide to leave the bed—while the alarm clock struck a quarter to seven—he heard a cautious knock on his door, close by his bed's head.

"Gregor," someone called—it was his mother—"It is a quarter to seven. Didn't you want to catch the train?"

What a soft voice! Gregor trembled as he heard his own voice reply. It was unmistakably his former voice, but with it could be heard, as if from below, a painful whining, which only allowed the words their real shape for a moment, immediately to confuse their sound so that one wondered if one had really heard aright. Gregor would have liked to answer fully and to give an explanation but, in these circumstances, he contented himself by saying, "Yes, yes, thank you, mother. I am just getting up." No doubt the door prevented her from judging the change in Gregor's voice, for the explanation reassured his mother, who went away, shuffling in her slippers. But because of this little dialogue the other members of the family had become aware that, contrary to custom, Gregor was still in the house, and his father started to knock on one of the side doors, softly, but with his fists.

"Gregor, Gregor," he cried, "what is the matter?" And, after a moment, in a warning tone, "Gregor! Gregor!"

At the other side door, the young man's sister softly called, "Gregor, aren't you well? Do you need anything?"

"I am getting ready," said Gregor, answering both sides and forcing himself to pronounce carefully and to separate each word with a long pause, to keep a natural voice.

His father went back to breakfast, but the sister still whispered, "Gregor, open the door, I beg you." But Gregor had no intention of answering this request; on the contrary, he complimented himself on having learned the habit of always locking his door, as if in a hotel.

He would get up quietly, without being bothered by anyone; he would dress, and above all, he would have breakfast; then would come the time to reflect, for he felt it was not in bed that a reasonable solution could be found. He recalled how often an unusual position adopted in bed had resulted in slight pains which proved imaginary as soon as he arose, and Gregor was curious to see his present hallucination gradually dissolve. As for the change in his voice, his private opinion was that it was the prelude to some serious quinsy, the occupational malady of travelers.

He had no difficulty in turning back the coverlet; he needed only to blow himself up a little, and it fell of its own accord. But beyond that he was impeded by his tremendous girth. To get up, he needed arms and hands; but he had only numerous little legs, in perpetual vibration, over which he had no control. Before he could bend one leg, he first had to stretch it out; and when at last he had performed the desired movement, all the other legs worked uncontrollably, in intensely painful agitation. "I must not stay uselessly in bed," said Gregor to himself.

To get his body out of bed, he first tried moving the hind part. But unfortunately this hind part, which he had not yet seen, and of which he could form no very precise idea, went so slowly it proved to be very difficult to move; he summoned all his strength to throw himself forward but, ill-calculating his course, he hurled himself violently against one of the bedposts, and the searing pain he felt showed that the lower part of his body was without doubt the most sensitive.

He then tried to start with the fore part of his body and cautiously turned his head toward the side of the bed. In this he succeeded quite easily, and the rest of his body, despite its weight and size, followed the direction of his head. But when his head left the bed and was hanging in mid-air, he was afraid to continue any further; if he were to fall in this position, it would be a miracle if he did not crack his head; and this was no moment to lose his senses—better to stay in bed.

But when, panting after his efforts, he again found himself stretched out just as before, when he saw his little legs struggling more wildly than ever, despairing of finding any means of bringing peace and order into this chaotic procedure, he once again realized that he absolutely could not stay in bed and that it was perfectly reasonable to sacrifice everything to the slightest chance of getting out. At the same time he did not forget that cool and wise reflection would be far better than desperate resolutions. Ordinarily, at such moments he turned his eyes to the window to gain encouragement and hope. But this day the fog prevented him from seeing the other side of the street; the window gave him neither confidence nor strength. "Seven o'clock already," he said as he listened once more to the sound of the alarm clock. "Seven o'clock already, and the fog has got no thinner!" He lay back again for a moment, breathing weakly, as though, in the complete silence, he could calmly await the return to his normal self.

Then he said, "Before a quarter past it is absolutely essential for me to be up. In any case, someone will be sent from the office to ask for me before then, for the place opens at seven." And he began to rock on his back in order to get his whole body out of bed in one movement. In this manner he would be able to protect his head by raising it sharply as he fell. His back seemed to be hard; nothing would be risked by falling on it to the floor; his only fear was that the noise of his fall, which must surely resound through the whole house, might arouse terror, or, at the very least, uneasiness. However, that would have to be risked.

When Gregor had half his body out of bed—the new method seemed more like a game than a task, for he had only to swing himself on his back—he began to think how easily he could have got up if only he had had a little assistance. Two strong people—he thought of his father and the servant girl—would have been quite enough; they would have needed only to pass their arms under his round back, raise it from the bed, quickly lean forward with their burden, and then wait carefully till he had completed the operation of settling himself on the ground, where he hoped his feet would at last find a way of working together. But even if the doors had not been closed, would it have been wise for him to call for help? At this idea, despite his misery, he could not repress a smile.

Now he had progressed so far that, by sharply accentuating his swinging movement, he felt he was nearly losing his balance; he would have to take a serious decision, for in five minutes it would be a quarter to eight—but suddenly there was a knock at the front door.

"Someone from the office," he said to himself, and he felt his blood run cold, while his little legs quickened their saraband. For a moment all was quiet.

"They're not going to the door," thought Gregor, in an access of absurd hope. But of course the maid, with a firm tread, went to the door and opened it. Gregor needed to hear only the caller's first words of greeting to know immediately who it was—the manager himself. Why was Gregor, particularly, condemned to work for a firm where the worst was suspected at the slightest inadvertence of the employees? Were the employees, without exception, all scoundrels? Was there among their number not one devoted, faithful servant, who, if it did so happen that by chance he missed a few hours work one morning, might have found himself so numbed with remorse that he just could not leave his bed? Would it not have been enough to send some apprentice to put things right—if, in any case, it was necessary to make inquiries at all—instead of the manager himself having to come, in order to let the whole innocent family know that the clearing-up of so suspicious an affair could only be entrusted to a person of his importance? These thoughts so irritated Gregor that he swung himself out of bed with all his might. This made a loud thud, but not the terrible crash that he had feared. The carpet somewhat softened the blow, and Gregor's back was more elastic than he had thought, and so his act was not accompanied by any din. Only his head had been slightly hurt. Gregor had not raised it enough, and it had been knocked in the fall. He turned over a little to rub it on the carpet, in pain and anger.

"Something fell in there just then," cried the manager, in the room on the left. Gregor tried to imagine his employer's face if such a mishap had occurred to him; for such a thing was possible, he had to admit. But, as if in brutal reply, the manager began pacing up and down in the next room, making his patent-leather boots creak.

And in the other room on the right, Gregor's sister whispered to warn her brother, "Gregor, the manager is here."

"I know," said Gregor to himself, but he dared not raise his voice enough for his sister to hear.

"Gregor," said his father in the room on the left, "the manager has come to find out why you didn't catch the early train. We don't know what to say. He wants to speak to you personally. So please open the door. I'm sure he will be kind enough to excuse the untidiness of your room."

"Good morning, good morning, Mr. Samsa," interrupted the manager, cordial and brisk.

"He is not well," said his mother to the manager, while his father went on shouting through the door. "Believe me, he is not well, sir. How else could Gregor have missed the train? The boy thinks of nothing but his work! It makes me upset to see how he never goes out after supper; do you know he's just spent a whole week here and been at home every evening! He sits down with us at the table and stays there, quietly reading the paper or studying his time-tables. His greatest indulgence is to do a little fret-work. Just lately he made a small picture frame. It was finished in two or three evenings, and you'd be surprised how pretty it is; it is hanging up in his room. As soon as Gregor opens his door, you will be able to see it. I am so glad you came, sir, because without you we would never have got Gregor to open his door, he is so obstinate; and surely he must be ill, even though he denied it this morning."

"I am just coming," said Gregor slowly and care-fully, but he continued to lie still, so as not to miss a word of the conversation.

"I can offer no other suggestion," declared the manager. "Let us only hope it is nothing serious. However, we businessmen must often—fortunately or not, as you will—get on with our jobs and ignore our little indispositions."

"Well, can the manager come in now?" asked his father impatiently, rapping on the door again.

"No," said Gregor. In the room on the left there was a painful silence; in that on the right the sister began to sob.

Why did she not go to the others? Possibly she had only just got out of bed and was not yet dressed. And why did she weep? Because he did not get up to let the manager in, because he risked losing his position, and because the boss would once more worry his parents about their old debts? These were misplaced troubles! Gregor was still there and had not the slightest intention of letting his family down. At this very moment he was stretched out on the carpet, and nobody seeing him in this state could seriously have demanded that he should let the man-ager enter his room. But it was not on account of this slight impoliteness—for which in normal times he could easily have made his excuses later—that Gregor would be dismissed. And he thought it would be more reasonable, just now, to leave him alone rather than to upset him with tears and speeches. But it was just this uncertainty which was making the others uneasy and which excused their behavior.

"Herr Samsa," now cried the manager, raising his voice, "What is the matter? You barricade yourself in your room, you don't answer yes or no, you needlessly upset your parents, and you neglect your professional duties in an unheard-of manner. I am speaking in the name of your employer and of your parents, and I beg you seriously to give us a satisfactory explanation immediately. I am astonished, astonished! I took you for a quiet, reasonable young man, and here you suddenly give yourself airs, behaving in an absolutely fantastic manner! The head of the firm, speaking to me this morning in your absence, suggested an explanation which I rejected; he mentioned the samples which were entrusted to you a while ago. I gave him my word of honor that this had nothing to do with the affair, but now that I have been witness to your obstinacy, I can assure you, Herr Samsa, that it deprives me of any wish to defend you. Your job is by no means safe! I had intended to tell you this in private but, since you oblige me to waste my time here for nothing, I see no reason for keeping quiet before your parents. I'd have you know that lately your work has been far from satisfactory; we realize, of course, that the time of the year is not propitious for big business, but you must understand, Herr Samsa, that a period with no business at all should not and can not be tolerated!"

Gregor was beside himself; in his anxiety he forgot everything else. "But, sir," he cried, "I will open the door immediately. I will open it. I felt a little ill; a slight giddiness prevented me from getting up. I am still in bed. But I feel better already. I am just get-ting up. Only a moment's patience. I am not quite so well as I thought. But I am all right, really. How can it be that illness should take one so quickly? Only yesterday I felt quite well, my parents can tell you; and then last evening I had a slight symptom. They must have noticed it. Why didn't I let them know at the office! But then, one always thinks one will be able to get rid of an illness without staying at home. Please, sir, spare my parents. The complaints you made just now are really without any foundation. No one has even suggested them before. Perhaps you have not seen the last orders I sent in. I will leave on the eight o'clock train; these few moments of rest have done me a great deal of good. Please don't stay, sir, I shall be at the office immediately; and please inform the director of what has happened and put in a good word for me."

And while Gregor hastily cried these words, scarcely realizing what he said, he had, with an ease due to his previous exertions, approached the chest of drawers, against which he now tried to raise himself. He wanted to open the door; he wanted to be seen and to speak with the manager. He was curious to know what impression he would make on these peo-ple who were so imperiously demanding his pres-ence. If he frightened them, that would be reas-suring, for he would stop being cross-questioned and be left in peace. If they took everything quietly, then he, too, need not be alarmed. And if he hurried he might still catch the eight o'clock train. The chest was polished, and Gregor slipped on it several times but, by a supreme effort, he managed to get upright. He paid no attention to the pains in his stomach, though they were hurting him. He let himself drop forward onto the top of a near-by chair and clung there with his little legs. Then, finding himself master of his body, he stayed very quiet in order to listen to what the manager had to say.

"Did you understand a word of what he said?" the manager asked the parents. "Is he trying to make fools of us?"

"Good heavens," cried the mother, already in tears. "Perhaps he is seriously ill, and here we are torturing him all this while! Grete! Grete!" she called.

"Mother!" cried the daughter from the other side. They were separated by Gregor's room.

"Fetch a doctor immediately. Gregor is ill. A doctor, quickly! Did you hear him speak?"

"It was an animal's voice," said the manager; after the cries of the women, his voice seemed curiously gentle.

"Anna, Anna!" shouted the father through the hall into the kitchen, clapping his hands. "Get a locksmith, quick!" And already the two young girls—how could his sister have dressed so soon?—ran along the corridor with rustling skirts and opened the front door. No one heard the door close; no doubt it had been left open, as is the custom in houses to which a great misfortune has come.

However, Gregor had become calmer. Doubtless they had not understood his words, though they had seemed clear enough to him, clearer, indeed, than the first time; perhaps his ears were becoming more accustomed to the sounds. But at least they were obliged to realize that his case was not normal, and they were ready, now, to help him. The assurance and resourcefulness with which the first steps had been taken comforted him considerably. He felt himself integrated into human society once again, and, without differentiating between them, he hoped for great and surprising things from the locksmith and the doctor. To clear his throat for the decisive conversation which he would have to hold soon, he coughed a little, but as quietly as possible, for he feared that even his cough might not sound human. Meanwhile, in the next room, it had become quiet. Perhaps his parents were sitting at table in a secret conference with the manager; perhaps everyone was leaning against the door, listening.

Gregor made his way slowly toward it with the chair; then he abandoned the chair and flung himself at the door, holding himself erect against the woodwork—for the bottoms of his feet secreted a sticky substance—and he rested a moment from his efforts. After this, he tried to turn the key in the lock with his mouth. Unfortunately, it seemed he had no proper teeth. How could he take hold of the key? In compensation, instead of teeth he possessed a pair of very strong mandibles and succeeded in seizing the key in the lock, regardless of the pain this caused him; a brownish liquid flowed out of his mouth, spread over the lock, and dropped to the floor.

"Listen!" said the manager in the next room. "He is just turning the key."

This was valuable encouragement for Gregor; he would have liked his father, his mother, everybody, to start calling to him, "Courage, Gregor, go on, push hard!" And, with the idea that everyone was following his efforts with passionate attention, he clutched the key with all the power of his jaws until he was nearly unconscious. Following the progress of the turning key, he twisted himself around the lock, hanging on by his mouth, and, clinging to the key, pressed it down again, whenever it slipped, with all the weight of his body. The clear click of the lock as it snapped back awoke Gregor from his momentary coma.

"I have dispensed with the locksmith," he thought, and sighed and leaned his head against the handle to open one panel of the double doors completely.

This method, the only possible one, prevented the others from seeing him for some time, even with the door open. Still erect, he had to grope his way round the door with great caution in order not to spoil his entry by falling flat on his back; so he was concentrating toward this end, with all his attention absorbed by the maneuver, when he heard the manager utter a sonorous, "Oh!" such as the roaring of the wind produces, and saw him—he was just by the door—press his hand over his open mouth and slowly stagger back as if some invisible and intensely powerful force were driving him from the spot. His mother—who, despite the presence of the manager, was standing by with her hair in curlers, still disordered by sleep—began to look at the father, clasping her hands; then she made two steps toward Gregor and fell backward into the family circle in the midst of a confusion of skirts which spread around her, while her face, falling on her breast, was concealed from sight. The father clenched his fists with a menacing air, as if to beat Gregor back into his room; then he looked around the dining room in perplexity, covered his eyes with his hand, and wept with great sobs which shook his powerful chest.

Gregor did not enter the room; he stood against the closed half of the double doors, allowing only a part of his body to be seen, while, above, he turned his head to one side to see what would happen. Meanwhile, it had grown much lighter; on either side of the street a part of the long, dark building opposite could clearly be seen—it was a hospital, with regular windows startlingly pitting its façade; it was still raining, but in great separate drops which fell to the ground, one by one. The breakfast crockery was spread all over the table, for breakfast was the most important meal of the day for Gregor's father; he would prolong it for hours while he read various newspapers. On the wall hung a photograph of Gregor in lieutenant's uniform, taken while he was in military service; he was smiling; his hand lay on the hilt of his sword. By his expression, he seemed happy to be alive; by his gesture, he appeared to command respect for his rank. The living-room door was ajar, and, as the front door was also open, the balcony and the first steps of the stairway could just be seen.

"Now," said Gregor, and he realized that he was the only one to have kept calm, "Now I will get dressed, collect my samples, and go. Will you, will you let me go? Surely you can now see, sir, that I am not obstinate, that I do mean to work; commercial traveling is tiresome, I admit, but without it I cannot live. Where are you going, sir? To the office? Yes? Will you give them a faithful account of what has happened? After all, anyone might find for a moment that they were incapable of resuming their work, but that's just a good opportunity to review the work they have been doing, and to bear in mind that, once the obstacle is removed, they will be able to return with twice the heart. I owe so much to the director, as you know very well. I have my parents and my sister to consider. I am in an awkward position, but I shall return to work. Only, please do not make things more difficult for me; they are hard enough as it is. Take my part at the office. I know only too well they don't like travelers. They think we earn our money too easily, that we lead too grand a life. I realize that the present situation doesn't encourage the removal of this prejudice; but you, sir, the manager, can judge the circumstances better than the rest of the staff, better than the director himself— though this is between ourselves—for in his executive capacity he is often easily misled by an employee's prejudice. You know quite well that the traveler, who is hardly ever in the office the whole year round, is often the victim of scandal, of a chance, undeserved complaint against which he is powerless to defend himself, for he does not even know that he is being accused; he only learns of it as he returns, exhausted, at the end of his trip, when the sad consequences of an affair, whose circumstances he can no longer recall, painfully confront him. Please, sir, don't leave me without a word to show that you think all this at least a little reasonable."

But, at Gregor's first words, the manager had turned away and only glanced back, with snarling lips, over his trembling shoulder. During Gregor's speech, he had not stood still for a moment; instead, he had retreated furtively, step by step, toward the door—always keeping Gregor in sight—as if some secret law forbade him to leave the room. He had already reached the hall and, as he took the very last step out of the living room, one would have thought the floor was burning his shoes, so sharply did he spring. Then he stretched his hand toward the balustrade, as if some unearthly deliverance awaited him at the foot of the stairs.

Gregor realized that, if he were to keep his job, on no account must the manager be allowed to leave in this condition. Unfortunately, his parents did not realize the position very clearly; they had for so long held the idea that Gregor was settled in the firm for life and were so taken up with their present troubles that they had little thought for such a contingency. But Gregor had more foresight. The manager must be stopped, calmed, convinced, and finally won over. The future of Gregor and of his family depended on it! If only his sister were there! She had understood, she had actually begun to weep while Gregor still lay quietly on his back. And the manager, who liked women, would have listened to her; he would have let himself be guided by her; she would have closed the door and would have proved to him, in the hall, how unreasonable his terror was. But she was not there; Gregor himself must manage this affair. And without even considering whether he would ever be able to return to work, nor whether his speech had been understood, he let go of the doorpost to glide through the opening and overtake the manager (who was clutching the balustrade with both hands in a ridiculous manner), vainly sought for a foothold, and, uttering a cry, he fell, with his frail little legs crumpled beneath him.

Suddenly, for the first time that whole morning, he experienced a feeling of physical well-being; his feet were on firm ground; he noticed with joy that his legs obeyed him wonderfully and were even eager to carry him wherever he might wish. But while, under the nervous influence of his need for haste, he hesitated on the spot, not far from his mother, he saw her suddenly jump, fainting though she seemed to be, and throw her arms about with outspread fingers, crying, "Help, for God's sake, help!" She turned her head, the better to see Gregor; then, in flagrant contradiction, she began to retreat madly, having forgotten that behind her stood the table, still laden with breakfast things. She staggered against it and sat down suddenly, like one distraught, regardless of the fact that, at her elbow, the overturned coffee-pot was making a pool of coffee on the carpet.

"Mother, mother," whispered Gregor, looking up at her. The manager had quite gone out of his mind. Seeing the coffee spilling, Gregor could not prevent himself from snapping his jaws several times in the air, as if he were eating. Thereupon his mother again began to shriek and quickly jumped up from the table and fell into the arms of the father, who had rushed up behind her. But Gregor had no time to bother about them. The manager was already on the stairs; with his chin on the balustrade, he was looking back for the last time.

Gregor summoned all his courage to try to bring him back; the manager must have suspected something of the sort, for he leaped several steps at a single bound and disappeared with a cry of, "Huh!" which resounded in the hollow of the stair well. This flight had the unfortunate effect of causing Gregor's father—who till now had remained master of himself —to lose his head completely; instead of running after the manager, or at least not interfering with Gregor in his pursuit, he seized in his right hand the manager's walking stick, which had been left behind on a chair with his overcoat and hat, took up in his left a newspaper from the table, and began stamping his feet and brandishing the newspaper and the cane to drive Gregor back into his room. Gregor's prayers were unavailing, were not even understood; he had turned to his father a supplicating head, but, meek though he showed himself, his father merely stamped all the louder. In the dining room, despite the cold, the mother had opened the window wide and was leaning out as far as possible, pressing her face in her hands. A great rush of air swept the space between the room and the stairway; the curtains billowed, the papers rustled, and a few sheets flew over the carpet. But the father pursued Gregor pitilessly, whistling and whooping like a savage, and Gregor, who was not used to walking backward, progressed but slowly.

Had he been able to turn around he could have reached his room quickly, but he feared to make his father impatient by the slowness of his turning and feared also that at any moment he might receive a mortal blow on his head or on his back from this menacing stick. Soon Gregor had no choice; for he realized with terror that when he was going backward he was not master of his direction and, still fearfully watching the attitude of his father out of the corner of his eye, he began his turning movement as quickly as possible, which was really only very slowly. Perhaps his father realized his good intention for, instead of hindering this move, he guided him

from a little distance away, helping Gregor with the tip of the stick. If only he had left off that insupportable whistling! Gregor was completely losing his head. He had nearly completed his turn when, bewildered by the din, he mistook his direction and began to go back to his former position. When at last, to his great joy, he found himself facing the half-opened double doors, he discovered that his body was too big to pass through without hurt. Naturally, it never occurred to his father, in his present state, to open the other half of the double doors in order to allow Gregor to pass. He was dominated by the one fixed idea that Gregor should be made to return to his room as quickly as possible. He would never have entertained the long-winded performance which Gregor would have needed to rear up and pass inside. Gregor heard him storming behind him, no doubt to urge him through as though there were no obstacle in his path; the hubbub no longer sounded like the voice of one single father. Now was no time to play, and Gregor—come what may—hurled himself into the doorway. There he lay, jammed in a slanting position, his body raised up on one side and his flank crushed by the door jamb, whose white paint was now covered with horrible brown stains. He was caught fast and could not free himself unaided; on one side his little legs fluttered in the air, on the other they were painfully pressed under his body; then his father gave him a tremendous blow from behind with the stick. Despite the pain, this was almost a relief; he was lifted bodily into the middle of the room and fell, bleeding thickly. The door was slammed by a thrust of the stick, and then, at last, all was still.

II

It was dusk when Gregor awoke from his heavy, deathlike sleep. Even had he not been disturbed, he would doubtless soon have awakened, for he felt he had had his fill of rest and sleep; however, he seemed to have been awakened by the cautious, furtive noise of a key turning in the lock of the hall door. The reflection of the electric tramway lay dimly here and there about the ceiling and on the upper parts of the furniture, but below, where Gregor was, it was dark. Slowly he dragged himself toward the door to ascertain what had happened and fumbled around clumsily with his feelers, whose use he was at last learning to appreciate. His left side seemed to him to be one long, irritating scar, and he limped about on his double set of legs. One of his legs had been seriously injured during the morning's events—it was a miracle that only one should be hurt—and it dragged lifelessly behind.

When he reached the door, he realized what had attracted him: the smell of food. For there was a bowl of sweetened milk in which floated little pieces of bread. He could have laughed with delight, his appetite had grown so since morning; he thrust his head up to the eyes in the milk. But he drew it back quickly; his painful left side gave him some difficulty, for he could only eat by convulsing his whole body and snorting; also, he could not bear the smell of milk, which once had been his favorite drink and which his sister had no doubt prepared for this special reason. He turned from the bowl in disgust and dragged himself to the middle of the room.

The gas was lit in the dining room; he could see it through the cracks of the door. Now was the time when, ordinarily, his father would read aloud to his family from the evening paper, but this time Gregor heard nothing. Perhaps this traditional reading, which his sister always retailed to him in her conversation and in her letters, had not lapsed entirely from the customs of the household. But everywhere was still, and yet surely someone was in the room.

"What a quiet life my family has led," thought Gregor, staring before him in the darkness, and he felt very proud, for it was to him that his parents and his sister owed so placid a life in so nice a flat. What would happen now, if this peace, this satisfaction, this well-being should end in terror and disaster? In order to dissipate such gloomy thoughts, Gregor began to take a little exercise and crawled back and forth over the floor.

Once during the evening he saw the door on the left open slightly, and once it was the door on the right; someone had wished to enter but had found the task too risky. Gregor resolved to stop by the dining-room door and to entice the hesitant visitor as best he might or at least to see who it was; but the door never opened again, and Gregor waited in vain. That morning, when the door had been locked, everyone had tried to invade his room; but now that they had succeeded in opening it no one came to see him; they had even locked his doors on the outside.

Not till late was the light extinguished, and Gregor could guess that his parents and his sister had been waiting till then, for he heard them all go off on tiptoe. Now no one would come to him till the morning, and so he would have the necessary time to reflect on the ordering of his new life; but his great room, in which he was obliged to remain flat on his stomach on the floor, frightened him in a way that he could not understand—for he had lived in it for the past five years—and, with a half-involuntary action of which he was a little ashamed, he hastily slid under the couch; he soon found that here his back was a little crushed and he could not raise his head; he only regretted that his body was too large to go entirely under the couch.

He spent the whole night there, sometimes in a half-sleep from which the pangs of hunger would wake him with a start, sometimes ruminating on his misfortune and his vague hopes, always concluding that his duty was to remain docile and to try to make things bearable for his family, whatever unpleasantness the situation might impose upon them.

Early in the morning he had a chance to test the strength of his new resolutions; it was still almost dark; his sister, already half dressed, opened the hall door and looked in curiously. She did not see Gregor at once but when she perceived him under the sofa —"Heavens, he must be somewhere; he can't have flown away!"—she was overcome by an unmanageable terror and rushed off, slamming the door. Then, repenting her gesture, she opened it again and entered on tiptoe, as if it were the room of a stranger or one seriously ill. Gregor stretched his head out from the side of the sofa and watched her. Would she notice that he had left the milk, and not from lack of appetite? Would she bring him something which suited his taste better? If she did not do so of her own accord, he would rather have died of hunger than draw her attention to these things, despite his overwhelming desire to rush out of his hiding place, to throw himself at his sister's feet, and to beg for something to eat. But suddenly the sister saw the full bowl in astonishment. A little milk had been spilled around it; using a piece of paper, she took up the bowl without touching it and carried it off to the kitchen. Gregor waited anxiously to see what she would bring him in its place and racked his brains to guess. But he had never realized to what lengths his sister's kindness would go. In order to discover her brother's likes, she brought a whole choice of eatables spread on an old newspaper. There were half-rotted stumps of vegetables, the bones of yesterday's dinner covered with a thick white sauce, a few currants and raisins, some almonds, some cheese that Gregor, a few days before, had declared uneatable, a stale loaf, a piece of salted bread and butter, and another without salt. Besides this she brought back the bowl which had become so important to Gregor. This time it was filled with water, and, guessing that her brother would not like to eat before her, she very kindly retired, closing and locking the door to show him that he might eat in peace. Now that his meal was ready, Gregor felt all his legs trembling. His wounds seemed cured, for he felt not the slightest hindrance, and he was astonished to remember that when he had been human and had cut his finger slightly only a few months ago, it had pained him for several days after.

"Have I become less sensitive?" he wondered; but already he had begun sucking at the cheese, which had suddenly and imperiously attracted him above all the other food. Gluttonously he swallowed in turn the cheese, the vegetables, and the sauce, his eyes moist with satisfaction; as to the fresh things, he wanted none of them; their smell repelled him, and, in order to eat, he separated them from the others.

When he had finished and was idly making up his mind to return to his place, his sister slowly began to turn the key in the lock to give him the signal for retreat. He was very frightened, though he was half asleep, and hurried to reach the sofa. It needed great determination to remain beneath it during the time, however short, that his sister was in the room; his heavy meal had so swollen his body that he could scarcely breathe in his retreat. Between two fits of suffocation he saw, with his eyes filled with tears, that his sister, intending no harm, was sweeping up the remains of his meal with the very things that he had not touched, as if he needed them no more; she put the refuse into a bucket, which she covered with a wooden lid and hastily carried away. Hardly had she turned the handle before Gregor struggled out from his hiding place to expand his body to its proper size.

So he was fed each day; in the morning, before his parents and the maid were awake, and in the afternoon, when lunch was over and while his parents were taking their nap and the maid had been provided with some task or other by his sister. Certainly they did not wish Gregor to die of hunger but perhaps they preferred to know nothing about his meals except by hearsay—they could not have borne to see him—perhaps, also, in order to diminish their disgust, his sister was taking pains to spare them the slightest trouble. He must realize that they, too, had their share of misfortune.

Gregor never learned what excuses they had made to rid themselves of the doctor and the locksmith, for, as no one attempted to understand him, no one, not even his sister, imagined that he could understand them. He had to be content, when she came into his room, to listen to her invoking the saints between her sighs. It was only much later, when Grete had become somewhat accustomed to the new situation—to which she never really became reconciled—that Gregor would occasionally overhear an expression which showed some kindness or allowed him to guess at such a meaning. When he had eaten all the food off the newspaper she would say, "He liked what I brought today"; at other times, when he had no appetite—and lately this had become more frequent—she would say, almost sadly, "Now he has left it all."

But even if he could learn no news directly, Gregor overheard a good deal of what was said in the dining room; as soon as he heard anyone speak, he would hurry to the most propitious door and press his whole body close against it. At first, especially, there was little conversation which did not bear more or less directly on his predicament. For two whole days, the mealtimes were given over to deliberating on the new attitude which must be maintained toward Gregor; even between meals they spoke mostly on the same theme, for now at least two members of the household always remained at home, each one fearing to remain alone and, particularly, to leave Gregor unwatched.

It was not very clear how much the maid knew of what had happened, but, on the very first day, she had fallen on her knees and begged his mother to let her go; and a quarter of an hour later she had left the house in tearful gratitude, as if her release were the greatest evidence of the kindness she had met with in the house; and of her own accord she took a long and boring oath never to reveal the secret to anyone. Now his sister and his mother had to look after the cooking; this entailed little trouble, for the appetite of the Samsa family had gone. Occasionally Gregor would hear one member of the family vainly exhorting another to eat. The reply was always the same: "Thank you, I have had enough," or some such phrase. Perhaps, also, they did not drink. Often his sister would ask her father if he would like some beer; she would cheerfully offer to fetch it, or, faced with her father's silence, she would say, to remove any scruples on his part, that the landlady could go for it, but her father would always reply with a loud, "No!" and nothing more would be said.

In the course of the very first day, the father had clearly explained their precise financial situation to his wife and daughter. From time to time he would get up from the table and hunt for some paper or account book in his Wertheim safe, which he had saved from the crash when his business had failed five years before. He could be heard opening the complicated locks of the safe and closing it again after he had taken out what he sought. Ever since he became a prisoner, nothing had given Gregor such pleasure as these financial explanations. He had always imagined that his father had been unable to save a penny from the ruins of his business; in any case, his father had never said anything to undeceive him, and Gregor had never questioned him upon the matter; he had done all he could to help his family to forget as quickly as possible the disaster which had plunged them into such despair.

He had set to work with splendid ardor; in less than no time, from being a junior clerk he had been promoted to the position of traveler, with all the benefits of such a post; and his successes were suddenly transformed into hard cash which could be spread on the table before the surprised and delighted eyes of his family. Those were happy times —they had never since recovered such a sense of delight, though Gregor now earned enough to feed the whole Samsa family. Everyone had grown accustomed to it, his family as much as himself; they took the money gratefully, he gave it willingly, but the act was accompanied by no remarkable effusiveness. Only his sister had remained particularly affectionate toward Gregor, and it was his secret plan to have her enter the conservatory next year regardless of the considerable cost of such an enterprise, which he would try to meet in some way; for, unlike him, Grete was very fond of music and wished to take up the study of the violin. This matter of the conservatory recurred often in the brief conversations between Gregor and his sister, whenever Gregor had a few days to spend with his family; they hardly ever spoke of it except as a dream impossible to realize; his parents did not much like the innocent allusions to the subject, but Gregor thought very seriously of it and had promised himself that he would solemnly announce his plan next Christmas eve.

It was ideas of this kind, ideas completely unsuited to his present situation, which now passed constantly through Gregor's mind while he held himself pressed erect against the door, listening. He would get so tired that he could no longer hear anything; then he would let himself go and allow his head to fall against the door; but he would draw it back immediately, for the slightest noise was noticed in the dining room and would be followed by an interval of silence.

"What can he be doing now?" his father would say after a moment's pause, turning, no doubt, toward the door; the interrupted conversation would only gradually be resumed.

His father was often obliged to repeat his explanations in order to recall forgotten details or to make them understood by his wife, who did not always grasp them the first time. Gregor thus learned, by what the father said, that, despite all their misfortunes, his parents had been able to save a certain amount from their former property—little enough, it is true, but it had been augmented, to some extent, by interest. Also, they had not spent all the money that Gregor, keeping only a few shillings for himself, had handed over to his family each week, enabling them to gather together a little capital. Behind his door, Gregor nodded his head in approval; he was so happy at this unexpected foresight and thrift. Doubtless, with these savings his father could have more rapidly paid off the debt he had contracted to

Gregor's employer, which would have brought nearer the date of Gregor's release; but under the circumstances it was much better that his father had acted as he had.

Unfortunately this money was not quite sufficient to enable the family to live on its interest; it would last a year, perhaps two, but no more. It was a sum which must not be touched, which must be kept for a case of urgent necessity. As for money on which to live, that would have to be earned. Now, despite his good health, the father was nevertheless an old man who had ceased to work five years before and who could not be expected to entertain any foolish hopes of getting employment; during these five years of retirement—his first holiday in a life entirely devoted to work and unsuccess—he had become very fat and moved with great difficulty. And the old mother would not be able to earn much, suffering as she did from asthma, for even now it was an effort for her to get about the house; she passed a good deal of her time each day lying on the sofa, panting and wheezing under the open window. And was the breadwinner to be the sister, who was still but a child, seventeen years old, so suited to the life she had led till then, nicely dressed, getting plenty of sleep, helping in the house, taking part in a few harmless little entertainments, and playing her violin? Whenever the conversation fell on this topic, Gregor left the door and lay on the leather sofa, whose coolness was so soothing to his body, burning as it was with anxiety and shame.

Often he lay all night, sleepless, and hearing no sound for hours on end save the creak of the leather as he turned. Or, uncomplainingly, he would push his armchair toward the window, crawl up on it, and, propped on the seat, he would lean against the window, not so much to enjoy the view as to recall the sense of release he once used to feel whenever he looked across the pavements; for now he was daily becoming more shortsighted, he could not even make out the hospital opposite, which he had cursed when he was human because he could see it all too clearly; and had he not known so well that he was living in Charlottenstrasse, a quiet but entirely urban street, he might have thought his window gave out on a desert, where the gray of the sky and the gray of the earth merged indistinguishably together. His attentive sister had only to see the armchair by the window twice to understand; from then on, each time she tidied the room she would push the armchair to the window, and would always leave its lower half open.

If only Gregor had been able to speak to his sister, to thank her for all she was doing for him, he could have borne her services easier; but as it was, they pained and embarrassed him. Grete naturally tried to hide any appearance of blame or trouble regarding the situation, and as time went on she played her part even better, but she could not prevent her brother from realizing his predicament more and more clearly. Each time she entered his room, it was terrible for Gregor. Hardly had she entered, when, despite the pains she always took to spare the others the sight of its interior, she would not even take time to shut the door but would run to the window, open it hastily with a single push, as if to escape imminent suffocation, and would stand there for a minute, however cold it might be, breathing deeply. Twice a day she terrified Gregor with this rush and clatter; he shrank trembling under the couch the whole time; he knew his sister would have spared him this had she been able to stand being in the room with him with the window shut.

One day—it must have been a month after Gregor's change, and his sister had no grounds for astonishment at his appearance—she came a little earlier than usual and found him looking out of the window, motionless and in such a position as to inspire terror. If she had not liked to enter, that would not have surprised Gregor, for his position prevented her from opening the window. But not only would she not enter; she sprang back, slammed the door, and locked it; a stranger might have thought that Gregor was lying in wait for his sister, to attack her. Naturally he hid himself under the couch immediately, but he had to wait till midday for Grete's return, and, when she did come, she appeared unusually troubled. He realized that his appearance was still disgusting to the poor girl, that it would always be so, and that she must fiercely resist her own impulse to flee the moment she caught sight of the tiniest part of Gregor's body protruding from under the sofa. To spare her this sight, he took a sheet on his back, dragged it to the sofa—a task which occupied some hours—and spread it in such a way that his sister could see nothing under the sofa, even if she stooped. Had she found this precaution unnecessary, she would have taken the sheet away, for she guessed that Gregor did not so completely shut himself away for pleasure; but she left the sheet where it lay, and Gregor, prudently parting the curtain with his head to see what impression this new arrangement had made upon his sister, thought he detected a look of gratitude in her face.

During the first fortnight his parents had not been able to bring themselves to enter his room, and he often heard them praising the zeal of his sister, whom they had regarded, so far, as a useless young girl and of whom they had often complained. But now, both his father and mother would wait quite frequently outside Gregor's door while his sister was tidying the room, and scarcely had she come out again before they would make her tell them in detail exactly how she had found the room, what Gregor had eaten, and, in detail, what he was doing at that moment; they would ask her, too, if there were the slightest signs of improvement. His mother seemed impatient to see Gregor, but the father and sister restrained her with argument to which she listened very attentively and with which she wholly agreed. Later, however, they had to use force, and when his mother began to cry, "Let me go to Gregor! My poor boy! Don't you understand that I must see him!" Gregor thought that perhaps it would be as well if his mother did come in, not every day, of course, but perhaps once a week; she would understand things better than his sister, who was but a child, for all her courage, and had perhaps taken on such a difficult task out of childish lightheartedness.

Gregor's wish to see his mother was soon realized. Gregor avoided showing himself at the window during the day, out of consideration to his parents; but his restricted walks around the floor did not fully compensate him for this self-denial, nor could he bear to lie still for long, even during the night; he took no more pleasure in eating, and it soon became his habit to distract himself by walking—around the room, back and forth along the walls, and across the ceiling, on which he would hang; it was quite a different matter from walking across the floor. His breathing became freer, a light, swinging motion went through his body, and he felt so elated that now and then, to his own surprise, he would let himself go and fall to the floor. But by now, knowing better how to manage his body, he succeeded in rendering these falls harmless. His sister soon noticed his new pastime, for he left sticky marks here and there in his track, and Grete took it into her head to help him in his walks by removing all the furniture likely to be a hindrance, particularly the chest and the desk. Unfortunately, she was not strong enough to manage this on her own and dared not ask the help of her father; as for the maid, she certainly would have refused, for if this sixteen-year-old child had worked bravely since the former cook had left, it was on condition that she could stay continually barricaded in the kitchen, whose doors she would only open on special demand. So there was nothing else for it; Grete would have to enlist the mother's help one day when the father was away.

The mother gladly consented, but her exclamations of joy were hushed before Gregor's door. The sister first made sure that everything was in order in the room; then she allowed the mother to enter. In his great haste, Gregor had pulled the sheet down further than usual, and the many folds in which it fell gave the scene the air of a still life. This time he refrained from peeping under the sheet to spy on his mother but he was delighted to have her near.

"You may come in; he is not in sight," said his sister; and, taking her mother by the hand, she led her into the room. Then Gregor heard the two frail women struggling to remove the heavy old chest; the sister undertook the hardest part of the task, despite the warnings of her mother, who feared she might do herself some harm. It took a long time. They had been struggling with the chest for four hours when the mother declared that it might be best to leave it where it was, that it was too heavy for them, that they would not finish moving it before the father returned, and that, with the chest in the middle of the room, Gregor would be considerably impeded in his movements, and, finally, who knew whether he might not be displeased by the removal of his furniture?

The mother thought he would be; the sight of the bare walls struck cold at her heart; might Gregor not feel the same, having long grown so accustomed to the furniture, and would he not feel forsaken in his empty room? "Isn't it a fact," said the mother in a low voice—she had spoken in whispers ever since she entered the room, so that Gregor whose hiding place she had not yet discovered, might not overhear, not so much what she was saying—for she was persuaded that he could not understand—but the very sound of her voice. "Isn't it a fact that when we remove the furniture, we seem to imply that we are giving up all hope of seeing him cured and are wickedly leaving him to his fate? I think it would be better to keep the room just as it was before, so that Gregor will find nothing changed when he comes back to us and will be able the more easily to forget what has happened meanwhile."

Hearing his mother's words, Gregor realized how these two monotonous months, in the course of which nobody had addressed a word to him, must have affected his mind; he could not otherwise explain his desire for an empty room. Did he really wish to allow this warm, comfortable room with its genial furniture to be transformed into a cavern in which, in rapid and complete forgetfulness of his human past, he might exercise his right to crawl all over the walls? It seemed he was already so near to forgetting; and it had required nothing less than his mother's voice, which he had not heard for so long, to rouse him. Nothing should be removed, everything must stay as it is, he could not bear to forego the good influence of his furniture, and, if it prevented him from indulging his crazy impulses, then so much the better.

Unfortunately, his sister was not of this opinion;

she had become accustomed to assume authority over her parents where Gregor was concerned—this not without cause—and now the mother's remarks were enough to make her decide to remove not only the desk and the chest—which till now had been their only aim—but all the other furniture as well, except the indispensable sofa. This was not the result of mere childish bravado, nor the outcome of that new feeling of self-confidence which she had just acquired so unexpectedly and painfully. No, she really believed that Gregor had need of plenty of room for exercise and that, as far as she could see, he never used the furniture. Perhaps, also, the romantic character of girls of her age was partly responsible for her decision, a sentiment which strove to satisfy itself on every possible occasion and which now drove her to dramatize her brother's situation to such an extent so that she could devote herself to Gregor even more passionately than hitherto; for in a room over whose bare walls Gregor reigned alone, no one but Grete dare enter and stay.

She did not allow herself to be turned from her resolve by her mother, made irresolute by the oppressive atmosphere of the room, and who did not hesitate now to remove the chest as best she could. Gregor could bear to see the chest removed, at a pinch, but the desk must stay. And hardly had the women left the room, panting as they pushed the chest, than Gregor put out his head to examine the possibilities of making a prudent and tactful appearance. But unfortunately it was his mother who returned first, while Grete, in the side room, her arms around the chest, was rocking it from side to side without being able to settle it in position. The mother was not used to the sight of Gregor; it might give her a serious shock. Terrified, he hastened to retreat to the other end of the sofa, but he could not prevent the sheet from fluttering slightly, which immediately attracted his mother's attention. She stopped short, stood stockstill for a moment, then hurried back to Grete.

Gregor assured himself that nothing extraordinary was happening—they were merely removing a few pieces of furniture—but the coming and going of the women, their little cries, the scraping of the furniture over the floor, seemed to combine in such an excruciating din that, however much he withdrew his head, contracted his legs, and pressed himself to the ground, he had to admit that he could not bear this torture much longer. They were emptying his room, taking away from him all that he loved; they had already removed the chest in which he kept his saw and his fretwork outfit; now they were shifting his desk, which had stood so solid and fast to the floor all the time it was in use, that desk on which he had written his lessons while he was at the commercial school, at the secondary school, even at the preparatory school. However, he could no longer keep pace with their intentions, for so absent minded had he become he had almost forgotten their existence, now that fatigue had quietened them and the clatter of the weary feet could no longer be heard.

So he came out—the women were only leaning against the desk in the next room, recovering their breath—and he found himself so bewildered that he changed his direction four times; he really could not decide what he should first salvage—when suddenly he caught sight of the picture of the woman in furs which assumed tremendous importance on the bare wall; he hastily climbed up and pressed himself against the glass, which stuck to his burning belly and refreshed him delightfully. This picture, at least, which Gregor entirely covered, should not be snatched away from him by anyone. He turned his head toward the dining-room door to observe the women as they returned.

They had had but a short rest and were already coming back; Grete's arm was round her mother's waist, supporting her.

"Well, what shall we take now?" said Grete, and she looked around. Her eyes met those of Gregor on the wall. If she succeeded in keeping her presence of mind, it was only for her mother's sake, toward whom she leaned her head to prevent her from seeing anything and said, a little too quickly and with a trembling voice, "Come, wouldn't it be better to go back to the living room for a minute?" The girl's intention was clear to Gregor: she wished to put her mother in a safe place and then to drive him from the wall. Well, let her try! He lay over his picture, and he would not let it go. He would rather leap into his sister's face.

But Grete had merely disquieted her mother; now she turned, saw the gigantic brown stain spread over the wallpaper and, before she realized that it was Gregor she was seeing, she cried, "O God! O God!" in a screaming, raucous voice, fell on the sofa with outspread arms in a gesture of complete renunciation, and gave no further sign of life. "You, Gregor!" cried the sister, raising her fist and piercing Gregor with a look. It was the first word she had addressed to him directly ever since his metamorphosis. Then she ran to get some smelling salts from the dining room to rouse her mother from her swoon. Gregor decided to help—there was still time to save the picture—alas, he found he had stuck fast to the glass and had to make a violent effort to detach himself; then he hurried into the dining room as if able to give his sister some good advice, but he was obliged to content himself with remaining passively behind

her while she rummaged among the bottles, and he frightened her so terribly when she turned around that a bottle fell and broke on the floor, a splinter wounded Gregor in the face, and a corrosive medicine flowed round his feet; then Grete hastily grabbed up all the bottles she could carry and rushed in to her mother, slamming the door behind her with her foot. Now Gregor was shut out from his mother, who perhaps was nearly dead through his fault; he dared not open the door lest he drive away his sister, who must stay by his mother; so there was nothing to do but wait, and, gnawed by remorse and distress, he began to wander over the walls, the furniture, and the ceilings so rapidly that everything began to spin around him, till in despair he fell heavily on to the middle of the huge table.

A moment passed; Gregor lay stretched there, around all was still; perhaps that was a good sign. But suddenly he heard a knock. The maid was naturally barricaded in her kitchen; Grete herself must go to the door. His father had returned. "What has happened?" were his first words; no doubt Grete's expression had explained everything.

The girl replied in a stifled voice—probably she leaned her face against her father's breast—"Mother fainted, but she is better now. Gregor has got out."

"I was waiting for that," said the father, "I told you all along, but you women will never listen."

Gregor realized by these words that his father had misunderstood Grete's brief explanation and imagined that his son had broken loose in some reprehensible way. There was no time to explain. Gregor had to find some way of pacifying his father, so he quickly crawled to the door of his room and pressed himself against it for his father to see, as he came in, how he had every intention of returning to his own room immediately and that it was not at all necessary to drive him back with violence; one had only to open the door and he would quickly withdraw.

But his father was in no mood to notice these fine points. As he entered he cried, "Ah!" in a tone at once of joy and anger; Gregor turned his head away from the door and lifted it toward his father. He was astonished. He had never imagined his father as he stood before him now; it is true that for some time now he had neglected to keep himself acquainted with the events of the house, preferring to devote himself to his new mode of existence, and he had therefore been unaware of a certain change of character in his family. And yet—and yet, was that really his father? Was it really the same man who once had lain wearily in bed when Gregor had been leaving on his journeys, who met him, on his return, in his nightshirt, seated in an armchair out of which he could not even lift himself, throwing his arms high to show

how pleased he was? Was this that same old man who, on the rare walks which the family would take together, two or three Sundays a year and on special holidays, would hobble between Gregor and his mother, while they walked slower and slower for him, as he, covered with an old coat, carefully set his stick before him and prudently worked his way forward; and yet, despite their slowness, he would be obliged to stop, whenever he wished to say anything, and call his escort back to him? How upstanding he had become since then!

Now he was wearing a blue uniform with gold buttons, without a single crease, just as you see the employees of banking houses wearing; above the big, stiff collar his double chin spread its powerful folds; under his bristly eyebrows the watchful expression of his black eyes glittered young and purposefully; his white hair, ordinarily untidy, had been carefully brushed till it shone. He threw on to the sofa his cap, ornamented with the gilded monogram of some bank, making it describe the arc of a circle across the room, and, with his hands in his trouser pockets, the long flaps of his coat turned back, he walked toward Gregor with a menacing air. He himself did not know what he was going to do; however, he raised his feet very high, and Gregor, astonished at the enormous size of the soles of his boots, took care to remain still, for he knew that, from the first day of his metamorphosis, his father had held the view that the greatest severity was the only attitude to take up toward Gregor. Then he began to beat a retreat before his father's approach, halting when the other stopped and beginning again at his father's slightest move. In this way they walked several times round the room without any decisive result; it did not even take on the appearance of a pursuit, so slow was their pace.

Gregor was provisionally keeping to the floor; he feared that if his father saw him climbing about the walls or rushing across the ceiling, he might take this maneuver for some refinement of bad behavior. However, he had to admit that he could not go on much longer in this way; in the little time his father needed to take a step, Gregor had to make a whole series of gymnastic movements and, as he had never had good lungs, he now began to pant and wheeze; he tried to recover his breath quickly in order to gather all his strength for a supreme effort, scarcely daring to open his eyes, so stupefied that he could think of no other way to safety than by pursuing his present course; he had already forgotten that the walls were at his disposal, and the carefully carved furniture, all covered with festoons of plush and lace as it was. Suddenly something flew sharply by him, fell to the ground, and rolled away. It was an apple, carelessly thrown;

a second one flew by. Paralyzed with terror, Gregor stayed still. It was useless to continue his course, now that his father had decided to bombard him. He had emptied the bowls of fruit on the sideboard, filled his pockets, and now threw apple after apple, without waiting to take aim.

These little red apples rolled about the floor as if electrified knocking against each other. One lightly-thrown apple struck Gregor's back and fell off without doing any harm, but the next one literally pierced his flesh. He tried to drag himself a little further away, as if a change of position could relieve the shattering agony he suddenly felt, but he seemed to be nailed fast to the spot and stretched his body helplessly, not knowing what to do. With his last, hopeless glance, he saw his door opened suddenly, and, in front of his sister, who was shouting at the top of her voice, his mother came running in, in her petticoat, for his sister had partly undressed her that she might breathe easier in her swoon. And his mother, who ran to the father, losing her skirts one by one, stumbled forward, thrust herself against her husband, embraced him, pressed him to her, and, with her hands clasped at the back of his neck—already Gregor could see no more—begged him to spare Gregor's life.

III

The apple which no one dared draw from Gregor's back remained embedded in his flesh as a palpable memory, and the grave wound which he now had borne for a month seemed to have reminded his father that Gregor, despite his sad and terrible change, remained none the less a member of the family and must not be treated as an enemy; on the contrary, duty demanded that disgust should be overcome and Gregor be given all possible help.

His wound had made him lose, irremediably, no doubt, much of his agility; now, merely to cross his room required a long, long time, as if he were an aged invalid; his walks across the walls could no longer be considered. But this aggravation of his state was largely compensated for, in his opinion, by the fact that now, every evening, the dining-room door was left open; for two hours he would wait for this. Lying in the darkness of his room, invisible to the diners, he could observe the whole family gathered round the table in the lamplight, and he could, by common consent, listen to all they had to say—it was much better than before.

It must be admitted that they no longer held those lively conversations of which, in former times, he had always thought with such sadness as he crept into his damp bed in some little hotel room. Most of the time, now, they discussed nothing in particular after dinner. The father would soon settle himself to doze in his armchair; the mother and daughter would bid each other be silent; the mother, leaning forward in the light, would sew at some fine needlework for a lingerie shop, and the sister, who had obtained a job as a shop assistant, would study shorthand or French in the hope of improving her position. Now and then the father would wake up and, as if he did not know that he had been asleep, would say to his wife, "How late you are sewing tonight!" and would fall off to sleep again, while the mother and sister would exchange a tired smile.

By some capricious obstinacy, the father always refused to take off his uniform, even at home; his dressing gown hung unused in the wardrobe, and he slept in his armchair in full livery, as if to keep himself always ready to carry out some order; even in his own home he seemed to await his superior's voice. Moreover, the uniform had not been new when it was issued to him and now each day it became more shabby, despite the care which the two women devoted to it; and Gregor often spent the evening staring dully at this coat, so spotted and stained, whose polished buttons always shone so brightly, and in which the old man slept, uncomfortably but peacefully.

As soon as the clock struck ten, the mother, in a low voice, tried to rouse her husband and to encourage him to go to bed, as it was impossible to get proper sleep in such a position, and he must sleep normally before returning to work at six the next morning. But, with the obstinacy which had characterized him ever since he had obtained his position at the bank, he would stay at the table although he regularly dropped off to sleep, and thus it would become more and more difficult to induce him to change his armchair for the bed. The mother and sister might insist with their little warnings; he stayed there just the same, slowly nodding his head, his eyes shut tight, and would not get up. The mother might shake him by the wrist, might whisper endearments in his ear; the daughter might abandon her work to assist her mother, but all in vain. The old man would merely sink deeper in his chair. At last the two women would have to take him under the arms to make him open his eyes; then he would look at each in turn and say, "What a life! Is this the hard-earned rest of my old days?" and, leaning on the two women, he would rise painfully, as if he were a tremendous weight, and would allow himself to be led to the door by his wife and daughter; then he would wave them off and continue alone, while the mother and sister, the one quickly throwing down her pen, the other her needle, would run after him to help.

Who in the overworked and overtired family had time to attend to Gregor, except for his most pressing needs? The household budget was ever more and more reduced; at last the maid was dismissed. In her place, a gigantic charwoman with bony features and white hair, which stood up all around her head, came, morning and evening, to do the harder work. The rest was done by the mother, over and above her interminable mending and darning. It even happened that they were obliged to sell various family trinkets which formerly had been worn proudly by the mother and sister at ceremonies and festivals, as Gregor discovered one evening when he heard them discussing the price they hoped to get. But their most persistent complaints were about this flat, which was so much larger than they needed and which had now become too expensive for the family purse; they could not leave, they said, for they could not imagine how Gregor could be moved. Alas, Gregor understood that it was not really he who was the chief obstacle to this removal, for he might easily have been transported in a large wooden box pierced with a few air holes. No, what particularly prevented the family from changing their residence was their own despair, the idea that they had been stricken by such a misfortune as had never before occurred in the family or within the circle of their acquaintances.

Of all the deprivations which the world imposes on poor people, not one had been spared them; the father took his day-time meals with the lesser employees of the bank, the mother was killing herself mending the linen of strangers, the sister ran here and there behind her counter at the customers' bidding; but the family had energy for nothing further. It seemed to poor Gregor that his wound reopened whenever his mother and sister, returning from putting the father to bed, would leave their work in disorder and bring their chairs nearer to each other, till they were sitting almost cheek to cheek; then the mother would say, pointing to Gregor's room, "Close the door, Grete," and he would once more be left in darkness, while, outside, the two women mingled their tears or, worse, sat at the table staring with dry eyes.

These days and nights brought Gregor no sleep. From time to time he thought of taking the family affairs in hand, as he once used, the very next time the door was opened; at the end of a long perspective of time he dimly saw in his mind his employer and the manager, the clerks and apprentices, the porter with his narrow ideas, two or three acquaintances from other offices, a provincial barmaid—a fleeting but dear memory—and a cashier in a hat shop, whom he had pursued earnestly but too slowly; they passed through his mind in confusion, mingled with unknown and forgotten faces; but none of them could bring help to him or his family; nothing was to be gained from them. He was pleased to be able to dismiss them from his mind but now he no longer cared what happened to his family; on the contrary, he only felt enraged because they neglected to tidy his room, and, though nothing imaginable could excite his appetite, he began making involved plans for a raid on the larder, with a view to taking such food as he had a right to, even if he was not hungry. Nowadays his sister no longer tried to guess what might please him; she made a hasty appearance twice a day, in the morning and in the afternoon, before going to her shop, and pushed a few scraps of food into the room with her foot; in the evening, without even bothering to see whether he had touched his meal or whether he had left it entirely—and this was usually the case—she would sweep up the remains with a whisk of the broom.

As for tidying up the room, which Grete now did in the evenings, it could not have been done in a more hasty manner. Great patches of dirt streaked the wall, little heaps of dust and ordure lay here and there about the floor. At first Gregor would place himself in the filthiest places whenever his sister appeared, so that this might seem a reproach to her. But he could have stayed there for weeks, and still Grete would not have altered her conduct; she saw the dirt as well as he but she had finally decided to take no further trouble. This did not prevent her from taking even more jealous care than ever to insure that no other member of the family should presume on her right to the tidying of the room.

Once the mother undertook to give Gregor's room a great cleaning which required several buckets of water, and this deluge deeply upset poor Gregor, crouched under his sofa in bitter immobility—but the mother's punishment soon came. Hardly had the sister, coming home in the evening, noticed the difference in Gregor's room, than, feeling deeply offended, she ran crying and screaming into the dining room, despite the appeal of her mother, who raised her hands in supplication; the father, who was quietly seated at table, leaped up, astonished but powerless to pacify her. Then he, too, became agitated; shouting, he began to attack the mother, on the one hand, for not leaving the care and cleaning of Gregor's room to the girl and, on the other hand, he forbade his daughter ever again to dare to clean it; the mother tried to draw the old man, quivering with anger as he was, into the bedroom; the daughter, shaken with sobs, was banging on the table with her little fists, while Gregor loudly hissed with rage to think that no one had the decency or consideration to close the door and thus spare him the sight of all this trouble and uproar.

But even if the sister, tired out by her work in the shop, could not bother to look after Gregor as carefully as hitherto, she could still have arranged that he should not be neglected without necessarily calling on the aid of her mother, for there was always the charwoman. This old woman, whose bony frame had helped her out of worse trouble during her long life, could not really be said to feel any disgust with Gregor. Though she was not inquisitive, she had opened his door one day and had stood with her hands folded over her stomach, astonished at the sight of Gregor, who began to trot here and there in his alarm, though she had no thought of chasing him. From that day, morning and evening, the old woman never lost an opportunity of opening the door a little to peer into the room.

At first she would call Gregor to make him come out, crying in a familiar tone, "Come on, you old cockroach!" or, "Hey, look at the old cockroach!" To such invitations Gregor would not respond; instead he remained motionless beneath his sofa as if the door had not been opened. If they had only ordered the charwoman to clean his room out each day instead of allowing her to go on teasing and upsetting him! Early one morning, when heavy rain—perhaps a sign of approaching spring—beat on the roofs, Gregor was so annoyed by the old woman as she began to bait him again that he suddenly turned on her, in a somewhat cumbersome and uncertain manner, it must be admitted, but with every intention of attacking her. She was not at all frightened of him; there was a chair by the door; she took it up and brandished it, opening wide her mouth with the obvious intention of not closing it until she had brought the chair down with a crash on Gregor's back. "Ah, is that all?" she asked, seeing him return to his former position, and she quietly put the chair back in its place.

Nowadays Gregor hardly ate at all. When, by some chance, he passed by his scraps, he would amuse himself by taking a piece of food in his mouth and keeping it there for hours, usually spitting it out in the end. At first he had thought that his loss of appetite was due to the misery into which the state of his room had plunged him; no doubt this was a mistake, for he had soon become reconciled to the squalor of his surroundings. His family had got into the habit of piling into his room whatever could not be accommodated elsewhere, and this meant a great deal, now that one of the rooms had been let to three lodgers. They were very earnest and serious men; all three had thick beards—as Gregor saw one day when he was peering through a crack in the door—and they were fanatically tidy; they insisted on order, not only in their own room, but also, now that they were living here, throughout the whole household, and especially in the kitchen.

They had brought with them all that they needed, and this rendered superfluous a great many things about the house which could neither be sold nor thrown away, and which were now all stacked in Gregor's room, as were the ash bucket and the rubbish bin. Everything that seemed for the moment useless would be dumped in Gregor's room by the charwoman, who was always in a breathless hurry to get through her work; he would just have time to see a hand brandishing some unwanted utensil, and then the door would slam again. Perhaps the old woman intended to return and find the objects she so carelessly relegated here when she needed them and had time to search; or perhaps she meant to throw them all away some day, but in actual fact they stayed in the room, on the very spot where they had first fallen, so that Gregor was obliged to pick his way among the rubbish to make a place for himself —a game for which his taste began to grow, in spite of the appalling misery and fatigue which followed these peregrinations, leaving him paralyzed for hours. As the lodgers sometimes dined at home in the living room, the door of this room would be shut on certain evenings; however, Gregor no longer attached any importance to this; for some while, now, he had ceased to profit by those evenings when the family would open the door and he would remain shrinking in the darkest corner of his room, where the family could not see him.

One day the woman forgot to close the dining-room door, and it was still ajar when the lodgers came in and lit the gas. They sat down at table in the places that previously had been occupied by the father, the mother, and Gregor; each unfolded his napkin and took up his knife and fork. Soon the mother appeared in the doorway with a plate of meat; the sister followed her, carrying a dish of potatoes. When their meal had been set before them the lodgers leaned over to examine it, and the one who was seated in the middle and who appeared to have some authority over the others, cut a piece of meat as it lay on the dish to ascertain whether it was tender or whether he should send it back to the kitchen. He seemed satisfied, however, and the two women, who had been anxiously watching, gave each other a smile of relief.

The family itself lived in the kitchen. However, the father, before going into the kitchen, always came into the dining room and bowed once with his cap in his hand, then made his way around the table. The boarders rose together and murmured something in their beards. Once they were alone, they began to eat in silence. It seemed curious to Gregor that he could hear the gnashing of their teeth above all the clatter of cutlery; it was as if they wanted to prove to him that one must have real teeth in order to eat properly, and that the best mandibles in the world were but an unsatisfactory substitute. "I am hungry," thought Gregor sadly, "but not for these things. How these lodgers can eat! And in the meantime I might die, for all they care."

He could not remember hearing his sister play since the arrival of the lodgers; but this evening the sound of the violin came from the kitchen. The lodgers had just finished their meal; the middle one had brought a newspaper and had given a page to each of the others; now they all three read, leaning back in their chairs and smoking. The sound of the violin attracted their attention, and they rose and walked on tiptoe toward the hall door, where they halted and remained very close together.

Apparently they had been heard in the kitchen, for the father cried, "Does the violin upset you gentlemen? We'll stop it immediately."

"On the contrary," said the man in the middle. "Would Fräulein Samsa not like to come in and play to us here in the dining room, where it is much nicer and more comfortable?"

"Oh, thank you," said the father, as if he were the violinist.

The gentlemen walked back across the room and waited. Soon the father came in with the music stand, the mother with the sheets of music, and the sister with the violin. The sister calmly prepared to play; her parents, who had never before let their rooms, were exaggeratedly polite to the boarders and were afraid to seem presumptuous by sitting in their own chairs; the father leaned against the door, his right hand thrust between two buttons of his livery coat; but one of the gentlemen offered the mother a chair in which she finally sat, not daring to move from her corner throughout the performance.

The girl now began to play, while her father and mother, from either side, watched the movement of her hands. Attracted by the music, Gregor had crawled forward a little and had thrust his head into the room. He was no longer astonished that nowadays he had entirely lost that consideration for others, that anxiety to cause no trouble that once had been his pride. Yet never had he more reason to remain hidden, for now, because of the dirt that lay about his room, flying up at the slightest movement, he was always covered with dust and fluff, with ends of cotton and hairs, and with morsels of stale food, which stuck to his back or to his feet and which he trailed after him wherever he went; his apathy had grown too great for him to bother anymore about cleaning himself several times a day by lying on his back and rubbing himself on the carpet, as once he used to do. And this filthy state did not prevent him from crawling over the spotless floor without a moment's shame.

So far, no one had noticed him. The family was too absorbed by the music of the violin, and the lodgers, who had first stood with their hands in their pockets, very close to the music stand—which disturbed the sister a great deal as she was obliged to see their image dancing amid the notes—had at last retired toward the window, where they stood speaking together half aloud, with lowered heads, under the anxious gaze of the father, who was watching attentively. It had become only too evident that they had been deceived in their hopes of hearing some beautiful violin piece, or at least some amusing little tune; it seemed that what the girl was playing bored them and that now they only tolerated her out of politeness. By the way in which they puffed the smoke of their cigars, by the energy with which they blew it toward the ceiling through the mouth or the nose, one could guess how fidgety they were becoming. And the sister was playing so nicely. Her face leaning to one side, her glance followed the score carefully and sadly. Gregor crawled forward a little more and put his head as near as possible to the floor to meet her gaze. Could it be that he was only an animal, when music moved him so? It seemed to him to open a way toward that unknown nourishment he so longed for. He resolved to creep up to his sister and to pull at her dress to make her understand that she must come with him, for no one here would appreciate her music as much as he. He would never let her out of his room—at least, while he lived—for once, his horrible shape would serve him some useful purpose; he would be at all doors at once, repulsing intruders with his raucous breath; but his sister would not be forced to stay there; she must live with him of her own accord; she would sit by him on the sofa, hearing what he had to say; then he would tell her in confidence that he had firmly intended to send her to the Conservatory and had planned to let everyone know last Christmas—was Christmas really past?—without listening to any objections, had his misfortune not overtaken him too soon. His sister, moved by this explanation, would surely burst into tears, and Gregor, climbing up on her shoulder, would kiss her neck; this would be all the easier, for she had worn neither collar nor ribbon ever since she had been working in the shop.

"Herr Samsa," cried the middle lodger, and he pointed at Gregor, who slowly came into the room. The violin was suddenly silenced, the middle lodger turned to his friends, grinning and shaking his head, then once more he stared at Gregor. The father seemed to consider it more urgent to reassure the lodgers than to drive his son from the room, though the lodgers did not seem to be at all upset by the spectacle; in fact, Gregor seemed to amuse them more highly than did the violin. The father hurried forward and, with outstretched arms, tried to drive them into their room, hiding Gregor from them with his body. Now they began to be really upset, but it is not known whether this was on account of the father's action or because they had been living with such a monstrous neighbor as Gregor without being made aware of it. They demanded explanations, waving their arms in the air; and, fidgeting nervously with their beards, they retreated toward their own door. Meanwhile the sister had recovered from the distress that the sudden interruption of her music had caused her; after remaining a moment completely at a loss, with the violin and the bow hanging from her helpless hands, following the score with her eyes as if she were still playing, she suddenly came back to life, laid the violin in her mother's lap—the mother sat suffocating in her chair, her lungs working violently—and rushed into the next room, toward which the lodgers were rapidly retreating before Herr Samsa's onslaught. One could see how quickly, under Grete's practised hand, pillows and covers were set in order on the beds. The lodgers had not yet reached the room when their beds were already prepared, and Grete had slipped out. The father seemed so possessed by his strange fury that he had quite forgotten the respect due to lodgers.

He drove them to the door of the room, where the middle lodger suddenly came to a stop, stamping thunderously on the floor. "I wish to inform you," said this man, raising his hand and looking around for the two women, "that in view of the disgusting circumstances which govern this family and this house"—and here he spat quickly on the carpet—"I hereby immediately give up my room. Naturally, you will not get a penny for the time I have been living here; on the contrary, I am considering whether I should not claim compensation from you, damages which should easily be awarded in any court of law; it is a matter about which I shall inquire, believe me." He was silent and stared into space, as if awaiting something. Accordingly, his two friends also spoke up: "We, too, give our notice." Thereupon the gentleman in the middle seized the door handle, and they went inside. The door closed with a crash.

The father stumbled toward his chair, put his trembling hands upon the arms, and let himself drop into it; he looked exactly as if he were settling himself for his customary evening nap, but the way his head drooped heavily from side to side showed that he was thinking of something other than sleep. All this time Gregor had stayed still on the spot where he had surprised the lodgers. He felt completely paralyzed with bewilderment at the checking of his plans—perhaps, also, with weakness due to his prolonged fasting. He feared that the whole household would fall upon him immediately; he foresaw the precise moment when this catastrophe would happen, and now he waited. Even the violin did not frighten him as it fell with a clatter from the trembling fingers of his mother, who until now had held it in her lap.

"My dear parents," said his sister, who beat with her hand on the table by way of introduction. "Things cannot go on like this. Even if you do not realize it, I can see it quite clearly. I will not mention my brother's name when I speak of this monster here; I merely want to say: we must find some means of getting rid of it. We have done all that is humanly possible to care for it, to put up with it; I believe that nobody could reproach us in the least."

"She's a thousand times right," said the father. But the mother, who had not yet recovered her breath, coughed helplessly behind her hand, her eyes haggard.

The sister hurried toward her mother and held her forehead. Grete's words seemed to have made up the father's mind, for now he sat up in his armchair and fidgeted with his cap among the dishes on the table, from which the lodgers' meal had not yet been cleared; from time to time he stared at Gregor.

"We must find a way of getting rid of it," repeated the sister, now speaking only to her father, for her mother, shaken by her coughing, could hear nothing. "It will bring you both to the grave. I can see it coming. When people have to work all day, as we must, we cannot bear this eternal torture each time we come home at night. I can stand it no longer." And she wept so bitterly that her tears fell on her mother's face, who wiped them off with a mechanical movement of her hand.

"But what can we do, child?" said the father in a pitiful voice. It was surprising to see how well he understood his daughter.

The sister merely shrugged her shoulders as a sign of the perplexity which, during her tears, had replaced her former assurance.

"If he could only understand us," said the father in a half-questioning tone, but the sister, through her tears, made a violent gesture with her hand as a sign that this was not to be thought of.

"If only he could understand us," repeated the father—and he shut his eyes as he spoke, as if to show that he agreed with the sister that such a thing was quite impossible. "If only he could understand us, perhaps there would be some way of coming to an agreement. But as it is . . ."

"It must go!" cried the sister. "That's the only way out. You must get the idea out of your head that this is Gregor. We have believed that for too long, and that is the cause of all our unhappiness. How could it be Gregor? If it were really he, he would long ago have realized that he could not live with human beings and would have gone off on his own accord. I haven't a brother any longer, but we can go on living and can honor his memory. In his place we have this monster that pursues us and drives away our lodgers; perhaps it wants the whole flat to itself, to drive us out into the streets. Look, father, look!" she suddenly screamed, "it's beginning again!" And in an access of terror, which Gregor could not understand, she let go her mother so suddenly that she bounced in the seat of the armchair; it seemed as if the sister would rather sacrifice her mother than stay near Gregor; she hastily took refuge behind her father, who was very upset by her behavior and now stood up, spreading his arms to protect her.

But Gregor had no thought of frightening anyone, least of all his sister. He had merely started to turn around in order to go back to his room; but it must be realized that this looked very alarming, for his weakness obliged him to assist his difficult turning movement with his head, which he raised and lowered many times, clutching at the carpet with his mandibles. At last he ceased and stared at the family. It seemed they realized his good intentions. They were watching him in mute sadness. The mother lay in her armchair, her outstretched legs pressed tightly together, her eyes nearly closed with fatigue; the father and sister were sitting side by side, and the girl's arm was round her father's neck.

"Now, perhaps, they will let me turn," thought Gregor, and he once more set about his task. He could not repress a sigh of weariness; he was obliged to rest from time to time. However, no one hurried him; they left him entirely alone. When he had completed his turn, he immediately beat a retreat, crawling straight ahead. He was astonished at the distance which separated him from his room; he did not realize that this was due merely to his weak state and that a little before he could have covered the distance without noticing it. His family did not disturb him by a single cry, a single exclamation; but this he did not even notice, so necessary was it to concentrate all his will on getting back to his room. It was only when he had at long last reached his door that he thought of turning his head, not completely, because his neck had become very stiff, but sufficiently to reassure himself that nothing had changed behind him; only his sister was not standing up. His last look was toward his mother, who, by this time, was fast asleep.

Hardly was he in his room before the door was slammed, locked, and double bolted. So sudden was the crash that Gregor's legs gave way. It was his sister who had rushed to the door. She had stood up so as to be ready immediately and at the right moment had run forward so lightly that he had not heard her come; as she turned the key in the lock, she cried to her parents, "At last!"

"What now?" asked Gregor, looking around himself in the darkness. He soon discovered that he could not move. This did not surprise him in the least; it seemed to him much more remarkable that such frail legs had hitherto been able to bear his weight. Now he experienced a feeling of relative comfort. True, his whole body ached, but it seemed that these aches became less and less until finally they disappeared. Even the rotted apple embedded in his back hardly hurt him now; no more did the inflammation of the surrounding parts, covered with fine dust, cause him any further discomfort. He thought of his family in tender solicitude. He realized that he must go, and his opinion on this point was even more firm, if possible, than that of his sister. He lay in this state of peaceful and empty meditation till the clock struck the third morning hour. He saw the landscape grow lighter through the window; then, against his will, his head fell forward and his last feeble breath streamed from his nostrils.

When the charwoman arrived early in the morning —and though she had often been forbidden to do so, she always slammed the door so loudly in her vigor and haste that once she was in the house it was impossible to get any sleep—she did not at first notice anything unusual as she paid her customary morning visit to Gregor. She imagined that he was deliberately lying motionless in order to play the role of an "injured party," as she herself would say—she deemed him capable of such refinements; as she had a long broom in her hand, she tried to tickle him from the doorway. Meeting with little success, she grew angry; she gave him one or two hard pushes, and it was only when his body moved unresistingly before her thrusts that she became curious. She quickly realized what had happened, opened her eyes wide, and whistled in astonishment, but she did not stay in the room; she ran to the bedroom, opened the door, and loudly shouted into the darkness, "Come and look! He's stone dead! He's lying there, absolutely dead as a doornail!"

Herr and Frau Samsa sat up in their bed and tried to calm each other; the old woman had frightened them so much and they did not realize the sense of

her message immediately. But now they hastily scrambled out of bed, Herr Samsa on one side, his wife on the other; Herr Samsa put the coverlet over his shoulders, Frau Samsa ran out, clad only in her nightdress; and it was thus that they rushed into Gregor's room. Meanwhile, the dining-room door was opened—Grete had been sleeping there since the arrival of the lodgers—she was fully dressed, as if she had not slept all night, and the pallor of her face seemed to bear witness to her sleeplessness.

"Dead?" said Frau Samsa, staring at the charwoman with a questioning look, though she could see as much for herself without further examination.

"I should say so," said the charwoman, and she pushed Gregor to one side with her broom, to support her statement. Frau Samsa made a movement as if to hold back the broom, but she did not complete her gesture.

"Well," said Herr Samsa, "we can thank God for that!" He crossed himself and signed the three women to do likewise.

Grete, whose eyes had never left the corpse, said, "Look how thin he was! It was such a long time since he had eaten anything. His meals used to come out of the room just as they were taken in." And, indeed, Gregor's body was quite flat and dry; this could be seen more easily now that he was no longer supported on his legs and there was nothing to deceive one's sight.

"Come with us a moment, Grete!" said Frau Samsa with a sad smile, and Grete followed her parents into their bedroom, not without turning often to gaze at the corpse. The charwoman closed the door and opened the French windows. Despite the early hour, the fresh morning air had a certain warmth. It was already the end of March.

The three lodgers came out of their room and gazed around in astonishment for their breakfast; they had been forgotten. "Where is our breakfast?" the middle lodger petulantly demanded of the old woman. But she merely laid her finger to her mouth and signed them, with a mute and urgent gesture, to follow her into Gregor's room. So they entered and stood around Gregor's corpse, with their hands in the pockets of their rather shabby coats, in the middle of the room already bright with sunlight.

Then the bedroom door opened and Herr Samsa appeared in his uniform with his wife on one arm, his daughter on the other. All seemed to have been weeping, and from time to time Grete pressed her face against her father's arm.

"Leave my house immediately!" said Herr Samsa, and he pointed to the door, while the women still clung to his arms.

Somewhat disconcerted, the middle lodger said with a timid smile, "Whatever do you mean?"

The two others clasped their hands behind their backs and kept on rubbing their palms together, as if they were expecting some great dispute which could only end in triumph for them.

"I mean exactly what I say!" answered Herr Samsa and, in line with the two women, he marched straight at the lodger. The latter, however, stood quietly in his place, his eyes fixed on the floor, as if reconsidering what he should do.

"Well, then, we will go," he said at last, raising his eyes to Herr Samsa as if searching, in a sudden access of humility, for some slight approval of his resolution.

Herr Samsa merely nodded several times, opening his eyes very wide. Thereupon the lodger walked away with big strides and soon reached the ante-room; his two friends, who for some while had ceased wringing their hands, now bounded after him, as if afraid Herr Samsa might reach the door before them and separate them from their leader. Once they had gained the hall, they took down their hats from the pegs, grabbed their sticks from the umbrella stand, bowed silently, and left the flat.

With a suspicion which, it appears, was quite unjustified, Herr Samsa ran out onto the landing after them with the women and leaned over the balustrade to watch the three men as they slowly, but steadily, descended the interminable stairway, disappearing once as they reached a certain point on each floor, and then, after a few seconds, coming into view again. As they went farther down the staircase, so the Samsa family's interest diminished, and when they had been met and passed by a butcher's boy who came proudly up the stairs with his basket on his head, Herr Samsa and the women quickly left the landing and went indoors again with an air of relief.

They decided to spend the whole day resting; perhaps they might take a walk in the country; they had earned a respite and needed it urgently. And so they sat down to the table to write three letters of excuse: Herr Samsa to the manager of the Bank, Frau Samsa to her employer, and Grete to the head of her department at the shop. The charwoman came in while they were writing and announced that her work was done and that she was going. The three writers at first merely nodded their heads, without raising their eyes, but, as the old woman did not leave, they eventually laid down their pens and looked crossly at her.

"Well?" asked Herr Samsa. The charwoman was standing in the doorway, smiling as if she had some very good news to tell them but which she would not impart till she had been begged to. The little ostrich feather which stood upright on her hat and which had always annoyed Herr Samsa so much ever since the old woman had entered their service, now waved lightly in all directions.

"Well, what is it?" asked Frau Samsa, toward whom the old woman had always shown so much more respect than to the others.

"Well . . ." she replied, and she laughed so much she could hardly speak for some while. "Well, you needn't worry about getting rid of that thing in there, I have fixed it already."

Frau Samsa and Grete leaned over the table as if to resume their letter-writing; Herr Samsa, noticing that the woman was about to launch forth into a detailed explanation, cut her short with a peremptory gesture of his outstretched hand. Then, prevented from speaking, she suddenly remembered that she was in a great hurry and, crying, "Goodbye, everyone," in a peevish tone, she half turned and was gone in a flash, savagely slamming the door behind her.

"This evening we must sack her," declared Herr Samsa; but neither his wife nor his daughter answered; the old woman had not been able to disturb their newly won tranquillity. They arose, went to the window, and stood there, with their arms around each other; Herr Samsa, turning toward them in his armchair, stared at them for a moment in silence. Then he cried, "Come, come, it's all past history now; you can start paying a little attention to me." The women immediately hurried to him, kissed him, and sat down to finish their letters.

Then they all left the apartment together, a thing they had been unable to do for many months past, and they boarded a tram which would take them some way into the country. There were no other passengers in the compartment, which was warm and bright in the sun. Casually leaning back in their seats, they began to discuss their future. On careful reflection, they decided that things were not nearly so bad as they might have been, for—and this was a point they had not hitherto realized—they had all three found really interesting occupations which looked even more promising in the future. They decided to effect what really should be the greatest improvement as soon as possible. That was to move from the flat they occupied at present. They would take a smaller, cheaper flat, but one more practical, and especially in a better neighborhood than the present one, which Gregor had chosen. Hearing their daughter speak in more and more lively tones, Herr and Frau Samsa noticed almost together that, during this affair, Grete had blossomed into a fine strapping girl, despite the make-up which made her cheeks look pale. They became calmer; almost unconsciously they exchanged glances; it occurred to both of them that it would soon be time for her to find a husband. And it seemed to them that their daughter's gestures were a confirmation of these new dreams of theirs, and encouragement for their good intentions, when, at the end of the journey, the girl rose before them and stretched her young body.

THE LOST BOY

THOMAS WOLFE

THOMAS WOLFE (1900–1938) was born in Asheville, North Carolina, graduated from the University of North Carolina, took his M.A. at Harvard, and taught English briefly at Washington Square College, New York University. He lived for a time in England and Europe. "A man must use the material and experience of his own life," he said, "if he is to create anything that has substantial value." The central problem for him as a writer was a sense of form, as he tells us in *The Story of a Novel* (1936). Among his books are *Look Homeward, Angel* (1929), *Of Time and the River* (1935), *From Death to Morning* (1935), and *You Can't Go Home Again* (1940). His collected letters were published in 1956.

I

LIGHT came and went and came again, the booming strokes of three o'clock beat out across the town in thronging bronze from the courthouse bell, light winds of April blew the fountain out in rainbow sheets, until the plume returned and pulsed, as Grover turned into the Square. He was a child, dark-eyed and grave, birthmarked upon his neck— a berry of warm brown—and with a gentle face, too quiet and too listening for his years. The scuffed boy's shoes, the thick-ribbed stockings gartered at the knees, the short knee pants cut straight with three small useless buttons at the side, the sailor blouse, the old cap battered out of shape, perched sideways up on top of the raven head, the old soiled canvas bag slung from the shoulder, empty now, but waiting for the crisp sheets of the afternoon—these friendly, shabby garments, shaped by Grover, uttered him. He turned and passed along the north side of the Square and in that moment saw the union of Forever and of Now.

Light came and went and came again, the great plume of the fountain pulsed and winds of April sheeted it across the Square in a rainbow gossamer of spray. The fire department horses drummed on the floors with wooden stomp, most casually, and with dry whiskings of their clean, coarse tails. The street cars ground into the Square from every portion of the compass and halted briefly like wound toys in their familiar quarter-hourly formula. A dray, hauled by a boneyard nag, rattled across the cobbles on the other side before his father's shop. The courthouse bell boomed out its solemn warning of immediate three, and everything was just the same as it had always been.

He saw that haggis of vexed shapes with quiet eyes —that hodgepodge of ill-sorted architectures that made up the Square, and he did not feel lost. For "Here," thought Grover, "here is the Square as it has always been—and papa's shop, the fire department and the City Hall, the fountain pulsing with its plume, the street cars coming in and halting at the quarter hour, the hardware store on the corner there, the row of old brick buildings on this side of the street, the people passing and the light that comes and changes and that always will come back again, and everything that comes and goes and changes in the Square, and yet will be the same again. And here," the boy thought, "is Grover with his paper bag. Here is old Grover, almost twelve years old. Here is the month of April, 1904. Here is the courthouse bell and three o'clock. Here is Grover on the Square that never changes. Here is Grover, caught upon this point of time."

It seemed to him that the Square, itself the accidental masonry of many years, the chance agglomeration of time and of disrupted strivings, was the center of the universe. It was for him, in his soul's picture, the earth's pivot, the granite core of changelessness, the eternal place where all things came and passed and yet abode forever and would never change.

He passed the old shack on the corner—the wooden fire-trap where S. Goldberg ran his wiener stand. Then he passed the Singer place next door, with its gleaming display of new machines. He saw them and admired them, but he felt no joy. They brought back to him the busy hum of housework and of women sewing, the intricacy of stitch and weave, the mystery of style and pattern, the memory of women bending over flashing needles, the pedaled tread, the busy whir. It was women's work: it filled him with unknown associations of dullness and of vague depression. And always, also, with a moment's twinge of horror, for his dark eye would always travel toward that needle stitching up and down so fast the eye could never follow it. And then he would remember how his mother once had told him she had driven the needle through her finger, and always, when he passed this place, he would remember it and for a moment crane his neck and turn his head away.

He passed on then, but had to stop again next door before the music store. He always had to stop by places that had shining perfect things in them. He loved hardware stores and windows full of accurate geometric tools. He loved windows full of hammers, saws, and planing boards. He liked windows full of strong new rakes and hoes, with unworn handles, of white perfect wood, and stamped hard and vivid with the maker's seal. He loved to see such things as these in the windows of hardware stores. And he would fairly gloat upon them and think that some day he would own a set himself.

Also, he always stopped before the music and piano store. It was a splendid store. And in the window was a small white dog upon his haunches, with head cocked gravely to one side, a small white dog that never moved, that never barked, that listened attentively at the flaring funnel of a horn to hear "His Master's Voice"—a horn forever silent, and a voice that never spoke. And within were many rich and shining shapes of great pianos, an air of splendor and of wealth.

And now, indeed, he *was* caught, held suspended. A waft of air, warm chocolate-laden, filled his nostrils. He tried to pass the white front of the little eight-foot shop; he paused, struggling with conscience; he could not go on. It was the little candy shop run by old Crocker and his wife. And Grover could not pass.

"Old stingy Crockers!" he thought scornfully. "I'll not go there anymore. But—" as the maddening fragrance of rich cooking chocolate touched him once again—"I'll just look in the window and see what they've got." He paused a moment, looking with his dark and quiet eyes into the window of the little candy shop. The window, spotlessly clean, was filled with trays of fresh-made candy. His eyes rested on a tray of chocolate drops. Unconsciously he licked his lips. Put one of them upon your tongue and it just melted there, like honeydew. And then the trays full of rich home-made fudge. He gazed longingly at the deep body of the chocolate fudge, reflectively at maple walnut, more critically, yet with longing, at the mints, the nougatines, and all the other dainties.

"Old stingy Crockers!" Grover muttered once again, and turned to go. "I wouldn't go in *there* again."

And yet he did not go away. "Old stingy Crockers" they might be; still they did make the best candy in town, the best, in fact, that he had ever tasted.

He looked through the window back into the little shop and saw Mrs. Crocker there. A customer had gone in and had made a purchase, and as Grover looked he saw Mrs. Crocker, with her little wrenny face, her pinched features, lean over and peer primly at the scales. She had a piece of fudge in her clean, bony, little fingers, and as Grover looked, she broke it, primly, in her little bony hands. She dropped a morsel down into the scales. They weighted down alarmingly, and her thin lips tightened. She snatched the piece of fudge out of the scales and broke it carefully once again. This time the scales wavered, went down very slowly, and came back again. Mrs. Crocker carefully put the reclaimed piece of fudge back in the tray, dumped the remainder in a paper bag, folded it and gave it to the customer, counted the money carefully and doled it out into the till, the pennies in one place, the nickels in another.

Grover stood there, looking scornfully. "Old stingy Crocker—afraid that she might give a crumb away!"

He grunted scornfully and again he turned to go. But now Mr. Crocker came out from the little partitioned place where they made all their candy, bearing a tray of fresh-made fudge in his skinny hands. Old Man Crocker rocked along the counter to the front and put it down. He really rocked along. He was a cripple. And like his wife, he was a wrenny, wizened little creature, with bony hands, thin lips, a pinched and meager face. One leg was inches shorter than the other, and on this leg there was an enormous thick-soled boot, with a kind of wooden, rocker-like arrangement, six inches high at least, to make up for the deficiency. On this wooden cradle Mr. Crocker rocked along, with a prim and apprehensive little smile, as if he were afraid he was going to lose something.

"Old stingy Crocker!" muttered Grover. "Humph! He wouldn't give you anything!"

And yet—he did not go away. He hung there curiously, peering through the window, with his dark and gentle face now focused and intent, alert and curious, flattening his nose against the glass. Unconsciously he scratched the thick-ribbed fabric of one stockinged leg with the scuffed and worn toe of his old shoe. The fresh, warm odor of the new-made fudge was delicious. It was a little maddening. Half consciously he began to fumble in one trouser pocket, and pulled out his purse, a shabby worn old black one with a twisted clasp. He opened it and prowled about inside.

What he found was not inspiring—a nickel and two pennies and—he had forgotten them—the stamps. He took the stamps out and unfolded them. There were five twos, eight ones, all that remained of the dollar-sixty-cents' worth which Reed, the pharmacist, had given him for running errands a week or two before.

"Old Crocker," Grover thought, and looked somberly at the grotesque little form as it rocked back into the shop again, around the counter, and up the other side. "Well—" again he looked indefinitely at the stamps in his hand—"he's had all the rest of them. He might as well take these."

So, soothing conscience with this sop of scorn, he went into the shop and stood looking at the trays in the glass case and finally decided. Pointing with a slightly grimy finger at the fresh-made tray of chocolate fudge, he said, "I'll take fifteen cents' worth of this, Mr. Crocker." He paused a moment, fighting with embarrassment, then he lifted his dark face and said quietly, "And please, I'll have to give you stamps again."

Mr. Crocker made no answer. He did not look at Grover. He pressed his lips together primly. He went rocking away and got the candy scoop, came back, slid open the door of the glass case, put fudge into the scoop, and, rocking to the scales, began to weigh the candy out. Grover watched him as he peered and squinted, he watched him purse and press his lips together, he saw him take a piece of fudge and break it in two parts. And then old Crocker broke two parts in two again. He weighed, he squinted, and he hovered, until it seemed to Grover that by calling *Mrs.* Crocker stingy he had been guilty of a rank injustice. But finally, to his vast relief, the job was over, the scales hung there, quivering apprehensively, upon the very hairline of nervous balance, as if even the scales were afraid that one more move from Old Man Crocker and they would be undone.

Mr. Crocker took the candy then and dumped it in a paper bag and, rocking back along the counter toward the boy, he dryly said: "Where are the stamps?" Grover gave them to him. Mr. Crocker relinquished his clawlike hold upon the bag and set it down upon the counter. Grover took the bag and dropped it in his canvas sack, and then remembered. "Mr. Crocker—" again he felt the old embarrassment that was almost like strong pain— "I gave you too much," Grover said. "There were eighteen cents in stamps. You—you can just give me three ones back."

Mr. Crocker did not answer. He was busy with his bony little hands, unfolding the stamps and flattening them out on top of the glass counter. When he had done so, he peered at them sharply for a moment, thrusting his scrawny neck forward and running his eye up and down, like a bookkeeper who totes up rows of figures.

When he had finished, he said tartly: "I don't like this kind of business. If you want candy, you should have the money for it. I'm not a post office. The next time you come in here and want anything, you'll have to pay me money for it."

Hot anger rose in Grover's throat. His olive face suffused with angry color. His tarry eyes got black and bright. He was on the verge of saying: "Then why did you take my other stamps? Why do you tell me now, when you have taken all the stamps I had, that you don't want them?"

But he was a boy, a boy of eleven years, a quiet, gentle, gravely thoughtful boy, and he had been taught how to respect his elders. So he just stood there looking with his tar-black eyes. Old Man Crocker, pursing at the mouth a little, without meeting Grover's gaze, took the stamps up in his thin, parched fingers and, turning, rocked away with them down to the till.

He took the twos and folded them and laid them in one rounded scallop, then took the ones and folded them and put them in the one next to it. Then he closed the till and started to rock off, down toward the other end. Grover, his face now quiet and grave, kept looking at him, but Mr. Crocker did not look at Grover. Instead he began to take some stamped cardboard shapes and fold them into boxes.

In a moment Grover said, "Mr. Crocker, will you give me the three ones, please?"

Mr. Crocker did not answer. He kept folding boxes, and he compressed his thin lips quickly as he did so. But Mrs. Crocker, back turned to her spouse, also folding boxes with her birdlike hands, muttered: "Hm! *I'd* give him nothing!"

Mr. Crocker looked up, looked at Grover, said, "What are you waiting for?"

"Will you give me the three ones, please?" Grover said.

"I'll give you nothing," Mr. Crocker said.

He left his work and came rocking forward along the counter. "Now you get out of here! Don't you come in here with any more of those stamps," said Mr. Crocker.

"I should like to know where he gets them—that's what *I* should like to know," said Mrs. Crocker.

She did not look up as she said these words. She inclined her head a little to the side, in Mr. Crocker's direction, and continued to fold the boxes with her bony fingers.

"You get out of here!" said Mr. Crocker. "And don't you come back here with any stamps. . . . Where did you get those stamps?" he said.

"That's just what *I've* been thinking," Mrs. Crocker said. "*I've* been thinking all along."

"You've been coming in here for the last two weeks with those stamps," said Mr. Crocker. "I don't like the look of it. Where did you get those stamps?" he said.

"That's what *I've* been thinking," said Mrs. Crocker, for a second time.

Grover had got white underneath his olive skin. His eyes had lost their luster. They looked like dull, stunned balls of tar. "From Mr. Reed," he said. "I got the stamps from Mr. Reed." Then he burst out desperately, "Mr. Crocker—Mr. Reed will tell you how I got the stamps. I did some work for Mr. Reed, he gave me those stamps two weeks ago."

"Mr. Reed," said Mrs. Crocker acidly. She did not turn her head. "I call it mighty funny."

"Mr. Crocker," Grover said, "if you'll just let me have three ones——"

"You get out of here!" cried Mr. Crocker, and he began rocking forward toward Grover. "Now don't you come in here again, boy! There's something funny about this whole business! I don't like the look of it," said Mr. Crocker. "If you can't pay as other people do, then I don't want your trade."

"Mr. Crocker," Grover said again, and underneath the olive skin his face was gray, "if you'll just let me have those three——"

"You get out of here!" Mr. Crocker cried, rocking down toward the counter's end. "If you don't get out, boy——"

"*I'd* call a policeman, that's what I'd do," Mrs. Crocker said.

Mr. Crocker rocked around the lower end of the counter. He came rocking up to Grover. "You get out," he said.

He took the boy and pushed him with his bony little hands, and Grover was sick and gray down to the hollow pit of his stomach.

"You've got to give me those three ones," he said.

"You get out of here!" shrilled Mr. Crocker. He seized the screen door, pulled it open, and pushed Grover out. "Don't you come back in here," he said, pausing for a moment, and working thinly at the lips. He turned and rocked back in the shop again. The screen door slammed behind him. Grover stood there on the pavement. And light came and went and came again into the Square.

The boy stood there, and a wagon rattled past. There were some people passing by, but Grover did not notice them. He stood there blindly, in the watches of the sun, feeling this was Time, this was the center of the universe, the granite core of changelessness, and feeling, this is Grover, this the Square, this is Now.

But something had gone out of day. He felt the overwhelming, soul-sickening guilt that all the children, all the good men of the earth, have felt since Time began. And even anger had died down, had been drowned out, in this swelling tide of guilt, and "This is the Square"—thought Grover as before— "This is Now. There is my father's shop. And all of it is as it has always been—save I."

And the Square reeled drunkenly around him, light went in blind gray motes before his eyes, the fountain sheeted out to rainbow iridescence and returned to its proud, pulsing plume again. But all the brightness had gone out of day, and "Here is the Square, and here is permanence, and here is Time—and all of it the same as it has always been, save I."

The scuffed boots of the lost boy moved and stumbled blindly. The numb feet crossed the pavement— reached the cobbled street, reached the plotted central square—the grass plots, and the flower beds, so soon to be packed with red geraniums.

"I want to be alone," thought Grover, "where I cannot go near him. . . . Oh God, I hope he never hears, that no one ever tells him——"

The plume blew out, the iridescent sheet of spray blew over him. He passed through, found the other side and crossed the street, and—"Oh God, if papa ever hears!" thought Grover, as his numb feet started up the steps into his father's shop.

He found and felt the steps—the width and thickness of old lumber twenty feet in length. He saw it all —the iron columns on his father's porch, painted with the dull anomalous black-green that all such columns in this land and weather come to; two angels, flyspecked, and the waiting stones. Beyond and all around, in the stonecutter's shop, cold shapes of white and marble, rounded stone, the languid angel with strong marble hands of love.

He went on down the aisle, the white shapes stood around him. He went on to the back of the workroom. This he knew—the little cast-iron stove in left-hand corner, caked, brown, heat-blistered, and the elbow of the long stack running out across the shop; the high and dirty window looking down across the Market Square toward Niggertown; the rude old shelves, plank-boarded, thick, the wood not smooth but pulpy, like the strong hair of an animal; upon the shelves the chisels of all sizes and a layer of stone dust; an emery wheel with pump tread; and a door that let out on the alleyway, yet the alleyway twelve feet below. Here in the room, two trestles of this coarse spiked wood upon which rested gravestones, and at one, his father at work.

The boy looked, saw the name was Creasman: saw the carved analysis of John, the symmetry of the s, the fine sentiment that was being polished off beneath the name and date: "John Creasman, November 7, 1903."

Gant looked up. He was a man of fifty-three, gaunt-visaged, mustache cropped, immensely long and tall and gaunt. He wore good dark clothes—heavy, massive—save he had no coat. He worked in shirt-sleeves with his vest on, a strong watch chain stretching across his vest, wing collar and black tie, Adam's apple, bony forehead, bony nose, light eyes, gray-green, undeep and cold, and, somehow, lonely-looking, a striped apron going up around his shoulders, and starched cuffs. And in one hand a tremendous rounded wooden mallet like a butcher's bole; and in his other hand, a strong cold chisel.

"How are you, son?"

He did not look up as he spoke. He spoke quietly, absently. He worked upon the chisel and the wooden mallet, as a jeweler might work on a watch, except that in the man and in the wooden mallet there was power too.

"What is it, son?" he said.

He moved around the table from the head, started up on "J" once again.

"Papa, I never stole the stamps," said Grover.

Gant put down the mallet, laid the chisel down. He came around the trestle.

"What?" he said.

As Grover winked his tar-black eyes, they brightened, the hot tears shot out. "I never stole the stamps," he said.

"Hey? What is this?" his father said. "What stamps?"

"That Mr. Reed gave me, when the other boy was sick and I worked there for three days. . . . And Old Man Crocker," Grover said, "he took all the stamps. And I told him Mr. Reed had given them to me. And now he owes me three ones—and Old Man Crocker says he don't believe that they were mine. He says—he says—that I must have taken them somewhere," Grover blurted out.

"The stamps that Reed gave you—hey?" the stonecutter said. "The stamps you had—" He wet his thumb upon his lips, threw back his head and slowly swung his gaze around the ceiling, then turned and strode quickly from his workshop out into the storeroom.

Almost at once he came back again, and as he passed the old gray painted-board partition of his office he cleared his throat and wet his thumb and said, "Now, I tell you——"

Then he turned and strode up toward the front again and cleared his throat and said, "I tell you now—" He wheeled about and started back, and as he came along the aisle between the marshaled rows of gravestones he said beneath his breath, "By God, now——"

He took Grover by the hand and they went out flying. Down the aisle they went by all the gravestones, past the fly-specked angels waiting there, and down the wooden steps and across the Square. The fountain pulsed, the plume blew out in sheeted iridescence, and it swept across them; an old gray horse, with a peaceful look about his torn lips, swucked up the cool mountain water from the trough as Grover and his father went across the Square, but they did not notice it.

They crossed swiftly to the other side in a direct line to the candy shop. Gant was still dressed in his long striped apron, and he was still holding Grover by the hand. He opened the screen door and stepped inside.

"Give him the stamps," Gant said.

Mr. Crocker came rocking forward behind the counter, with the prim and careful look that now was somewhat like a smile. "It was just—" he said.

"Give him the stamps," Gant said, and threw some coins down on the counter.

Mr. Crocker rocked away and got the stamps. He came rocking back. "I just didn't know—" he said.

The stonecutter took the stamps and gave them to the boy. And Mr. Crocker took the coins.

"It was just that—" Mr. Crocker began again, and smiled.

Gant cleared his throat: "You never were a father," he said. "You never knew the feelings of a father, or understood the feelings of a child; and that is why you acted as you did. But a judgment is upon you. God has cursed you. He has afflicted you. He has made you lame and childless as you are—and lame and childless, miserable as you are, you will go to your grave and be forgotten!"

And Crocker's wife kept kneading her bony little hands and said, imploringly, "Oh, no—oh don't say that, please don't say that."

The stonecutter, the breath still hoarse in him, left the store, still holding the boy tightly by the hand. Light came again into the day.

"Well, son," he said, and laid his hand on the boy's back. "Well, son," he said, "now don't you mind."

They walked across the Square, the sheeted spray of iridescent light swept out on them, the horse swizzled at the water-trough, and "Well, son," the stonecutter said.

And the old horse sloped down, ringing with his hoofs upon the cobblestones.

"Well, son," said the stonecutter once again, "be a good boy."

And he trod his own steps then with his great stride and went back again into his shop.

The lost boy stood upon the Square, hard by the porch of his father's shop.

"This is Time," thought Grover. "Here is the Square, here is my father's shop, and here am I."

And light came and went and came again—but now not quite the same as it had done before. The boy saw the pattern of familiar shapes and knew that they were just the same as they had always been. But something had gone out of day, and something had come in again. Out of the vision of those quiet eyes some brightness had gone, and into their vision had come some deeper color. He could not say, he did not know through what transforming shadows life had passed within that quarter hour. He only knew that something had been lost—something forever gained.

Just then a buggy curved out through the Square, and fastened to the rear end was a poster, and it said "St. Louis" and "Excursion" and "The Fair."

II—The Mother

As we went down through Indiana—you were too young, child, to remember it—but I always think of all of you the way you looked that morning, when we went down through Indiana, going to the Fair. All of the apple trees were coming out, and it was April; it was the beginning of spring in southern Indiana and everything was getting green. Of course we don't have farms at home like those in Indiana. The children had never seen such farms as those, and I reckon, kidlike, they had to take it in.

So all of them kept running up and down the aisle —well, no, except for you and Grover. *You* were too young, Eugene. You were just three, I kept you with me. As for Grover—well, I'm going to tell you about that.

But the rest of them kept running up and down the aisle and from one window to another. They kept calling out and hollering to each other every time they saw something new. They kept trying to look out on all sides, in every way at once as if they wished they had eyes at the back of their heads. It was the first time any of them had ever been in Indiana, and I reckon that it all seemed strange and new.

And so it seemed they couldn't get enough. It seemed they never could be still. They kept running up and down and back and forth, hollering and shouting to each other, until—"I'll vow! You children! I never saw the beat of you!" I said. "The way that you keep running up and down and back and forth and never can be quiet for a minute beats all I ever saw," I said.

You see, they were excited about going to St. Louis, and so curious over everything they saw. They couldn't help it, and they wanted to see everything. But—"I'll vow!" I said. "If you children don't sit down and rest you'll be worn to a frazzle before we ever get to see St. Louis and the Fair!"

Except for Grover! He—no, sir! not him. Now, boy, I want to tell you—I've raised the lot of you—and if I do say so, there wasn't a numbskull in the lot. But *Grover!* Well, you've all grown up now, all of you have gone away, and none of you are children anymore. . . . And of course, I hope that, as the fellow says, you reached the dignity of man's estate. I suppose you have the judgment of grown men. . . . But *Grover! Grover* had it even then!

Oh, even as a child, you know—at a time when I was almost afraid to trust the rest of you out of my sight—I could depend on Grover. He could go anywhere, I could send him anywhere, and I'd always know he'd get back safe, and do exactly what I told him to!

Why, I didn't even have to tell him. You could send that child to market and tell him what you wanted, and he'd come home with *twice* as much as you could get yourself for the same money!

Now you know, I've always been considered a good trader. But *Grover!*—why, it got so finally that I wouldn't even tell him. Your papa said to me: "You'd be better off if you'd just tell him what you want and leave the rest to him. For," your papa says, "damned if I don't believe he's a better trader than you are. He gets more for the money than anyone I ever saw."

Well, I had to admit it, you know. I had to own up then. Grover, even as a child, was a far better trader than I was. . . . Why, yes, they told it on him all over town, you know. They said all of the market men, all of the farmers, knew him. They'd begin to laugh when they saw him coming—they'd say: "Look out! Here's Grover! Here's one trader you're not going to fool!"

And they were right! *That* child! I'd say, "Grover, suppose you run uptown and see if they've got anything good to *eat* today"—and I'd just wink at him, you know, but he'd know what I meant. I wouldn't let on that I *wanted* anything exactly, but I'd say, "Now it just occurs to me that some good fresh stuff may be coming in from the country, so suppose you take this dollar and just see what you can do with it."

Well, sir, that was all that was needed. The minute you told that child that you depended on his judgment, he'd have gone to the ends of the earth for you —and, let me tell you something, he wouldn't *miss*, either!

His eyes would get as black as coals—oh! the way that child would look at you, the intelligence and sense in his expression. He'd say: "Yes, *ma'am!* Now don't you worry, mama. You leave it all to me—and I'll do *good!*" said Grover.

And he'd be off like a streak of lightning and—oh Lord! As your father said to me, "I've been living in this town for almost thirty years," he said—"I've seen it grow up from a crossroads village, and I thought I knew everything there was to know about it—but that child—" your papa says—"he knows places that I never heard of!" . . . Oh, he'd go right down there to that place below your papa's shop where the draymen and the country people used to park their wagons—or he'd go down there to those old lots on Concord Street where the farmers used to keep their wagons. And, child that he was, he'd go right in among them, sir—*Grover* would!—go right in and barter with them like a grown man!

And he'd come home with things he'd bought that would make your eyes stick out. . . . Here he comes one time with another boy, dragging a great bushel basket full of ripe termaters between them. "Why, Grover!" I says. "How on earth are we ever going to use them? Why they'll go bad on us before we're half way through with them." "Well, mama," he says, "I know—" oh, just as solemn as a judge—"but they were the last the man had," he says, "and he wanted to go home, and so I got them for ten cents," he says. "They were so cheap," said Grover, "I thought it was a shame to let 'em go, and I figgered that what we couldn't eat—why," says Grover, "you could *put up!*" Well, the way he said it—so earnest and so serious— I had to laugh. "But I'll vow!" I said. "If you don't beat all!" . . . But that was *Grover!*—the way he was in *those* days! As everyone said, boy that he was, he had the sense and judgment of a grown man. . . . Child, child, I've seen you all grow up, and all of you were bright enough. There were no half-wits in *my* family. But for all-round intelligence, judgment, and general ability, Grover surpassed the whole crowd. I've never seen his equal, and everyone who knew him as a child will say the same.

So that's what I tell them now when they ask me about all of you. I have to tell the truth. I always said that *you* were smart enough, Eugene—but when they come around and brag to me about you, and about how you have got on and have a kind of name—I don't let on, you know. I just sit there and let them talk. I don't brag on you—if *they* want to brag on you, that's *their* business. I never bragged on one of my own children in my life. When father raised us up, we were all brought up to believe that it was not good breeding to brag about your kin. "If the others want to do it," father said, "well, let *them* do it. Don't ever let on by a word or sign that you know what they are talking about. Just let *them* do the talking, and say nothing."

So when they come around and tell me all about the things *you've* done—I don't let on to them, I never say a word. Why yes!—why, here, you know—oh, along about a month or so ago, this feller comes—a well-dressed man, you know—he looked intelligent, a good substantial sort of person. He said he came from New Jersey, or somewhere up in that part of the country, and he began to ask me all sorts of questions—what you were like when you were a boy, and all such stuff as that.

I just pretended to study it all over and then I said, "Well, yes"—real serious-like, you know—"well, yes— I reckon I ought to know a little something about him. Eugene was my child, just the same as all the others were. I brought him up just the way I brought up all the others. And," I says—oh, just as solemn as you please—"he wasn't a *bad* sort of a boy. Why," I says, "up to the time that he was twelve years old he was just about the same as any other boy—a good, average, normal sort of fellow."

"Oh," he says, "But didn't you notice something? Wasn't there something kind of strange?" he says— "something different from what you noticed in the other children?"

I didn't let on, you know—I just took it all in and looked as solemn as an owl—I just pretended to study it all over, just as serious as you please.

"Why no," I says, real slow-like, after I'd studied it all over. "As I remember it, he was a good, ordinary, normal sort of boy, just like all the others."

"Yes," he says—oh, all excited-like, you know—"But didn't you notice how brilliant he was? Eugene must have been more brilliant than the rest!"

"Well, now," I says, and pretended to study that all over too. "Now let me see. . . . Yes," I says—I just looked him in the eye, as solemn as you please— "he did pretty well. . . . Well, yes," I says, "I guess he was a fairly bright sort of a boy. I never had no complaints to make of him on that score. He was bright enough," I says. "The only trouble with him was that he was lazy."

"Lazy!" he says—oh, you should have seen the look upon his face, you know—he jumped like someone had stuck a pin in him. "Lazy!" he says. "Why, you don't mean to tell me——"

"Yes," I says—oh, I never cracked a smile—"I was

telling him the same thing myself the last time that I saw him. I told him it was a mighty lucky thing for him that he had the gift of gab. Of course, he went off to college and read a lot of books, and I reckon that's where he got this flow of language they say he has. But as I said to him the last time that I saw him: 'Now look a-here,' I said. 'If you can earn your living doing a light, easy class of work like this you do,' I says, 'you're mighty lucky, because none of the rest of your people,' I says, 'had any such luck as that. They had to work hard for a living.' "

Oh, I told him, you know. I came right out with it. I made no bones about it. And I tell you what—I wish you could have seen his face. It was a study.

"Well," he says, at last, "you've got to admit this, haven't you—he was the brightest boy you had, now wasn't he?"

I just looked at him a moment. I had to tell the truth. I couldn't fool him any longer. "No," I says. "He was a good, bright boy—I got no complaint to make about him on that score—but the brightest boy I had, the one that surpassed all the rest of them in sense, and understanding, and in judgment—the best boy I had—the smartest boy I ever saw—was—well, it wasn't Eugene," I said. "It was another one."

He looked at me a moment, then he said, "Which boy was that?"

Well, I just looked at him, and smiled. I shook my head, you know. I wouldn't tell him. "I never brag about my own," I said. "You'll have to find out for yourself."

But—I'll have to tell *you*—and you know yourself, I brought the whole crowd up, I knew you all. And you can take my word for it—the best one of the lot was—*Grover!*

And when I think of Grover as he was along about that time, I always see him sitting there, so grave and earnest-like with his nose pressed to the window, as we went down through Indiana in the morning, to the Fair.

All through that morning we were going down along beside the Wabash River—the Wabash River flows through Indiana, it is the river that they wrote the song about—so all that morning we were going down along the river. And I sat with all you children gathered about me as we went down through Indiana, going to St. Louis, to the Fair.

And Grover sat there, so still and earnest-like, looking out the window, and he didn't move. He sat there like a man. He was just eleven and a half years old, but he had more sense, more judgment, and more understanding than any child I ever saw.

So here he sat beside this gentleman and looked out the window. I never knew the man—I never asked his name—but I tell you what! He was cer-tainly a fine-looking, well-dressed, good, substantial sort of man, and I could see that he had taken a great liking to Grover. And Grover sat there looking out, and then turned to this gentleman, as grave and earnest as a grown-up man, and says, "What kind of crops grow here, sir?" Well, this gentleman threw his head back and just hah-hahed. "Well, I'll see if I can tell you," says this gentleman, and then, you know, he talked to him, they talked together, and Grover took it all in, as solemn as you please, and asked this gentleman every sort of question—what the trees were, what was growing there, how big the farms were—all sorts of questions, which this gentleman would answer, until I said: "Why, I'll vow, Grover! You shouldn't ask so many questions. You'll bother the very life out of this gentleman."

The gentleman threw his head back and laughed right out. "Now you leave that boy alone. He's all right," he said. "He doesn't bother me a bit, and if I know the answers to his questions I will answer him. And if I don't know, why, then, I'll tell him so. But he's *all right*," he said, and put his arm round Grover's shoulders. "You leave him alone. He doesn't bother me a bit."

And I can still remember how he looked that morning, with his black eyes, his black hair, and with the birthmark on his neck—so grave, so serious, so earnest-like—as he sat by the train window and watched the apple trees, the farms, the barns, the houses, and the orchards, taking it all in, I reckon, because it was strange and new to him.

It was so long ago, but when I think of it, it all comes back, as if it happened yesterday. Now all of you have either died or grown up and gone away, and nothing is the same as it was then. But all of you were there with me that morning and I guess I should remember how the others looked, but somehow I don't. Yet I can still see Grover just the way he was, the way he looked that morning when we went down through Indiana, by the river, to the Fair.

III—THE SISTER

Can you remember, Eugene, how Grover used to look? I mean the birthmark, the black eyes, the olive skin. The birthmark always showed because of those open sailor blouses kids used to wear. But I guess you must have been too young when Grover died. . . . I was looking at that old photograph the other day. You know the one I mean—that picture showing mama and papa and all of us children before the house on Woodson Street. *You* weren't there, Eugene. *You* didn't get in. *You* hadn't arrived when that was taken. . . . You remember how mad you used to get when we'd tell you that you were only a dishrag hanging out in Heaven when something happened?

You were the baby. That's what you get for being the baby. You don't get in the picture, do you? . . . I was looking at that old picture just the other day. There we were. And, my God, what is it all about? I mean, when you see the way we were—Daisy and Ben and Grover, Steve and all of us—and then how everyone either dies or grows up and goes away— and then—look at us now! Do you ever get to feeling funny? You know what I mean—do you ever get to feeling *queer*—when you try to figure these things out? You've been to college and you ought to know the answer—and I wish you'd tell me if you know.

My Lord, when I think sometimes of the way I used to be—the dreams I used to have. Playing the piano, practicing seven hours a day, thinking that some day I would be a great pianist. Taking singing lessons from Aunt Nell because I felt that some day I was going to have a great career in opera. . . . Can you beat it now? Can you imagine it? *Me!* In grand opera! . . . Now I want to ask you. I'd like to know.

My Lord! When I go uptown and walk down the street and see all these funny-looking little boys and girls hanging around the drug store—do you suppose any of them have ambitions the way we did? Do you suppose any of these funny-looking little girls are thinking about a big career in opera? . . . Didn't you ever see that picture of us? I was looking at it just the other day. It was made before the old house down on Woodson Street, with papa standing there in his swallow-tail, and mama there beside him—and Grover, and Ben, and Steve, and Daisy, and myself, with our feet upon our bicycles. Luke, poor kid, was only four or five. *He* didn't have a bicycle like us. But there he was. And there were all of us together.

Well, there I was, and my poor old skinny legs and long white dress, and two pigtails hanging down my back. And all the funny-looking clothes we wore, with the doo-lolley business on them. . . . But I guess you can't remember. You weren't born.

But, well, we were a right nice-looking set of people, if I do say so. And there was "86" the way it used to be, with the front porch, the grape vines, and the flower beds before the house—and "Miss Eliza" standing there by papa, with a watch charm pinned upon her waist. . . . I shouldn't laugh, but "Miss Eliza"—well, mama was a pretty woman then. Do you know what I mean? "Miss Eliza" was a right good-looking woman, and papa in his swallow-tail was a good-looking man. Do you remember how he used to get dressed up on Sunday? And how grand we thought he was? And how he let me take his money out and count it? And how rich we all thought he was? And how wonderful that dinkey little shop

on the Square looked to us? . . . Can you beat it, now? Why we thought that papa was the biggest man in town and—oh, you can't tell me! You can't tell me! He had his faults, but papa was a wonderful man. You know he was!

And there was Steve and Ben and Grover, Daisy, Luke, and me lined up there before the house with one foot on our bicycles. And I got to thinking back about it all. It all came back.

Do you remember anything about St. Louis? You were only three or four years old then, but you must remember something. . . . Do you remember how you used to bawl when I would scrub you? How you'd bawl for Grover? Poor kid, you used to yell for Grover every time I'd get you in the tub. . . . He was a sweet kid and he was crazy about you—he almost brought you up.

That year Grover was working at the Inside Inn out on the Fair Grounds. Do you remember the old Inside Inn? That big old wooden thing inside the Fair? And how I used to take you there to wait for Grover when he got through working? And old fat Billy Pelham at the newsstand—how he always used to give you a stick of chewing gum?

They were all crazy about Grover. Everybody liked him. . . . And how proud Grover was of you! Don't you remember how he used to show you off? How he used to take you around and make you talk to Billy Pelham? And Mr. Curtis at the desk? And how Grover would try to make you talk and get you to say "Grover"? And you couldn't say it—you couldn't pronounce the "r." You'd say "Gova." Have you forgotten that? You shouldn't forget *that*, because—you were a *cute* kid, then—Ho-ho-ho-ho-ho—I don't know where it's gone to, but you were a big hit in those days. . . . I tell you, boy, you were Somebody back in those days.

And I was thinking of it all the other day when I was looking at that photograph. How we used to go and meet Grover there, and how he'd take us to the Midway. Do you remember the Midway? The Snake-Eater and the Living Skeleton, the Fat Woman and the Chute-the-chute, the Scenic Railway and the Ferris Wheel? How you bawled the night we took you up on the Ferris Wheel? You yelled your head off—I tried to laugh it off, but I tell you, I was scared myself. Back in those days, that was Something. And how Grover laughed at us and told us there was no danger. . . . My Lord! poor little Grover. He wasn't quite twelve years old at the time, but he seemed so grown up to us. I was two years older, but I thought he knew it all.

It was always that way with him. Looking back now, it sometimes seems that it was Grover who brought us up. He was always looking after us, telling us what to do, bringing us something—some ice cream or some candy, something he had bought out of the poor little money he'd gotten at the Inn.

Then I got to thinking of the afternoon we sneaked away from home. Mama had gone out somewhere. And Grover and I got on the street car and went downtown. And my Lord, we thought that we were going Somewhere. In those days, that was what we called a *trip*. A ride in the street car was something to write home about in those days. . . . I hear that it's all built up around there now.

So we got on the car and rode the whole way down into the business section of St. Louis. We got out on Washington Street and walked up and down. And I tell you, boy, we thought that that was Something. Grover took me into a drug store and set me up to soda water. Then we came out and walked around some more, down to the Union Station and clear over to the river. And both of us half scared to death at what we'd done and wondering what mama would say if she found out.

We stayed down there till it was getting dark, and we passed by a lunchroom—an old one-armed joint with one-armed chairs and people sitting on stools and eating at the counter. We read all the signs to see what they had to eat and how much it cost, and I guess nothing on the menu was more than fifteen cents, but it couldn't have looked grander to us if it had been Delmonico's. So we stood there with our noses pressed against the window looking in. Two skinny little kids, both of us scared half to death, getting the thrill of a lifetime out of it. You know what I mean? And smelling everything with all our might and thinking how good it all smelled. . . . Then Grover turned to me and whispered: "Come on, Helen. Let's go in. It says fifteen cents for pork and beans. And I've got the money," Grover said. "I've got sixty cents."

I was so scared I couldn't speak. I'd never been in a place like that before. But I kept thinking, "Oh Lord, if mama should find out!" I felt as if we were committing some big crime. . . . Don't you know how it is when you're a kid? It was the thrill of a lifetime. . . . I couldn't resist. So we both went in and sat down on those high stools before the counter and ordered pork and beans and a cup of coffee. I suppose we were too frightened at what we'd done really to enjoy anything. We just gobbled it all up in a hurry, and gulped our coffee down. And I don't know whether it was the excitement—I guess the poor kid was already sick when we came in there and didn't know it. But I turned and looked at him, and he was white as death. . . . And when I asked him what was the matter, he wouldn't tell me. He was too proud. He said he was all right, but I could

see that he was sick as a dog. . . . So he paid the bill. It came to forty cents—I'll never forget *that* as long as I live. . . . And sure enough, we no more than got out the door—he hardly had time to reach the curb—before it all came up.

And the poor kid was so scared and so ashamed. And what scared him so was not that he had gotten sick, but that he had spent all that money and it had come to nothing. And mama would find out. . . . Poor kid, he just stood there looking at me and he whispered: "Oh Helen, don't tell mama. She'll be mad if she finds out." Then we hurried home, and he was still white as a sheet when we got there.

Mama was waiting for us. She looked at us—you know how "Miss Eliza" looks at you when she thinks you've been doing something that you shouldn't. Mama said, "Why, where on earth have you two children been?" I guess she was all set to lay us out. Then she took one look at Grover's face. That was enough for her. She said, "Why, child, what in the world!" She was white as a sheet herself. . . . And all that Grover said was—"Mama, I feel sick."

He was sick as a dog. He fell over on the bed, and we undressed him and mama put her hand upon his forehead and came out in the hall—she was so white you could have made a black mark on her face with chalk—and whispered to me, "Go get the doctor quick, he's burning up."

And I went chasing up the street, my pigtails flying, to Dr. Packer's house. I brought him back with me. When he came out of Grover's room he told mama what to do but I don't know if she even heard him.

Her face was white as a sheet. She looked at me and looked right through me. She never saw me. And oh, my Lord, I'll never forget the way she looked, the way my heart stopped and came up in my throat. I was only a skinny little kid of fourteen. But she looked as if she was dying right before my eyes. And I knew that if anything happened to him, she'd never get over it if she lived to be a hundred.

Poor old mama. You know, he always was her eyeballs—you know that, don't you?—not the rest of us! —no, sir! I know what I'm talking about. It always has been Grover—she always thought more of him than she did of any of the others. And—poor kid!—he was a sweet kid. I can still see him lying there, and remember how sick he was, and how scared I was! I don't know why I was so scared. All we'd done had been to sneak away from home and go into a lunchroom—but I felt guilty about the whole thing, as if it was my fault.

It all came back to me the other day when I was looking at that picture, and I thought, my God, we were two kids together, and I was only two years older than Grover was, and now I'm forty-six. . . . Can you believe it? Can you figure it out—the way we grow up and change and go away? . . . And my Lord, Grover seemed so grown-up to me. He was such a quiet kid—I guess that's why he seemed older than the rest of us.

I wonder what Grover would say now if he could see that picture. All my hopes and dreams and big ambitions have come to nothing, and it's all so long ago, as if it happened in another world. Then it comes back, as if it happened yesterday. . . . Sometimes I lie awake at night and think of all the people who have come and gone, and how everything is different from the way we thought that it would be. Then I go out on the street next day and see the faces of the people that I pass. . . . Don't they look strange to you? Don't you see something funny in people's eyes, as if all of them were puzzled about something? As if they were wondering what had happened to them since they were kids? Wondering what it is that they have lost? . . . Now am I crazy, or do you know what I mean? You've been to college, Gene, and I want you to tell me if you know the answer. Now do they look that way to you? I never noticed that look in people's eyes when I was a kid—did you?

My God, I wish I knew the answer to these things. I'd like to find out what is wrong—what has changed since then—and if we have the same queer look in our eyes, too. Does it happen to us all, to everyone? . . . Grover and Ben, Steve, Daisy, Luke, and me—all standing there before that house on Woodson Street in Altamont—there we are, and you see the way we were—and how it all gets lost. What is it, anyway, that people lose?

How is it that nothing turns out the way we thought it would be? It all gets lost until it seems that it has never happened—that it is something we dreamed somewhere. . . . You see what I mean? . . . It seems that it must be something we heard somewhere—that it happened to someone else. And then it all comes back again.

And suddenly you remember just how it was, and see again those two funny, frightened, skinny little kids with their noses pressed against the dirty window of that lunchroom thirty years ago. You remember the way it felt, the way it smelled, even the strange smell in the old pantry in that house we lived in then. And the steps before the house, the way the rooms looked. And those two little boys in sailor suits who used to ride up and down before the house on tricycles. . . . And the birthmark on Grover's neck. . . . The Inside Inn. . . . St. Louis and the Fair.

It all comes back as if it happened yesterday. And then it goes away again, and seems farther off and stranger than if it happened in a dream.

IV—THE BROTHER

"*This* is King's Highway," the man said.

And then Eugene looked and saw that it was just a street. There were some big new buildings, a large hotel, some restaurants and "bar-grill" places of the modern kind, the livid monotone of neon lights, ceaseless traffic of motor cars—all this was new, but it was just a street. And he knew that it had always been just a street and nothing more—but somehow— well, he stood there looking at it, wondering what else he had expected to find.

The man kept looking at him with inquiry in his eyes, and Eugene asked him if the Fair had not been out this way.

"Sure, the Fair was out beyond here," the man said. "Out where the park is now. But this street you're looking for—don't you remember the name of it or nothing?" the man said.

Eugene said he thought the name of the street was Edgemont, but that he wasn't sure. Anyhow it was something like that. And he said the house was on the corner of that street and of another street.

Then the man said: "What was that other street?"

Eugene said he did not know, but that King's Highway was a block or so away, and that an interurban line ran past about half a block from where he once had lived.

"What line was this?" the man said, and stared at him.

"The interurban line," Eugene said.

Then the man stared at him again, and finally, "I don't know no interurban line," he said.

Eugene said it was a line that ran behind some houses, and that there were board fences there and grass beside the tracks. But somehow he could not say that it was summer in those days and that you could smell the ties, a wooden, tarry smell, and feel a kind of absence in the afternoon after the car had gone. He only said the interurban line was back behind somewhere between the backyards of some houses and some old board fences, and that King's Highway was a block or two away.

He did not say that King's Highway had not been a street in those days but a kind of road that wound from magic out of some dim and haunted land, and that along the way it had got mixed in with Tom the Piper's son, with hot cross buns, with all the light that came and went, and with coming down through Indiana in the morning, and the smell of engine smoke, the Union Station, and most of all with voices lost and far and long ago that said "King's Highway."

He did not say these things about King's Highway because he looked about him and he saw what King's Highway was. All he could say was that the street was near King's Highway, and was on the corner, and that the interurban trolley line was close to there. He said it was a stone house, and that there were stone steps before it, and a strip of grass. He said he thought the house had had a turret at one corner, he could not be sure.

The man looked at him again, and said, "This is King's Highway, but I never heard of any street like that."

Eugene left him then, and went on till he found the place. And so at last he turned into the street, finding the place where the two corners met, the huddled block, the turret, and the steps, and paused a moment, looking back, as if the street were Time.

For a moment he stood there, waiting—for a word, and for a door to open, for the child to come. He waited but no words were spoken; no one came.

Yet all of it was just as it had always been, except that the steps were lower, the porch less high, the strip of grass less wide, than he had thought. All the rest of it was as he had known it would be. A gray-stone front, three-storied, with a slant slate roof, the side red brick and windowed, still with the old arched entrance in the center for the doctor's use.

There was a tree in front, and a lamp post; and behind and to the side, more trees than he had known there would be. And all the slatey turret gables, all the slatey window gables, going into points, and the two arched windows, in strong stone, in the front room.

It was all so strong, so solid, and so ugly—and all so enduring and so good, the way he had remembered it, except he did not smell the tar, the hot and caulky dryness of the old cracked ties, the boards of backyard fences and the coarse and sultry grass, and absence in the afternoon when the street car had gone, and the twins, sharp-visaged in their sailor suits, pumping with furious shrillness on tricycles up and down before the house, and the feel of the hot afternoon, and the sense that everyone was absent at the Fair.

Except for this, it all was just the same; except for this and for King's Highway, which was now a street; except for this, and for the child that did not come.

It was a hot day. Darkness had come. The heat rose up and hung and sweltered like a sodden blanket in St. Louis. It was wet heat, and one knew that there would be no relief or coolness in the night. And when one tried to think of the time when the heat would go away, one said: "It cannot last. It's bound to go away," as we always say it in America.

But one did not believe it when he said it. The heat soaked down and men sweltered in it; the faces of the people were pale and greasy with the heat. And in their faces was a patient wretchedness, and one felt the kind of desolation that one feels at the end of a hot day in a great city in America—when one's home is far away, across the continent, and he thinks of all that distance, all that heat, and feels, "Oh God! but it's a big country!"

And he feels nothing but absence, absence, and the desolation of America, the loneliness and sadness of the high, hot skies, and evening coming on across the Middle West, across the sweltering and heat-sunken land, across all the lonely little towns, the farms, the fields, the oven swelter of Ohio, Kansas, Iowa, and Indiana at the close of day, and voices, casual in the heat, voices of the little stations, quiet, casual, somehow faded into that enormous vacancy and weariness of heat, of space, and of the immense, the sorrowful, the most high and awful skies.

Then he hears the engine and the wheel again, the wailing whistle and the bell, the sound of shifting in the sweltering yard, and walks the street, and walks the street, beneath the clusters of hard lights, and by the people with sagged faces, and is drowned in desolation and in no belief.

He feels the way one feels when one comes back, and knows that he should not have come, and when he sees that, after all, King's Highway is—a street; and St. Louis—the enchanted name—a big, hot, common town upon the river, sweltering in wet, dreary heat, and not quite South, and nothing else enough to make it better.

It had not been like this before. He could remember how it would get hot, and how good the heat was, and how he would lie out in the backyard on an airing mattress, and how the mattress would get hot and dry and smell like a hot mattress full of sun, and how the sun would make him want to sleep, and how, sometimes, he would go down into the basement to feel coolness, and how the cellar smelled as cellars always smell—a cool, stale smell, the smell of cobwebs and of grimy bottles. And he could remember, when you opened the door upstairs, the smell of the cellar would come up to you—cool, misty, stale and dank and dark—and how the thought of the dark cellar always filled him with a kind of numb excitement, a kind of visceral expectancy.

He could remember how it got hot in the afternoons, and how he would feel a sense of absence and vague sadness in the afternoons, when everyone had gone away. The house would seem so lonely and sometimes he would sit inside, on the second step of the hall stairs, and listen to the sound of silence and of absence in the afternoon. He could smell the oil upon the floor and on the stairs, and see the sliding doors with their brown varnish and the beady chains across the door, and thrust his hands among the beady chains, and gather them together in his arms, and let them clash, and swish with light beady swishings all around him. He could feel darkness, absence, varnished darkness, and stained light within the house, through the stained glass of the window on the stairs, through the small stained glasses by the door, stained light and absence, silence and the smell of floor oil and vague sadness in the house on a hot mid-afternoon. And all these things themselves would have a kind of life: would seem to wait attentively, to be most living and most still.

He would sit there and listen. He could hear the girl next door practice her piano lessons in the afternoon, and hear the street car coming by between the backyard fences, half a block away, and smell the dry and sultry smell of backyard fences, the smell of coarse hot grasses by the car tracks in the afternoon, the smell of tar, of dry caulked ties, the smell of bright worn flanges, and feel the loneliness of backyards in the afternoon and the sense of absence when the car was gone.

Then he would long for evening and return, the slant of light, and feet along the street, the sharp-faced twins in sailor suits upon their tricycles, the smell of supper and the sound of voices in the house again, and Grover coming from the Fair.

That is how it was when he came into the street, and found the place where the two corners met, and turned at last to see if Time was there. He passed the house: some lights were burning, the door was open, and a woman sat upon the porch. And presently he turned, came back, and stopped before the house again. The corner light fell blank upon the house. He stood looking at it, and put his foot upon the step.

Then he said to the woman who was sitting on the porch: "This house—excuse me—but could you tell me, please, who lives here in this house?"

He knew his words were strange and hollow, and he had not said what he wished to say. She stared at him a moment, puzzled.

Then she said: "I live here. Who are you looking for?"

He said, "Why, I am looking for——"

And then he stopped, because he knew he could not tell her what it was that he was looking for.

"There used to be a house—" he said.

The woman was now staring at him hard.

He said, "I think I used to live here."

She said nothing.

In a moment he continued, "I used to live here in this house," he said, "when I was a little boy."

She was silent, looking at him, then she said: "Oh. Are you sure this was the house? Do you remember the address?"

"I have forgotten the address," he said, "but it was Edgemont Street, and it was on the corner. And I know this is the house."

"This isn't Edgemont Street," the woman said. "The name is Bates."

"Well, then, they changed the name of the street," he said, "but this is the same house. It hasn't changed."

She was silent a moment, then she nodded: "Yes. They did change the name of the street. I remember when I was a child they called it something else," she said. "But that was a long time ago. When was it that you lived here?"

"In 1904."

Again she was silent, looking at him. Then presently: "Oh. That was the year of the Fair. You were here then?"

"Yes." He now spoke rapidly, with more confidence. "My mother had the house, and we were here for seven months. And the house belonged to Dr. Packer," he went on. "We rented it from him."

"Yes," the woman said, and nodded, "this was Dr. Packer's house. He's dead now, he's been dead for many years. But this was the Packer house, all right."

"That entrance on the side," he said, "where the steps go up, that was for Dr. Packer's patients. That was the entrance to his office."

"Oh," the woman said, "I didn't know that. I've often wondered what it was. I didn't know what it was for."

"And this big room in front here," he continued, "that was the office. And there were sliding doors, and next to it, a kind of alcove for his patients——"

"Yes, the alcove is still there, only all of it has been made into one room now—and I never knew just what the alcove was for."

"And there were sliding doors on this side, too, that opened on the hall—and a stairway going up upon this side. And halfway up the stairway, at the landing, a little window of colored glass—and across the sliding doors here in the hall, a kind of curtain made of strings of beads."

She nodded, smiling. "Yes, it's just the same—we still have the sliding doors and the stained glass window on the stairs. There's no bead curtain any more," she said, "but I remember when people had them. I know what you mean."

"When we were here," he said, "we used the doctor's office for a parlor—except later on—the last month or two—and then we used it for—a bedroom."

"It is a bedroom now," she said. "I run the house— I rent rooms—all of the rooms upstairs are rented—

but I have two brothers and they sleep in this front room."

Both of them were silent for a moment, then Eugene said, "My brother stayed there too."

"In the front room?" the woman said.

He answered, "Yes."

She paused, then said: "Won't you come in? I don't believe it's changed much. Would you like to see?"

He thanked her and said he would, and he went up the steps. She opened the screen door to let him in.

Inside it was just the same—the stairs, the hallway, the sliding doors, the window of stained glass upon the stairs. And all of it was just the same, except for absence, the stained light of absence in the afternoon, and the child who once had sat there, waiting on the stairs.

It was all the same except that as a child he had sat there feeling things were *Somewhere*—and now he *knew*. He had sat there feeling that a vast and sultry river was somewhere—and now he knew! He had sat there wondering what King's Highway was, where it began, and where it ended—now he knew! He had sat there haunted by the magic word "downtown"—now he knew!—and by the street car, after it had gone—and by all things that came and went and came again, like the cloud shadows passing in a wood, that never could be captured.

And he felt that if he could only sit there on the stairs once more, in solitude and absence in the afternoon, he would be able to get it back again. Then would he be able to remember all that he had seen and been—the brief sum of himself, the universe of his four years, with all the light of Time upon it—that universe which was so short to measure, and yet so far, so endless, to remember. Then would he be able to see his own small face again, pooled in the dark mirror of the hall, and peer once more into the grave eyes of the child that he had been, and discover there in his quiet three-years' self the lone integrity of "I," knowing: "Here is the House, and here House listening; here is Absence, Absence in the afternoon; and here in this House, this Absence, is my core, my kernel—here am I!"

But as he thought it, he knew that even if he could sit here alone and get it back again, it would be gone as soon as seized, just as it had been then—first coming like the vast and drowsy rumors of the distant and enchanted Fair, then fading like cloud shadows on a hill, going like faces in a dream—coming, going, coming, possessed and held but never captured, like lost voices in the mountains long ago—and like the dark eyes and quiet face of the dark, lost boy, his brother, who, in the mysterious rhythms of his life and work, used to come into this house, then go, and return again.

The woman took Eugene back into the house and through the hall. He told her of the pantry, told her where it was and pointed to the place, but now it was no longer there. And he told her of the backyard, and of the old board fence around the yard. But the old board fence was gone. And he told her of the carriage house, and told her it was painted red. But now there was a small garage. And the backyard was still there, but smaller than he thought, and now there was a tree.

"I did not know there was a tree," he said. "I do not remember any tree."

"Perhaps it was not there," she said. "A tree could grow in thirty years." And then they came back through the house again and paused at the sliding doors.

"And could I see this room?" he said.

She slid the doors back. They slid open smoothly, with a rolling heaviness, as they used to do. And then he saw the room again. It was the same. There was a window at the side, the two arched windows at the front, the alcove and the sliding doors, the fireplace with the tiles of mottled green, the mantel of dark mission wood, the mantel posts, a dresser and a bed, just where the dresser and the bed had been so long ago.

"Is this the room?" the woman said. "It hasn't changed?"

He told her that it was the same.

"And your brother slept here where my brothers sleep?"

"This is his room," he said.

They were silent. He turned to go, and said, "Well, thank you. I appreciate your showing me."

She said that she was glad and that it was no trouble. "And when you see your family, you can tell them that you saw the house," she said. "My name is Mrs. Bell. You can tell your mother that a Mrs. Bell has the house now. And when you see your brother, you can tell him that you saw the room he slept in, and that you found it just the same."

He told her then that his brother was dead.

The woman was silent for a moment. Then she looked at him and said: "He died here, didn't he? In this room?"

He told her that it was so.

"Well, then," she said, "I knew it. I don't know how. But when you told me he was here, I knew it."

He said nothing. In a moment the woman said, "What did he die of?"

"Typhoid."

She looked shocked and troubled, and said involuntarily, "My two brothers——"

"That was a long time ago," he said. "I don't think you need to worry now."

"Oh, I wasn't thinking about that," she said. "It was just hearing that a little boy—your brother—was—was in this room that my two brothers sleep in now——"

"Well, maybe I shouldn't have told you then. But he was a good boy—and if you'd known him you wouldn't mind."

She said nothing, and he added quickly: "Besides, he didn't stay here long. This wasn't really his room—but the night he came back with my sister he was so sick—they didn't move him."

"Oh," the woman said, "I see." And then: "Are you going to tell your mother you were here?"

"I don't think so."

"I—I wonder how she feels about this room."

"I don't know. She never speaks of it."

"Oh. . . . How old was he?"

"He was twelve."

"You must have been pretty young yourself."

"I was not quite four."

"And—you just wanted to see the room, didn't you? That's why you came back."

"Yes."

"Well—" indefinitely—"I guess you've seen it now."

"Yes, thank you."

"I guess you don't remember much about him, do you? I shouldn't think you would."

"No, not much."

The years dropped off like fallen leaves: the face came back again—the soft dark oval, the dark eyes, the soft brown berry on the neck, the raven hair, all bending down, approaching—the whole appearing to him ghostwise, intent and instant.

"Now say it—*Grover!*"

"Gova."

"No—not Gova.—*Grover!* . . . Say it!"

"Gova."

"Ah-h—you didn't say it. You said Gova. *Grover*—now say it!"

"Gova."

"Look, I tell you what I'll do if you say it right. Would you like to go down to King's Highway? Would you like Grover to set you up? All right, then. If you say Grover and say it right, I'll take you to King's Highway and set you up to ice cream. Now say it right—*Grover!*"

"Gova."

"Ah-h, you-u. You're the craziest little old boy I ever did see. Can't you even say Grover?"

"Gova."

"Ah-h, you-u. Old Tongue-Tie, that's what you are. . . . Well, come on, then, I'll set you up anyway."

It all came back, and faded, and was lost again. Eugene turned to go, and thanked the woman and said good-bye.

"Well, then, good-bye," the woman said, and they shook hands. "I'm glad if I could show you. I'm glad if—" She did not finish, and at length she said: "Well, then, that was a long time ago. You'll find everything changed now, I guess. It's all built up around here now—and way out beyond here, out beyond where the Fair Grounds used to be. I guess you'll find it changed."

They had nothing more to say. They just stood there for a moment on the steps, and then shook hands once more.

"Well, good-bye."

And again he was in the street, and found the place where the corners met, and for the last time turned to see where Time had gone.

And he knew that he would never come again, and that lost magic would not come again. Lost now was all of it—the street, the heat, King's Highway, and Tom the Piper's son, all mixed in with the vast and drowsy murmur of the Fair, and with the sense of absence in the afternoon, and the house that waited, and the child that dreamed. And out of the enchanted wood, that thicket of man's memory, Eugene knew that the dark eye and the quiet face of his friend and brother—poor child, life's stranger, and life's exile, lost like all of us, a cipher in blind mazes, long ago—the lost boy was gone forever, and would not return.

THE RED PONY I

THE GIFT

JOHN STEINBECK

JOHN STEINBECK (1902–   ) was born in Salinas, California, studied biology as a special student at Stanford and worked at many odd jobs while beginning to write. He has displayed in much of his mature work a deep sympathy with simple and deprived people, at the same time viewing their actual condition with a realistic eye. His style ranges from an almost cruel realism to the lyrical. Among his books are *Tortilla Flat* (1935), *In Dubious Battle* (1936), *Of Mice and Men* (1937), *The Long Valley* (1938), *Grapes of Wrath* (1939), which won the Pulitzer Prize, *The Moon is Down* (1942), *Cannery Row* (1945), *East of Eden* (1952), *The Winter of our Discontent* (1961), which was mentioned when he was awarded the Nobel Prize for Literature in 1962, and *Travels with Charley* (1962).

AT DAYBREAK Billy Buck emerged from the bunkhouse and stood for a moment on the porch looking up at the sky. He was a broad, bandy-legged little man with a walrus mustache, with square hands; puffed and muscled on the palms. His eyes were a contemplative, watery grey and the hair which protruded from under his Stetson hat was spiky and weathered. Billy was still stuffing his shirt into his blue jeans as he stood on the porch. He unbuckled his belt and tightened it again. The belt showed, by the worn shiny places opposite each hole, the gradual increase of Billy's middle over a period of years. When he had seen to the weather, Billy cleared each nostril by holding its mate closed with his forefinger and blowing fiercely. Then he walked down to the barn, rubbing his hands together. He curried and brushed two saddle horses in the stalls, talking quietly to them all the time; and he had hardly finished when the iron triangle started ringing at the ranch house. Billy stuck the brush and curry-comb together and laid them on the rail, and went up to breakfast. His action had been so deliberate and yet so wasteless of time that he came to the house while Mrs. Tiflin was still ringing the triangle. She nodded her grey head to him and withdrew into the kitchen. Billy Buck sat down on the steps, because he was a cow-hand, and it wouldn't be fitting that he should go first into the dining-room. He heard Mr. Tiflin in the house, stamping his feet into his boots.

The high jangling note of the triangle put the boy Jody in motion. He was only a little boy, ten years old, with hair like dusty yellow grass and with shy polite grey eyes, and with a mouth that worked when he thought. The triangle picked him up out of sleep. It didn't occur to him to disobey the harsh note. He never had: no one he knew ever had. He brushed the tangled hair out of his eyes and skinned his nightgown off. In a moment he was dressed—blue chambray shirt and overalls. It was late in the summer, so of course there were no shoes to bother with. In the kitchen he waited until his mother got from in front of the sink and went back to the stove. Then he washed himself and brushed back his wet hair with his fingers. His mother turned sharply on him as he left the sink. Jody looked shyly away.

"I've got to cut your hair before long," his mother said. "Breakfast's on the table. Go on in, so Billy can come."

Jody sat at the long table which was covered with white oilcloth washed through to the fabric in some places. The fried eggs lay in rows on their platter. Jody took three eggs on his plate and followed with three thick slices of crisp bacon. He carefully scraped a spot of blood from one of the egg yolks.

Billy Buck clumped in. "That won't hurt you," Billy explained. "That's only a sign the rooster leaves."

Jody's tall stern father came in then and Jody knew from the noise on the floor that he was wearing boots, but he looked under the table anyway, to make sure. His father turned off the oil lamp over the table, for plenty of morning light now came through the windows.

Jody did not ask where his father and Billy Buck were riding that day, but he wished he might go along. His father was a disciplinarian. Jody obeyed him in everything without questions of any kind.

Now, Carl Tiflin sat down and reached for the egg platter.

"Got the cows ready to go, Billy?" he asked.

"In the lower corral," Billy said. "I could just as well take them in alone."

"Sure you could. But a man needs company. Besides your throat gets pretty dry." Carl Tiflin was jovial this morning.

Jody's mother put her head in the door. "What time do you think to be back, Carl?"

"I can't tell. I've got to see some men in Salinas. Might be gone till dark."

The eggs and coffee and big biscuits disappeared rapidly. Jody followed the two men out of the house. He watched them mount their horses and drive six old milk cows out of the corral and start over the hill toward Salinas. They were going to sell the old cows to the butcher.

When they had disappeared over the crown of the ridge Jody walked up the hill in back of the house. The dogs trotted around the house corner hunching their shoulders and grinning horribly with pleasure. Jody patted their heads—Doubletree Mutt with the big thick tail and yellow eyes, and Smasher, the shepherd, who had killed a coyote and lost an ear in doing it. Smasher's one good ear stood up higher than a collie's ear should. Billy Buck said that always happened. After the frenzied greeting the dogs lowered their noses to the ground in a businesslike way and went ahead, looking back now and then to make sure that the boy was coming. They walked up through the chicken yard and saw the quail eating with the chickens. Smasher chased the chickens a little to keep in practice in case there should ever be sheep to herd. Jody continued on through the large vegetable patch where the green corn was higher than his head. The cow-pumpkins were green and small yet. He went on to the sagebrush line where the cold spring ran out of its pipe and fell into a round wooden tub. He leaned over and drank close to the green mossy wood where the water tasted best. Then he turned and looked back on the ranch, on the low, whitewashed house girded with red geraniums, and on the long bunkhouse by the cypress tree where Billy Buck lived alone. Jody could see the great black kettle under the cypress tree. That was where the pigs were scalded. The sun was coming over the ridge now, glaring on the whitewash of the houses and barns, making the wet grass blaze softly. Behind him, in the tall sagebrush, the birds were scampering on the ground, making a great noise among the dry leaves; the squirrels piped shrilly on the side-hills. Jody looked along at the farm buildings. He felt an uncertainty in the air, a feeling of change and of loss and of the gain of new and unfamiliar things. Over

the hillside two big black buzzards sailed low to the ground and their shadows slipped smoothly and quickly ahead of them. Some animal had died in the vicinity. Jody knew it. It might be a cow or it might be the remains of a rabbit. The buzzards overlooked nothing. Jody hated them as all decent things hate them, but they could not be hurt because they made away with carrion.

After a while the boy sauntered down hill again. The dogs had long ago given him up and gone into the brush to do things in their own way. Back through the vegetable garden he went, and he paused for a moment to smash a green muskmelon with his heel, but he was not happy about it. It was a bad thing to do, he knew perfectly well. He kicked dirt over the ruined melon to conceal it.

Back at the house his mother bent over his rough hands, inspecting his fingers and nails. It did little good to start him clean to school for too many things could happen on the way. She sighed over the black cracks on his fingers, and then gave him his books and his lunch and started him on the mile walk to school. She noticed that his mouth was working a good deal this morning.

Jody started his journey. He filled his pockets with little pieces of white quartz that lay in the road, and every so often he took a shot at a bird or at some rabbit that had stayed sunning itself in the road too long. At the crossroads over the bridge he met two friends and the three of them walked to school together, making ridiculous strides and being rather silly. School had just opened two weeks before. There was still a spirit of revolt among the pupils.

It was four o'clock in the afternoon when Jody topped the hill and looked down on the ranch again. He looked for the saddle horses, but the corral was empty. His father was not back yet. He went slowly, then, toward the afternoon chores. At the ranch house, he found his mother sitting on the porch, mending socks.

"There's two doughnuts in the kitchen for you," she said. Jody slid to the kitchen, and returned with half of one of the doughnuts already eaten and his mouth full. His mother asked him what he had learned in school that day, but she didn't listen to his doughnut-muffled answer. She interrupted, "Jody, tonight see you fill the wood-box clear full. Last night you crossed the sticks and it wasn't only about half full. Lay the sticks flat tonight. And Jody, some of the hens are hiding eggs, or else the dogs are eating them. Look about in the grass and see if you can find any nests."

Jody, still eating, went out and did his chores. He saw the quail come down to eat with the chickens when he threw out the grain. For some reason his father was proud to have them come. He never allowed any shooting near the house for fear the quail might go away.

When the wood-box was full, Jody took his twenty-two rifle up to the cold spring at the brush line. He drank again and then aimed the gun at all manner of things, at rocks, at birds on the wing, at the big black pig kettle under the cypress tree, but he didn't shoot for he had no cartridges and wouldn't have until he was twelve. If his father had seen him aim the rifle in the direction of the house he would have put the cartridges off another year. Jody remembered this and did not point the rifle down the hill again. Two years was enough to wait for cartridges. Nearly all of his father's presents were given with reservations which hampered their value somewhat. It was good discipline.

The supper waited until dark for his father to return. When at last he came in with Billy Buck, Jody could smell the delicious brand on their breaths. Inwardly he rejoiced, for his father sometimes talked to him when he smelled of brandy, sometimes even told things he had done in the wild days when he was a boy.

After supper, Jody sat by the fireplace and his shy polite eyes sought the room corners, and he waited for his father to tell what it was he contained, for Jody knew he had news of some sort. But he was disappointed. His father pointed a stern finger at him.

"You'd better go to bed, Jody. I'm going to need you in the morning."

That wasn't so bad. Jody liked to do the things he had to do as long as they weren't routine things. He looked at the floor and his mouth worked out a question before he spoke it. "What are we going to do in the morning, kill a pig?" he asked softly.

"Never you mind. You better get to bed."

When the door was closed behind him, Jody heard his father and Billy Buck chuckling and he knew it was a joke of some kind. And later, when he lay in bed, trying to make words out of murmurs in the other room, he heard his father protest, "But, Ruth, I didn't give much for him."

Jody heard the hoot-owls hunting mice down by the barn, and he heard a fruit tree limb tap-tapping against the house. A cow was lowing when he went to sleep.

When the triangle sounded in the morning, Jody dressed more quickly even than usual. In the kitchen, while he washed his face and combed back his hair, his mother addressed him irritably. "Don't you go out until you get a good breakfast in you."

He went into the dining-room and sat at the long white table. He took a steaming hotcake from the platter, arranged two fried eggs on it, covered them with another hotcake and squashed the whole thing with his fork.

His father and Billy Buck came in. Jody knew from the sound of the floor that both of them were wearing flatheeled shoes, but he peered under the table to make sure. His father turned off the oil lamp, for the day had arrived, and he looked stern and disciplinary, but Billy Buck didn't look at Jody at all. He avoided the shy questioning eyes of the boy and soaked a whole piece of toast in his coffee.

Carl Tiflin said crossly, "You come with us after breakfast!"

Jody had trouble with his food then, for he felt a kind of doom in the air. After Billy had tilted his saucer and drained the coffee which had slopped into it, and had wiped his hands on his jeans, the two men stood up from the table and went out into the morning light together, and Jody respectfully followed a little behind them. He tried to keep his mind from running ahead, tried to keep it absolutely motionless.

His mother called, "Carl! Don't you let it keep him from school."

They marched past the cypress, where a singletree hung from a limb to butcher the pigs on, and past the black iron kettle, so it was not a pig killing. The sun shone over the hill and threw long, dark shadows of the trees and buildings. They crossed a stubble-field to shortcut to the barn. Jody's father unhooked the door and they went in. They had been walking toward the sun on the way down. The barn was black as night in contrast and warm from the hay and from the beasts. Jody's father moved over toward the one box stall. "Come here!" he ordered. Jody could begin to see things now. He looked into the box stall and then stepped back quickly.

A red pony colt was looking at him out of the stall. Its tense ears were forward and a light of disobedience was in its eyes. Its coat was rough and thick as an airedale's fur and its mane was long and tangled. Jody's throat collapsed in on itself and cut his breath short.

"He needs a good currying," his father said, "and if I ever hear of you not feeding him or leaving his stall dirty, I'll sell him off in a minute."

Jody couldn't bear to look at the pony's eyes any more. He gazed down at his hands for a moment, and he asked very shyly, "Mine?" No one answered him. He put his hands out toward the pony. Its grey nose came close, sniffing loudly, and then the lips drew back and the strong teeth closed on Jody's fingers. The pony shook its head up and down and seemed to laugh with amusement. Jody regarded his bruised fingers. "Well," he said with pride— "Well, I guess he can bite all right." The two men laughed, somewhat in relief. Carl Tiflin went out of the barn and walked up a sidehill to be by himself, for he was embarrassed, but Billy Buck stayed. It was easier to talk to Billy Buck. Jody asked again—"Mine?"

Billy became professional in tone. "Sure! That is, if you look out for him and break him right. I'll show you how. He's just a colt. You can't ride him for some time."

Jody put out his bruised hand again, and this time the red pony let his nose be rubbed. "I ought to have a carrot," Jody said. "Where'd we get him, Billy?"

"Bought him at a sheriff's auction," Billy explained. "A show went broke in Salinas and had debts. The sheriff was selling off their stuff."

The pony stretched out his nose and shook the forelock from his wild eyes. Jody stroked the nose a little. He said softly, "There isn't a—saddle?"

Billy Buck laughed. "I'd forgot. Come along."

In the harness room he lifted down a little saddle of red morocco leather. "It's just a show saddle," Billy Buck said disparagingly. "It isn't practical for the brush, but it was cheap at the sale."

Jody couldn't trust himself to look at the saddle either, and he couldn't speak at all. He brushed the shining red leather with his fingertips, and after a long time he said, "It'll look pretty on him though." He thought of the grandest and prettiest things he knew. "If he hasn't a name already, I think I'll call him Gabilan Mountains," he said.

Billy Buck knew how he felt. "It's a pretty long name. Why don't you just call him Gabilan? That means hawk. That would be a fine name for him." Billy felt glad. "If you will collect tail hair, I might be able to make a hair rope for you sometime. You could use it for a hackamore."

Jody wanted to go back to the box stall. "Could I lead him to school, do you think—to show the kids?"

But Billy shook his head. "He's not even halter-broke yet. We had a time getting him here. Had to almost drag him. You better be starting for school though."

"I'll bring the kids to see him here this afternoon," Jody said.

Six boys came over the hill half an hour early that afternoon, running hard, their heads down, their forearms working, their breath whistling. They swept by the house and cut across the stubble-field to the barn. And then they stood self-consciously before the pony, and then they looked at Jody with eyes in which there was a new admiration and a new respect. Before today Jody had been a boy, dressed in overalls and a blue shirt—quieter than most, even suspected of being a little cowardly. And now he was different. Out of a thousand centuries they drew the ancient admiration of the footman for the horseman They knew instinctively that a man on a horse is spiritually as well as physically bigger than a man on foot. They knew that Jody had been miraculously lifted out of equality with them, and had been placed over them. Gabilan put his head out of the stall and sniffed them.

"Why'nt you ride him?" the boys cried. "Why'nt you braid his tail with ribbons like in the fair?" "When you going to ride him?"

Jody's courage was up. He too felt the superiority of the horseman. "He's not old enough. Nobody can ride him for a long time. I'm going to train him on the long halter. Billy Buck is going to show me how."

"Well, can't we even lead him around a little?"

"He isn't even halter-broke," Jody said. He wanted to be completely alone when he took the pony out the first time. "Come and see the saddle."

They were speechless at the red morocco saddle, completely shocked out of comment. "It isn't much use in the brush," Jody explained. "It'll look pretty on him though. Maybe I'll ride bareback when I go into the brush."

"How you going to rope a cow without a saddle horn?"

"Maybe I'll get another saddle for every day. My father might want me to help him with the stock." He let them feel the red saddle, and showed them the brass chain throat-latch on the bridle and the big brass buttons at each temple where the headstall and brow band crossed. The whole thing was too wonderful. They had to go away after a little while, and each boy, in his mind, searched among his possessions for a bribe worthy of offering a return for a ride on the red pony when the time should come.

Jody was glad when they had gone. He took brush and currycomb from the wall, took down the barrier of the box stall and stepped cautiously in. The pony's eyes glittered, and he edged around into kicking position. But Jody touched him on the shoulder and rubbed his high arched neck as he had always seen Billy Buck do, and he crooned, "So-o-o Boy," in a deep voice. The pony gradually relaxed his tenseness. Jody curried and brushed until a pile of dead hair lay in the stall and until the pony's coat had taken on a deep red shine. Each time he finished he thought it might have been done better. He braided the mane into a dozen little pigtails, and he braided the forelock, and then he undid them and brushed the hair out straight again.

Jody did not hear his mother enter the barn. She was angry when she came, but when she looked in at the pony and at Jody working over him, she felt a curious pride rise up in her. "Have you forgot the wood-box?" she asked gently. "It's not far off from dark and there's not a stick of wood in the house, and the chickens aren't fed."

Jody quickly put up his tools. "I forgot, ma'am."

"Well, after this do your chores first. Then you won't forget. I expect you'll forget lots of things now if I don't keep an eye on you."

"Can I have carrots from the garden for him, ma'am?"

She had to think about that. "Oh—I guess so, if you only take the big tough ones."

"Carrots keep the coat good," he said, and again she felt the curious rush of pride.

Jody never waited for the triangle to get him out of bed after the coming of the pony. It became his habit to creep out of bed even before his mother was awake, to slip into his clothes and go quietly to the barn to see Gabilan. In the grey quiet mornings when the land and the brush and the houses and the trees were silver-grey and black like a photograph nega-tive, he stole toward the barn, past the sleeping stones and the sleeping cypress tree. The turkeys, roosting in the tree out of coyotes' reach, clicked drowsily. The fields glowed with a grey frost-like light and in the dew the tracks of rabbits and of field mice stood out sharply. The good dogs came stiffly out of their little houses, hackles up and deep growls in their throats. Then they caught Jody's scent, and their stiff tails rose up and waved a greet-ing—Doubletree Mutt with the big thick tail, and Smasher, the incipient shepherd—then went lazily back to their warm beds.

It was a strange time and mysterious journey, to Jody—an extension of a dream. When he first had the pony he liked to torture himself during the trip by thinking Gabilan would not be in his stall, and worse, would never have been there. And he had other deli-cious little self-induced pains. He thought how the rats had gnawed ragged holes in the red saddle, and how the mice had nibbled Gabilan's tail until it was stringy and thin. He usually ran the last little way to the barn. He unlatched the rusty hasp of the barn door and stepped in, and no matter how quietly he opened the door, Gabilan was always looking at him over the barrier of the box stall and Gabilan whin-nied softly and stamped his front foot, and his eyes had big sparks of red fire in them like oakwood embers.

Sometimes, if the work horses were to be used that day, Jody found Billy Buck in the barn harnessing and currying. Billy stood with him and looked long at Gabilan and he told Jody a great many things about horses. He explained that they were terribly afraid for their feet, so that one must make a practice of lifting the legs and patting the hooves and ankles to remove their terror. He told Jody how horses love conversation. He must talk to the pony all the time, and tell him the reasons for everything. Billy wasn't sure a horse could understand everything that was said to him, but it was impossible to say how much was understood. A horse never kicked up a fuss if some one he liked explained things to him. Billy could give examples, too. He had known, for in-stance, a horse nearly dead beat with fatigue to perk up when told it was only a little farther to his desti-nation. And he had known a horse paralyzed with fright to come out of it when his rider told him what it was that was frightening him. While he talked in the mornings, Billy Buck cut twenty or thirty straws into neat three-inch lengths and stuck them into his hatband. Then during the whole day, if he wanted to pick his teeth or merely to chew on something, he had only to reach up for one of them.

Jody listened carefully, for he knew and the whole country knew that Billy Buck was a fine hand with horses. Billy's own horse was a stringy cayuse with a hammer head, but he nearly always won the first prizes at the stock trials. Billy could rope a steer, take a double half-hitch about the horn with his riata, and dismount, and his horse would play the steer as an angler plays a fish, keeping a tight rope until the steer was down or beaten.

Every morning, after Jody had curried and brushed the pony, he let down the barrier of the stall, and Gabilan thrust past him and raced down the barn and into the corral. Around and around he galloped, and sometimes he jumped forward and landed on stiff legs. He stood quivering, stiff ears forward, eyes rolling so that the whites showed, pretending to be frightened. At last he walked snorting to the water-trough and buried his nose in the water up to the nostrils. Jody was proud then, for he knew that was the way to judge a horse. Poor horses only touched their lips to the water, but a fine spirited beast put his whole nose and mouth under, and only left room to breathe.

Then Jody stood and watched the pony, and he saw things he had never noticed about any other horse, the sleek, sliding flank muscles and the cords of the buttocks, which flexed like a closing fist, and the shine the sun put on the red coat. Having seen horses all his life, Jody had never looked at them very closely before. But now he noticed the moving ears which gave expression and even inflection of ex-pression to the face. The pony talked with his ears. You could tell exactly how he felt about everything by the way his ears pointed. Sometimes they were stiff and upright and sometimes lax and sagging. They went back when he was angry or fearful, and forward when he was anxious and curious and pleased; and their exact position indicated which emotion he had.

Billy Buck kept his word. In the early fall the training began. First there was the halter-breaking, and that was the hardest because it was the first thing. Jody held a carrot and coaxed and promised and pulled on the rope. The pony set his feet like a burro when he felt the strain. But before long he learned. Jody walked all over the ranch leading him. Gradually he took to dropping the rope until the pony followed him unled wherever he went.

And then came the training on the long halter. That was slower work. Jody stood in the middle of a circle, holding the long halter. He clucked with his tongue and the pony started to walk in a big circle, held in by the long rope. He clucked again to make the pony trot, and again to make him gallop. Around and around Gabilan went thundering and enjoying it immensely. Then he called, "Whoa," and the pony stopped. It was not long until Gabilan was perfect at it. But in many ways he was a bad pony. He bit Jody in the pants and stomped on Jody's feet. Now and then his ears went back and he aimed a tremendous kick at the boy. Every time he did one of these bad things, Gabilan settled back and seemed to laugh to himself.

Billy Buck worked at the hair rope in the evenings before the fireplace. Jody collected tail hair in a bag, and he sat and watched Billy slowly constructing the rope, twisting a few hairs to make a string and rolling two strings together for a cord, and then braiding a number of cords to make the rope. Billy rolled the finished rope on the floor under his foot to make it round and hard.

The long halter work rapidly approached perfection. Jody's father, watching the pony stop and start and trot and gallop, was a little bothered by it.

"He's getting to be almost a trick pony," he complained. "I don't like trick horses. It takes all the—dignity out of a horse to make him do tricks. Why, a trick horse is kind of like an actor—no dignity, no character of his own." And his father said, "I guess you better be getting him used to the saddle pretty soon."

Jody rushed for the harness-room. For some time he had been riding the saddle on a sawhorse. He changed the stirrup length over and over, and could never get it just right. Sometimes, mounted on the sawhorse in the harness-room, with collars and hames and tugs hung all about him, Jody rode out beyond the room. He carried his rifle across the pommel. He saw the fields go flying by, and he heard the beat of the galloping hoofs.

It was a ticklish job, saddling the pony the first time. Gabilan hunched and reared and threw the saddle off before the cinch could be tightened. It had to be replaced again and again until at last the pony let it stay. And the cinching was difficult, too. Day by day Jody tightened the girth a little more until at last the pony didn't mind the saddle at all.

Then there was the bridle. Billy explained how to use a stick of licorice for a bit until Gabilan was used to having something in his mouth. Billy explained, "Of course we could force-break him to everything, but he wouldn't be as good a horse if we did. He'd always be a little bit afraid, and he wouldn't mind because he wanted to."

The first time the pony wore the bridle he whipped his head about and worked his tongue against the bit until the blood oozed from the corners of his mouth. He tried to rub the headstall off on the manger. His ears pivoted about and his eyes turned red with fear and with general rambunctiousness. Jody rejoiced, for he knew that only a mean-souled horse does not resent training.

And Jody trembled when he thought of the time when he would first sit in the saddle. The pony would probably throw him off. There was no disgrace in that. The disgrace would come if he did not get right up and mount again. Sometimes he dreamed that he lay in the dirt and cried and couldn't make himself mount again. The shame of the dream lasted until the middle of the day.

Gabilan was growing fast. Already he had lost the long-leggedness of the colt; his mane was getting longer and blacker. Under the constant currying and brushing his coat lay as smooth and gleaming as orange-red lacquer. Jody oiled the hoofs and kept them carefully trimmed so they would not crack.

The hair rope was nearly finished. Jody's father gave him an old pair of spurs and bent in the side bars and cut down the strap and took up the chainlets until they fitted. And then one day Carl Tiflin said:

"The pony's growing faster than I thought. I guess you can ride him by Thanksgiving. Think you can stick on?"

"I don't know," Jody said shyly. Thanksgiving was only three weeks off. He hoped it wouldn't rain, for rain would spot the red saddle.

Gabilan knew and liked Jody by now. He nickered when Jody came across the stubble-field, and in the pasture he came running when his master whistled for him. There was always a carrot for him every time.

Billy Buck gave him riding instructions over and over. "Now when you get up there, just grab tight with your knees and keep your hands away from the saddle, and if you get throwed, don't let that stop you. No matter how good a man is, there's always some horse can pitch him. You just climb up again before he gets to feeling smart about it. Pretty soon, he won't throw you no more, and pretty soon he *can't* throw you no more. That's the way to do it."

"I hope it don't rain before," Jody said.

"Why not? Don't want to get throwed in the mud?"

That was partly it, and also he was afraid that in the flurry of bucking Gabilan might slip and fall on him and break his leg or his hip. He had seen that happen to men before, had seen how they writhed on the ground like squashed bugs, and he was afraid of it.

He practiced on the sawhorse how he would hold the reins in his left hand and a hat in his right hand. If he kept his hands thus busy, he couldn't grab the horn if he felt himself going off. He didn't like to think of what would happen if he did grab the horn. Perhaps his father and Billy Buck would never speak to him again, they would be so ashamed. The news would get about and his mother would be ashamed too. And in the school yard—it was too awful to contemplate.

He began putting his weight in a stirrup when Gabilan was saddled, but he didn't throw his leg over the pony's back. That was forbidden until Thanksgiving.

Every afternoon he put the red saddle on the pony and cinched it tight. The pony was learning already to fill his stomach out unnaturally large while the cinching was going on, and then to let it down when the straps were fixed. Sometimes Jody led him up to the brush line and let him drink from the round green tub, and sometimes he led him up through the stubble-field to the hilltop from which it was possible to see the white town of Salinas and the geometric fields of the great valley, and the oak trees clipped by the sheep. Now and then they broke through the brush and came to little cleared circles so hedged in that the world was gone and only the sky and the circle of brush were left from the old life. Gabilan liked these trips and showed it by keeping his head very high and by quivering his nostrils with interest. When the two came back from an expedition they smelled of the sweet sage they had forced through.

Time dragged on toward Thanksgiving, but winter came fast. The clouds swept down and hung all day over the land and brushed the hilltops, and the winds blew shrilly at night. All day the dry oak leaves drifted down from the trees until they covered the ground, and yet the trees were unchanged.

Jody had wished it might not rain before Thanksgiving, but it did. The brown earth turned dark and the trees glistened. The cut ends of the stubble turned black with mildew; the haystacks grayed from exposure to the damp, and on the roofs the moss, which had been all summer as grey as lizards, turned a brilliant yellow-green. During the week of rain, Jody kept the pony in the box stall out of the dampness, except for a little time after school when he took him out for exercise and to drink at the water-trough in the upper corral. Not once did Gabilan get wet.

The wet weather continued until little new grass appeared. Jody walked to school dressed in a slicker and short rubber boots. At length one morning the sun came out brightly. Jody, at his work in the box stall, said to Billy Buck, "Maybe I'll leave Gabilan in the corral when I go to school today."

"Be good for him to be out in the sun," Billy assured him. "No animal likes to be cooped up too long. Your father and me are going back on the hill to clean the leaves out of the spring." Billy nodded and picked his teeth with one of his little straws.

"If the rain comes, though—" Jody suggested.

"Not likely to rain today. She's rained herself out." Billy pulled up his sleeves and snapped his arm bands. "If it comes on to rain—why a little rain don't hurt a horse."

"Well, if it does come on to rain, you put him in, will you, Billy? I'm scared he might get cold so I couldn't ride him when the time comes."

"Oh sure! I'll watch out for him if we get back in time. But it won't rain today."

And so Jody, when he went to school left Gabilan standing out in the corral.

Billy Buck wasn't wrong about many things. He couldn't be. But he was wrong about the weather that day, for a little after noon the clouds pushed over the hills and the rain began to pour down. Jody heard it start on the schoolhouse roof. He considered holding up one finger for permission to go to the outhouse and, once outside, running for home to put the pony in. Punishment would be prompt both at school and at home. He gave it up and took ease from Billy's assurance that rain couldn't hurt a horse. When school was finally out, he hurried home through the dark rain. The banks at the sides of the road spouted little jets of muddy water. The rain slanted and swirled under a cold and gusty wind. Jody dog-trotted home, slopping through the gravelly mud of the road.

From the top of the ridge he could see Gabilan standing miserably in the corral. The red coat was almost black, and streaked with water. He stood head down with his rump to the rain and wind. Jody arrived running and threw open the barn door and led the wet pony in by his forelock. Then he found a gunny sack and rubbed the soaked hair and rubbed the legs and ankles. Gabilan stood patiently, but he trembled in gusts like the wind.

When he had dried the pony as well as he could, Jody went up to the house and brought hot water down to the barn and soaked the grain in it. Gabilan was not very hungry. He nibbled at the hot mash, but he was not very much interested in it, and he still shivered now and then. A little steam rose from his damp back.

It was almost dark when Billy Buck and Carl Tiflin came home. "When the rain started we put up at Ben Herche's place, and the rain never let up all afternoon," Carl Tiflin explained. Jody looked reproachfully at Billy Buck and Billy felt guilty.

"You said it wouldn't rain," Jody accused him.

Billy looked away. "It's hard to tell, this time of year," he said, but his excuse was lame. He had no right to be fallible, and he knew it.

"The pony got wet, got soaked through."

"Did you dry him off?"

"I rubbed him with a sack and I gave him hot grain."

Billy nodded in agreement.

"Do you think he'll take cold, Billy?"

"A little rain never hurt anything," Billy assured him.

Jody's father joined the conversation then and lectured the boy a little. "A horse," he said, "isn't any lap-dog kind of thing." Carl Tiflin hated weakness and sickness, and he held a violent contempt for helplessness.

Jody's mother put a platter of steaks on the table and boiled potatoes and boiled squash, which clouded the room with their steam. They sat down to eat. Carl Tiflin still grumbled about weakness put into animals and men by too much coddling.

Billy Buck felt bad about his mistake. "Did you blanket him?" he asked.

"No. I couldn't find any blanket. I laid some sacks over his back."

"We'll go down and cover him up after we eat, then." Billy felt better about it then. When Jody's father had gone in to the fire and his mother was washing dishes, Billy found and lighted a lantern. He and Jody walked through the mud to the barn. The barn was dark and warm and sweet. The horses still munched their evening hay. "You hold the lantern!" Billy ordered. And he felt the pony's legs and tested the heat of the flanks. He put his cheek against the pony's grey muzzle and then he rolled up the eyelids to look at the eyeballs and he lifted the lips to see the gums, and he put his fingers inside the ears. "He

don't seem so chipper," Billy said. "I'll give him a rub-down."

Then Billy found a sack and rubbed the pony's legs violently and he rubbed the chest and the withers. Gabilan was strangely spiritless. He submitted patiently to the rubbing. At last Billy brought an old cotton comforter from the saddle-room, and threw it over the pony's back and tied it at neck and chest with string.

"Now he'll be all right in the morning," Billy said.

Jody's mother looked up when he got back to the house. "You're late up from bed," she said. She held his chin in her hard hand and brushed the tangled hair out of his eyes and she said, "Don't worry about the pony. He'll be all right. Billy's as good as any horse doctor in the country."

Jody hadn't known she could see his worry. He pulled gently away from her and knelt down in front of the fireplace until it burned his stomach. He scorched himself through and then went in to bed, but it was a hard thing to go to sleep. He awakened after what seemed a long time. The room was dark but there was a greyness in the window like that which precedes the dawn. He got up and found his overalls and searched for the legs, and then the clock in the other room struck two. He laid his clothes down and got back into bed. It was broad daylight when he awakened again. For the first time he had slept through the ringing of the triangle. He leaped up, flung on his clothes and went out of the door still buttoning his shirt. His mother looked after him for a moment and then went quietly back to her work. Her eyes were brooding and kind. Now and then her mouth smiled a little but without changing her eyes at all.

Jody ran on toward the barn. Halfway there he heard the sound he dreaded, the hollow rasping cough of a horse. He broke into a sprint then. In the barn he found Billy Buck with the pony. Billy was rubbing its legs with his strong thick hands. He looked up and smiled gaily.

"He just took a little cold," Billy said. "We'll have him out of it in a couple of days."

Jody looked at the pony's face. The eyes were half closed and the lids thick and dry. In the eye corners a crust of hard mucus stuck. Gabilan's ears hung loosely sideways and his head was low. Jody put out his hand, but the pony did not move close to it. He coughed again and his whole body constricted with the effort. A little stream of thin fluid ran from his nostrils.

Jody looked back at Billy Buck. "He's awful sick, Billy."

"Just a little cold, like I said," Billy insisted. "You

go get some breakfast and then go back to school. I'll take care of him."

"But you might have to do something else. You might leave him."

"No, I won't. I won't leave him at all. Tomorrow's Saturday. Then you can stay with him all day." Billy had failed again, and he felt badly about it. He had to cure the pony now.

Jody walked up to the house and took his place listlessly at the table. The eggs and bacon were cold and greasy, but he didn't notice it. He ate his usual amount. He didn't even ask to stay home from school. His mother pushed his hair back when she took his plate. "Billy'll take care of the pony," she assured him.

He moped through the whole day at school. He couldn't answer any questions nor read any words. He couldn't even tell anyone the pony was sick, for that might make him sicker. And when school was finally out he started home in dread. He walked slowly and let the other boys leave him. He wished he might continue walking and never arrive at the ranch.

Billy was in the barn, as he had promised, and the pony was worse. His eyes were almost closed now, and his breath whistled shrilly past an obstruction in his nose. A film covered that part of the eyes that was visible at all. It was doubtful whether the pony could see anymore. Now and then he snorted, to clear his nose, and by the action seemed to plug it tighter. Jody looked dispiritedly at the pony's coat. The hair lay rough and unkempt and seemed to have lost all of its old luster. Billy stood quietly besides the stall. Jody hated to ask, but he had to know.

"Billy, is he—is he going to get well?"

Billy put his fingers between the bars under the pony's jaw and felt about. "Feel here," he said and he guided Jody's fingers to a large lump under the jaw. "When that gets bigger, I'll open it up and then he'll get better."

Jody looked quickly away, for he had heard about that lump. "What is it the matter with him?"

Billy didn't want to answer, but he had to. He couldn't be wrong three times. "Strangles," he said shortly, "but don't you worry about that. I'll pull him out of it. I've seen them get well when they were worse than Gabilan is. I'm going to steam him now. You can help."

"Yes," Jody said miserably. He followed Billy into the grain room and watched him make the steaming bag ready. It was a long canvas nose bag with straps to go over a horse's ears. Billy filled it one-third full of bran and then he added a couple of handfuls of dried hops. On top of the dry substance he poured a little carbolic acid and a little turpentine. "I'll be mix-

ing it all up while you run to the house for a kettle of boiling water," Billy said.

When Jody came back with the steaming kettle, Billy buckled the straps over Gabilan's head and fitted the bag tightly around his nose. Then through a little hole in the side of the bag he poured the boiling water on the mixture. The pony started away as a cloud of strong steam rose up, but then the soothing fumes crept through his nose and into his lungs, and the sharp steam began to clear out the nasal passages. He breathed loudly. His legs trembled in an ague, and his eyes closed against the biting cloud. Billy poured in more water and kept the steam rising for fifteen minutes. At last he set down the kettle and took the bag from Gabilan's nose. The pony looked better. He breathed freely, and his eyes were open wider than they had been.

"See how good it makes him feel," Billy said. "Now we'll wrap him up in the blanket again. Maybe he'll be nearly well by morning."

"I'll stay with him tonight," Jody suggested.

"No. Don't you do it. I'll bring my blankets down here and put them in the hay. You can stay tomorrow and steam him if he needs it."

The evening was falling when they went to the house for their supper. Jody didn't even realize that some one else had fed the chickens and filled the wood-box. He walked up past the house to the dark brush line and took a drink of water from the tub. The spring water was so cold that it stung his mouth and drove a shiver through him. The sky above the hills was still light. He saw a hawk flying so high that it caught the sun on its breast and shone like a spark. Two blackbirds were driving him down the sky, glittering as they attacked their enemy. In the west, the clouds were moving in to rain again.

Jody's father didn't speak at all while the family ate supper, but after Billy Buck had taken his blankets and gone to sleep in the barn, Carl Tiflin built a high fire in the fireplace and told stories. He told about the wild man who ran naked through the country and had a tail and ears like a horse, and he told about the rabbit-cats of Moro Cojo that hopped into the trees for birds. He revived the famous Maxwell brothers who found a vein of gold and hid the traces of it so carefully that they could never find it again.

Jody sat with his chin in his hands; his mouth worked nervously, and his father gradually became aware that he wasn't listening very carefully. "Isn't that funny?" he asked.

Jody laughed politely and said, "Yes, sir." His father was angry and hurt, then. He didn't tell any more stories. After awhile, Jody took a lantern and went down to the barn. Billy Buck was asleep in the hay, and, except that his breath rasped a little in his lungs, the pony seemed to be much better. Jody stayed a little while, running his fingers over the red rough coat, and then he took up the lantern and went back to the house. When he was in bed his mother came into the room.

"Have you enough covers on? It's getting winter."

"Yes, ma'am."

"Well, get some rest tonight." She hesitated to go out, stood uncertainly. "The pony will be all right," she said.

Jody was tired. He went to sleep quickly and didn't awaken until dawn. The triangle sounded, and Billy Buck came up from the barn before Jody could get out of the house.

"How is he?" Jody demanded.

Billy always wolfed his breakfast. "Pretty good. I'm going to open that lump this morning. Then he'll be better maybe."

After breakfast, Billy got out his best knife, one with a needle point. He whetted the shining blade a long time on a little carborundum stone. He tried the point and the blade again and again on his calloused thumb-ball, and at last he tried it on his upper lip.

On the way to the barn, Jody noticed how the young grass was up and how the stubble was melting day by day into the new green crop of volunteer. It was a cold sunny morning.

As soon as he saw the pony, Jody knew he was worse. His eyes were closed and sealed shut with dried mucus. His head hung so low that his nose almost touched the straw of his bed. There was a little groan in each breath, a deep-seated, patient groan.

Billy lifted the weak head and made a quick slash with the knife. Jody saw the yellow pus run out. He held up the head while Billy swabbed out the wound with weak carbolic acid salve.

"Now he'll feel better," Billy assured him. "That yellow poison is what makes him sick."

Jody looked unbelieving at Billy Buck. "He's awful sick."

Billy thought a long time what to say. He nearly tossed off a careless assurance, but he saved himself in time. "Yes, he's pretty sick," he said at last. "I've seen worse ones get well. If he doesn't get pneumonia, we'll pull him through. You stay with him. If he gets worse, you can come and get me."

For a long time after Billy went away, Jody stood beside the pony, stroking him behind the ears. The pony didn't flip his head the way he had done when he was well. The groaning in his breathing was becoming more hollow.

Doubletree Mutt looked into the barn, his big tail waving provocatively, and Jody was so incensed at

his health that he found a hard black clod on the floor and deliberately threw it. Doubletree Mutt went yelping away to nurse a bruised paw.

In the middle of the morning, Billy Buck came back and made another steam bag. Jody watched to see whether the pony improved this time as he had before. His breathing eased a little, but he did not raise his head.

The Saturday dragged on. Late in the afternoon Jody went to the house and brought his bedding down and made up a place to sleep in the hay. He didn't ask permission. He knew from the way his mother looked at him that she would let him do almost anything. That night he left a lantern burning on a wire over the box stall. Billy had told him to rub the pony's legs every little while.

At nine o'clock the wind sprang up and howled around the barn. And in spite of his worry, Jody grew sleepy. He got into his blankets and went to sleep, but the breathy groans of the pony sounded in his dreams. And in his sleep he heard a crashing noise which went on and on until it awakened him. The wind was rushing through the barn. He sprang up and looked down the lane of stalls. The barn door had blown open, and the pony was gone.

He caught the lantern and ran outside into the gale, and he saw Gabilan weakly shambling away into the darkness, head down, legs working slowly and mechanically. When Jody ran up and caught him by the forelock, he allowed himself to be led back and put into his stall. His groans were louder, and a fierce whistling came from his nose. Jody didn't sleep anymore then. The hissing of the pony's breath grew louder and sharper.

He was glad when Billy Buck came in at dawn. Billy looked for a time at the pony as though he had never seen him before. He felt the ears and flanks. "Jody," he said, "I've got to do something you won't want to see. You run up to the house for a while."

Jody grabbed him fiercely by the forearm. "You're not going to shoot him?"

Billy patted his hand. "No. I'm going to open a little hole in his windpipe so he can breathe. His nose is filled up. When he gets well, we'll put a little brass button in the hole for him to breathe through."

Jody couldn't have gone away if he had wanted to. It was awful to see the red hide cut, but infinitely more terrible to know it was being cut and not to see it. "I'll stay right here," he said bitterly. "You sure you got to?"

"Yes. I'm sure. If you stay, you can hold his head. If it doesn't make you sick, that is."

The fine knife came out again and was whetted again just as carefully as it had been the first time. Jody held the pony's head up and the throat taut, while Billy felt up and down for the right place. Jody sobbed once as the bright knife point disappeared into the throat. The pony plunged weakly away and then stood still, trembling violently. The blood ran thickly out and up the knife and across Billy's hand and into his shirtsleeve. The sure square hand sawed out a round hole in the flesh, and the breath came bursting out of the hole, throwing a fine spray of blood. With the rush of oxygen, the pony took a sudden strength. He lashed out with his hind feet and tried to rear, but Jody held his head down while Billy mopped the new wound with carbolic salve. It was a good job. The blood stopped flowing and the air puffed out of the hole and sucked it in regularly with a little bubbling noise.

The rain brought in by the night wind began to fall on the barn roof. Then the triangle rang for breakfast. "You go up and eat while I wait," Billy said. "We've got to keep this hole from plugging up."

Jody walked slowly out of the barn. He was too dispirited to tell Billy how the barn door had blown open and let the pony out. He emerged into the wet grey morning and sloshed up to the house, taking a perverse pleasure in splashing through all the puddles. His mother fed him and put dry clothes on. She didn't question him. She seemed to know he couldn't answer questions. But when he was ready to go back to the barn she brought him a pan of steaming meal. "Give him this," she said.

But Jody did not take the pan. He said, "He won't eat anything," and ran out of the house. At the barn, Billy showed him how to fix a ball of cotton on a stick, with which to swab out the breathing hole when it became clogged with mucus.

Jody's father walked into the barn and stood with them in front of the stall. At length he turned to the boy. "Hadn't you better come with me? I'm going to drive over the hill." Jody shook his head. "You better come on, out of this," his father insisted.

Billy turned on him angrily. "Let him alone. It's his pony, isn't it?"

Carl Tiflin walked away without saying another word. His feelings were badly hurt.

All morning Jody kept the wound open and the air passing in and out freely. At noon the pony lay wearily down on his side and stretched his nose out.

Billy came back. "If you're going to stay with him tonight, you better take a little nap," he said. Jody went absently out of the barn. The sky had cleared to a hard thin blue. Everywhere the birds were busy with worms that had come to the damp surface of the ground.

Jody walked to the brush line and sat on the edge of the mossy tub. He looked down at the house and at the old bunkhouse and at the dark cypress tree.

The place was familiar, but curiously changed. It wasn't itself anymore, but a frame for things that were happening. A cold wind blew out of the east now, signifying that the rain was over for a little while. At his feet Jody could see the little arms of new weeds spreading out over the ground. In the mud about the spring were thousands of quail tracks.

Doubletree Mutt came sideways and embarrassed up through the vegetable patch, and Jody, remembering how he had thrown the clod, put his arm about the dog's neck and kissed him on his wide black nose. Doubletree Mutt sat still, as though he knew some solemn thing was happening. His big tail slapped the ground gravely. Jody pulled a swollen tick out of Mutt's neck and popped it dead between his thumbnails. It was a nasty thing. He washed his hands in the cold spring water.

Except for the steady swish of the wind, the farm was very quiet. Jody knew his mother wouldn't mind if he didn't go in to eat his lunch. After a little while he went slowly back to the barn. Mutt crept into his own little house and whined softly to himself for a long time.

Billy Buck stood up from the box and surrendered the cotton swab. The pony still lay on his side and the wound in his throat bellowsed in and out. When Jody saw how dry and dead the hair looked, he knew at last that there was no hope for the pony. He had seen the dead hair before on dogs and on cows, and it was a sure sign. He sat heavily on the box and let down the barrier of the box stall. For a long time he kept his eyes on the moving wound, and at last he dozed, and the afternoon passed quickly. Just before dark his mother brought a deep dish of stew and left it for him and went away. Jody ate a little of it, and, when it was dark, he set the lantern on the floor by the pony's head so he could watch the wound and keep it open. And he dozed again until the night chill awakened him. The wind was blowing fiercely, bringing the north cold with it. Jody brought a blanket from his bed in the hay and wrapped himself in it. Gabilan's breathing was quiet at last; the hole in his throat moved gently. The owls flew through the hayloft, shrieking and looking for mice. Jody put his hands down on his head and slept. In his sleep he was aware that the wind had increased. He heard it slamming about the barn.

It was daylight when he awakened. The barn door had swung open. The pony was gone. He sprang up and ran out into the morning light.

The pony's tracks were plain enough, dragging through the frostlike dew on the young grass, tired tracks with little lines between them where the hoofs had dragged. They headed for the brush line halfway up the ridge. Jody broke into a run and followed them. The sun shone on the sharp white quartz that stuck through the ground here and there. As he followed the plain trail, a shadow cut across in front of him. He looked up and saw a high circle of black buzzards, and the slowly revolving circle dropped lower and lower. The solemn birds soon disappeared over the ridge. Jody ran faster then, forced on by panic and rage. The trail entered the brush at last and followed a winding route among the tall sage bushes.

At the top of the ridge Jody was winded. He paused, puffing noisily. The blood pounded in his ears. Then he saw what he was looking for. Below, in one of the little clearings in the brush, lay the red pony. In the distance, Jody could see the legs moving slowly and convulsively. And in a circle around him stood the buzzards, waiting for the moment of death they know so well.

Jody leaped forward and plunged down the hill. The wet ground muffled his steps and the brush hid him. When he arrived, it was all over. The first buzzard sat on the pony's head and its beak had just risen dripping with dark eye fluid. Jody plunged into the circle like a cat. The black brotherhood arose in a cloud, but the big one on the pony's head was too late. As it hopped along to take off, Jody caught its wing tip and pulled it down. It was nearly as big as he was. The free wing crashed into his face with the force of a club, but he hung on. The claws fastened on his leg and the wing elbows battered his head on either side. Jody groped blindly with his free hand. His fingers found the neck of the struggling bird. The red eyes looked into his face, calm and fearless and fierce; the naked head turned from side to side. Then the beak opened and vomited a stream of putrefied fluid. Jody brought up his knee and fell on the great bird. He held the neck to the ground with one hand while his other found a piece of sharp white quartz. The first blow broke the beak sideways and black blood spurted from the twisted, leathery mouth corners. He struck again and missed. The red fearless eyes still looked at him, impersonal and unafraid and detached. He struck again and again, until the buzzard lay dead, until its head was a red pulp. He was still beating the dead bird when Billy Buck pulled him off and held him tightly to calm his shaking.

Carl Tiflin wiped the blood from the boy's face with a red bandana. Jody was limp and quiet now. His father moved the buzzard with his toe. "Jody," he explained, "the buzzard didn't kill the pony. Don't you know that?"

"I know it," Jody said wearily.

It was Billy Buck who was angry. He had lifted Jody in his arms, and had turned to carry him home. But he turned back on Carl Tiflin. " 'Course he knows it," Billy said furiously, "Jesus Christ! man, can't you see how he'd feel about it?"

OF THIS TIME, OF THAT PLACE

LIONEL TRILLING

LIONEL TRILLING (1905–   ) was born in New York City and received his education, including the doctorate in philosophy, from Columbia University. A sensitive and creative critic, and a writer of fiction as well, he has served as advisor to the editorial boards of the *Kenyon Review* and the *Partisan Review*. Among his books are *E. M. Forster* (1943), *The Liberal Imagination* (1950), *The Opposing Self* (1955), *A Gathering of the Fugitives* (1956), and *Beyond Culture* (1965).

IT WAS a fine September day. By noon it would be summer again, but now it was true autumn with a touch of chill in the air. As Joseph Howe stood on the porch of the house in which he lodged, ready to leave for his first class of the year, he thought with pleasure of the long indoor days that were coming. It was a moment when he could feel glad of his profession.

On the lawn the peach tree was still in fruit and

young Hilda Aiken was taking a picture of it. She held the camera tight against her chest. She wanted the sun behind her, but she did not want her own long morning shadow in the foreground. She raised the camera, but that did not help, and she lowered it, but that made things worse. She twisted her body to the left, then to the right. In the end she had to step out of the direct line of the sun. At last she snapped the shutter and wound the film with intense care.

Howe, watching her from the porch, waited for her to finish and called good morning. She turned, startled, and almost sullenly lowered her glance. In the year Howe had lived at the Aikens', Hilda had accepted him as one of her family, but since his absence of the summer she had grown shy. Then suddenly she lifted her head and smiled at him, and the humorous smile confirmed his pleasure in the day. She picked up her bookbag and set off for school.

The handsome houses on the streets to the college were not yet fully awake, but they looked very friendly. Howe went by the Bradby house where he would be a guest this evening at the first dinner party of the year. When he had gone the length of the picket fence, the whitest in town, he turned back. Along the path there was a fine row of asters and he went through the gate and picked one for his buttonhole. The Bradbys would be pleased if they happened to see him invading their lawn and the knowledge of this made him even more comfortable.

He reached the campus as the hour was striking. The students were hurrying to their classes. He himself was in no hurry. He stopped at his dim cubicle of an office and lit a cigarette. The prospect of facing his class had suddenly presented itself to him and his hands were cold; the lawful seizure of power he was about to make seemed momentous. Waiting did not help. He put out his cigarette, picked up a pad of theme paper, and went to his classroom.

As he entered, the rattle of voices ceased, and the twenty-odd freshmen settled themselves and looked at him appraisingly. Their faces seemed gross, his heart sank at their massed impassivity, but he spoke briskly.

'My name is Howe,' he said, and turned and wrote it on the blackboard. The carelessness of the scrawl confirmed his authority. He went on, 'My office is 412 Slemp Hall, and my office-hours are Monday, Wednesday and Friday from eleven-thirty to twelve-thirty.'

He wrote, 'M., W., F., 11:30-12:30.' He said, 'I'll be very glad to see any of you at that time. Or if you can't come then, you can arrange with me for some other time.'

He turned again to the blackboard and spoke over his shoulder. 'The text for the course is Jarman's *Modern Plays*, revised edition. The Co-op has it in stock.' He wrote the name, underlined 'revised edition' and waited for it to be taken down in the new notebooks.

When the bent heads were raised again he began his speech of prospectus. 'It is hard to explain—' he said, and paused as they composed themselves. 'It is hard to explain what a course like this is intended to do. We are going to try to learn something about modern literature and something about prose composition.'

As he spoke, his hands warmed and he was able to look directly at the class. Last year on the first day the faces had seemed just as cloddish, but as the term wore on they became gradually alive and quite likable. It did not seem possible that the same thing could happen again.

'I shall not lecture in this course,' he continued. 'Our work will be carried on by discussion and we will try to learn by an exchange of opinion. But you will soon recognize that my opinion is worth more than anyone else's here.'

He remained grave as he said it, but two boys understood and laughed. The rest took permission from them and laughed too. All Howe's private ironies protested the vulgarity of the joke, but the laughter made him feel benign and powerful.

When the little speech was finished, Howe picked up the pad of paper he had brought. He announced that they would write an extemporaneous theme. Its subject was traditional, 'Who I am and why I came to Dwight College.' By now the class was more at ease and it gave a ritualistic groan of protest. Then there was a stir as fountain pens were brought out and the writing-arms of the chairs were cleared, and the paper was passed about. At last, all the heads bent to work, and the room became still.

Howe sat idly at his desk. The sun shone through the tall clumsy windows. The cool of the morning was already passing. There was a scent of autumn and of varnish and the stillness of the room was deep and oddly touching. Now and then a student's head was raised and scratched in the old, elaborate students' pantomime that calls the teacher to witness honest intellectual effort.

Suddenly a tall boy stood within the frame of the open door. 'Is this,' he said, and thrust a large nose into a college catalogue, 'is this the meeting place of English 1A? The section instructed by Dr. Joseph Howe?'

He stood on the very sill of the door, as if refusing to enter until he was perfectly sure of all his rights. The class looked up from work, found him absurd and gave a low mocking cheer.

The teacher and the new student, with equal pointedness, ignored the disturbance. Howe nodded to the boy, who pushed his head forward and then jerked it back in a wide elaborate arc to clear his brow of a heavy lock of hair. He advanced into the room and halted before Howe, almost at attention. In a loud, clear voice he announced, 'I am Tertan, Ferdinand R., reporting at the direction of Head of Department Vincent.'

The heraldic formality of this statement brought

forth another cheer. Howe looked at the class with a sternness he could not really feel, for there was indeed something ridiculous about this boy. Under his displeased regard the rows of heads dropped to work again. Then he touched Tertan's elbow, led him up to the desk and stood so as to shield their conversation from the class.

'We are writing an extemporaneous theme,' he said. 'The subject is, "Who I am and why I came to Dwight College." '

He stripped a few sheets from the pad and offered them to the boy. Tertan hesitated and then took the paper, but he held it only tentatively. As if with the effort of making something clear, he gulped, and a slow smile fixed itself on his face. It was at once knowing and shy.

'Professor,' he said, 'to be perfectly fair to my classmates'—he made a large gesture over the room— 'and to you'—he inclined his head to Howe—'this would not be for me an extemporaneous subject.'

Howe tried to understand. 'You mean you've already thought about it—you've heard we always give the same subject? That doesn't matter.'

Again the boy ducked his head and gulped. It was the gesture of one who wishes to make a difficult explanation with perfect candor. 'Sir,' he said, and made the distinction with great care, 'the topic I did not expect, but I have given much ratiocination to the subject.'

Howe smiled and said, 'I don't think that's an unfair advantage. Just go ahead and write.'

Tertan narrowed his eyes and glanced sidewise at Howe. His strange mouth smiled. Then in quizzical acceptance, he ducked his head, threw back the heavy, dank lock, dropped into a seat with a great loose noise and began to write rapidly.

The room fell silent again and Howe resumed his idleness. When the bell rang, the students who had groaned when the task had been set now groaned again because they had not finished. Howe took up the papers, and held the class while he made the first assignment. When he dismissed it, Tertan bore down on him, his slack mouth held ready for speech.

'Some professors,' he said, 'are pedants. They are Dryasdusts. However, some professors are free souls and creative spirits. Kant, Hegel and Nietzsche were all professors.' With this pronouncement he paused. 'It is my opinion,' he continued, 'that you occupy the second category.'

Howe looked at the boy in surprise and said with good-natured irony, 'With Kant, Hegel and Nietzsche?'

Not only Tertan's hand and head but his whole awkward body waved away the stupidity. 'It is the

kind and not the quantity of the kind,' he said sternly.

Rebuked, Howe said as simply and seriously as he could, 'It would be nice to think so.' He added, 'Of course I am not a professor.'

This was clearly a disappointment but Tertan met it. 'In the French sense,' he said with composure. 'Generically, a teacher.'

Suddenly he bowed. It was such a bow, Howe fancied, as a stage-director might teach an actor playing a medieval student who takes leave of Abelard—stiff, solemn, with elbows close to the body and feet together. Then, quite as suddenly, he turned and left.

A queer fish, and as soon as Howe reached his office, he sifted through the batch of themes and drew out Tertan's. The boy had filled many sheets with his unformed headlong scrawl. 'Who am I?' he had begun. 'Here, in a mundane, not to say commercialized academe, is asked the question which from time long immemorably out of mind has accreted doubts and thoughts in the psyche of man to pester him as a nuisance. Whether in St. Augustine (or Austin as sometimes called) or Miss Bashkirtsieff or Frederic Amiel or Empedocles, or in less lights of the intellect than these, this posed question has been ineluctable.'

Howe took out his pencil. He circled 'academe' and wrote 'vocab.' in the margin. He underlined 'time long immemorably out of mind' and wrote 'Diction!' But this seemed inadequate for what was wrong. He put down his pencil and read ahead to discover the principle of error in the theme. 'Today as ever, in spite of gloomy prophets of the dismal science (economics) the question is uninvalidated. Out of the starry depths of heaven hurtles this spear of query demanding to be caught on the shield of the mind ere it pierces the skull and the limbs be unstrung.'

Baffled but quite caught, Howe read on. 'Materialism, by which is meant the philosophic concept and not the moral idea, provides no aegis against the question which lies beyond the tangible (metaphysics). Existence without alloy is the question presented. Environment and heredity relegated aside, the rags and old clothes of practical life discarded, the name and the instrumentality of livelihood do not, as the prophets of the dismal science insist on in this connection, give solution to the interrogation which not from the professor merely but veritably from the cosmos is given. I think, therefore I am (cogito etc.) but who am I? Tertan I am, but what is Tertan? Of this time, of that place, of some parentage, what does it matter?'

Existence without alloy: the phrase established

itself. Howe put aside Tertan's paper and at random picked up another. 'I am Arthur J. Casebeer, Jr.,' he read. 'My father is Arthur J. Casebeer and my grandfather was Arthur J. Casebeer before him. My mother is Nina Wimble Casebeer. Both of them are college graduates and my father is in insurance. I was born in St. Louis eighteen years ago and we still make our residence there.'

Arthur J. Casebeer, who knew who he was, was less interesting than Tertan, but more coherent. Howe picked up Tertan's paper again. It was clear that none of the routine marginal comments, no 'sent. str.' or 'punct.' or 'vocab.' could cope with this torrential rhetoric. He read ahead, contenting himself with underscoring the errors against the time when he should have the necessary 'conference' with Tertan.

It was a busy and official day of cards and sheets, arrangements and small decisions, and it gave Howe pleasure. Even when it was time to attend the first of the weekly Convocations he felt the charm of the beginning of things when intention is still innocent and uncorrupted by effort. He sat among the young instructors on the platform, and joined in their humorous complaints at having to assist at the ceremony, but actually he got a clear satisfaction from the ritual of prayer, and prosy speech, and even from wearing his academic gown. And when the Convocation was over the pleasure continued as he crossed the campus, exchanging greetings with men he had not seen since the spring. They were people who did not yet, and perhaps never would, mean much to him, but in a year they had grown amiably to be part of his life. They were his fellow-townsmen.

The day had cooled again at sunset, and there was a bright chill in the September twilight. Howe carried his voluminous gown over his arm, he swung his doctoral hood by its purple neckpiece, and on his head he wore his mortarboard with its heavy gold tassel bobbing just over his eye. These were the weighty and absurd symbols of his new profession and they pleased him. At twenty-six Joseph Howe had discovered that he was neither so well off nor so bohemian as he had once thought. A small income, adequate when supplemented by a sizable cash legacy, was genteel poverty when the cash was all spent. And the literary life—the room at the Lafayette, or the small apartment without a lease, the long summers on the Cape, the long afternoons and the social evenings—began to weary him. His writing filled his mornings, and should perhaps have filled his life, yet it did not. To the amusement of his friends, and with a certain sense that he was betraying his own freedom, he had used the last of his legacy for a year at Harvard. The small but respectable reputation of his two volumes of verse had proved useful—he continued at Harvard on a fellowship and when he emerged as Doctor Howe he received an excellent appointment, with prospects, at Dwight.

He had his moments of fear when all that had ever been said of the dangers of the academic life had occurred to him. But after a year in which he had tested every possibility of corruption and seduction he was ready to rest easy. His third volume of verse, most of it written in his first years of teaching, was not only ampler but, he thought, better than its predecessors.

There was a clear hour before the Bradby dinner party, and Howe looked forward to it. But he was not to enjoy it, for lying with his mail on the hall table was a copy of this quarter's issue of *Life and Letters,* to which his landlord subscribed. Its severe cover announced that its editor, Frederic Woolley, had this month contributed an essay called 'Two Poets,' and Howe, picking it up, curious to see who the two poets might be, felt his own name start out at him with cabalistic power—Joseph Howe. As he continued to turn the pages his hand trembled.

Standing in the dark hall, holding the neat little magazine, Howe knew that his literary contempt for Frederic Woolley meant nothing, for he suddenly understood how he respected Woolley in the way of the world. He knew this by the trembling of his hand. And of the little world as well as the great, for although the literary groups of New York might dismiss Woolley, his name carried high authority in the academic world. At Dwight it was even a revered name, for it had been here at the college that Frederic Woolley had made the distinguished scholarly career from which he had gone on to literary journalism. In middle life he had been induced to take the editorship of *Life and Letters,* a literary monthly not widely read but heavily endowed, and in its pages he had carried on the defense of what he sometimes called the older values. He was not without wit, he had great knowledge and considerable taste, and even in the full movement of the 'new' literature he had won a certain respect for his refusal to accept it. In France, even in England, he would have been connected with a more robust tradition of conservatism, but America gave him an audience not much better than genteel. It was known in the college that to the subsidy of *Life and Letters* the Bradbys contributed a great part.

As Howe read, he saw that he was involved in nothing less than an event. When the Fifth Series of *Studies in Order and Value* came to be collected, this latest of Frederic Woolley's essays would not be merely another step in the old direction. Clearly and unmistakably, it was a turning point. All his literary life Woolley had been concerned with the relation of literature to morality, religion, and the private and delicate pieties, and he had been unalterably opposed to all that he had called 'inhuman humanitarianism.' But here, suddenly, dramatically late, he had made an about-face, turning to the public life and to the humanitarian politics he had so long despised. This was the kind of incident the histories of literature make much of. Frederic Woolley was opening for himself a new career and winning a kind of new youth. He contrasted the two poets, Thomas Wormser, who was admirable, Joseph Howe, who was almost dangerous. He spoke of the 'precious subjectivism' of Howe's verse. 'In times like ours,' he wrote, 'with millions facing penury and want, one feels that the qualities of the *tour d'ivoire* are well-nigh inhuman, nearly insulting. The *tour d'ivoire* becomes the *tour d'ivresse,* and it is not self-intoxicated poets that our people need.' The essay said more: 'The problem is one of meaning. I am not ignorant that the creed of the esoteric poets declares that a poem does not and should not *mean* anything, that it *is* something. But poetry is what the poet makes it, and if he is a true poet he makes what his society needs. And what is needed now is the tradition in which Mr. Wormser writes, the true tradition of poetry. The Howes do no harm, but they do no good when positive good is demanded of all responsible men. Or do the Howes indeed do no harm? Perhaps Plato would have said they do, that in some ways theirs is the Phrygian music that turns men's minds from the struggle. Certainly it is true that Thomas Wormser writes in the lucid Dorian mode which sends men into battle with evil.'

It was easy to understand why Woolley had chosen to praise Thomas Wormser. The long, lilting lines of *Corn Under Willows* hymned, as Woolley put it, the struggle for wheat in the Iowa fields, and expressed the real lives of real people. But why out of the dozen more notable examples he had chosen Howe's little volume as the example of 'precious subjectivism' was hard to guess. In a way it was funny, this multiplication of himself into 'the Howes.' And yet this becoming the multiform political symbol by whose creation Frederic Woolley gave the sign of a sudden new life, this use of him as a sacrifice whose blood was necessary for the rites of rejuvenation, made him feel oddly unclean.

Nor could Howe get rid of a certain practical resentment. As a poet he had a special and respectable place in the college life. But it might be another thing to be marked as the poet of a wilful and selfish obscurity.

As he walked to the Bradbys', Howe was a little tense and defensive. It seemed to him that all the world knew of the 'attack' and agreed with it. And, indeed, the Bradbys had read the essay but Professor Bradby, a kind and pretentious man, said, 'I see my old friend knocked you about a bit, my boy,' and his wife Eugenia looked at Howe with her childlike blue eyes and said, 'I shall *scold* Frederic for the untrue things he wrote about you. You aren't the least obscure.' They beamed at him. In their genial snobbery they seemed to feel that he had distinguished himself. He was the leader of Howeism. He enjoyed the dinner party as much as he had thought he would.

And in the following days, as he was more preoccupied with his duties, the incident was forgotten. His classes had ceased to be mere groups. Student after student detached himself from the mass and required or claimed a place in Howe's awareness. Of them all it was Tertan who first and most violently signaled his separate existence. A week after classes had begun Howe saw his silhouette on the frosted glass of his office door. It was motionless for a long time, perhaps stopped by the problem of whether or not to knock before entering. Howe called, 'Come in!' and Tertan entered with his shambling stride.

He stood beside the desk, silent and at attention. When Howe asked him to sit down, he responded with a gesture of head and hand, as if to say that such amenities were beside the point. Nevertheless, he did take the chair. He put his ragged, crammed briefcase between his legs. His face, which Howe now observed fully for the first time, was confusing, for it was made up of florid curves, the nose arched in the bone and voluted in the nostril, the mouth loose and soft and rather moist. Yet the face was so thin and narrow as to seem the very type of asceticism. Lashes of unusual length veiled the eyes and, indeed, it seemed as if there were a veil over the whole countenance. Before the words actually came, the face screwed itself into an attitude of preparation for them.

'You can confer with me now?' Tertan said.

'Yes, I'd be glad to. There are several things in your two themes I want to talk to you about.' Howe reached for the packet of themes on his desk and sought for Tertan's. But the boy was waving them away.

'These are done perforce,' he said. 'Under the pressure of your requirement. They are not significant; mere duties.' Again his great hand flapped vaguely to dismiss his themes. He leaned forward and gazed at his teacher.

'You are,' he said, 'a man of letters? You are a poet?' It was more declaration than question.

'I should like to think so,' Howe said.

At first Tertan accepted the answer with a show of appreciation, as though the understatement made a secret between himself and Howe. Then he chose to misunderstand. With his shrewd and disconcerting control of expression, he presented to Howe a puzzled grimace. 'What does that mean?' he said.

Howe retracted the irony. 'Yes. I am a poet.' It sounded strange to say.

'That,' Tertan said, 'is a wonder.' He corrected himself with his ducking head. 'I mean that is wonderful.'

Suddenly, he dived at the miserable briefcase between his legs, put it on his knees, and began to fumble with the catch, all intent on the difficulty it presented. Howe noted that his suit was worn thin, his shirt almost unclean. He became aware, even, of a vague and musty odor of garments worn too long in unaired rooms. Tertan conquered the lock and began to concentrate upon a search into the interior. At last he held in his hand what he was after, a torn and crumpled copy of *Life and Letters*.

'I learned it from here,' he said, holding it out.

Howe looked at him sharply, his hackles a little up. But the boy's face was not only perfectly innocent, it even shone with a conscious admiration. Apparently nothing of the import of the essay had touched him except the wonderful fact that his teacher was a 'man of letters.' Yet this seemed too stupid, and Howe, to test it, said, 'The man who wrote that doesn't think it's wonderful.'

Tertan made a moist hissing sound as he cleared his mouth of saliva. His head, oddly loose on his neck, wove a pattern of contempt in the air. 'A critic,' he said, 'who admits *prima facie* that he does not understand.' Then he said grandly, 'It is the inevitable fate.'

It was absurd, yet Howe was not only aware of the absurdity but of a tension suddenly and wonderfully relaxed. Now that the 'attack' was on the table between himself and this strange boy, and subject to the boy's funny and absolutely certain contempt, the hidden force of his feeling was revealed to him in the very moment that it vanished. All unsuspected, there had been a film over the world, a transparent but discoloring haze of danger. But he had no time to stop over the brightened aspect of things. Tertan was going on. 'I also am a man of letters. Putative.'

'You have written a good deal?' Howe meant to be no more than polite, and he was surprised at the tenderness he heard in his words.

Solemnly the boy nodded, threw back the dank lock, and sucked in a deep, anticipatory breath. 'First, a work of homiletics, which is a defense of the principles of religious optimism against the pessi-

mism of Schopenhauer and the humanism of Nietzsche.'

'Humanism? Why do you call it humanism?'

'It is my nomenclature for making a deity of man,' Tertan replied negligently. 'Then three fictional works, novels. And numerous essays in science, combating materialism. Is it your duty to read these if I bring them to you?'

Howe answered simply, 'No, it isn't exactly my duty, but I shall be happy to read them.'

Tertan stood up and remained silent. He rested his bag on the chair. With a certain compunction—for it did not seem entirely proper that, of two men of letters, one should have the right to blue-pencil the other, to grade him or to question the quality of his 'sentence structure'—Howe reached for Tertan's papers. But before he could take them up, the boy suddenly made his bow-to-Abelard, the stiff inclination of the body with the hands seeming to emerge from the scholar's gown. Then he was gone.

But after his departure something was still left of him. The timbre of his curious sentences, the downright finality of so quaint a phrase as 'It is the inevitable fate' still rang in the air. Howe gave the warmth of his feeling to the new visitor who stood at the door announcing himself with a genteel clearing of the throat.

'Doctor Howe, I believe?' the student said. A large hand advanced into the room and grasped Howe's hand. 'Blackburn, sir, Theodore Blackburn, vice-president of the Student Council. A great pleasure, sir.'

Out of a pair of ruddy cheeks a pair of small eyes twinkled good-naturedly. The large face, the large body were not so much fat as beefy and suggested something 'typical'—monk, politician, or innkeeper.

Blackburn took the seat beside Howe's desk. 'I may have seemed to introduce myself in my public capacity, sir,' he said. 'But it is really as an individual that I came to see you. That is to say, as one of your students to be.'

He spoke with an English intonation and he went on, 'I was once an English major, sir.'

For a moment Howe was startled, for the roast-beef look of the boy and the manner of his speech gave a second's credibility to one sense of his statement. Then the collegiate meaning of the phrase asserted itself, but some perversity made Howe say what was not really in good taste even with so forward a student, 'Indeed? What regiment?'

Blackburn stared and then gave a little pouf-pouf of laughter. He waved the misapprehension away. '*Very* good, sir. It certainly is an ambiguous term.' He chuckled in appreciation of Howe's joke, then cleared his throat to put it aside. 'I look forward to taking your course in the romantic poets, sir,' he said earnestly. 'To me the romantic poets are the very crown of English literature.'

Howe made a dry sound, and the boy, catching some meaning in it, said, 'Little as I know them, of course. But even Shakespeare who is so dear to us of the Anglo-Saxon tradition is in a sense but the preparation for Shelley, Keats and Byron. And Wadsworth.'

Almost sorry for him, Howe dropped his eyes. With some embarrassment, for the boy was not actually his student, he said softly, 'Wordsworth.'

'Sir?'

'Wordsworth, not Wadsworth. You said Wadsworth.'

'Did I, sir?' Gravely he shook his head to rebuke himself for the error. 'Wordsworth, of course—slip of the tongue.' Then, quite in command again, he went on. 'I have a favor to ask of you, Doctor Howe. You see, I began my college course as an English major,'—he smiled—'as I said.'

'Yes?'

'But after my first year I shifted. I shifted to the social sciences. Sociology and government—I find them stimulating and very *real*.' He paused, out of respect for reality. 'But now I find that perhaps I have neglected the other side.'

'The other side?' Howe said.

'Imagination, fancy, culture. A well-rounded man.' He trailed off as if there were perfect understanding between them. 'And so, sir, I have decided to end my senior year with your course in the romantic poets.'

His voice was filled with an indulgence which Howe ignored as he said flatly and gravely, 'But that course isn't given until the spring term.'

'Yes, sir, and that is where the favor comes in. Would you let me take your romantic prose course? I can't take it for credit, sir, my program is full, but just for background it seems to me that I ought to take it. I do hope,' he concluded in a manly way, 'that you will consent.'

'Well, it's no great favor, Mr. Blackburn. You can come if you wish, though there's not much point in it if you don't do the reading.'

The bell rang for the hour and Howe got up.

'May I begin with this class, sir?' Blackburn's smile was candid and boyish.

Howe nodded carelessly and together, silently, they walked to the classroom down the hall. When they reached the door Howe stood back to let his student enter, but Blackburn moved adroitly behind him and grasped him by the arm to urge him over the threshold. They entered together with Blackburn's hand firmly on Howe's biceps, the student

inducting the teacher into his own room. Howe felt a surge of temper rise in him and almost violently he disengaged his arm and walked to the desk, while Blackburn found a seat in the front row and smiled at him.

II

The question was, At whose door must the tragedy be laid?

All night the snow had fallen heavily and only now was abating in sparse little flurries. The windows were valanced high with white. It was very quiet; something of the quiet of the world had reached the class, and Howe found that everyone was glad to talk or listen. In the room there was a comfortable sense of pleasure in being human.

Casebeer believed that the blame for the tragedy rested with heredity. Picking up the book he read, 'The sins of the fathers are visited on their children.' This opinion was received with general favor. Nevertheless, Johnson ventured to say that the fault was all Pastor Manders' because the Pastor had made Mrs. Alving go back to her husband and was always hiding the truth. To this Hibbard objected with logic enough, 'Well then, it was really all her husband's fault. He *did* all the bad things.' De Witt, his face bright with an impatient idea, said that the fault was all society's. 'By society I don't mean upper-crust society,' he said. He looked around a little defiantly, taking in any members of the class who might be members of upper-crust society. 'Not in that sense. I mean the social unit.'

Howe nodded and said, 'Yes, of course.'

'If the society of the time had progressed far enough in science,' De Witt went on, 'then there would be no problem for Mr. Ibsen to write about. Captain Alving plays around a little, gives way to perfectly natural biological urges, and he gets a social disease, a venereal disease. If the disease is cured, no problem. Invent salvarsan and the disease is cured. The problem of heredity disappears and li'l Oswald just doesn't get paresis. No paresis, no problem—no problem, no play.'

This was carrying the ark into battle, and the class looked at De Witt with respectful curiosity. It was his usual way and on the whole they were sympathetic with his struggle to prove to Howe that science was better than literature. Still, there was something in his reckless manner that alienated them a little.

'Or take birth-control, for instance,' De Witt went on. 'If Mrs. Alving had some knowledge of contraception, she wouldn't have had to have li'l Oswald at all. No li'l Oswald, no play.'

The class was suddenly quieter. In the back row Stettenhover swung his great football shoulders in a righteous sulking gesture, first to the right, then to the left. He puckered his mouth ostentatiously. Intellect was always ending up by talking dirty.

Tertan's hand went up, and Howe said, 'Mr. Tertan.' The boy shambled to his feet and began his long characteristic gulp. Howe made a motion with his fingers, as small as possible, and Tertan ducked his head and smiled in apology. He sat down. The class laughed. With more than half the term gone, Tertan had not been able to remember that one did not rise to speak. He seemed unable to carry on the life of the intellect without this mark of respect for it. To Howe the boy's habit of rising seemed to accord with the formal shabbiness of his dress. He never wore the casual sweaters and jackets of his classmates. Into the free and comfortable air of the college classroom he brought the stuffy sordid strictness of some crowded, metropolitan high school.

'Speaking from one sense,' Tertan began slowly, 'there is no blame ascribable. From the sense of determinism, who can say where the blame lies? The preordained is the preordained and it cannot be said without rebellion against the universe, a palpable absurdity.'

In the back row Stettenhover slumped suddenly in his seat, his heels held out before him, making a loud, dry, disgusted sound. His body sank until his neck rested on the back of his chair. He folded his hands across his belly and looked significantly out of the window, exasperated not only with Tertan, but with Howe, with the class, with the whole system designed to encourage this kind of thing. There was a certain insolence in the movement and Howe flushed. As Tertan continued to speak, Howe stalked casually toward the window and placed himself in the line of Stettenhover's vision. He stared at the great fellow, who pretended not to see him. There was so much power in the big body, so much contempt in the Greek-athlete face under the crisp Greek-athlete curls, that Howe felt almost physical fear. But at last Stettenhover admitted him to focus and under his disapproving gaze sat up with slow indifference. His eyebrows raised high in resignation, he began to examine his hands. Howe relaxed and turned his attention back to Tertan.

'Flux of existence,' Tertan was saying, 'produces all things, so that judgment wavers. Beyond the phenomena, what? But phenomena are adumbrated and to them we are limited.'

Howe saw it for a moment as perhaps it existed in the boy's mind—the world of shadows which are cast by a great light upon a hidden reality as in the old myth of the Cave. But the little brush with Stetten-hover had tired him, and he said irritably, 'But come to the point, Mr. Tertan.'

He said it so sharply that some of the class looked at him curiously. For three months he had gently carried Tertan through his verbosities, to the vaguely respectful surprise of the other students, who seemed to conceive that there existed between this strange classmate and their teacher some special understanding from which they were content to be excluded. Tertan looked at him mildly, and at once came brilliantly to the point. 'This is the summation of the play,' he said and took up his book and read, ' "Your poor father never found any outlet for the overmastering joy of life that was in him. And I brought no holiday into his home, either. Everything seemed to turn upon duty and I am afraid I made your poor father's home unbearable to him, Oswald." Spoken by Mrs. Alving.'

Yes that was surely the 'summation' of the play and Tertan had hit it, as he hit, deviously and eventually, the literary point of almost everything. But now, as always, he was wrapping it away from sight. 'For most mortals,' he said, 'there are only joys of biological urgings, gross and crass, such as the sensuous Captain Alving. For certain few there are the transmutations beyond these to a contemplation of the utter whole.'

Oh, the boy was mad. And suddenly the word, used in hyperbole, intended almost for the expression of exasperated admiration, became literal. Now that the word was used, it became simply apparent to Howe that Tertan was mad.

It was a monstrous word and stood like a bestial thing in the room. Yet it so completely comprehended everything that had puzzled Howe, it so arranged and explained what for three months had been perplexing him that almost at once its horror became domesticated. With this word Howe was able to understand why he had never been able to communicate to Tertan the value of a single criticism or correction of his wild, verbose themes. Their conferences had been frequent and long but had done nothing to reduce to order the splendid confusion of the boy's ideas. Yet, impossible though its expression was, Tertan's incandescent mind could always strike for a moment into some dark corner of thought.

And now it was suddenly apparent that it was not a faulty rhetoric that Howe had to contend with. With his new knowledge he looked at Tertan's face and wondered how he could have so long deceived himself. Tertan was still talking, and the class had lapsed into a kind of patient unconsciousness, a coma of respect for words which, for all that most of them knew, might be profound. Almost with a suffusion of shame, Howe believed that in some dim way the class had long ago had some intimation of Tertan's madness. He reached out as decisively as he could to seize the thread of Tertan's discourse before it should be entangled further.

'Mr. Tertan says that the blame must be put upon whoever kills the joy of living in another. We have been assuming that Captain Alving was a wholly bad man, but what if we assume that he became bad only because Mrs. Alving, when they were first married, acted toward him in the prudish way she says she did?'

It was a ticklish idea to advance to freshmen and perhaps not profitable. Not all of them were following.

'That would put the blame on Mrs. Alving herself, whom most of you admire. And she herself seems to think so.' He glanced at his watch. The hour was nearly over. 'What do you think, Mr. De Witt?'

De Witt rose to the idea; he wanted to know if society couldn't be blamed for educating Mrs. Alving's temperament in the wrong way. Casebeer was puzzled, Stettenhover continued to look at his hands until the bell rang.

Tertan, his brows louring in thought, was making as always for a private word. Howe gathered his books and papers to leave quickly. At this moment of his discovery and with the knowledge still raw, he could not engage himself with Tertan. Tertan sucked in his breath to prepare for speech and Howe made ready for the pain and confusion. But at that moment Casebeer detached himself from the group with which he had been conferring and which he seemed to represent. His constituency remained at a tactful distance. The mission involved the time of an assigned essay. Casebeer's presentation of the plea—it was based on the freshmen's heavy duties at the fraternities during Carnival Week—cut across Tertan's preparations for speech. 'And so some of us fellows thought,' Casebeer concluded with heavy solemnity, 'that we could do a better job, give our minds to it more, if we had more time.'

Tertan regarded Casebeer with mingled curiosity and revulsion. Howe not only said that he would postpone the assignment but went on to talk about the Carnival, and even drew the waiting constituency into the conversation. He was conscious of Tertan's stern and astonished stare, then of his sudden departure.

Now that the fact was clear, Howe knew that he must act on it. His course was simple enough. He must lay the case before the Dean. Yet he hesitated. His feeling for Tertan must now, certainly, be in some way invalidated. Yet could he, because of a word, hurry to assign to official and reasonable solici-

tude what had been, until this moment, so various and warm? He could at least delay and, by moving slowly, lend a poor grace to the necessary, ugly act of making his report.

It was with some notion of keeping the matter in his own hands that he went to the Dean's office to look up Tertan's records. In the outer office the Dean's secretary greeted him brightly, and at his request brought him the manila folder with the small identifying photograph pasted in the corner. She laughed. 'He was looking for the birdie in the wrong place,' she said.

Howe leaned over her shoulder to look at the picture. It was as bad as all the Dean's-office photographs were, but it differed from all that Howe had ever seen. Tertan, instead of looking into the camera, as no doubt he had been bidden, had, at the moment of exposure, turned his eyes upward. His mouth, as though conscious of the trick played on the photographer, had the sly superior look that Howe knew.

The secretary was fascinated by the picture. 'What a funny boy,' she said. 'He looks like Tartuffe!'

And so he did, with the absurd piety of the eyes and the conscious slyness of the mouth and the whole face bloated by the bad lens.

'Is he *like* that?' the secretary said.

'Like Tartuffe? No.'

From the photograph there was little enough comfort to be had. The records themselves gave no clue to madness, though they suggested sadness enough. Howe read of a father, Stanislaus Tertan, born in Budapest and trained in engineering in Berlin, once employed by the Hercules Chemical Corporation—this was one of the factories that dominated the sound end of the town—but now without employment. He read of a mother Erminie (Youngfellow) Tertan, born in Manchester, educated at a Normal School at Leeds, now housewife by profession. The family lived on Greenbriar Street which Howe knew as a row of once elegant homes near what was now the factory district. The old mansion had long ago been divided into small and primitive apartments. Of Ferdinand himself there was little to learn. He lived with his parents, had attended a Detroit high school and had transferred to the local school in his last year. His rating for intelligence, as expressed in numbers, was high, his scholastic record was remarkable, he held a college scholarship for his tuition.

Howe laid the folder on the secretary's desk. 'Did you find what you wanted to know?' she asked.

The phrases from Tertan's momentous first theme came back to him. 'Tertan I am, but what is Tertan? Of this time, of that place, of some parentage, what does it matter?'

'No, I didn't find it,' he said.

Now that he had consulted the sad, half-meaningless record he knew all the more firmly that he must not give the matter out of his own hands. He must not release Tertan to authority. Not that he anticipated from the Dean anything but the greatest kindness for Tertan. The Dean would have the experience and skill which he himself could not have. One way or another the Dean could answer the question, 'What is Tertan?' Yet this was precisely what he feared. He alone could keep alive—not forever but for a somehow important time—the question, 'What is Tertan?' He alone could keep it still a question. Some sure instinct told him that he must not surrender the question to a clean official desk in a clear official light to be dealt with, settled and closed.

He heard himself saying, 'Is the Dean busy at the moment? I'd like to see him.'

His request came thus unbidden, even forbidden, and it was one of the surprising and startling incidents of his life. Later when he reviewed the events, so disconnected in themselves, or so merely odd, of the story that unfolded for him that year, it was over this moment, on its face the least notable, that he paused longest. It was frequently to be with fear and never without a certainty of its meaning in his own knowledge of himself that he would recall this simple, routine request, and the feeling of shame and freedom it gave him as he sent everything down the official chute. In the end, of course, no matter what he did to 'protect' Tertan, he would have had to make the same request and lay the matter on the Dean's clean desk. But it would always be a landmark of his life that, at the very moment when he was rejecting the official way, he had been, without will or intention, so gladly drawn to it.

After the storm's last delicate flurry, the sun had come out. Reflected by the new snow, it filled the office with a golden light which was almost musical in the way it made all the commonplace objects of efficiency shine with a sudden sad and noble significance. And the light, now that he noticed it, made the utterance of his perverse and unwanted request even more momentous.

The secretary consulted the engagement pad. 'He'll be free any minute. Don't you want to wait in the parlor?'

She threw open the door of the large and pleasant room in which the Dean held his Committee meetings, and in which his visitors waited. It was designed with a homely elegance on the masculine side of the eighteenth-century manner. There was a small coal fire in the grate and the handsome mahogany table was strewn with books and magazines. The large windows gave on the snowy lawn, and there was such a fine width of window that the white case-ments and walls seemed at this moment but a continuation of the snow, the snow but an extension of casement and walls. The outdoors seemed taken in and made safe, the indoors seemed luxuriously freshened and expanded.

Howe sat down by the fire and lighted a cigarette. The room had its intended effect upon him. He felt comfortable and relaxed, yet nicely organized, some young diplomatic agent of the eighteenth century, the newly fledged Swift carrying out Sir William Temple's business. The rawness of Tertan's case quite vanished. He crossed his legs and reached for a magazine.

It was that famous issue of *Life and Letters* that his idle hand had found and his blood raced as he sifted through it, and the shape of his own name, Joseph Howe, sprang out at him, still cabalistic in its power. He tossed the magazine back on the table as the door of the Dean's office opened and the Dean ushered out Theodore Blackburn.

'Ah, Joseph!' the Dean said.

Blackburn said, 'Good morning, Doctor.' Howe winced at the title and caught the flicker of amusement over the Dean's face. The Dean stood with his hand high on the door-jamb and Blackburn, still in the doorway, remained standing almost under the long arm.

Howe nodded briefly to Blackburn, snubbing his eager deference. 'Can you give me a few minutes?' he said to the Dean.

'All the time you want. Come in.' Before the two men could enter the office, Blackburn claimed their attention with a long full 'er.' As they turned to him, Blackburn said, 'Can *you* give *me* a few minutes, Doctor Howe?' His eyes sparkled at the little audacity he had committed, the slightly impudent play with hierarchy. Of the three of them Blackburn kept himself the lowest, but he reminded Howe of his subaltern relation to the Dean.

'I mean, of course,' Blackburn went on easily, 'when you've finished with the Dean.'

'I'll be in my office shortly,' Howe said, turned his back on the ready 'Thank you, sir,' and followed the Dean into the inner room.

'Energetic boy,' said the Dean. 'A bit beyond himself but very energetic. Sit down.'

The Dean lighted a cigarette, leaned back in his chair, sat easy and silent for a moment, giving Howe no signal to go ahead with business. He was a young Dean, not much beyond forty, a tall handsome man with sad, ambitious eyes. He had been a Rhodes scholar. His friends looked for great things from him, and it was generally said that he had notions of education which he was not yet ready to try to put into practice.

His relaxed silence was meant as a compliment to Howe. He smiled and said, 'What's the business, Joseph?'

'Do you know Tertan—Ferdinand Tertan, a freshman?'

The Dean's cigarette was in his mouth and his hands were clasped behind his head. He did not seem to search his memory for the name. He said, 'What about him?'

Clearly the Dean knew something, and he was waiting for Howe to tell him more. Howe moved only tentatively. Now that he was doing what he had resolved not to do, he felt more guilty at having been so long deceived by Tertan and more need to be loyal to his error.

'He's a strange fellow,' he ventured. He said stubbornly, 'In a strange way he's very brilliant.' He concluded, 'But very strange.'

The springs of the Dean's swivel chair creaked as he came out of his sprawl and leaned forward to Howe. 'Do you mean he's so strange that it's something you could give a name to?'

Howe looked at him stupidly. 'What do you mean?' he said.

'What's his trouble?' the Dean said more neutrally.

'He's very brilliant, in a way. I looked him up and he has a top intelligence rating. But somehow, and it's hard to explain just how, what he says is always on the edge of sense and doesn't quite make it.'

The Dean looked at him and Howe flushed up. The Dean had surely read Woolley on the subject of 'the Howes' and the *tour d'ivresse*. Was that quick glance ironical?

The Dean picked up some papers from his desk, and Howe could see that they were in Tertan's impatient scrawl. Perhaps the little gleam in the Dean's glance had come only from putting facts together.

'He sent me this yesterday,' the Dean said. 'After an interview I had with him. I haven't been able to do more than glance at it. When you said what you did, I realized there was something wrong.'

Twisting his mouth, the Dean looked over the letter. 'You seem to be involved,' he said without looking up. 'By the way, what did you give him at mid-term?'

Flushing, setting his shoulders, Howe said firmly, 'I gave him A-minus.'

The Dean chuckled. 'Might be a good idea if some of our nicer boys went crazy—just a little.' He said, 'Well,' to conclude the matter and handed the papers to Howe. 'See if this is the same thing you've been finding. Then we can go into the matter again.'

Before the fire in the parlor, in the chair that Howe had been occupying, sat Blackburn. He sprang to his feet as Howe entered.

'I said my office, Mr. Blackburn.' Howe's voice was sharp. Then he was almost sorry for the rebuke, so clearly and naively did Blackburn seem to relish his stay in the parlor, close to authority.

'I'm in a bit of a hurry, sir,' he said, 'and I did want to be sure to speak to you, sir.'

He was really absurd, yet fifteen years from now he would have grown up to himself, to the assurance and mature beefiness. In banks, in consular offices, in brokerage firms, on the bench, more seriously affable, a little sterner, he would make use of his ability to be administered by his job. It was almost reassuring. Now he was exercising his too-great skill on Howe. 'I owe you an apology, sir,' he said.

Howe knew that he did, but he showed surprise.

'I mean, Doctor, after your having been so kind about letting me attend your class, I stopped coming.' He smiled in deprecation. 'Extracurricular activities take up so much of my time. I'm afraid I undertook more than I could perform.'

Howe had noticed the absence and had been a little irritated by it after Blackburn's elaborate plea. It was an absence that might be interpreted as a comment on the teacher. But there was only one way for him to answer. 'You've no need to apologize,' he said. 'It's wholly your affair.'

Blackburn beamed. 'I'm so glad you feel that way about it, sir. I was worried you might think I had stayed away because I was influenced by—' he stopped and lowered his eyes.

Astonished, Howe said, 'Influenced by what?'

'Well, by—' Blackburn hesitated and for answer pointed to the table on which lay the copy of *Life and Letters*. Without looking at it, he knew where to direct his hand. 'By the unfavorable publicity, sir.' He hurried on. 'And that brings me to another point, sir. I am secretary of Quill and Scroll, sir, the student literary society, and I wonder if you would address us. You could read your own poetry, sir, and defend your own point of view. It would be very interesting.'

It was truly amazing. Howe looked long and cruelly into Blackburn's face, trying to catch the secret of the mind that could have conceived this way of manipulating him, this way so daring and inept—but not entirely inept—with its malice so without malignity. The face did not yield its secret. Howe smiled broadly and said, 'Of course I don't think you were influenced by the unfavorable publicity.'

'I'm still going to take—regularly, for credit—your romantic poets course next term,' Blackburn said.

'Don't worry, my dear fellow, don't worry about it.'

Howe started to leave and Blackburn stopped him with, 'But about Quill, sir?'

'Suppose we wait until next term? I'll be less busy then.'

And Blackburn said, 'Very good, sir, and thank you.'

In his office the little encounter seemed less funny to Howe, was even in some indeterminate way disturbing. He made an effort to put it from his mind by turning to what was sure to disturb him more, the Tertan letter read in the new interpretation. He found what he had always found, the same florid leaps beyond fact and meaning, the same headlong certainty. But as his eye passed over the familiar scrawl it caught his own name, and for the second time that hour he felt the race of his blood.

'The Paraclete,' Tertan had written to the Dean, 'from a Greek word meaning to stand in place of, but going beyond the primitive idea to mean traditionally the helper, the one who comforts and assists, cannot without fundamental loss be jettisoned. Even if taken no longer in the supernatural sense, the concept remains deeply in the human consciousness inevitably. Humanitarianism is no reply, for not every man stands in the place of every other man for this other comrade's comfort. But certain are chosen out of the human race to be the consoler of some other. Of these, for example, is Joseph Barker Howe, Ph.D. Of intellects not the first yet of true intellect and lambent instructions, given to that which is intuitive and irrational, not to what is logical in the strict word, what is judged by him is of the heart and not the head. Here is one chosen, in that he chooses himself to stand in the place of another for comfort and consolation. To him more than another I give my gratitude, with all respect to our Dean who reads this, a noble man, but merely dedicated, not consecrated. But not in the aspect of the Paraclete only is Dr. Joseph Barker Howe established, for he must be the Paraclete to another aspect of himself, that which is driven and persecuted by the lack of understanding in the world at large, so that he in himself embodies the full history of man's tribulations and, overflowing upon others, notably the present writer, is the ultimate end.'

This was love. There was no escape from it. Try as Howe might to remember that Tertan was mad and all his emotions invalidated, he could not destroy the effect upon him of his student's stern, affectionate regard. He had betrayed not only a power of mind but a power of love. And, however firmly he held before his attention the fact of Tertan's madness, he could do nothing to banish the physical sensation of gratitude he felt. He had never thought of himself as 'driven and persecuted' and he did not now. But still he could not make meaningless his sensation of gratitude. The pitiable Tertan sternly pitied him, and comfort came from Tertan's never-to-be-comforted mind.

III

In an academic community, even an efficient one, official matters move slowly. The term drew to a close with no action in the case of Tertan, and Joseph Howe had to confront a curious problem. How should he grade his strange student, Tertan?

Tertan's final examination had been no different from all his other writing, and what did one 'give' such a student? De Witt must have his A, that was clear. Johnson would get a B. With Casebeer it was a question of a B-minus or a C-plus, and Stettenhover, who had been crammed by the team tutor to fill half a blue-book with his thin feminine scrawl, would have his C-minus which he would accept with mingled indifference and resentment. But with Tertan it was not so easy.

The boy was still in the college process and his name could not be omitted from the grade sheet. Yet what should a mind under suspicion of madness be graded? Until the medical verdict was given, it was for Howe to continue as Tertan's teacher and to keep his judgment pedagogical. Impossible to give him an F: he had not failed. B was for Johnson's stolid mediocrity. He could not be put on the edge of passing with Stettenhover, for he exactly did not pass. In energy and richness of intellect he was perhaps even De Witt's superior, and Howe toyed grimly with the notion of giving him an A; but that would lower the value of the A De Witt had won with his beautiful and clear, if still arrogant, mind. There was a notation which the Registrar recognized—Inc., for Incomplete, and in the horrible comedy of the situation, Howe considered that. But really only a mark of M for Mad would serve.

In his perplexity, Howe sought the Dean, but the Dean was out of town. In the end, he decided to maintain the A-minus he had given Tertan at midterm. After all, there had been no falling away from that quality. He entered it on the grade sheet with something like bravado.

Academic time moves quickly. A college year is not really a year, lacking as it does three months. And it is endlessly divided into units which, at their beginning, appear larger than they are—terms, half-terms, months, weeks. And the ultimate unit, the hour, is not really an hour, lacking as it does ten minutes. And so the new term advanced rapidly, and one day the fields about the town were all brown, cleared of even the few thin patches of snow which had lingered so long.

Howe, as he lectured on the romantic poets, became conscious of Blackburn emanating wrath. Blackburn did it well, did it with enormous dignity.

He did not stir in his seat, he kept his eyes fixed on Howe in perfect attention, but he abstained from using his notebook, there was no mistaking what he proposed to himself as an attitude. His elbow on the writing-wing of the chair, his chin on the curled fingers of his hand, he was the embodiment of intellectual indignation. He was thinking his own thoughts, would give no public offense, yet would claim his due, was not to be intimidated. Howe knew that he would present himself at the end of the hour.

Blackburn entered the office without invitation. He did not smile; there was no cajolery about him. Without invitation he sat down beside Howe's desk. He did not speak until he had taken the blue-book from his pocket. He said, 'What does this mean, sir?'

It was a sound and conservative student tactic. Said in the usual way it meant, 'How could you have so misunderstood me?' or 'What does this mean for my future in the course?' But there were none of the humbler tones in Blackburn's way of saying it.

Howe made the established reply, 'I think that's for you to tell me.'

Blackburn continued icy. 'I'm sure I can't, sir.'

There was a silence between them. Both dropped their eyes to the blue-book on the desk. On its cover Howe had penciled: 'F. This is very poor work.'

Howe picked up the blue-book. There was always the possibility of injustice. The teacher may be bored by the mass of papers and not wholly attentive. A phrase, even the student's handwriting, may irritate him unreasonably. 'Well,' said Howe, 'Let's go through it.'

He opened the first page. 'Now here: you write, "In *The Ancient Mariner,* Coleridge lives in and transports us to a honey-sweet world where all is rich and strange, a world of charm to which we can escape from the humdrum existence of our daily lives, the world of romance. Here, in this warm and honey-sweet land of charming dreams we can relax and enjoy ourselves." '

Howe lowered the paper and waited with a neutral look for Blackburn to speak. Blackburn returned the look boldly, did not speak, sat stolid and lofty. At last Howe said, speaking gently, 'Did you mean that, or were you just at a loss for something to say?'

'You imply that I was just "bluffing"?' The quotation marks hung palpable in the air about the word.

'I'd like to know. I'd prefer believing that you were bluffing to believing that you really thought this.'

Blackburn's eyebrows went up. From the height of a great and firm-based idea he looked at his teacher. He clasped the crags for a moment and then pounced, craftily, suavely. 'Do you mean, Doctor Howe, that there aren't two opinions possible?'

It was superbly done in its air of putting all of Howe's intellectual life into the balance. Howe remained patient and simple. 'Yes, many opinions are possible, but not this one. Whatever anyone believes of *The Ancient Mariner,* no one can in reason believe that it represents a—a honey-sweet world in which we can relax.'

'But that is what I *feel,* sir.'

This was well-done, too. Howe said, 'Look, Mr. Blackburn. Do you really relax with hunger and thirst, the heat and the sea-serpents, the dead men with staring eyes, Life in Death and the skeletons? Come now, Mr. Blackburn.'

Blackburn made no answer, and Howe pressed forward. 'Now, you say of Wordsworth, "Of peasant stock himself, he turned from the effete life of the salons and found in the peasant the hope of a flaming revolution which would sweep away all the old ideas. This is the subject of his best poems." '

Beaming at his teacher with youthful eagerness, Blackburn said, 'Yes, sir, a rebel, a bringer of light to suffering mankind. I see him as a kind of Prothemeus.'

'A kind of what?'

'Prothemeus, sir.'

'Think, Mr. Blackburn. We were talking about him only today and I mentioned his name a dozen times. You don't mean Prothemeus. You mean—' Howe waited, but there was no response.

'You mean Prometheus.'

Blackburn gave no assent, and Howe took the reins. 'You've done a bad job here, Mr. Blackburn, about as bad as could be done.' He saw Blackburn stiffen and his genial face harden again. 'It shows either a lack of preparation or a complete lack of understanding.' He saw Blackburn's face begin to go to pieces and he stopped.

'Oh, sir,' Blackburn burst out, 'I've never had a mark like this before, never anything below a B, never. A thing like this has never happened to me before.'

It must be true, it was a statement too easily verified. Could it be that other instructors accepted such flaunting nonsense? Howe wanted to end the interview. 'I'll set it down to lack of preparation,' he said. 'I know you're busy. That's not an excuse, but it's an explanation. Now, suppose you really prepare, and then take another quiz in two weeks. We'll forget this one and count the other.'

Blackburn squirmed with pleasure and gratitude. 'Thank you, sir. You're really very kind, very kind.'

Howe rose to conclude the visit. 'All right, then— in two weeks.'

It was that day that the Dean imparted to Howe the conclusion of the case of Tertan. It was simple and a little anti-climactic. A physician had been called in, and had said the word, given the name.

'A classic case, he called it,' the Dean said. 'Not a doubt in the world,' he said. His eyes were full of miserable pity, and he clutched at a word. 'A classic case, a classic case.' To his aid and to Howe's there came the Parthenon and the form of the Greek drama, the Aristotelian logic, Racine and the Well-Tempered Clavichord, the blueness of the Aegean and its clear sky. Classic—that is to say, without a doubt, perfect in its way, a veritable model, and, as the Dean had been told, sure to take a perfectly predictable and inevitable course to a foreknown conclusion.

It was not only pity that stood in the Dean's eyes. For a moment there was fear too. 'Terrible,' he said, 'it is simply terrible.'

Then he went on briskly. 'Naturally, we've told the boy nothing. And, naturally, we won't. His tuition's paid by his scholarship, and we'll continue him on the rolls until the end of the year. That will be kindest. After that the matter will be out of our control. We'll see, of course, that he gets into the proper hands. I'm told there will be no change, he'll go on like this, be as good as this, for four to six months. And so we'll just go along as usual.'

So Tertan continued to sit in Section 5 of English 1A, to his classmates still a figure of curiously dignified fun, symbol to most of them of the respectable but absurd intellectual life. But to his teacher he was now very different. He had not changed—he was still the greyhound casting for the scent of ideas, and Howe could see that he was still the same Tertan, but he could not feel it. What he felt as he looked at the boy sitting in his accustomed place was the hard blank of a fact. The fact itself was formidable and depressing. But what Howe was chiefly aware of was that he had permitted the metamorphosis of Tertan from person to fact.

As much as possible he avoided seeing Tertan's upraised hand and eager eye. But the fact did not know of its mere factuality, it continued its existence as if it were Tertan, hand up and eye questioning, and one day it appeared in Howe's office with a document.

'Even the spirit who lives egregiously, above the herd, must have its relations with the fellowman,' Tertan declared. He laid the document on Howe's desk. It was headed 'Quill and Scroll Society of Dwight College. Application for Membership.'

'In most ways these are crass minds,' Tertan said, touching the paper. 'Yet as a whole, bound together in their common love of letters, they transcend their intellectual lacks since it is not a paradox that the whole is greater than the sum of its parts.'

'When are the elections?' Howe asked.

'They take place tomorrow.'

'I certainly hope you will be successful.'

'Thank you. Would you wish to implement that hope?' A rather dirty finger pointed to the bottom of the sheet. 'A faculty recommender is necessary,' Tertan said stiffly, and waited.

'And you wish me to recommend you?'

'It would be an honor.'

'You may use my name.'

Tertan's finger pointed again. 'It must be a written sponsorship, signed by the sponsor.' There was a large blank space on the form under the heading, 'Opinion of Faculty Sponsor.'

This was almost another thing and Howe hesitated. Yet there was nothing else to do and he took out his fountain pen. He wrote, 'Mr. Ferdinand Tertan is marked by his intense devotion to letters and by his exceptional love of all things of the mind.' To this he signed his name, which looked bold and assertive on the white page. It disturbed him, the strange affirming power of a name. With a business-like air, Tertan whipped up the paper, folding it with decision, and put it into his pocket. He bowed and took his departure, leaving Howe with the sense of having done something oddly momentous.

And so much now seemed odd and momentous to Howe that should not have seemed so. It was odd and momentous, he felt, when he sat with Blackburn's second quiz before him, and wrote in an excessively firm hand the grade of C-minus. The paper was a clear, an indisputable failure. He was carefully and consciously committing a cowardice. Blackburn had told the truth when he had pleaded his past record. Howe had consulted it in the Dean's office. It showed no grade lower than a B-minus. A canvass of some of Blackburn's previous instructors had brought vague attestations to the adequate powers of a student imperfectly remembered, and sometimes surprise that his abilities could be questioned at all.

As he wrote the grade, Howe told himself that his cowardice sprang from an unwillingness to have more dealings with a student he disliked. He knew it was simpler than that. He knew he feared Blackburn; that was the absurd truth. And cowardice did not solve the matter after all. Blackburn, flushed with a first success, attacked at once. The minimal passing grade had not assuaged his feelings and he sat at Howe's desk and again the blue-book lay between them. Blackburn said nothing. With an enormous impudence, he was waiting for Howe to speak and explain himself.

At last Howe said sharply and rudely, 'Well?' His throat was tense and the blood was hammering in his head. His mouth was tight with anger at himself for his disturbance.

Blackburn's glance was almost baleful. 'This is impossible, sir.'

'But there it is,' Howe answered.

'Sir?' Blackburn had not caught the meaning but his tone was still haughty.

Impatiently Howe said, "There it is, plain as day. Are you here to complain again?'

'Indeed I am, sir.' There was surprise in Blackburn's voice that Howe should ask the question.

'I shouldn't complain if I were you. You did a thoroughly bad job on your first quiz. This one is a little, only a very little, better.' This was not true. If anything, it was worse.

'That might be a matter of opinion, sir.'

'It is a matter of opinion. Of my opinion.'

'Another opinion might be different, sir.'

'You really believe that?' Howe said.

'Yes.' The omission of the 'sir' was monumental.

'Whose, for example?'

'The Dean's, for example.' Then the fleshy jaw came forward a little. 'Or a certain literary critic's, for example.'

It was colossal and almost too much for Blackburn himself to handle. The solidity of his face almost crumpled under it. But he withstood his own audacity and went on. 'And the Dean's opinion might be guided by the knowledge that the person who gave me this mark is the man whom a famous critic, the most eminent judge of literature in this country, called a drunken man. The Dean might think twice about whether such a man is fit to teach Dwight students.'

Howe said in quiet admonition, 'Blackburn, you're mad,' meaning no more than to check the boy's extravagance.

But Blackburn paid no heed. He had another shot in the locker. 'And the Dean might be guided by the information, of which I have evidence, documentary evidence,'—he slapped his breast pocket twice—'that this same person personally recommended to the college literary society, the oldest in the country, that he personally recommended a student who is crazy, who threw the meeting into an uproar—a psychiatric case. The Dean might take that into account.'

Howe was never to learn the details of that 'uproar.' He had always to content himself with the dim but passionate picture which at that moment sprang into his mind, of Tertan standing on some abstract height and madly denouncing the multitude of Quill and Scroll who howled him down.

He sat quiet a moment and looked at Blackburn. The ferocity had entirely gone from the student's face. He sat regarding his teacher almost benevolently. He had played a good card and now, scarcely at all unfriendly, he was waiting to see the effect. Howe took up the blue-book and negligently sifted through it. He read a page, closed the book, struck out the C-minus and wrote an F.

'Now you may take the paper to the Dean,' he said. 'You may tell him that after reconsidering it, I lowered the grade.'

The gasp was audible. 'Oh, sir!' Blackburn cried. 'Please!' His face was agonized. 'It means my graduation, my livelihood, my future. Don't do this to me.'

'It's done already.'

Blackburn stood up. 'I spoke rashly, sir, hastily. I had no intention, no real intention, of seeing the Dean. It rests with you—entirely, entirely. I *hope* you will restore the first mark.'

'Take the matter to the Dean or not, just as you choose. The grade is what you deserve and it stands.'

Blackburn's head dropped. 'And will I be failed at mid-term, sir?'

'Of course.'

From deep out of Blackburn's great chest rose a cry of anguish. 'Oh, sir, if you want me to go down on my knees to you, I will, I will.'

Howe looked at him in amazement.

'I will, I will. On my knees, sir. This mustn't, mustn't happen.'

He spoke so literally, meaning so very truly that his knees and exactly his knees were involved and seeming to think that he was offering something of tangible value to his teacher, that Howe, whose head had become icy clear in the nonsensical drama, thought, 'The boy is mad,' and began to speculate fantastically whether something in himself attracted or developed aberration. He could see himself standing absurdly before the Dean and saying, 'I've found another. This time it's the vice-president of the Council, the manager of the debating team and secretary of Quill and Scroll.'

One more such discovery, he thought, and he himself would be discovered! And there, suddenly, Blackburn was on his knees with a thump, his huge thighs straining his trousers, his hand outstretched in a great gesture of supplication.

With a cry, Howe shoved back his swivel chair and it rolled away on its casters half across the little room. Blackburn knelt for a moment to nothing at all, then got to his feet.

Howe rose abruptly. He said, 'Blackburn, you will stop acting like an idiot. Dust your knees off, take your paper and get out. You've behaved like a fool and a malicious person. You have half a term to do a decent job. Keep your silly mouth shut and try to do it. Now get out.'

Blackburn's head was low. He raised it and there was a pious light in his eyes. 'Will you shake hands, sir?' he said. He thrust out his hand.

'I will not,' Howe said.

Head and hand sank together. Blackburn picked up his blue-book and walked to the door. He turned and said, 'Thank you, sir.' His back, as he departed, was heavy with tragedy and stateliness.

IV

After years of bad luck with the weather, the College had a perfect day for Commencement. It was wonderfully bright, the air so transparent, the wind so brisk that no one could resist talking about it.

As Howe set out for the campus he heard Hilda calling from the back yard. She called, 'Professor, professor,' and came running to him.

Howe said, 'What's this "professor" business?'

'Mother told me,' Hilda said. 'You've been promoted. And I want to take your picture.'

'Next year,' said Howe. 'I won't be a professor until next year. And you know better than to call anybody "professor." '

'It was just in fun,' Hilda said. She seemed disappointed.

'But you can take my picture if you want. I won't look much different next year.' Still, it was frightening. It might mean that he was to stay in this town all his life.

Hilda brightened. 'Can I take it in this?' she said, and touched the gown he carried over his arm.

Howe laughed. 'Yes, you can take it in this.'

'I'll get my things and meet you in front of Otis,' Hilda said. 'I have the background all picked out.'

On the campus the Commencement crowd was already large. It stood about in eager, nervous little family groups. As he crossed, Howe was greeted by a student, capped and gowned, glad of the chance to make an event for his parents by introducing one of his teachers. It was while Howe stood there chatting that he saw Tertan.

He had never seen anyone quite so alone, as though a circle had been woven about him to separate him from the gay crowd on the campus. Not that Tertan was not gay, he was the gayest of all. Three weeks had passed since Howe had last seen him, the weeks of examination, the lazy week before Commencement, and this was now a different Tertan. On his head he wore a panama hat, broad-brimmed and fine, of the shape associated with South American planters. He wore a suit of raw silk, luxurious, but yellowed with age and much too tight, and he sported a whangee cane. He walked sedately, the hat tilted at a devastating angle, the stick coming up and down in time to his measured tread. He had, Howe guessed, outfitted himself to greet the day in the clothes of that ruined father whose existence was on record in the Dean's office. Gravely and arrogantly he surveyed the scene—in it, his whole bearing seemed to say, but not of it. With his haughty step, with his flashing eye, Tertan was coming nearer. Howe did not wish to be seen. He shifted his position slightly. When he looked again, Tertan was not in sight.

The chapel clock struck the quarter hour. Howe detached himself from his chat and hurried to Otis Hall at the far end of the campus. Hilda had not yet come. He went up into the high portico and, using the glass of the door for a mirror, put on his gown, adjusted the hood on his shoulders and set the mortarboard on his head. When he came down the steps, Hilda had arrived.

Nothing could have told him more forcibly that a year had passed than the development of Hilda's photographic possessions from the box camera of the previous fall. By a strap about her neck was hung a leather case, so thick and strong, so carefully stitched and so molded to its contents that it could only hold a costly camera. The appearance was deceptive, Howe knew, for he had been present at the Aikens' pre-Christmas conference about its purchase. It was only a fairly good domestic camera. Still, it looked very impressive. Hilda carried another leather case from which she drew a collapsible tripod. Decisively she extended each of its gleaming legs and set it up on the path. She removed the camera from its case and fixed it to the tripod. In its compact efficiency the camera almost had a life of its own, but Hilda treated it with easy familiarity, looked into its eye, glanced casually at its gauges. Then from a pocket she took still another leather case and drew from it a small instrument through which she looked first at Howe, who began to feel inanimate and lost, and then at the sky. She made some adjustment on the instrument, then some adjustment on the camera. She swept the scene with her eye, found a spot and pointed the camera in its direction. She walked to the spot, stood on it and beckoned to Howe. With each new leather case, with each new instrument, and with each new adjustment she had grown in ease and now she said, 'Joe, will you stand here?'

Obediently Howe stood where he was bidden. She had yet another instrument. She took out a tape-measure on a mechanical spool. Kneeling down before Howe, she put the little metal ring of the tape under the tip of his shoe. At her request, Howe pressed it with his toe. When she had measured her distance, she nodded to Howe who released the tape. At a touch, it sprang back into the spool. 'You have to be careful if you're going to get what you want,' Hilda said. 'I don't believe in all this snap-snap-snapping,' she remarked loftily. Howe nodded in agreement, although he was beginning to think Hilda's care excessive.

Now at last the moment had come. Hilda squinted into the camera, moved the tripod slightly. She stood to the side, holding the plunger of the shutter-cable. 'Ready,' she said. 'Will you relax, Joseph, please?' Howe realized that he was standing frozen. Hilda stood poised and precise as a setter, one hand holding the little cable, the other extended with curled dainty fingers like a dancer's, as if expressing to her subject the precarious delicacy of the moment. She pressed the plunger and there was the click. At once she stirred to action, got behind the camera, turned a new exposure. 'Thank you,' she said. 'Would you stand under that tree and let me do a character study with light and shade?'

The childish absurdity of the remark restored Howe's ease. He went to the little tree. The pattern the leaves made on his gown was what Hilda was after. He had just taken a satisfactory position when he heard in the unmistakable voice, 'Ah, Doctor! Having your picture taken?'

Howe gave up the pose and turned to Blackburn who stood on the walk, his hands behind his back, a little too large for his bachelor's gown. Annoyed that Blackburn should see him posing for a character study in light and shade, Howe said irritably, 'Yes, having my picture taken.'

Blackburn beamed at Hilda. 'And the little photographer?' he said. Hilda fixed her eyes on the ground and stood closer to her brilliant and aggressive camera. Blackburn, teetering on his heels, his hands behind his back, wholly prelatical and benignly patient, was not abashed at the silence. At last Howe said, 'If you'll excuse us, Mr. Blackburn, we'll go on with the picture.'

'Go right ahead, sir. I'm running along.' But he only came closer. 'Doctor Howe,' he said fervently, 'I want to tell you how glad I am that I was able to satisfy your standards at last.'

Howe was surprised at the hard, insulting brightness of his own voice, and even Hilda looked up curiously as he said, 'Nothing you have ever done has satisfied me, and nothing you could ever do would satisfy me, Blackburn.'

With a glance at Hilda, Blackburn made a gesture as if to hush Howe—as though all his former bold malice had taken for granted a kind of understanding between himself and his teacher, a secret which must not be betrayed to a third person. 'I only meant, sir,' he said, 'that I was able to pass your course after all.'

Howe said, 'You didn't pass my course. I passed you out of my course. I passed you without even reading your paper. I wanted to be sure the college would be rid of you. And when all the grades were in and I did read your paper, I saw I was right not to have read it first.'

Blackburn presented a stricken face. 'It was very bad, sir?'

But Howe had turned away. The paper had been fantastic. The paper had been, if he wished to see it so, mad. It was at this moment that the Dean came up behind Howe and caught his arm. 'Hello, Joseph,' he said. 'We'd better be getting along, it's almost late.'

He was not a familiar man, but when he saw Blackburn, who approached to greet him, he took Blackburn's arm, too. 'Hello, Theodore,' he said. Leaning forward on Howe's arm and on Blackburn's, he said, 'Hello, Hilda dear.' Hilda replied quietly, 'Hello, Uncle George.'

Still clinging to their arms, still linking Howe and Blackburn, the Dean said, 'Another year gone, Joe, and we've turned out another crop. After you've been here a few years, you'll find it reasonably upsetting—you wonder how there can be so many graduating classes while you stay the same. But of course you don't stay the same.' Then he said, 'Well,' sharply, to dismiss the thought. He pulled Blackburn's arm and swung him around to Howe. 'Have you heard about Teddy Blackburn?' he asked. 'He has a job already, before graduation—the first man of his class to be placed.' Expectant of congratulations, Blackburn beamed at Howe. Howe remained silent.

'Isn't that good?' the Dean said. Still Howe did not answer and the Dean, puzzled and put out, turned to Hilda. 'That's a very fine-looking camera, Hilda.' She touched it with affectionate pride.

'Instruments of precision,' said a voice. 'Instruments of precision.' Of the three with joined arms, Howe was the nearest to Tertan, whose gaze took in all the scene except the smile and the nod which Howe gave him. The boy leaned on his cane. The broad-brimmed hat, canting jauntily over his eye, confused the image of his face that Howe had established, suppressed the rigid lines of the ascetic and brought out the baroque curves. It made an effect of perverse majesty.

'Instruments of precision,' said Tertan for the last time, addressing no one, making a casual comment to the universe. And it occurred to Howe that Tertan might not be referring to Hilda's equipment. The sense of the thrice-woven circle of the boy's loneliness smote him fiercely. Tertan stood in majestic jauntiness, superior to all the scene, but his isolation made Howe ache with a pity of which Tertan was more the cause than the object, so general and indiscriminate was it.

Whether in his sorrow he made some unintended movement toward Tertan which the Dean checked, or whether the suddenly tightened grip on his arm was the Dean's own sorrow and fear, he did not know. Tertan watched them in the incurious way people watch a photograph being taken, and suddenly the thought that, to the boy, it must seem that the three were posing for a picture together made Howe detach himself almost rudely from the Dean's grasp.

'I promised Hilda another picture,' he announced—needlessly, for Tertan was no longer there, he had vanished in the last sudden flux of visitors who, now that the band had struck up, were rushing nervously to find seats.

'You'd better hurry,' the Dean said. 'I'll go along, it's getting late for me.' He departed and Blackburn walked stately by his side.

Howe again took his position under the little tree which cast its shadow over his face and gown. 'Just hurry, Hilda, won't you?' he said. Hilda held the cable at arm's length, her other arm crooked and her fingers crisped. She rose on her toes and said 'Ready,' and pressed the release. 'Thank you,' she said gravely and began to dismantle her camera as he hurried off to join the procession.

BABYLON REVISITED

F. SCOTT FITZGERALD

F. SCOTT FITZGERALD (1896–1940) was born in St. Paul, Minnesota, entered Princeton in 1913 but left to enlist in the Army in 1917. His first novel, *This Side of Paradise* (1920), a tale of the jazz age following the First World War, was a great success. He lived for a number of years on the Riviera and in Rome. His last three years were lived in Hollywood, where he wrote for the motion pictures. Among his books are *The Beautiful and Damned* (1921); *The Great Gatsby* (1925), his most popular novel; *Tender Is the Night* (1934); *The Last Tycoon* (1941), an unfinished novel; *The Crack-Up* (1945) and *Afternoon of an Author* (1957), collections of his last writings; and *The Letters of F. Scott Fitzgerald* (1963).

A ND where's Mr. Campbell?" Charlie asked.

"Gone to Switzerland. Mr. Campbell's a pretty sick man, Mr. Wales."

"I'm sorry to hear that. And George Hardt?" Charlie inquired.

"Back in America, gone to work."

"And where is the Snow Bird?"

"He was in here last week. Anyway, his friend, Mr. Schaeffer, is in Paris."

Two familiar names from the long list of a year and a half ago. Charlie scribbled an address in his notebook and tore out the page.

"If you see Mr. Schaeffer, give him this," he said. "It's my brother-in-law's address. I haven't settled on a hotel yet."

He was not really disappointed to find Paris was so empty. But the stillness in the Ritz bar was strange and portentous. It was not an American bar any more —he felt polite in it, and not as if he owned it. It had gone back into France. He felt the stillness from the moment he got out of the taxi and saw the doorman, usually in a frenzy of activity at this hour, gossiping with a *chasseur* by the servants' entrance.

Passing through the corridor, he heard only a single, bored voice in the once-clamorous women's room. When he turned into the bar he travelled the twenty feet of green carpet with his eyes fixed straight ahead by old habit; and then, with his foot firmly on the rail, he turned and surveyed the room, encountering only a single pair of eyes that fluttered up from a newspaper in the corner. Charlie asked for the head barman, Paul, who in the latter days of the bull market had come to work in his own custom-built car—disembarking, however, with due nicety

at the nearest corner. But Paul was at his country house today and Alix giving him information.

"No, no more," Charlie said, "I'm going slow these days."

Alix congratulated him: "You were going pretty strong a couple of years ago."

"I'll stick to it all right," Charlie assured him. "I've stuck to it for over a year and a half now."

"How do you find conditions in America?"

"I haven't been to America for months. I'm in business in Prague, representing a couple of concerns there. They don't know about me down there."

Alix smiled.

"Remember the night of George Hardt's bachelor dinner here?" said Charlie. "By the way, what's become of Claude Fessenden?"

Alix lowered his voice confidentially: "He's in Paris, but he doesn't come here any more. Paul doesn't allow it. He ran up a bill of thirty thousand francs, charging all his drinks and his lunches, and usually his dinner, for more than a year. And when Paul finally told him he had to pay, he gave him a bad check."

Alix shook his head sadly.

"I don't understand it, such a dandy fellow. Now he's all bloated up—" He made a plump apple of his hands.

Charlie watched a group of strident queens installing themselves in a corner.

"Nothing affects them," he thought. "Stocks rise and fall, people loaf or work, but they go on forever." The place oppressed him. He called for the dice and shook with Alix for the drink.

"Here for long, Mr. Wales?"

"I'm here for four or five days to see my little girl."

"Oh-h! You have a little girl?"

Outside, the fire-red, gas-blue, ghost-green signs shone smokily through the tranquil rain. It was late afternoon and the streets were in movement; the *bistros* gleamed. At the corner of the Boulevard des Capucines he took a taxi. The Place de la Concorde moved by in pink majesty; they crossed the logical Seine, and Charlie felt the sudden provincial quality of the left bank.

Charlie directed his taxi to the Avenue de l'Opera, which was out of his way. But he wanted to see the blue hour spread over the magnificent facade, and imagine that the cab horns, playing endlessly the first few bars of *Le Plus que Lent*, were the trumpets of the Second Empire. They were closing the iron grill in front of Brentano's Book-store, and people were already at dinner behind the trim little bourgeois hedge of Duval's. He had never eaten at a really cheap restaurant in Paris. Five-course dinner, four francs fifty, eighteen cents, wine included. For some odd reason he wished that he had.

As they rolled on to the Left Bank and he felt its sudden provincialism, he thought, "I spoiled this city for myself. I didn't realize it, but the days came along one after another, and then two years were gone, and everything was gone, and I was gone."

He was thirty-five, and good to look at. The Irish mobility of his face was sobered by a deep wrinkle between his eyes. As he rang his brother-in-law's bell in the Rue Palatine, the wrinkle deepened till it pulled down his brows; he felt a cramping sensation in his belly. From behind the maid who opened the door darted a lovely little girl of nine who shrieked "Daddy!" and flew up, struggling like a fish, into his arms. She pulled his head around by one ear and set her cheek against his.

"My old pie," he said.

"Oh, daddy, daddy, daddy, daddy, dads, dads, dads!"

She drew him into the salon, where the family waited, a boy and girl his daughter's age, his sister-in-law and her husband. He greeted Marion with his voice pitched carefully to avoid either feigned enthusiasm or dislike, but her response was more frankly tepid, though she minimized her expression of unalterable distrust by directing her regard toward his child. The two men clasped hands in a friendly way and Lincoln Peters rested his for a moment on Charlie's shoulder.

The room was warm and comfortably American. The three children moved intimately about, playing through the yellow oblongs that led to other rooms; the cheer of six o'clock spoke in the eager smacks of the fire and the sounds of French activity in the kitchen. But Charlie did not relax; his heart sat up rigidly in his body and he drew confidence from his daughter, who from time to time came close to him, holding in her arms the doll he had brought.

"Really extremely well," he declared in answer to Lincoln's question. "There's a lot of business there that isn't moving at all, but we're doing even better than ever. In fact, damn well. I'm bringing my sister over from America next month to keep house for me. My income last year was bigger than it was when I had money. You see, the Czechs——"

His boasting was for a specific purpose; but after a moment, seeing a faint restiveness in Lincoln's eye, he changed the subject:

"Those are fine children of yours, well brought up, good manners."

"We think Honoria's a great little girl too."

Marion Peters came back from the kitchen. She was a tall woman with worried eyes, who had once possessed a fresh American loveliness. Charlie had never been sensitive to it and was always surprised when people spoke of how pretty she had been. From the first there had been an instinctive antipathy between them.

"Well, how do you find Honoria?" she asked.

"Wonderful. I was astonished how much she's grown in ten months. All the children are looking well."

"We haven't had a doctor for a year. How do you like being back in Paris?"

"It seems very funny to see so few Americans around."

"I'm delighted," Marion said vehemently. "Now at least you can go into a store without their assuming you're a millionaire. We've suffered like everybody, but on the whole it's a good deal pleasanter."

"But it was nice while it lasted," Charlie said. "We were a sort of royalty, almost infallible, with a sort of magic around us. In the bar this afternoon"—he stumbled, seeing his mistake—"there wasn't a man I knew."

She looked at him keenly. "I should think you'd have had enough of bars."

"I only stayed a minute. I take one drink every afternoon, and no more."

"Don't you want a cocktail before dinner?" Lincoln asked.

"I take only one drink every afternoon, and I've had that."

"I hope you keep to it," said Marion.

Her dislike was evident in the coldness with which she spoke, but Charlie only smiled; he had larger plans. Her very aggressiveness gave him an advantage, and he knew enough to wait. He wanted them to initiate the discussion of what they knew had brought him to Paris.

At dinner he couldn't decide whether Honoria was most like him or her mother. Fortunate if she didn't combine the traits of both that had brought them to disaster. A great wave of protectiveness went over him. He thought he knew what to do for her. He believed in character; he wanted to jump back a whole generation and trust in character again as the eternally valuable element. Everything wore out.

He left soon after dinner, but not to go home. He was curious to see Paris by night with clearer and more judicious eyes than those of other days. He bought a *strapontin* for the Casino and watched Josephine Baker go through her chocolate arabesques.

After an hour he left and strolled toward Montmartre, up the Rue Pigalle into the Place Blanche. The rain had stopped and there were a few people in evening clothes disembarking from taxis in front of cabarets, and *cocottes* prowling singly or in pairs, and many Negroes. He passed a lighted door from which issued music, and stopped with the sense of familiarity; it was Bricktop's, where he had parted with so many hours and so much money. A few doors farther on he found another ancient rendezvous and incautiously put his head inside. Immediately an eager orchestra burst into sound, a pair of professional dancers leaped to their feet and a maître d'hôtel swooped toward him, crying, "Crowd just arriving, sir!" But he withdrew quickly.

"You have to be damn drunk," he thought.

Zelli's was closed, the bleak and sinister cheap hotels surrounding it were dark; up in the Rue Blanche there was more light and a local, colloquial French crowd. The Poet's Cave had disappeared, but the two great mouths of the Café of Heaven and the Café of Hell still yawned—even devoured, as he watched, the meagre contents of a tourist bus—a German, a Japanese, and an American couple who glanced at him with frightened eyes.

So much for the effort and ingenuity of Montmartre. All the catering to vice and waste was on an utterly childish scale, and he suddenly realized the meaning of the word "dissipate"—to dissipate into thin air; to make nothing out of something. In the little hours of the night every move from place to place was an enormous human jump, an increase of paying for the privilege of slower and slower motion.

He remembered thousand-franc notes given to an orchestra for playing a single number, hundred-franc notes tossed to a doorman for calling a cab.

But it hadn't been given for nothing.

It had been given, even the most wildly squandered sum, as an offering to destiny that he might not remember the things most worth remembering, the things that now he would always remember—his child taken from his control, his wife escaped to a grave in Vermont.

In the glare of a *brasserie* a woman spoke to him. He bought her some eggs and coffee, and then, eluding her encouraging stare, gave her a twenty-franc note and took a taxi to his hotel.

II

He woke upon a fine fall day—football weather. The depression of yesterday was gone and he liked the people on the streets. At noon he sat opposite Honoria at Le Grand Vatel, the only restaurant he could think of not reminiscent of champagne dinners and long luncheons that began at two and ended in a blurred and vague twilight.

"Now, how about vegetables? Oughtn't you to have some vegetables?"

"Well, yes."

"Here's *épinards* and *chou-fleur* and carrots and *haricots*."

"I'd like *chou-fleur*."

"Wouldn't you like to have two vegetables?"

"I usually only have one at lunch."

The waiter was pretending to be inordinately fond of children. "*Qu'elle est mignonne la petite? Elle parle exactement comme une Française.*"

"How about dessert? Shall we wait and see?"

The waiter disappeared. Honoria looked at her father expectantly.

"What are we going to do?"

"First, we're going to that toy store in the Rue Saint-Honoré and buy you anything you like. And then we're going to the vaudeville at the Empire."

She hesitated. "I like it about the vaudeville, but not the toy store."

"Why not?"

"Well, you brought me this doll." She had it with her. "And I've got lots of things. And we're not rich any more, are we?"

"We never were. But today you are to have anything you want."

"All right," she agreed resignedly.

When there had been her mother and a French nurse he had been inclined to be strict; now he extended himself, reached out for a new tolerance; he must be both parents to her and not shut any of her out of communication.

"I want to get to know you," he said gravely. "First let me introduce myself. My Name is Charles J. Wales, of Prague."

"Oh, daddy!" her voice cracked with laughter.

"And who are you, please?" he persisted, and she accepted a rôle immediately: "Honoria Wales, Rue Palatine, Paris."

"Married or single?"

"No, not married. Single."

He indicated the doll. "But I see you have a child, madame."

Unwilling to disinherit it, she took it to her heart and thought quickly: "Yes, I've been married, but I'm not married now. My husband is dead."

He went on quickly, "And the child's name?"

"Simone. That's after my best friend at school."

"I'm very pleased that you're doing so well at school."

"I'm third this month," she boasted. "Elsie"—that was her cousin—"is only about eighteenth, and Richard is about at the bottom."

"You like Richard and Elsie, don't you?"

"Oh, yes. I like Richard quite well and I like her all right."

Cautiously and casually he asked: "And Aunt Marion and Uncle Lincoln—which do you like best?"

"Oh, Uncle Lincoln, I guess."

He was increasingly aware of her presence. As they came in, a murmur of ". . . adorable" followed them, and now the people at the next table bent all their silences upon her, staring as if she were something no more conscious than a flower.

"Why don't I live with you?" she asked suddenly. "Because mamma's dead?"

"You must stay here and learn more French. It would have been hard for daddy to take care of you so well."

"I don't really need much taking care of any more. I do everything for myself."

Going out of the restaurant, a man and a woman unexpectedly hailed him!

"Well, the old Wales!"

"Hello there, Lorraine. . . . Dunc."

Sudden ghosts out of the past: Duncan Schaeffer, a friend from college. Lorraine Quarrles, a lovely, pale blonde of thirty; one of a crowd who had helped them make months into days in the lavish times of three years ago.

"My husband couldn't come this year," she said, in answer to his question. "We're poor as hell. So he gave me two hundred a month and told me I could do my worst on that. . . . This your little girl?"

"What about coming back and sitting down?" Duncan asked.

"Can't do it." He was glad for an excuse. As always, he felt Lorraine's passionate, provocative attraction, but his own rhythm was different now.

"Well, how about dinner?" she asked.

"I'm not free. Give me your address and let me call you."

"Charlie, I believe you're sober," she said judi-

cially. "I honestly believe he's sober, Dunc. Pinch him and see if he's sober."

Charlie indicated Honoria with his head. They both laughed.

"What's your address?" said Duncan sceptically.

He hesitated, unwilling to give the name of his hotel.

"I'm not settled yet. I'd better call you. We're going to see the vaudeville at the Empire."

"There! That's what I want to do," Lorraine said. "I want to see some clowns and acrobats and jugglers. That's just what we'll do, Dunc."

"We've got to do an errand first," said Charlie. "Perhaps we'll see you there."

"All right, you snob. . . . Good-by, beautiful little girl."

"Good-by."

Honoria bobbed politely.

Somehow, an unwelcome encounter. They liked him because he was functioning, because he was serious; they wanted to see him, because he was stronger than they were now, because they wanted to draw a certain sustenance from his strength.

At the Empire, Honoria proudly refused to sit upon her father's folded coat. She was already an individual with a code of her own, and Charlie was more and more absorbed by the desire of putting a little of himself into her before she crystallized utterly. It was hopeless to try to know her in so short a time.

Between the acts they came upon Duncan and Lorraine in the lobby where the band was playing.

"Have a drink?"

"All right, but not up at the bar. We'll take a table."

"The perfect father."

Listening abstractedly to Lorraine, Charlie watched Honoria's eyes leave their table, and he followed them wistfully about the room, wondering what they saw. He met her glance and she smiled.

"I like that lemonade," she said.

What had she said? What had he expected? Going home in a taxi afterward, he pulled her over until her head rested against his chest.

"Darling, do you ever think about your mother?"

"Yes, sometimes," she answered vaguely.

"I don't want you to forget her. Have you got a picture of her?"

"Yes, I think so. Anyhow, Aunt Marion has. Why don't you want me to forget her?"

"She loved you very much."

"I loved her too."

They were silent for a moment.

"Daddy, I want to come and live with you," she said suddenly.

His heart leaped; he had wanted it to come like this.

"Aren't you perfectly happy?"

"Yes, but I love you better than anybody. And you love me better than anybody, don't you, now that mummy's dead?"

"Of course I do. But you won't always like me best, honey. You'll grow up and meet somebody your own age and go marry him and forget you ever had a daddy."

"Yes, that's true," she agreed tranquilly.

He didn't go in. He was coming back at nine o'clock and he wanted to keep himself fresh and new for the thing he must say then.

"When you're safe inside, just show yourself in that window."

"All right. Good-by, dads, dads, dads, dads."

He waited in the dark street until she appeared, all warm and glowing, in the window above and kissed her fingers out into the night.

III

They were waiting. Marion sat behind the coffee service in a dignified black dinner dress that just faintly suggested mourning. Lincoln was walking up and down with the animation of one who had already been talking. They were as anxious as he was to get into the question. He opened it almost immediately:

"I suppose you know what I want to see you about—why I really came to Paris."

Marion played with the black stars on her necklace and frowned.

"I'm awfully anxious to have a home," he continued. "And I'm awfully anxious to have Honoria in it. I appreciate your taking in Honoria for her mother's sake, but things have changed now"—he hesitated and then continued more forcibly—"changed radically with me, and I want to ask you to reconsider the matter. It would be silly for me to deny that about three years ago I was acting badly——"

Marion looked up at him with hard eyes.

"—but all that's over. As I told you, I haven't had more than a drink a day for over a year, and I take that drink deliberately, so that the idea of alcohol won't get too big in my imagination. You see the idea?"

"No," said Marion succinctly.

"It's a sort of stunt I set myself. It keeps the matter in proportion."

"I get you," said Lincoln. "You don't want to admit it's got any attraction for you."

"Something like that. Sometimes I forget and don't take it. But I try to take it. Anyhow, I couldn't afford to drink in my position. The people I represent are more than satisfied with what I've done, and I'm bringing my sister over from Burlington to keep house for me, and I want awfully to have Honoria too. You know that even when her mother and I weren't getting along well we never let anything that happened touch Honoria. I know she's fond of me and I know I'm able to take care of her and—well, there you are. How do you feel about it?"

He knew that now he would have to take a beating. It would last an hour or two hours, and it would be difficult, but if he modulated his inevitable resentment to the chastened attitude of the reformed sinner, he might win his point in the end.

Keep your temper, he told himself. You don't want to be justified. You want Honoria.

Lincoln spoke first: "We've been talking it over ever since we got your letter last month. We're happy to have Honoria here. She's a dear little thing, and we're glad to be able to help her, but of course that isn't the question——"

Marion interrupted suddenly. "How long are you going to stay sober, Charlie?" she asked.

"Permanently, I hope."

"How can anybody count on that?"

"You know I never did drink heavily until I gave up business and came over here with nothing to do. Then Helen and I began to run around with——"

"Please leave Helen out of it. I can't bear to hear you talk about her like that."

He stared at her grimly; he had never been certain how fond of each other the sisters were in life.

"My drinking only lasted about a year and a half—from the time we came over until I—collapsed."

"It was time enough."

"It was time enough," he agreed.

"My duty is entirely to Helen," she said. "I try to think what she would have wanted me to do. Frankly, from the night you did that terrible thing you haven't really existed for me. I can't help that. She was my sister."

"Yes."

"When she was dying she asked me to look out for Honoria. If you hadn't been in a sanitarium then, it might have helped matters."

He had no answer.

"I'll never in my life be able to forget the morning when Helen knocked at my door, soaked to the skin and shivering, and said you'd locked her out."

Charlie gripped the sides of the chair. This was more difficult than he expected; he wanted to launch out into a long expostulation and explanation, but he only said: "The night I locked her out—" and she interrupted, "I don't feel up to going over that again."

After a moment's silence Lincoln said: "We're getting off the subject. You want Marion to set aside her legal guardianship and give you Honoria. I think the main point for her is whether she has confidence in you or not."

"I don't blame Marion," Charlie said slowly, "but I think she can have entire confidence in me. I had a good record up to three years ago. Of course, it's within human possibilities I might go wrong any time. But if we wait much longer I'll lose Honoria's childhood and my chance for a home." He shook his head, "I'll simply lose her, don't you see?"

"Yes, I see," said Lincoln.

"Why didn't you think of all this before?" Marion asked.

"I suppose I did, from time to time, but Helen and I were getting along badly. When I consented to the guardianship, I was flat on my back in a sanitarium and the market had cleaned me out. I knew I'd acted badly, and I thought if it would bring any peace to Helen, I'd agree to anything. But now it's different. I'm functioning, I'm behaving damn well, so far as——"

"Please don't swear at me," Marion said.

He looked at her, startled. With each remark the force of her dislike became more and more apparent. She had built up all her fear of life into one wall and faced it toward him. This trivial reproof was possibly the result of some trouble with the cook several hours before. Charlie became increasingly alarmed at leaving Honoria in this atmosphere of hostility against himself; sooner or later it would come out, in a word here, a shake of the head there, and some of that distrust would be irrevocably implanted in Honoria. But he pulled his temper down out of his face and shut it up inside him; he had won a point, for Lincoln realized the absurdity of Marion's remark and asked her lightly since when she had objected to the word "damn."

"Another thing," Charlie said: "I'm able to give her certain advantages now. I'm going to take a French governess to Prague with me. I've got a lease on a new apartment——"

He stopped, realizing that he was blundering. They couldn't be expected to accept with equanimity the fact that his income was again twice as large as their own.

"I suppose you can give her more luxuries than we can," said Marion. "When you were throwing away money we were living along watching every ten francs. . . . I suppose you'll start doing it again."

"Oh, no," he said. "I've learned. I worked hard for ten years, you know—until I got lucky in the market, like so many people. Terribly lucky. It didn't seem any use working any more, so I quit. It won't happen again."

There was a long silence. All of them felt their nerves straining, and for the first time in a year Charlie wanted a drink. He was sure now that Lincoln Peters wanted him to have his child.

Marion shuddered suddenly; part of her saw that Charlie's feet were planted on the earth now, and her own maternal feeling recognized the naturalness of his desire; but she had lived for a long time with a prejudice—a prejudice founded on a curious disbelief in her sister's happiness, and which, in the shock of one terrible night, had turned to hatred for him. It had all happened at a point in her life where the discouragement of ill health and adverse circumstances made it necessary for her to believe in tangible villainy and a tangible villain.

"I can't help what I think!" she cried out suddenly. "How much you were responsible for Helen's death, I don't know. It's something you'll have to square with your own conscience."

An electric current of agony surged through him; for a moment he was almost on his feet, an unuttered sound echoing in his throat. He hung on to himself for a moment, another moment.

"Hold on there," said Lincoln uncomfortably. "I never thought you were responsible for that."

"Helen died of heart trouble," Charlie said dully.

"Yes, heart trouble." Marion spoke as if the phrase had another meaning for her.

Then, in the flatness that followed her outburst, she saw him plainly and she knew he had somehow arrived at control over the situation. Glancing at her husband, she found no help from him, and as abruptly as if it were a matter of no importance, she threw up the sponge.

"Do what you like!" she cried, springing up from her chair. "She's your child. I'm not the person to stand in your way. I think if it were my child I'd rather see her—" She managed to check herself. "You two decide it. I can't stand this. I'm sick. I'm going to bed."

She hurried from the room; after a moment Lincoln said:

"This has been a hard day for her. You know how strongly she feels—" His voice was almost apologetic: "When a woman gets an idea in her head."

"Of course."

"It's going to be all right. I think she sees now that you—can provide for the child, and so we can't very well stand in your way or Honoria's way."

"Thank you, Lincoln."

"I'd better go along and see how she is."

"I'm going."

He was still trembling when he reached the street,

but a walk down the Rue Bonaparte to the quais set him up, and as he crossed the Seine, fresh and new by the quai lamps, he felt exultant. But back in his room he couldn't sleep. The image of Helen haunted him. Helen whom he had loved so until they had senselessly begun to abuse each other's love, tear it into shreds. On that terrible February night that Marion remembered so vividly, a slow quarrel had gone on for hours. There was a scene at the Florida, and then he attempted to take her home, and then she kissed young Webb at a table; after that there was what she had hysterically said. When he arrived home alone he turned the key in the lock in wild anger. How could he know she would arrive an hour later alone, that there would be a snowstorm in which she wandered about in slippers, too confused to find a taxi? Then the aftermath, her escaping pneumonia by a miracle, and all the attendant horror. They were "reconciled," but that was the beginning of the end, and Marion, who had seen with her own eyes and who imagined it to be one of many scenes from her sister's martyrdom, never forgot.

Going over it again brought Helen nearer, and in the white, soft light that steals upon half sleep near morning he found himself talking to her again. She said that he was perfectly right about Honoria and that she wanted Honoria to be with him. She said she was glad he was being good and doing better. She said a lot of other things—very friendly things—but she was in a swing in a white dress, and swinging faster and faster all the time, so that at the end he could not hear clearly all that she said.

IV

He woke up feeling happy. The door of the world was open again. He made plans, vistas, futures for Honoria and himself, but suddenly he grew sad, remembering all the plans he and Helen had made. She had not planned to die. The present was the thing—work to do and someone to love. But not to love too much, for he knew the injury that a father can do to a daughter or a mother to a son by attaching them too closely; afterward, out in the world, the child would seek in the marriage partner the same blind tenderness and, failing probably to find it, turn against love and life.

It was another bright, crisp day. He called Lincoln Peters at the bank where he worked and asked if he could count on taking Honoria when he left for Prague. Lincoln agreed that there was no reason for delay. One thing—the legal guardianship. Marion wanted to retain that a while longer. She was upset by the whole matter, and it would oil things if she

felt that the situation was still in her control for another year. Charlie agreed, wanted only the tangible, visible child.

Then the question of a governess. Charlie sat in a gloomy agency and talked to a cross Bernaise and to a buxom Breton peasant, neither of whom he could have endured. There were others whom he would see tomorrow.

He lunched with Lincoln Peters at Griffons, trying to keep down his exultation.

"There's nothing quite like your own child," Lincoln said. "But you understand how Marion feels too."

"She's forgotten how hard I worked for seven years there," Charlie said. "She just remembers one night."

"There's another thing." Lincoln hesitated. "While you and Helen were tearing around Europe throwing money away, we were just getting along. I didn't touch any of the prosperity because I never got ahead enough to carry anything but my insurance. I think Marion felt there was some kind of injustice in it—you not even working toward the end, and getting richer and richer."

"It went just as quick as it came," said Charlie.

"Yes, a lot of it stayed in the hands of *chasseurs* and saxophone players and maîtres d'hôtel—well, the big party's over now. I just said that to explain Marion's feeling about those crazy years. If you drop in about six o'clock tonight before Marion's too tired, we'll settle the details on the spot."

Back at his hotel, Charlie found a *pneumatique* that had been redirected from the Ritz bar where Charlie had left his address for the purpose of finding a certain man.

Dear Charlie: You were so strange when we saw you the other day that I wondered if I did something to offend you. If so, I'm not conscious of it. In fact, I have thought about you too much for the last year, and it's always been in the back of my mind that I might see you if I came over here. We *did* have such good times that crazy spring, like the night you and I stole the butcher's tricycle, and the time we tried to call on the president and you had the old derby rim and the wire cane. Everybody seems so old lately, but I don't feel old a bit. Couldn't we get together some time today for old time's sake? I've got a vile hang-over for the moment, but will be feeling better this afternoon and will look for you about five in the sweat-shop at the Ritz.

Always devotedly,

LORRAINE.

His first feeling was one of awe that he had actually, in his mature years, stolen a tricycle and pedalled Lorraine all over the Étoile between the small hours and dawn. In retrospect it was a nightmare. Locking out Helen didn't fit in with any other act of his life, but the tricycle incident did—it was one of many. How many weeks or months of dissipation to arrive at that condition of utter irresponsibility?

He tried to picture how Lorraine had appeared to him then—very attractive; Helen was unhappy about it, though she said nothing. Yesterday, in the restaurant, Lorraine had seemed trite, blurred, worn away. He emphatically did not want to see her, and he was glad Alix had not given away his hotel address. It was a relief to think, instead, of Honoria, to think of Sundays spent with her and of saying good morning to her and of knowing she was there in his house at night, drawing her breath in the darkness.

At five he took a taxi and bought presents for all the Peters—a piquant cloth doll, a box of Roman soldiers, flowers for Marion, big linen handkerchiefs for Lincoln.

He saw, when he arrived in the apartment, that Marion had accepted the inevitable. She greeted him now as though he were a recalcitrant member of the family, rather than a menacing outsider. Honoria had been told she was going; Charlie was glad to see that her tact made her conceal her excessive happiness. Only on his lap did she whisper her delight and the question "When?" before she slipped away with the other children.

He and Marion were alone for a minute in the room, and on an impulse he spoke out boldly:

"Family quarrels are bitter things. They don't go according to any rules. They're not like aches or wounds; they're more like splits in the skin that won't heal because there's not enough material. I wish you and I could be on better terms."

"Some things are hard to forget," she answered. "It's a question of confidence." There was no answer to this and presently she asked, "When do you propose to take her?"

"As soon as I can get a governess. I hoped the day after tomorrow."

"That's impossible. I've got to get her things in shape. Not before Saturday."

He yielded. Coming back into the room, Lincoln offered him a drink.

"I'll take my daily whisky," he said.

It was warm here, it was a home, people together by a fire. The children felt very safe and important; the mother and father were serious, watchful. They had things to do for the children more important than his visit here. A spoonful of medicine was, after all, more important than the strained relations between Marion and himself. They were not dull people, but they were very much in the grip of life and circumstances. He wondered if he couldn't do something to get Lincoln out of his rut at the bank.

A long peal at the door-bell; the *bonne à toute faire* passed through and went down the corridor. The door opened upon another long ring, and then voices, and the three in the salon looked up expectantly; Richard moved to bring the corridor within his range of vision, and Marion rose. Then the maid came back along the corridor, closely followed by the voices, which developed under the light into Duncan Schaeffer and Lorraine Quarrles.

They were gay, they were hilarious, they were roaring with laughter. For a moment Charlie was astounded; unable to understand how they ferreted out the Peters' address.

"Ah-h-h!" Duncan wagged his finger roguishly at Charlie. "Ah-h-h!"

They both slid down another cascade of laughter. Anxious and at a loss, Charlie shook hands with them quickly and presented them to Lincoln and Marion. Marion nodded, scarcely speaking. She had drawn back a step toward the fire; her little girl stood beside her, and Marion put an arm about her shoulder.

With growing annoyance at the intrusion, Charlie waited for them to explain themselves. After some concentration Duncan said:

"We came to invite you out to dinner. Lorraine and I insist that all this chichi, cagy business 'bout your address got to stop."

Charlie came closer to them, as if to force them backward down the corridor.

"Sorry, but I can't. Tell me where you'll be and I'll phone you in half an hour."

This made no impression. Lorraine sat down suddenly on the side of a chair, and focussing her eyes on Richard, cried, "Oh, what a nice little boy! Come here, little boy." Richard glanced at his mother, but did not move. With a perceptible shrug of her shoulders, Lorraine turned back to Charlie:

"Come and dine. Sure your cousins won' mine. See you so sel'om. Or solemn."

"I can't," said Charlie sharply. "You two have dinner and I'll phone you."

Her voice became suddenly unpleasant. "All right, we'll go. But I remember once when you hammered on my door at four A.M. I was enough of a good sport to give you a drink. Come on, Dunc."

Still in slow motion, with blurred, angry faces, with uncertain feet, they retired along the corridor.

"Good night," Charlie said.

"Good night!" responded Lorraine emphatically.

When he went back into the salon Marion had not moved, only now her son was standing in the circle of her other arm. Lincoln was still swinging Honoria back and forth like a pendulum from side to side.

"What an outrage!" Charlie broke out. "What an absolute outrage!"

Neither of them answered. Charlie dropped into an armchair, picked up his drink, set it down again and said:

"People I haven't seen for two years having the colossal nerve——"

He broke off. Marion had made the sound "Oh!" in one swift, furious breath, turned her body from him with a jerk and left the room.

Lincoln set down Honoria carefully.

"You children go in and start your soup," he said, and when they obeyed, he said to Charlie:

"Marion's not well and she can't stand shocks. That kind of people make her really physically sick."

"I didn't tell them to come here. They wormed your name out of somebody. They deliberately——"

"Well, it's too bad. It doesn't help matters. Excuse me a minute."

Left alone, Charlie sat tense in his chair. In the next room he could hear the children eating, talking in monosyllables, already oblivious to the scene between their elders. He heard a murmur of conversation from a farther room and then the ticking bell of a telephone receiver picked up, and in a panic he moved to the other side of the room and out of earshot.

In a minute Lincoln came back. "Look here, Charlie. I think we'd better call off dinner for tonight. Marion's in bad shape."

"Is she angry with me?"

"Sort of," he said, almost roughly. "She's not strong and——"

"You mean she's changed her mind about Honoria?"

"She's pretty bitter right now. I don't know. You phone me at the bank tomorrow."

"I wish you'd explain to her I never dreamed these people would come here. I'm just as sore as you are."

"I couldn't explain anything to her now."

Charlie got up. He took his coat and hat and started down the corridor. Then he opened the door of the dining room and said in a strange voice, "Good night, children."

Honoria rose and ran around the table to hug him.

"Good night, sweetheart," he said vaguely, and then trying to make his voice more tender, trying to conciliate something, "Good night, dear children."

V

Charlie went directly to the Ritz bar with the furious idea of finding Lorraine and Duncan, but they were not there, and he realized that in any case there was nothing he could do. He had not touched his drink at the Peters', and now he ordered a whisky-and-soda. Paul came over to say hello.

"It's a great change," he said sadly. "We do about half the business we did. So many fellows I hear about back in the States lost everything, maybe not in the first crash, but then in the second. Your friend George Hardt lost every cent, I hear. Are you back in the States?"

"No, I'm in business in Prague."

"I heard that you lost a lot in the crash."

"I did," and he added grimly, "but I lost everything I wanted in the boom."

"Selling short."

"Something like that."

Again the memory of those days swept over him like a nightmare—the people they had met travelling; then people who couldn't add a row of figures or speak a coherent sentence. The little man Helen had consented to dance with at the ship's party, who had insulted her ten feet from the table; the women and girls carried screaming with drink or drugs out of public places——

—The men who locked their wives out in the snow, because the snow of twenty-nine wasn't real snow. If you didn't want it to be snow, you just paid some money.

He went to the phone and called the Peters' apartment; Lincoln answered.

"I called up because this thing is on my mind. Has Marion said anything definite?"

"Marion's sick," Lincoln answered shortly. "I know this thing isn't altogether your fault, but I can't have her go to pieces about it. I'm afraid we'll have to let it slide for six months; I can't take the chance of working her up to this state again."

"I see."

"I'm sorry, Charlie."

He went back to his table. His whisky glass was empty, but he shook his head when Alix looked at it questioningly. There wasn't much he could do now except send Honoria some things; he would send her a lot of things tomorrow. He thought rather angrily that this was just money—he had given so many people money. . . .

"No, no more," he said to another waiter. "What do I owe you?"

He would come back some day; they couldn't make him pay forever. But he wanted his child, and nothing was much good now, beside that fact. He wasn't young any more, with a lot of nice thoughts and dreams to have by himself. He was absolutely sure Helen wouldn't have wanted him to be so alone.